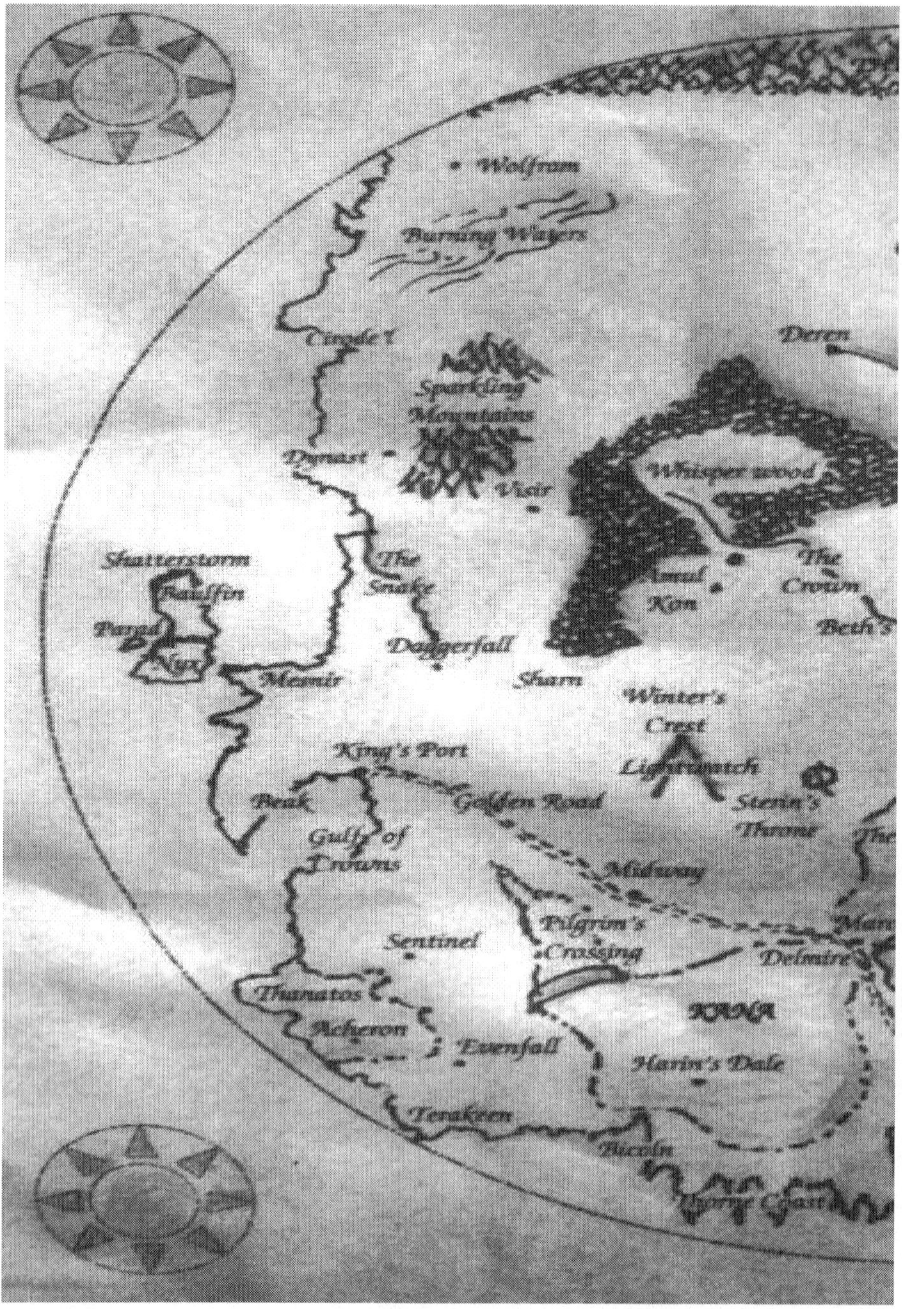
Wolfram
Burning Waters
Sparkling Mountains
Deren
Visir
Whisperwood
The Crown
Shatterstorm
Nux
The Snake
Daggerfall
Memir
Sharn
Winter's Crest
King's Port
Beak
Golden Road
Midway
Pilgrim's Crossing
Sentinel
Delmire
Thanatos
Acheron
Evenfall
Harin's Dale
Tenakeen

The Land of Càrin

Twilight of Ages

J.D. Reding

Twilight of Ages
Copyright © 2010 by Joshua Reding

ISBN (9780983423300)

Seven Men, Three Stories, One Destiny

Dedication

This book is dedicated to my father Rick, who taught me to never, ever take my eye off the ball and without whom this story would not exist.

Dramatis Personae

Aurum Guilden's Tale

Joven- Human Wizard, Brother of Aurum
Grey- Human Wizard, Brother of Aurum
Rayn- Human Wizard, Brother of Aurum
Dorian- Human Wizard, Brother of Aurum
Rikard- Human Wizard, Brother of Aurum
Dane- Centaur Warrior
Qel of the Thousand Hammers- Unu Clansmaster
The Red Man- Unknown

Tendra Sumenel's Tale

Jeric Tybius- Human Light Monk, Fiancé of Tendra
Jethro Sumenel- Human King, Father of Tendra
Jakob Sumenel- Human Prince, Brother of Tendra
Vizien Traenor- Human Grand Inquisitor
Rowen- Human Wizard, Brother of Aurum

Galeerial Strongwind's Tale

Ezekiel Gracefall- Skyguard Raptor
Veriel Stormrise- Skyguard Lord Commander
Gabriel Highflight- Skyguard
The Wither- Unknown

Table of Contents

Foreword

Welcome to the Land of Carin, a fantastic world filled with wizards, angels, demons, giants, kings and queens embroiled in a war that can only end in extinction and exultation. The only question is...who will be left standing. Twilight of Ages is the first book of a high fantasy series called, The Heart Quest Saga. This is the chronicle of three heroic characters, whose lives are intertwined in this epic struggle between good and evil.

From the very first page, all your senses will be assailed as you find yourself drawn into the first battle between a fearsome feral race of ravenous beasts and humanity. A band of brothers, magicians all hail from a distant land across an impassable mountain range, known as The Rift, to orchestrate the end of the world as they know it. The Seven, as they are called, are led by Aurum Guilden, the first of three main characters. Aurum is an Arthurian character tormented by loved ones lost, and his unwavering commitment to lead his brothers on this seemingly not so noble quest.

Galeerial Strongwind, a member in low standing among his angelic race, The Skyguard, who live in airy high places and majestic mountain cathedrals in the clouds above Carin, is the next main character that you will be introduced to. Galeerial immediately brings to mind what one would imagine the biblical archangels would look like. Only this angelic race has fallen from grace under the deception of a Luciferian creature named, Veriel. Galeerial has uncovered his traitorous scheme and is determined to expose his true identity.

The last of the three main characters is a woman of intrigue, Tendra Sumenel, princess of humanity and second in line to the throne in Gemport. Her father, Jethro, is a power hungry king who is obsessed with controlling all of Carin and will do anything to have it, even sacrificing his own son, Jakob to get it. Tendra's importance grows with the story, from what appears to be a minor role that connects the reader with the true emotions of the moment, to what may be the very fabric that all the main characters are so keenly woven into. The author does a masterful job of drawing the reader into the lives of each character and whets your appetite for more, only to be re-directed to the next storyline.

At first glance, Carin could easily be mistaken as one of those mythological lands imagined beyond the edge of the known world during the Dark Ages of Western Europe here on Earth. True romantics, who love nothing more than to curl up on a comfy couch or nestle into the comforter on their bed to read a good book, will love this read and will yearn for the sequel, Dawn of Darkness. Even the casual reader will easily become captivated with this book and want more.

What makes this world and this book so intriguing to me is that it was created from the imagination of a teenage author with very little real life experience to draw from. It conjures up images of a creative young heart and mind connecting with his Creator on a never-ending adventure called imagination. What touches my own heart is the fact that this aspiring young author is my son, Joshua D. Reding.

With the renewed global interest in high fantasy and incredible success of feature films, J.R.R. Tolkien's *The Lord of The Rings* and C.S. Lewis' *Chronicles of Narnia*, I am confident that Joshua Reding's Twilight of Ages and The Heart Quest Saga will be well received by enthusiasts around the world. As of this printing, Joshua has finished the manuscript of the sequel, Dawn of Darkness, and it is even better than Twilight of Ages.

Rick Reding
Proverbs 23:24

Preface

I thought I would write a new preface for this third, and, hopefully, final edition. Twilight of Ages has now been worked on for seven years. It hasn't always been my highest priority, or even in the top five, as evidenced by the fact that the last draft I published was in 2012, but it has always been in my thoughts. This book, and this series of books, known as The Heart Quest Saga, for reasons that will be made apparent as you read, represents my first foray into the world of writing. It isn't always pretty, in fact, a lot of the characters are rough outlines of who they will later become, but I wanted to leave the spirit of this first effort intact for this edition. The book is rough around the edges, because I was rough around the edges when I wrote it. The characters meander sometimes, because I was meandering when I wrote them. This story is a reflection of my most formative years. I hope you enjoy it. It is a piece of my soul. A soul that was still finding itself through literature. I'd like to end this the same way that I have ended every edition of this book I have published with a confession and a greeting.

This book is my mind, my heart, and my soul. Welcome to the world of Carin. Welcome to The Heart Quest Saga.

Nothing is True, Everything is Permitted
One

The first thing you notice in a battle is the sound...the sound of swords scraping as they move through flesh and bone...the sound of the screams: first as challenges, and then the cries of the dying as blood gurgles from open wounds...the sound of thunder. In every battle, I hear thunder.

Next, you notice the sights. The sky is bright above us; the sun is at its apex in the summer sky. The world is sharp in a battle. You see every enemy soldier in front of you vividly...your focus is wide, and the battlefield is entirely within your grasp. You see the shine on stainless armor...armor soon to lose that sheen. You see fear in the faces of some...anticipation, glee, hope, and resignation in the eyes of others. You see the future...your own death, the deaths of your enemies, the deaths

1

of your friends, the joys of victory, and the horrors of capture. Then, there is a shift, and suddenly the world blends back together into a cornucopia of brilliance and the danger that was once so abstract is now so very real.

I hear all this and more. I see all this and more.

I see hordes of ferals standing several hundred yards away from me. No feral stands above six feet tall, so I can never look them in the eye. An unholy amalgamation of man and wolf, the ferals can walk on two legs or gallop using their arms that stretch almost to their knees. Brown fur covered the ferals' bodies, but only small tufts protruded from the tops or sides of their breastplates and leggings. Their thin eyes sit above wolfish snouts full of snarling teeth. Their curved swords of cruel iron strapped to their backs with pikes and spears in their hands. I hear the sway of the grass in the light wind. I see the blood already staining my blade.

I pull my sword from the chest of the feral in front of me. Its white blood drips down the blade to my hand. The feral captain sinks to the ground, an expression of shock on his face. It is my first kill of the day and the first of many to come. But it isn't my first kill, and it is going to be far from my last. The smell is sickeningly, gloriously sweet. I shake my blade and watch as blood sprays off of it. I feel a hand on my shoulder pulling me back towards our army, which stands to the west. Suddenly, I am no longer entranced in the one moment. Now, the battle was on.

"Aurum, we've got to move!" I turned to see my brother Dorian urging me back. Beyond him, Rikard stood atop the body of the feral general, and his mighty bull mount…both dead by his blade. Rikard squared his shoulders and stared at the opposing army. There were over three hundred ferals standing opposite us…all warriors in the army of the Kingdom of Fangs.

I began to run. Our plan was very specific and required utter precision, but I stopped when I heard Rikard: when I heard him roar. It was terrifying, the sound of death's approach. I smiled. It was deep and raw, wordless…a challenge hurled out in defiance. A dare to come and face the ones who had just slaughtered your leaders so callously, and the Army of Fangs was more than ready to meet this challenge. They screamed in retaliation and charged.

They became a mass of moving flesh that rippled with the contours of the ground, a wave of fur and bone and steel. Rikard leapt from the body of the bull and sprinted after us. The seven of us fled from Sterin's Throne, where our confrontation had taken place. The massive black stone monolith stretched a hundred feet into the air, and it loomed high, as a specter above the battlefield. We hurled back towards our meager army, which held its ground a hundred yards from the solid stone tower.

"Split!" Joven yelled as the seven of us hurtled back to the forty-five men. Our ragtag army was full of farmers and millers and smiths…no soldiers. That would have defeated the purpose. They were here to serve as cannon fodder, something to distract the ferals from us.

The men hurriedly broke into their groups, six cells of seven men and one group of three. The group of three, our rangers, ran back to where their horses were waiting and leapt aboard. They would pick off any ferals who attempted to flee.

As they rushed to their circles, each headlined by one of us, they nocked arrows into their bowstrings and fired them off at the approaching horde. I stood center stage with Sterin's Throne directly in front of me. To the left of me stood Rikard and Dorian; behind me, Joven took his place, and to my right were Rayn, Grey and Rowen. I stood in front of my seven men; I couldn't remember any of their names, but I could hear the fear in their breathing and see it in their hands. They were right to

3

fear, but their fear would avail them not, for every one of them would die this day. We were as actors upon a stage, each with our designated place. Their place was to die, and ours was to triumph.

"On my mark," Rayn called out. It was his plan, and so he called the shots. Arrows flew by my face as the men behind fired one after another. I watched as most of them flew short and embedded in the ground, but a few of them found their marks. My skin tingled with anticipation. There was electricity in the air. We could all feel it. I trained my eyes forward, watching as they hurtled towards us. I looked down and saw the X burned into the ground in front of me. Grey had read something about X marking the spot in some story years ago and had henceforth attempted to include it in all that he did, no matter how inappropriate the circumstances. I was not amused.

"Steady." Two hundred yards, they crested the hill behind the Throne. The leaders sprinted ahead, loping on four legs, while the slower pike and spearmen lagged behind.

"Steady." They had reached Sterin's Throne. They would be upon us in thirty seconds. I knew that some of the men would barely be able to contain their enthusiasm. For some, this was their first kill, but for me, death was a gift that I had given out to many in the last seven years. Each time it had been easier and easier.

"Steady." Rayn called out. The main force had reached the break.

"Mark." His voice was calm and focused. We raised our staffs in unison and smashed them into the ground. The result was immediate. The world exploded into a shower of red glass and flying dirt as the explosion rippled through the Fields of Corug. A resounding crash shook my teeth as the shock wave slammed into us, followed quickly by the heat. Even though I was over a hundred yards from the explosion, I could still feel it singe my exposed skin.

The screams began again, screams of surprise transforming into victory from our men, and screams of pain from the enemy. The explosion had cut a giant swath in the feral's ranks. About forty had made it through the explosion, and they were bearing down upon us with all due speed.

"Break!" Rayn roared, and then they were upon us.

I swept my sword up to meet the opening overhead strike. The weight of the blow ran down the blade and into my right arm, shaking my wrist. I swept around with my staff and knocked the feral from its feet before reversing my grip and thrusting down into its chest. As I jutted out my staff, I whispered, causing lightning to arc from its tip and leaving a smoking crater where the head of another soldier had been not a second before.

My men formed around me. They were good-not great, but good enough for their designated task. They weren't fighters though, and two of them fell before the onslaught of the nine ferals attacking us. My brothers and I had taught them how to fight, but it had only been a week's worth of training. I whipped off my cloak to reveal chain mail. It was light enough to allow for full range of movement, but it would still protect me. I raised my staff as the second wave arrived.

"I need a lane!" I cried, and the three men in front of me ducked to the ground. "Splinter!" Lightning once again arced from the top of my staff, this time in a forked pattern that skewered several approaching ferals. I heard a gurgle as one of my men took an arrow to the throat and fell, with blood gushing from the wound. Half a second later, I saw two more fall from the sword slashes of multiple foes.

Only a blur was left in my wake as I moved from one foe to the next, never straying far from the center of my cell. My men did what they were told to do: they defended my flanks in close ranks as well as they could, but they weren't fast enough.

Once the last of my soldiers had fallen, I halted my bloody advance and twirled my sword around before slamming it into the ground. I gripped my staff in both hands, holding it high into the air. The ferals circled me carefully. Perfect. They were curious.

I was the calm center of a maelstrom. There was a pounding in my ears, but I was too fueled with adrenaline to notice. I didn't move. I merely looked at my enemies. They weren't sure what to do. I could see it in their faces. They knew I was dangerous and that-that alone, stayed their onslaught for the briefest of seconds. My hands were almost shaking due to the volume of adrenaline coursing through me.

They snarled at me with their hateful, frothing mouths. They raised their spears: sharp and bloody. "Push!" I threw my hand out towards the enemy before me, and three of the ferals went flying into the air. Their corpses came crashing back down to the ground, bodies broken twenty meters away. I lunged to the left at another group still gaping at their flying companions.

I swept my staff under the legs of one of the ferals and slammed it down into its throat; I could almost imagine the sound of the larynx collapsing inward. I deflected two sword slashes with the wood of my staff before sliding my hands down to grip it like a club and swinging it hard into the temple of one the ferals and snap kicking the second in the chest.

I saw a flash of fur and three leapt in unison towards my back. I dropped my staff at the feet of my blade and put my palms up.

"Burn!" I screamed and gouts of flame erupted from my hands. I stared into the eyes of the feral soldiers as their faces melted from their skulls. I forced myself to disengage from the flowing flesh, forcing myself to turn to the other wolves sur-

6

rounding me. I swept my arms out, spraying the surrounding beasts and encircling myself in fire. The smell of overcooked flesh and singed hair filled my nostrils. I breathed in deep.

I reached for my sword and was barely able to get it up in defense, as a crazed feral burst through the flames. I blocked his leap and rode the swing all the way over my head as he came down in a roll before returning to his feet. He wore the eight link chain of a commander, and we circled each other warily.

I had only to look at the way the feral carried himself to determine that this was not the usual rabble. This was a warrior. The other ferals that I had crossed blades with today were inexperienced in the ways of true warfare. They were used to the random pillaging and burning of farms against helpless peasants, not fighting well-trained warriors. But this feral, this feral knew how to wield a blade. I snapped back to attention as I focused on his black curved blade. Our eyes met, and then he was on top of me. I fended off a wave of furious thrusts parrying and redirecting, but always on the defensive. He was pushing me towards the brushfire that I had started a moment earlier. He was too fast, and my broadsword was too big and clumsy to be much help against someone like this, someone fast and agile in close quarters.

Again, he came at me lunging in as a feint before quickly reversing back into a sweep at my left leg. This time though, I was ready. I flipped the sword around and slammed it into the ground to block his advance and then slid my twin daggers from their sheaths in the sleeves of my armor. I dove forward, stabbing the feral quickly in the leg with one blade while cutting its hand from its wrist with the other.

I pulled my two blades with me, cutting a ragged hole into his leg and rolled to my feet. The feral stumbled from its leg wound and fell to the ground. I back-flipped to where my sword was sitting and pulled it from the ground. The feral scrambled back to his feet, and I sliced down hard, seeking to bisect him from head to foot, but he twisted out of the way and all I hit was his arm, which joined his hand on the ground. The feral captain turned and ran, stumbling and rolling through the circle of fire and away from the battle. His tortured cry as his fur caught fire and mixed with copious amounts of blood convinced me of his imminent demise. I thought no more of him as I searched for more targets, but surprisingly enough, there were none. The rest of the ferals had retreated from my circle of death.

I wiped the sweat from my brow and thrust my daggers into the ground to clean them before returning them to their sheaths. I gathered my strength, strapped my staff to my sweat-covered back, and gripped my sword in hand. I backed away and took a running start to leap out of the circle of fire, which enshrined me. I covered my face with my arms and snapped into a quick roll as I emerged from the flames. I rose smoothly back to my feet and began to run.

Chaos was everywhere, and the smoke from a dozen fires filled the air. My brothers had done their job well, and the sounds of the dying were a testament to this fact. Men and ferals were strewn about like children's toys after a tantrum. My eyes stung and watered. The air was thick.

As I ran toward the massive stone monolith that was Sterin's Throne, I whirled and stabbed one, two, three more ferals through the chest. I searched for my brothers as I went along. I dragged my sword as I ran, and it swept through the top of one feral's head that lay twitching on the ground. I saw four of the others moving in conjunction with me towards the Throne. They were all alone as well.

Rikard tossed pellets of wildfyre with impunity as he ran. It would burn and burn and burn with only a lack of fuel to put it out. It was dangerous, and I hesitated to use it, but Rikard was casting it like candy to greedy children. What struck me most was his laughter…it was the sound of a madman.

As I ran, I watched for ferals still breathing and out of the corner of my eye, saw a flicker of motion right before my left leg buckled, and I flew forward, face planting into the ground. My leg screamed in pain from the impact, and I looked back to see the shattered remnants of a spear strewn out behind me. An astonished feral watched gaping as I slowly rose back up to my feet. The spear hadn't penetrated, but the skin and muscle screamed with pain. I gritted my teeth.

"Strike!" I said pointing my staff at the feral, and a lightning blast left a gaping hole in its stomach. I spat out a mouthful of dirt as I turned away from the smoking corpse.

By this time, the crows had arrived. In truth, they could have been here for some time, but I hadn't noticed them until now. They swooped in to feast on the flesh of the fallen as well as the not yet fallen. The sky was black with them…every crow within a hundred miles had answered our call.

I saw Dorian hurtling down to where Joven and Rikard now stood at the base of Sterin's Throne. The large stone tower loomed high above me as I approached; I was less than a hundred feet from it now and I smiled. Where the battle began, so here it would end.

As I arrived, Dorian, Joven, and Rikard were already there. Rayn was making a slow advance towards us, fighting along the way. Rowen and Grey were nowhere to be seen, but I knew they would be coming from the other side of Sterin's Throne.

Joven, the next oldest brother after me, gestured for me to watch the flank on the other side of the Throne to see if the others were coming and to watch for a counter-attack. The field to the east was slanted upward and reached its apex in a hill, whereas everywhere else was flat surrounding the Throne. Grey and Rowen came trotting down the hill and I greeted them as they arrived. Grey had a large toothy grin on his soot-covered face. Rarely did I know the man to now be grinning, though it seemed obviously out of place on the battlefield. Though being a historian, Grey himself was out of place on the battlefield. One day long ago, I would have been too.

"What's the word?" I asked.

"Nothing, it's over." Rowen smiled with relief. "We did it. Not that there was any doubt of course, at least not with me here." His grin was unaffected by the rolling of my eyes.

"A few ferals escaped, most so wounded they won't make it back to Long Fang, but a few of them will live long enough to spread the word and the fear." Joven said joining us.

"Casualties from our forces?" Joven asked.

"Every human we brought with us is dead." Dorian confirmed. I nodded my head in acknowledgement. It was unfortunate, but neither unanticipated, nor undesirable. No one would remember those men who had followed us, and none of them would be alive to remind the world of what they had done. I leaned heavily on my staff as the adrenaline began to seep from my body, and the pain in my leg began to throb. I gritted my teeth and along with the rest of my brothers, we made our way up the hill. What I was greeted with was glorious.

Death greeted us: three hundred and sixty degrees of it. The world was awash with color: the flickering red of fires, the constant red of human blood, the white blood of the lupine ferals, and the black wings of crows. The last things you notice in battle are the sights. I see the future before me-our future. The one we had brought with us, the future of Carin, one of endings and steel and ruin and fire and blood. I see a future of change. I see a future of men. I looked at everything we had made, and it was very good.

"My lord, a messenger from the Fields of Corug has arrived." The snarling voice of the gatekeeper Tarth called out. Lord Kaelish, king of the Kingdom of Fangs, glared down from his throne. It was a throne made from the jawbone of Rirnef, the largest wolf to ever walk the earth. Legend said that in ages past it had drunk the sound from the Island of Silence which was, an age ago, known as Nyx and was still called so on the old maps. Now, no words could be spoken on that island's shores. Lord Kaelish didn't believe those myths, but there was no denying the power that was extruded from the garish teeth that were covered in silver and its bronze jawbone. Kaelish sat on this throne now just as he had sat when General Syrn had walked out at dawn, and here he sat long past sun fall. Kaelish was not an intimidating king in physical stature or in fierceness. He had guile though, and he had powerful friends.

Three days ago, a human arrived bearing the heads of a hundred feral rangers, but he came also with a challenge: seven Wizards against the entirety of the Kingdom of Fangs. Initially, Kaelish had scoffed at the proposition; magic was a myth. Wizards. The sheer absurdity of it had made him laugh. Yet something stayed his hand, something made him pause. For, in the last five or so years, there had been whispers.

Every story was different, yet they all had one underlying thread. Magic and humans, always paired together. These whispers were what stayed his hand from outright dismissal. They made him hesitate, and so the King of Fangs had sent three hundred and fifty of his men along with one of his three generals to deal with the problem. But now, he wasn't so sure even that had been enough.

Kaelish felt something in his gut; it was something he had felt all too often these days. It was the feeling of fear: fear of

11

the unknown, the fear that something had gone terribly, horribly wrong. Syrn had not been heard from since he had left this morning at sunrise. Kaelish should have heard something-anything, and now he would discover exactly what had occurred.

"Enter, and be heard." Kaelish hissed. The feral that was brought before him was not what he had expected, but rather what he had feared. This pathetic feral had one arm hanging limply at its side, while the other was nonexistent, and blood caked the fur of its head. Its fur was burned to ash, and it stood all but naked in front of him. It stumbled down the length of the chamber until it arrived at the throne, where it collapsed to its knees.

"Lord, I bring word from Sterin's Throne. They...they are all dead. Every last one of them! The wizards, they killed them all." Kaelish's blood ran cold.

"Speak. Your life will be weighed by your tale." Kaelish said in a low tone.

"Yes my..." The feral coughed and wheezed out blood and saliva, "...liege. Syrn led us to the Fields of Corug; we arrived between sunrise and the apex of the sun. He rode out on his bull with the four captains to demand their surrender as is custom. Seven men strode out to meet him. Following them, were maybe fifty humans at most." The feral spat out the word 'humans.' "The wizards wore heavy robes and carried long staffs. They met with Syrn and his aides. We could not hear what was said, but we watched as out of nowhere, the beasts attacked them. They...they butchered them. All of them. I have never seen humans move so fast." The feral coughed twice, and then spat blood out on the floor. Kaelish sat stoically as he listened.

"When they fell, we...were shocked. We didn't know what to do. There was chaos in the ranks; we all stood and watched as they turned and began to run, all but one. One among their number stood on the back of the dead bull and screamed a challenge at us. Some among our ranks began to scream battle cries, and we charged at them. I was swept along with the others. It was madness, mindless havoc; nobody knew what to do. All that we knew was to kill. There was no plan, no order, just blood lust. We hurtled at them, drawing our weapons. The archers hung back and arrows began to fly. The wizards retreated back beyond Sterin's Throne to where their men awaited. As we approached, the whole world exploded. Light flashed, and I watched as all around me ferals were thrown into the air. Fires began to erupt, but we continued forward. Then we were on them. The men fell like wheat before us. They were just humans, but the wizards..." He coughed again, and his body collapsed to the ground.

"Rise." Kaelish commanded. The exertion was evident on the feral's face. It struggled up to its knees. "Finish."

"The wizards' staffs spewed lightning, and their hands poison and fire. Their swords flashed and struck like thunderbolts. They moved so fast. We never even got close. We fell in droves while they never sustained a scratch. I lost an arm attacking one of them one on one. My every strike he blocked. He moved so fast. I never even saw the sword cut through my flesh." His left leg gave out again, and he fell to the ground. Two guards moved to help him.

"Stop! I told you to rise, captain." Kaelish said. Once again he struggled up to his feet, and Kaelish knew that he was almost gone.

"Then the crows came. En masse they descended upon us, attacking even those who hadn't fallen. They were crazed, wild, ferocious. They feasted on all but Them. I watched as they slaughtered all of us-the wounded, those crying their surrender, all of them. I ran as fast as I could, and it still took me an eternity to arrive here. They followed me here I know, I saw them." The feral's eyes grew wild, and Kaelish knew that now all he would get was paranoia and fear.

"They are here…in Long Fang! They are spirits of death, three hundred men against fifty, and they received not a scratch. They are not men, but Horrors." The feral captain sputtered out his last word before collapsing into unconsciousness. A pool of blood had marshaled around where he lay. Kaelish sat brooding on his throne.

"Leave me. Tend his wounds; he is valuable and will be useful in the future." Two guards strode forward and lifted the captain from the ground and pulled him out of the Hall. His words were disturbing, to say the least.

"Close the gates, no one in or out. Double the night watch, anything out of the ordinary is to be killed. No chances. Now leave me, all of you." The guards nodded their understanding, and the rest of his cabinet bowed gracefully before removing themselves from the chamber. Kaelish felt a shiver run up his spine. Things had changed. Magic, long the domain of children's tales and *The Stone*, was once again real. *Humans. How dare they? How dare they do this to me?* Kaelish seethed. King Jethro would burn for this. This meant one thing…war. Kaelish knew it. This changed things. The Heart of Fires had been found, and it was in the hands of humanity.

The Dread would not be pleased.

Death Flies on Dark Wings

Two

"Ezekiel?" Galeerial Strongwind inquired as he landed gracefully upon the platform, which led into their shared aerie. The air was thin up here at the top of the mountain where the city of Cloud Breach was built: thin and cold. As a Skyguard, Galeerial barely felt it. His long white, feathered wings connected at his shoulder blades folded in behind him as he entered their dwelling.

"Yes Galeerial, no need to shout." Ezekiel Gracefall called down lazily from his hammock, which was slung from the ceiling. Galeerial's best friend acknowledged him with only a finger to his lips, while his eyes remained firmly entrenched in

15

his book. "Hush, it is worship hour, Galeerial; calm yourself." Ezekiel was in some ways a mirror to Galeerial, and in others polar opposite. He was patient and relaxed to Galeerial's rasher temperament. However, they shared the same long blonde hair and violet eyes as all members of their species. Though Galeerial's was a good deal more tussled. Ezekiel was stronger in build though; he enjoyed having his feet on the ground almost as much as he enjoyed flying. Galeerial had never understood his friend's disposition towards walking, but it showed in his more toned legs.

"Come now, you know that every hour here is worship hour. Besides look what you're reading." Galeerial rebuked. Ezekiel shrugged as he went back to his book, *Endless*. It told the story of seven immortals who wandered the earth for a thousand years before despairing and hurling themselves into the Rift. Yet even that could not kill them, and there within that bottomless abyss they still wait for the Ravishing of the World, the day when the world was destroyed again.

"I have read *The Stone* so many times that I know every word of it by soul." Ezekiel responded.

"You know, but do you truly understand?" Galeerial replied in a holier-than-thou voice, which they often used as representing the High Clerics, the leaders of the Skyguard. This brought both a grin and chuckle out of Ezekiel.

"Well?" Ezekiel asked inquisitively ignoring Galeerial's question.

"Well what?" Galeerial responded innocently.

"You are in far too good a mood for any kind of a normal day, so tell me what new revelation has been imparted upon you concerning the Heart Quest?" The Heart Quest was their code phrase. About seven years ago, Galeerial began to have suspicions that the Lord Commander of the Shining Host was not all that he seemed. Veriel was his name, and he was an irregular-

16

ity among the Skyguard. He was the only one that anyone in Cloud Breach knew to have visited all three of the divine cathedrals.

Veriel had arrived in Cloud Breach about two hundred and fifty years ago with claims of coming from the city, Soaring, and spreading a message of peace and self-sufficiency of the Skyguard: a message that promoted the worth of the Skyguard above all else. Now, he was the Lord Commander, a rank second only to the High Clerics.

Since Veriel's arrival, slowly but steadily changes had begun to occur that had aroused Galeerial's suspicions. About five years ago, Galeerial had first brought these suspicions to Ezekiel, and they had compiled them all together into a book. They had plenty of suspicious evidence, but nothing solid, nothing definitive, and it seemed to Ezekiel that Galeerial had finally found it.

"This could be the one, Ezekiel. This could decide everything." The grin on Galeerial's face was wide enough to bridge the Rift.

"You are going to make me beg aren't you?" Ezekiel clicked his tongue. "Fine." He rolled off his hammock and floated down to the ground spreading his wings out behind him to slow his fall. Galeerial just stood there watching him approach. Ezekiel's feet touched the ground, and he walked up to Galeerial, who was still perched right at the edge of the doorway and shoved him hard back out the door. Galeerial pin-wheeled his arms in a desperate effort to keep his balance but the force was too great and he fell.

"So that's how you want to play?" Galeerial said with a smile as he rolled with the fall and let his momentum carry him earthward, relishing the feeling of the wind on his face as he folded his wings in behind him, picking up speed with Ezekiel in hot pursuit. It was an old game...first to the city gates wins the crown. Not only that, but the loser would have to do one thing that the winner wanted, which usually meant going out on illegal rangings for various items. Today though, Galeerial would reveal his hunch, his grand idea. If it turned out to be true, it would mean that not only was Veriel a liar and a traitor, but that he was not even a Skyguard. Galeerial knew that he would tell Ezekiel regardless of the outcome, but he wanted to win nonetheless.

He opened his wings a fraction of a second before he hit the ground and pulled up into a tight glide that used his momentum to carry him up about three yards above the ground zooming tightly in between the towers of the Skyguard, which contained barracks and forges and bakeries and other places of creation. A Skyguard walked out of his aerie and into Galeerial's path, and Galeerial had to throw his weight right and raise his wings to toss himself out of the other Skyguard's way. Galeerial crashed into the wall and dropped into a roll and took back off running with a string of muttering following him. He grinned, but knew that he would surely be chastised for that later.

Galeerial glanced up and saw Ezekiel about ten yards above him and fifteen in front, reclining on his back and waving at him. Galeerial sprinted forward and leapt into the air, beating his wings to try to gain back his momentum. He thrashed his wings hard behind him in order to make up the gap. He wove behind Ezekiel, trying hard to make up ground but not succeeding.

The Dead Gates arose in front of him, and he knew that this was one race that he was going to lose. He saw Ezekiel descend lightly and sighed. The gates stood before Tenbraun, the ascending road. In the days of old it had been crowded with traders from all over the land of Carin coming to witness the spectacle of the towering Cathedral of Light or trade for the burned glass for which the Skyguard were so famous. But no longer were outsiders welcome in Cloud Breach.

"Pity." Galeerial said as he landed next to his friend.

"Say it." Ezekiel prodded.

"The Crown passes to you, after fourteen days of being under the rule of Galeerial the Magnificent, the Benevolent, the…"

"Blowhard?" Ezekiel interrupted, and they chuckled.

"Good enough," Ezekiel said nodding his head towards the old guard tower. "Now let us chat about what exactly it is that you found."

"After you, my liege." Galeerial said with an exaggerated bow and a mocking tone. Ezekiel shook his head but, nonetheless, walked into the guard tower followed by Galeerial.

Inside, everything was old. Years upon years rested heavily upon the stone guard tower. Ivy crept up the walls, and dust smothered everything within.

To the left existed a decrepit bookshelf, which held, among other books, *The Stone:* the foundation upon which the faith in Supremor was wrought. It had been written just after the Reforging of the World, mostly by Crestian, the telos secondborn son of Garen, the first man. Their evidence lied between pages 342 and 345, at the end of the chapter "Fireheart", which told of Garen's funeral and of the binding of magic to the Heart of Fires. This missing page detailed the final resting place of that stone.

In the original writing of *The Stone*, which had actually been carved into stone, those two pages had been shattered by some unknown force before the book had been copied and were lost forever to the annals of history.

The file was twelve fully scripted pages long, detailing everything that had occurred since Veriel had arrived that could be listed as evidence of a possible conspiracy. Everything from the prohibition of ranging to the forced isolation from the other races of the world to the limited contact between the Skyguard and the Clerics to several mysterious deaths…all of this and more was contained within. While Ezekiel settled down into one of the simple wooden chairs, Galeerial went for the wine they had stashed behind a particularly heavy grove of ivy that had grown up the side of one of the craggy walls. Galeerial popped the cork. It was nigh impossible to get wine anymore, and thus only opened in times of great sorrow or greater joy. Today was one of those days. It was one of forty-nine bottles they discovered about eighty years ago. Sadly, they were down to two…and now only one. Galeerial took his time sitting down and getting comfortable.

"What have you discovered?" The eagerness in Ezekiel's voice could not be mistaken. Galeerial took pleasure in his friend's anticipation and took his time in filling his draught before enjoying a long drink. The sweetness filled his mouth, and it slid smoothly down his throat. It was delicious. A treat that was far too brief to be fully enjoyed. He passed the bottle to the impatient Ezekiel.

"Not discovered, realized. It is so simple that I cannot believe we forgot to look for it…the Aer."

"I do not understand." Ezekiel said.

"Bear with me. You know how we have talked about how Veriel does not look quite right? He looks a little too perfect, too idealized. What if, Veriel is not a Skyguard, but just looks like one?" A puzzled look gave way to a grin of realization, which spread over Ezekiel's face, and Galeerial felt a thrill of elation flow through him. The Aer was the name given to the soul that all Skyguard were imbued with. Skyguard don't bleed, for the Aer runs through their veins. It is what keeps them alive. Each Skyguard's Aer held the entirety of his or her life it was the song of his or her soul that would echo through the holy Cathedral when he or she died.

"He would not be able to swallow the Charist." Ezekiel pondered. The Charist was a holy drink that Skyguard needed to consume every week or else they would die. It replenished and rejuvenated their Aer. No other race could drink it. Galeerial nodded his head in response. "Sunday is in two days; we can verify it then." Galeerial nodded his head, and Ezekiel took a sip.

"Exactly, and if he does not, then I think it is time to approach the High Clerics." Galeerial said, his voice falling back down to an acceptable speaking level.

"You think...You think? Of course it is. If he does not swallow it this Sunday at the service, then we nail his wings to the wall the next day." Galeerial felt a sense of uneasiness come over him. Ezekiel noted the subtle change in his mood. "What is it?" Ezekiel asked, concerned.

"Let us think about how we should do this. If Veriel really is not one of us, then that means he has been deceiving the High Clerics for over two hundred years. Who has that kind of power? To lie while standing before the shiftstone idol, I didn't think such an act was possible. Unless..."

"Unless what?" Ezekiel inquired.

"You do not know as much history as I do," Ezekiel gave him a disproving look, "do not look at me like that. You have grown lax in your studies, we both know it. During the Dread War, there was a being that traveled with the Dread all those years ago: a being called the Wither. No one really knew what he looked like, but he vanished after the assassination of the Dread at Amul Kon. He was one of the principal lieutenants of the Dread...and whispers were that he was not one of the children of Garen. What if Veriel is the Wither? It would make sense." Ezekiel looked at him.

"Why him?"

"Excuse me?" Galeerial asked confused.

21

"Well, there are still Horrors out there. Who is to say that Veriel is not one of them? What is it about the Wither that drew you to him?"

"I do not know. It is just one of the untold stories of history. Who or what was the Wither? Nobody knew. No one knows still. It is one of the great mysteries of the world."

"Okay well, let us think about it then…what was the goal of the Wither? What did he do within the army of the Dread? What was his purpose, Mr. History?" Ezekiel asked with a smile.

"Like I said, nobody knew. I mean the goal of Veriel is obviously to render the Skyguard impotent, if not completely and utterly indebted to him. Or maybe he just wants to destroy us all. As for the Wither, there just is nothing in history that is really written about him beyond his presence. He was obviously important… the Dread had five lieutenants, that much we know. The Wither is the only one that there is no solid accounting of about his life or his death, outside of brief mentions in books like *Shadowed Stars* and *Juniper*. However, there is a poem written about him." Ezekiel looked at him expectedly. Galeerial sighed and called the poem from the depths.

"Dusty bones
Ashy eyes
Dies
All dies
Born of Garen
NO!
Thrice cursed
Never!
The end of order
The agent of chaos ends
Bends
Trends

22

Fends
Himself over all
Slick as shadow
Loyalties folly
Honors mockery
Snake no plans
Can ever see
All, know all, be none
Firesoft, waterbound
Death in every form
Annihilation's bride"

"Well, I understood none of that." Ezekiel said with a smile.

"Wait…Mr. Cryptic Prophecies cannot understand a simple poem written a thousand years ago?" Galeerial asked, a mask of shock on his face. Ezekiel merely rolled his eyes.

"Well, it does not help our situation knowing who he is anyway. It does not matter who or what Veriel is; if he is truly not a Skyguard, then he must be judged." Ezekiel said pointedly.

"So what are we going to do?" Galeerial asked.

"We cannot hide this." Ezekiel said with conviction.

"I know that." Galeerial snapped.

"The High Clerics cannot ignore this, but Veriel will fight tooth and nail. If we are right about him, he has been laying these plans for hundreds of years."

"If we are right." Galeerial echoed. "They will use the Five Eye. They must." The Five Eye was a pendant that was held by the Supreme Cleric, the lord of all Skyguard. No one knew who he was. The anonymity was supposed to ensure that all Skyguard treated each other with the utmost of dignity and respect. Neither Galeerial nor Ezekiel had ever seen the Five Eye, but they knew of its power. Any Skyguard could wield it.

23

"If he is not one of us, the Five Eye will not work." Ezekiel responded.

"Exactly!"

"So, that is it then? In three days, we could be the greatest heroes that the Skyguard has ever known." Ezekiel said with a smile.

"No, now you are just being silly. If we are heroes, it makes you sad for the glory days... the days when our forces blocked the midday sun...when the Hailing Harp and the Trumpets of Wrath and the Horn of Seventeen Sorrows rang out in a cacophony that heralded the destruction of some deadly foe...when the Skyguard were the arbiters of justice and reason throughout the land. When these gates," Galeerial swung the half emptied bottle of wine in a wide gesture to the walls around him, "were filled with the songs of humans and unu and giants and centaurs and Iron Men. A time of heroes and legends...a time of great darkness and even greater light." A sober mood fell over Galeerial, "a time long gone, but never forgotten." It was a final toast, and Galeerial took one last swig before handing it over to Ezekiel, who sat silently listening to his friend.

"I fear those times are soon to be upon us again, my friend."

"You fear? You fear glory and honor and-"

"Death? How about war and strife and famine? You may know history, my friend, but I know the prophecies of the world far better than anyone else: living or dead." With that Ezekiel began a low hum, which lead into ominous words.

"A Twilight of Ages
When the second Pillar is strangled by itself
And fear grips the world
When seven emerge from shadow
And two share a single face
When lies break truth's fragile hold

24

When alliances are formed in death's name
And plans buried bear fruit
The silent kingdom dawns.
Summer will fall to winter's bite
And the Skyguard will pass into the night."

"You speak from the book of final prophecies. You speak from the Book of Arestephan. You say the end of the world is upon us then? The Ravishing is coming?" Galeerial said quietly. Night time had descended upon them as they spoke, and the last vestiges of light had begun to fade from view. Ezekiel nodded.

"Then, if the days we live in truly be those times...if the Ravishing of the World truly is within our grasp, then we of the Skyguard welcome it. Now come," Galeerial said, helping his friend to his feet as the last of the bottle was drained. Ezekiel held the empty bottle upside down, and a single drop fell from its rim. It hit the ground with a small splash. They walked together out into the night sky. There was only one thing left to do. Wait

*   *   *

Galeerial sat perched atop one of the many spires that adorned the great Cathedral of Light. They had been right; Veriel hadn't swallowed the Charist, though his deception had been almost entirely complete, and Galeerial knew why they had missed it, for it was extraordinarily well-practiced. After he had drunk from the golden goblet, he had bowed his head and kept his mouth firmly shut seemingly deep within the throes of earnest prayer to Supremor. But as is said, "when you stare into the looking glass, the looking glass stares back," and Galeerial was sure that Veriel had noticed his gaze. When he had shared his thoughts with Ezekiel, they agreed that Veriel was to be under a keen eye at all times.

25

So, here he sat, watching Veriel fly quickly and quietly out from his loft and down across the Plaza of the Fallen, pull into a tight loop and descend into the massive pit in the center of the plaza that extended deep into the heart of the mountain where the stone cells lay dark. Galeerial gave a slight start. That he had not expected. He had expected something, but certainly not that. The stone cells had been created in ancient times to house the enemies of the Skyguard.

"What are you doing down there, Veriel?" Galeerial muttered to himself. He knew that he should go and wake Ezekiel, but Ezekiel had only woken him an hour and a half ago. He waited another minute to allow Veriel enough of a head start such that he would not be waiting for him when he arrived at the bottom of the shaft.

"Sixty." He murmured, followed by a short prayer of protection to Supremor, before leaping from his perch and following Veriel down into the deep darkness of the mountain. Instantly, Galeerial felt a tightness grip his chest as he descended. The air was close, and the sheer presence of the stone weighed heavily upon him. His breath grew shallow. He had to force himself to bring it back under control. He looked behind him and saw the pinpoints of light that were the stars high above him. He slowly began to spread his wings out to slow his descent. The last thing that he wanted was to crash into the bottom. He could still barely see anything, but his eyes could make out the flickering light of a fire about another hundred meters below him.

He beat his wings as slowly as he could in order to halt his flight and landed quietly upon the ground. He heard the murmur of voices as he crept down the hallway to where the old cells lay, unused for centuries.

"...need a catalyst."

"I may have something. A group of humans have been preparing for some kind of event. My master's book is disturbingly vague on them, but I have been able to watch them through their interactions with others. This event will occur in midsummer." This was a second voice, one that was wholly unlike anything that Galeerial had ever heard before. It was harmonic and sullen. And pronounced the 'T's in words very precisely.

"Interesting. Though that is still six months away. I can manufacture an event if need be, but if these humans are willing, we can use them. And the Skyguard?" This was a third player. Galeerial crept down the corridor until he was right at the edge of the doorway. He did not dare look. He could not risk getting caught.

"They will fall in line, just like they always have. Just like they always have."

"Cloud Breach will follow me wherever I lead, and the other two cathedrals will fall into step. I will allow these agents of chaos to perform their duty for a short while before sending the Skyguard into battle, and, when the ranks of the world have been suitably diminished, my army will sweep down from Wolfram to obliterate whatever opposition is left." *His army? Wolfram?* Wolfram was a city in the far away times. Back before the War of Unending Flames had resulted in the Burning Waters destroying the entire northwest region of Carin. "It will be simple to convince the Clerics that the humans have desecrated Garen's tomb and must be destroyed. The Clerics worship Garen almost as much as they do Supremor. Who will they strike against?"

"The ferals." The second voice replied.

"Kaelish is the king, is he not?" There was a pause. "Tell me about him."

"The ferals have long resented the disservice given them by the other races in the world, especially for their alliance with the Dread, and the races' belief that the Dread created them. Kaelish is no different."

27

"Contact him. Give him a way out, make him feel important. Use the world's prejudices to offer him safety and security. He will resist, but with the right catalyst, he will fall in line."

"I am not a lackey, Veriel." The voice grew low and threatening.

"I did not mean to insinuate as such. However, our goals are mutually aligned, and it was you who sought me out originally and not the other way around." Veriel replied coolly. *Interesting*. There was bickering within the ranks of the leadership.

"Just remember that I don't serve you. Our paths coincide right now, but my master is far beyond even you."

"So you may think, and though your master is important in our game, I am one of the players. More than that, you know what I am capable of and that your power has no sway over me, but mine might just be enough to kill you. We tread many of the same paths, which is why you are here, and because it is your fate. You know this to be true as much as I do."

"Indeed, but unlike you, I can exist beyond your limits. I can go where even your power becomes meaningless, and my master's book knows things even you do not. You need me Veriel, you need what is mine, and what is my masters." There was a slight pause.

"What about him?"

"Galeerial?" Veriel questioned, and Galeerial missed the response.

He knows me...Dreadspawn! Galeerial swallowed. A thousand thoughts per second blazed through his mind, but, through it all, one thought rose to the surface. *This was it.*

No more delays were tolerable. He would have to go to the Clerics immediately. He tuned back into the conversation just in time.

"Everything goes according to plan with him."

28

"Well, just be aware that he has heard the majority of this conversation." Galeerial's eyes opened wide as he heard Veriel begin to curse, but he was already hurtling towards the exit. Galeerial ran the ten meters to the base of the shaft, bent his legs and hurled himself up into the air. He shot up into the still air of the tunnel beating his wings furiously behind him.

The starlight was but a small pinpoint when he began his ascent, but it was slowly growing bigger and bigger. But not fast enough. Galeerial's face grew taut, and he stretched his wings as hard as he could. He knew that the slipstream from his wings would force Veriel back and buy him more time, but he didn't know if it would be enough. He saw the hole of sky that was freedom loom large ahead of him, and he thought he heard a snarl beneath him. Terrified, he pounded his wings one final time and SWOOSH!

He was free!

He shot into the air, rising a few dozen yards into the sky before angling his wings to send him hurtling towards the Cathedral of Light. He would find sanctuary there. No matter what Veriel was, even he would dare not commit murder within its hallowed walls.

He pounded his wings forward. He saw one of the small gateways that allowed entrance into one of the cathedral's higher levels…another thirty yards, and he was there. Just then, a wraith entered Galeerial's periphery, and he turned just in time to get the wind knocked out of him as a shadow slammed him against the wall of the cathedral.

30

Aftershock
Three

I sat alone within the way-station. Three raids were going to be staged tonight...led by three pairs of us, Joven and Rayn, Dorian and Grey, and Rowen and Rikard. In the meantime, because of my wounded leg, I was forced to sit this one out. I roved around our small way-station. It was a twenty-foot-long, eight-foot-high and ten-foot-wide underground lair at the base of the mountain of Lightwatch. This was way-station number twelve, codenamed The Boar. These were designed to be so well hidden that no one would ever find them, but occasionally accidents had happened. Two years ago someone had stumbled upon The Flare, a way-station which was located on the west side of Lake Lefron. We had been forced to take extreme steps to preserve the safety and security of that station.

I paced back and forth in The Boar until finally settling down to read from *The Stone*. It was an amazing piece of work, and even with seven years' worth of reading, there were still stories to be told within it that were astounding…stories from back at the beginning of the world, even some from before the Reforging, as it was called. I thumbed through the book to Threshold 4:12-46:

And those of pride took up their arms across the lands in crusade against their maker. They strode to His Hallowed Halls and into the Room where the All-Creator, Supremor, dwelt. Weapons of fire and ice and earth and sky were brought to bear and those assembled quaked in fear as they approached the mighty throne which was turned from them. They came into view of their Creator and all assembled dropped their weapons in fright.

Before them sat an empty throne and a voice rang out in blinding light.

'Oh you of foolishness and audacity and pride. You who hath been corrupted and now bear arms against me. You hath done naught but to rain death upon your families and your peoples. Your animals will be slaughtered and your lands brought to doom.' And the men shook with fear and fell to their knees in sorrow. But it was too late.

So great was the wrath of Supremor that the world was rent asunder and scattered across the stars, and the race of the Proud were reduced to naught but a single man and woman. Garen and Meren. A man and woman so pure of heart and spirit that Supremor spared them. They lived through the Breaking by the grace of Supremor's mercy. But they were changed. They were gifted with a land of their own, where, in the old order, they had been the lowliest of peasants. For so great was Supremor's mercy that the lowest became the highest, and the world was made clean once again.

32

I set the book down. Threshold was the last book before the new world, after the Reforging...an odd name considering Carin was bound on all sides by the Rift and was still rent apart, though not quite as far away as some might presume. I stood up: restless. The others would not return for several hours, and I knew that I wouldn't sleep until they returned. I fashioned my sword to my back and emerged from The Boar.

I pulled the hood of my dark brown cloak up. There was a tavern a few miles south of here where I could find a drink and, more importantly, information. It was late enough that all the chores would be done. So the farmhands and even the bosses would be enjoying a drink. And the owner, Gabin, was a good source of information if you had the coin.

It was a long, ponderous walk. My ankle had been healing nicely, but it was still swollen, and I didn't want to agitate it any further. I made sure, however, that I didn't look like I was injured. The broadsword would deter most thieves. The majority of knights and lords used hand-and-half swords or even sabers. If you had a broadsword, it meant that you were rich, but if you carried it, then it also meant that you knew how to use it.

The lanterns of the tavern were visible from far off-a beacon that seemed perpetually out of reach. When I finally arrived at the *Lingering Ocean,* I really needed a drink. I pushed open the door and caught quite a few stares as I made my way up to the bar. I knew the broadsword would attract attention, but I wanted to look like a traveler, and a traveler with no weapon was a fool.

I took a seat next to a young man, probably eighteen or nineteen, who looked rather perturbed that I was sitting next to him. He was tall and lean, not real muscular. His face, though, made him look more like a noble, with his blonde hair and long face, and his smooth hands confirmed his spoiled nature.

"May I help you?" He said to me indignantly.

"Maybe. Depends on how stupid you are." I replied without even bothering to meet his gaze. A hush fell over the bar as Gabin strode over to where we were sitting.

"Listen fella, we're all friends here. Got a name?" Gabin cut in. He was a short stocky man with a large chest and a big smile. His face was quite unusual; he had only half of it working right. Rayn had told me that Gabin's right ear had been cut off in a duel many years ago, and his right eye had been burned out in a later fracas. The blonde-haired boy still looked angry that I was sitting next to him, and I realized why a second later when I turned as the doors opened to reveal a very pretty young woman.

"Damaen...Damaen Longshore." I replied, it was the name I had used when traveling along the Thorne Coast, and the name most of the world knew me by, at least for the moment. I heard a couple of whispers at that name, and I smiled. People knew the name, and they feared it. The girl had curly brown hair that flowed down past her shoulders. She strode around behind the bar, giving Gabin a kiss on the cheek.

"Rose, would you get our friend Damaen here a drink while I speak with young master Yorin for a moment?" Gabin gestured with his eyes, and Yorin removed himself stiltedly to the far end of the bar.

"Of course." She said, flashing me a smile. "What'll it be?"

"Firewine, indigo if you have it...gold if you don't." She nodded and turned to find the appropriate bottle.

"So, where are you from? You've got an interesting accent. I haven't heard anything quite like it before, and believe me, I've heard a lot of accents." She said casually while she pulled one of the bottles down from the shelf.

34

"To be honest, there is no place that I really call home. I've been wandering all over Carin for the last few years. Most recently, I'm out of Shezon."

"Oh? How's Chancellor Hop doing? Still embezzling from the royal coffers?" I smiled. It was bait. For all her pretty looks, she knew what to ask. Hop died a couple of months back, and his son Jeffris looked to be the one to replace him, though right now the city was under the control of the council.

"Not unless he is doing it from the grave." I replied, and she gave me a slightly odd look as she poured my drink. I smiled, half because I had defied her expectations and half because the wine was indigo.

"So what brings you here?" She asked, still slightly off balance at being proven wrong. *Amateur.*

"I heard rumors that something big was going down. I've been hearing reports that a band of men took down a superior force of ferals over at the Throne. Thought maybe I could pick them up. My business is always looking to expand."

"You heard right. Though it wasn't just men, there were a group of magi with 'em as well." I cocked an eyebrow. Before I could respond, a hand came to rest on my shoulder. I turned and saw the angry young man standing there.

"That's my girl you're talking to, stranger. I don't like it when men talk to my girl in such a cavalier manner."

"Yorin!" Rose said exasperated.

"You pick fights with every guy that talks to the barkeep?" I said turning back around to my drink.

"Only ones who I don't like the look of." He replied sharply.

"If you want to keep your hand boy, you'll remove it. I'm just passing through looking for some information about that little ruckus over at the Throne, that's all. But I can make my business a lot less pleasant." Out of the corner of my eye I saw

Gabin over in the corner shaking his head. I knew that he had just warned this young man not to do what he had just done.

"I think it is time for you to leave." He said in a voice that I would imagine to him sounded firm, but to me it just sounded scared.

"Last chance, boy." I waited for a moment, but the hand remained firmly clamped to my shoulder. I sighed. "Better tell your girl to turn around. She won't want to see this."

"Do you know who I am? I am Magistrate Uman's nephew. He holds province over these lands, which includes you while you are in them." Aha, that explained it. He was a noble, I smiled in acknowledgment of the correctness of my earlier thoughts. I didn't know why he was dawdling amongst the farm folk, besides the pretty face, but it was clear by a glance around the tavern that everybody was just waiting to see him get beaten down. I turned around and stood up, grabbing him by the front of the shirt.

"What makes you think I care what breeding stock you hail from?" I asked pulling him close to my face. I saw a shadow of fear cross over his face. It gave me a modicum of satisfaction to know that this moron wasn't completely devoid of common sense. I hadn't come here looking for a fight, but from the looks on people's faces, the folk here might be more inclined to talk if I did bloody him just a bit to teach him a lesson. A knock on the door caused me to turn, and I saw a centaur walk in. I immediately dropped the boy and silently cursed. I did not need this right now. No one in the bar moved. Everyone just stared. The centaur bowed by bringing his right elbow to his knee.

"My name is Dane, and I seek information about the Seven Sorcerers. I am prepared to reward anyone handsomely for any information that you have on them." I saw Gabin move away from one of the bar's patrons and a moment later saw that self-same individual call out to the centaur, who proceeded to walk over to the table. He had to bend his head down to make it under the rafters. I turned back to the bar and quickly finished my drink. I started to rise, but Gabin strode over to give me another glass. He bent his head low across the bar, and I leaned in.

"I know you're one of 'em." He whispered to me. "I left the door to the storeroom unlocked. Make your way back there and take flight, while I stall him."

"No, I'll leave the same way I came in just like any other customer. Anything suspicious, and he may very well burn down your establishment with everyone in it." I laid a coin on the bar for the drinks. "Before I go," I whispered, "are the people with us?" Gabin nodded affirmatively.

"Nobody's complaining that the ferals got what they deserved, but some of us are a little angry that none of the men who volunteered came back alive. But, nobody's asking too many questions. They're just celebrating the fact that the world has fewer ferals to deal with. Listen, I don't know how you do what you do, but thank you. It's about time somebody fought back. You've given us some hope." I nodded in thanks before rising up from my chair. I made it to the door in six steps, nodding to Rose as I left and flipping her another coin.

"Excuse me, sir?" I was one step from the door, but I stopped and turned slowly.

"Yes?" The centaur walked in front of me. I was of a respectable height for a human, yet the centaur dwarfed me by almost a foot and a half. "What do you want?"

"Do you have any information on the whereabouts of these Seven Sorcerers?"

"I've actually been looking for them myself. I hear they are quite the fighters, and a man like me is always looking for good fighting men. If you find them be sure to send 'em my way. If there's anything left of you once they are done, of course." The centaur bristled. He was wearing armor, including twin blades crisscrossed on his back. He wasn't a messenger, but rather a soldier.

"And what kind of man are you exactly?" The centaur asked eying me.

"The kind you don't want to ask too many questions about."

"That sounds like the men I am looking for."

"Must be why I'm interested. Now, if you'll excuse me. I'm leaving."

"Do you have a name, sir?"

"Why yes…yes I do. I do indeed." I replied. The centaur waited, but I simply turned on my heel and pushed the doors open in front of me.

I walked out into the cool night sky. I made sure to travel west before traveling north. I watched carefully as the centaur followed me. It didn't surprise me that he did so; only that he was so obvious about it. I walked until I was almost directly south of our camp; there were a scattering of trees, and I managed to find enough wood to start up a small fire. I slept under the stars that night, and when I awoke the centaur was nowhere to be seen.

I rose quickly and scouted around, before making my way back to The Boar. I was within two hundred feet when I heard the sound of pounding behind me. I turned around and saw the same centaur that had been at the tavern riding up behind me. I regarded him coolly as he rode up beside me.

"Any luck?" I asked, stopping and staring at him as he approached.

"Possibly. I'll know for sure soon. We have two gallowglass out looking as we speak." I saw him watching me closely, and I took care not to show any emotion. Inwardly, though I grimaced. *That was fast.* The centaurs must have sent hawks to Daggerfall, the home of the mercenary gallowglass, in order to get them on our trail so fast. It had only been a ten days since our first encounter with the ferals. If they had gallowglass here then we had maybe a two days before they found us. Gallowglass weren't cheap. The centaurs wanted to find us bad if they were willing to pay for two of them to find us.

"You think I'm one of 'em, don't you?" I was stating the obvious. Might as well, this idiot wasn't going to take the hint unless I served it to him on a silver platter.

"Am I wrong?"

"I look like some kind o' wizard to you?"

"Yes." He said matter-of-factly. I shrugged.

"I'm honored. Now, if there is nothing else, you really need to leave me alone." I said shortly.

"You are a human of modest to large build, you carry a broadsword and, from the exchange that I interrupted in the bar, you are not from around these parts. And, you happen to show up at this exact time?" He was reaching, but I hadn't implicated myself. Now he was trying to present a case by correlation. He strode up next to me and was now keeping pace with me. We were fifty feet from the entrance to The Boar. By now, Rowen would have the centaur in his arrow sights. I stopped suddenly and turned to him as he reigned himself backwards to adjust. I sighed.

"How about this?" I said looking at him annoyed. "You go that way," I said pointing north towards the Boar, "and I'll go this way," pointing south, "and maybe we might find them."

"What are you so afraid of?" He asked, and I eyed him carefully.

"I am afraid that I am going to have to kill you if you don't leave me alone."

"For someone who shares my goal, you seem more inclined to get rid of me than you are to find the Seven."

"Listen, I don't know if you are stupid or stubborn, and I don't know if you have noticed, but there wasn't a soul in that bar that wanted to help a krin like you." The centaur bristled at the slur. "People don't trust your kind. They tolerate you, which is more than they give the ferals."

"And what about you? You said they. Do you believe in that same doctrine?" I chuckled.

"Why do you think I'm looking for the Seven? As far as I'm concerned, the death of the ferals is just the start of a glorious new day for humans. First, the wolves, then the barbarians, then we'll come for you krins. 'Bout time if you ask me." An angry look darkened over the centaur's face, and I thought that I really was going to have to kill him. He seemed to find his calm though and backed away.

"Very well then, I can only pray that the Seven are less akin to wholesale slaughter than you are." I shook my head and took a drink from the water skin hanging from my belt.

"Why would you pray that? If they aren't as 'akin to slaughter,' as you put it, then they won't be much good to you against the ferals."

"You may think what you wish about our purposes, human. I care not." With that, he wheeled around and galloped off to the east. I stood there and watched as he rode away before shaking my head.

I slid down into The Boar a few minutes later to a large group of annoyed stares and one furious one. I sighed...this was going to be fun.

"What in Supremor's name are you doing, Aurum? Where have you been, and why was there a centaur on our doorstep?" Joven bombarded me. I blinked heavily and then took a deep breath.

"First of all, I was gathering information while you were all gallivanting out on your night raid. As for your other ques-

40

tions, the centaur followed me from *Ocean*'s, so I stayed the night outside. When I woke up, he was there…so I had to scare him off."

"And you didn't think for a second that maybe he was going to get the rest of his troupe to come and fish us out of here?" Joven demanded.

"No, I was able to convince him that I was a bigot quite effectively, and if not, then we will simply tell them that we aren't ready to go with them yet."

"Oh dread, Aurum!" Joven ran a hand through his hair. "We are trying to make friends with these beings right now, not antagonize them."

"You haven't earned the right to speak to me in that tone." I said with dark eyes. "What were my alternatives? Kill him? Or better yet, bring him down here now? Oh yes, that would have been fabulous. Look at this place." I gestured around at the mess of weapons and equipment scattered about The Boar. Joven shook his head reluctantly. "No, I did the one thing I could. We will deal with them soon enough."

"I hope you're right, because you may have jeopardized our entire plan by your careless actions."

"I've done no such thing, and if you ever accuse me of doing that again…" I let the threat hang in the air. Joven knew what I had sacrificed for this; he knew the price I had paid. He backed down.

"I misspoke. I apologize." Joven sighed. "What did you uncover?"

"The centaurs are here. I don't know how many, but they brought gallowglass with them." I saw Rikard smile as Rowen cursed. "But the people believe in us enough to celebrate the fact that we killed forty-five of them last week. I was also recognized; even using Damaen Longshore they knew me. We're not as invisible as we'd like to be."

41

"Anything else?"

"And, that the *Lingering Ocean* actually serves a decent port." Grey snickered, but the rest merely shook their heads at my attempt to bring a little humor into their dreary lives.

"Please, please Aurum, humor is much more effective when it is shades of Grey." Grey said, which merely served to elicit a few groans as the others went back to their tasks.

"Aurum, swear to me that you won't go out again…I need your word." Joven said as he pulled me to the far corner of the pit. I stared him in the eyes.

"You have my word. I apologize, but I felt like one of us should see what the response was among the people. We sacrificed forty-five of their own men, and they still seemed to support us overwhelmingly."

"I don't want to make a habit out of killing humans." Joven replied.

"Neither do I, but this is good news for us nonetheless. We've captured their imaginations, Joven. They watched our battle. They watched us slaughter the feral troops. They believe in us. And, they're all going to be dead soon because of it." Joven nodded solemnly. I put my hands on his shoulders. "Don't take this on your shoulders. I am the eldest. Everything we do here-the blame and guilt rests upon my shoulders and mine alone. You are the mind of the team; let me be the conscience."

"We should have made Rikard the conscience; he doesn't have one, it would have been an easy job." Joven said with a grin.

"True, but he has no responsibility either. Speaking of Rikard, why is he still here? He should have left for the coast last night." I asked.

"I know…I know. But when we got back and you weren't here, I was afraid that we might have to change our plans. He is leaving as soon as the coast is clear."

"Good. He needs to be firmly entrenched in case the worst happens." Joven nodded. "Relax, Joven, we've made our opening gambits in this game. The pieces are all set and only we know the rules." Joven smiled.

"I hope you're right. No, I pray you're right." I smiled as he turned around and began issuing orders for today's mission and, more importantly, tonight's.

"Pray? When did you find religion, Joven?" I called out to him.

"The moment our plans fell into place."

"Yes, well. I don't know how much good prayers will do me. But I'll take any help I can get." I muttered under my breath.

Blood Will Run

Four

"My lady?" The royal physician Domini entered into the small tower room. There was nothing extravagant about the small dormitory, nothing to express the magnitude of the rank of the person who lay dying within, nor that of the person next to him.

"How is he?" The princess of humanity, Tendra Sumenel, asked. She sat in the small chair beside the man's bed staring into his face. The man had just seen his twenty-fifth birthday, and his youthful face contrasted heavily with the masque of death that now held thrall over him. She held his right hand in her own. The skin was coarse, like it had been covered in sand, and was as white as new-fallen snow. She blinked heavily in an effort to maintain her composure before the doctor and the fully armed and armored knights that stood outside the doorway.

"Prince Jakob grows worse. Yesterday, he began to cry tears of blood. He is almost gone, my lady. He has not eaten in four days, and we can barely force him to keep water down. The White is spreading through his body. I am sorry, my lady. I have done what I can; Jeric has as well. We can keep him alive as long as possible, but...he won't last much longer." Domini said. Tendra felt his hand touch her shoulder lightly. The gesture of pity was acknowledged, but she didn't want pity. She wanted answers, she wanted to know why her brother was dying.

"How long?" She asked.

"My lady..." Domini began.

"How long?" She replied firmly .

"No more than a month. I can't tell you for sure. But, we won't stop trying."

"Thank you." For the first time her eyes left Jakob's face, and her piercing green eyes drilled into the doctor with anything but gratitude in them, "for everything." The doctor nodded and bowed before excusing himself.

He looked so fragile. Before he had been struck, Jakob looked like he could hold the whole world in his strong hands. The White had leeched the blood from his veins, and he was slowly dying from atrophy. He was so pale. His short brown hair had begun to fall out of his head, leaving it motley and scattered. It had only been three weeks since the plague had swept through Gemport, killing over six thousand people during the two-week period that it had infected them...and then it had vanished, almost overnight, from everyone but her brother. Jakob had been one of the first to be infected; yet he had languished on the doorway to death's realm. She squeezed his hand in her own.

"Sister?" His voice was so weak, like it would be lost within a light wind.

"Yes, Jakob, it is I. Hush now, it wounds you to speak, and you need all your strength. Jeric says that you are getting better. It won't be long now and you will be riding and ranging...and raging through the kingdom." She forced a smile, but knew her words were choked. She watched as a thin line of red began to make its way from his eye down the side of his head. She quickly wiped the blood away. She shuddered.

"Why do you give the prince false hope, my lady? It is no use; the White spares none. No matter your station." She looked up as Sir Terrance Greenhorn and three of his bannermen strode through the door.

"I do not recall you being summoned." Tendra replied curtly, rising from her seat. The four men took up positions at the foot of Jakob's bed. Tendra glared out at the guards, but they were nowhere to be seen. "In fact, I know for a fact you weren't. He will not suffer the likes of you in here. Nor will I."

"It seems to me like the prince is merely suffering, my lady; why not just put him out of his misery? You and I both know that the White is rotting him. He dies each and every day in agony." Sir Terrance stepped forward to face her, not a foot from her face. "I could do it," his hand strayed to his sword, "it would be quick and painless."

"Just like your beheading would be for such treason."

"Treason! Ha!" His laughter was short and cold. "I believe that, by line of succession, my family is next after that boy is dead. With no living sons, the Sumenel bloodline vanishes."

"As long as I live, our bloodline is secure and strong. Now, I asked you once to leave. Do not make me do it again." Tendra glared at the men. The Greenhorn was a large man, and was one of the best fighters in the south. His lordship extended over a large swath of land near Illuvium, and his title made him believe that he was far more important than he actually was. It was true what he said about the line of succession, but the

47

Greenhorn would not sit the throne. That honor belonged to Magistrate Kay of Bicoln.

"Or what? Your father is a decrepit old man, and your brother is in even worse condition, and if rumors from the north are true, we will need a real king to sit on the Unyielding Throne. Not some woman and her sickly family."

"Speak another word and I will cut your head from your shoulders." He smiled and backed away from Tendra, throwing his hands out.

"You just go ahead and try it, my lady." The mocking was evident in his voice. "Show me what you can do, my lady." The challenge in his voice was naught but a joke to him. She was naught but a joke to him. Very well then, she would show him what she was. Tendra slipped the small dagger from her sleeve, lowered her head, and took a breath. She mouthed an apology to her brother when she heard a sound like a nail being driven into wood followed by a crash. She started as her brain finally processed the crossbow bolt that had embedded itself in the Greenhorn's chest, and had knocked him to the ground.

"I suggest you gentlemen leave...Immediately!" She turned and saw a mountain of a man standing in the doorway. His shoulders were as broad as a bull's, and he towered over her by almost a foot. He had a broadsword slung across his back, and the crossbow in his right hand had already been locked with another quarrel.

The men accompanying Terrance hurriedly grabbed him by his arms and pulled him to his feet. Blood was seeping from the wound, and he had a stupidly shocked look on his face that Tendra couldn't help but laugh at. Jeric Tybius, her betrothed, fixed her with a disproving eye. He stepped out of their way as they dragged Terrance out the door and down the stairs. "I missed his heart by four inches; take him down to Domini. He will dress the wound and save his wretched life, though he de-

48

serves none of it." He called to them. As they dragged Terrance out and shouted curses at Jeric, "and you... should not take such pleasure in other's suffering." Jeric said to Tendra disapprovingly.

"Why didn't you let me handle him?"

"Because letting me handle him means that he gets to walk away." He offered her a smile and kissed her forehead. "He is a good soldier, foolish, but good nonetheless, and if what the news from the north portends, then we will soon need all the soldiers we can muster."

"Tell me." Jeric nodded his head towards the door, and she leaned down and kissed Jakob's forehead. "Tomorrow, brother." Tendra walked around his bed and followed Jeric out into the hall.

"Well, what happened?"

"From all the rumors we have heard, everything from the second coming of Garen...to magic being wielded by mysterious men of valor...to dragons screaming from the sky crying for our blood." Tendra fixed him with a look that told him to cut to the chase. He nodded his head. "The most reliable of sources says that one week ago, seven men defeated over three hundred ferals," he paused, "using magic."

"Impossible!"

"Which part? I know what it seems, but nevertheless, the rotting corpses of hundreds of ferals that litter the Fields of Corug around Sterin's Throne beg to differ. Now Tendra, I need an answer, an honest one, is this your father's doing?"

"What?" She asked startled.

"Nothing happens in the world of men that your father is not aware of. He is the king, and his hands stretch long over this world."

"I can't believe you are even considering this."

49

"Yes, well, listen to me." Jeric grabbed her shoulders and turned her to face him. "Magic was sealed away in the Heart of Fires seventeen hundred years ago when Garen was killed. If Jethro has somehow found it-if he has unsealed it-the potential for disaster could be catastrophic. I need to know, Tendra." She wrested herself from his grip, and from his gaze.

"Why? Why must you know?" She asked angrily. She saw his face soften.

"Because I can't protect you from what I don't know about."

"That's sweet, but I don't need protecting. My father... he isn't some kind of cleric or mystic. He never has been. He is rooted in the tangible-the physical. He lives in a world of swords and steel and scepters, not of sorcery and spirits and shadows. Now let's go." Jeric wisely kept silent as they moved down the stairs and through the winding hallways towards their fated destination, for which she was grateful. It gave her some time to think. What Jeric had said was unfathomable.

Magic? The Stone said that Garen had wielded all the powers of the elements and more. Yet *The Stone* also said that, in the year 145, Garen had been killed, and his body sealed in a tomb called the Heart of Fires. When Garen had died, his secondborn sons of all races had gathered and sealed all magic away with his body as a show of the great sorrow throughout the world. But, if father had found the Heart of Fires, well, despite what the Greenhorn had said, Jethro was far from an old man. He was ambitious, driven and... manipulative. Even if he weren't directly responsible, he would find some way to get his hands into whatever these seven men were doing.

"I'm sorry, beloved." Jeric said quietly behind her, "I didn't mean to insinuate anything, but I am a Light Monk and this use of magic by those men has the entire Order in an uproar. Your father is frustrated with mankind's position in the world and, to be frank, he is a little bit xenophobic. And as for your brother, I...the fact that I can't do anything for him...it makes me feel so impotent, and to be honest hearing these whispers-whispers of real honest-to-Garen magic. It gives me hope that maybe we can save him. Maybe they can do what I couldn't." He bowed his head, and Tendra reached out and took his hand.

"You have done everything that you could-everything that was asked of you and more. The White is not your fault; you can't fight an illness. Beloved, I love you, and if you believe that these men can help Jakob, then I believe as well. But you're right; we need to confront my father. He must know something about this, even if he isn't responsible."

The doors of the throne room were pulled open in front of them, and they entered side by side. Jeric disengaged his hand from hers, and she smiled.

Silly man! She thought. The throne room was long, a hundred meters long. It was called the Walk of Eternity. Imperial Sentinels with spears seven feet tall and garbed in crimson stood guard at every five yards.

The throne room itself was lined with stone pillars and had a high curved ceiling. The stone of the entire palace was stark white marble, and it sparkled from the sunlight streaming through the giant circular glass window that was directly over the Unyielding Throne itself. The throne was made from a type of metal whose very name was no longer known and was so heavy it took an entire fleet of giants to move. It was forged by Titus the Smith and, ironically enough, it had only yielded when the capitol of humankind had switched voluntarily from King's Port to Gemport. Tapestries hung from the walls depicted the greatest moments in mankind's history, and at the end of it all stood six men and sat one man, the royal counselors and the royal himself, Tendra's father Jethro.

51

"No more business today my royal sycophants…get out! I have family business to attend to." Tendra and Jeric strode up together to the throne. "Ah, my lovely child and child to be. Welcome." Jethro stood from his throne and threw his arms out in welcome but made no move to actually embrace them.

"Hello father." Tendra said curtseying.

"My liege." Jeric bowed.

"I suppose you have heard about them already haven't you, Jeric? Your order's spies are everywhere. So, tell your king what you know about them." He didn't even bother to say who they were; yet it was quite obvious to whom he was referring.

"They're dangerous. As far as we know the final death count was somewhere nigh three hundred and fifty ferals, and if what my agents tell me is true, they killed them with magic, which means that they found the Heart of Fires. They also tell me that currently, both the ferals and the centaurs are hunting for them extensively. Now, it's your turn. What do you know, Sire?" Jeric looked pointedly at the king. Jethro backed up into his throne. His eyes grew dark.

Then a grin came over her father's face. Tendra had heard the whispers of the belief that perhaps her father was mad but had never put stock in them until now. That smile, coupled with his eyes. It unnerved her.

"What I know is that the world has changed. I changed it. Seven men. Seven assassins. Seven warriors. My seven warriors are on their way to start a war, and when they are through, mankind will rule Carin over the ashes of the other races."

"What are you talking about?" Tendra asked, a chill falling down the length of her spine.

"The seven, they are the future. I had them trained specifically for this purpose. The magic is a recent addition I will admit, but this is what they were bred for. They are perfect warriors, each one capable of taking on legions of regulars. And, it

appears like they performed quite admirably in their first test."
Jethro smiled.

"Why wasn't I told? No, don't answer that. You found the Heart of Fires, didn't you? How? Where? When?" Jeric demanded. Jethro chuckled.

"Oh Jeric, yes, I found it. But if you had known, you would never have let me unseal it."

"Father! Do you know what you have unleashed?"

"Of course!" He said with a smirk. "I have given humanity the chance to rise above the rest of the races that infest our world. We were the Template. Garen was made as human and then shaped and mutilated into those other blasphemous creatures. But now," he smiled deviously, "now my agents of chaos have entered into the fray. They have upset the balance, and the unu won't allow for that. The centaurs have already expressed their interest in the wizard's quest, just like I planned. There will be war! There will be a reckoning...and the ferals and the telos will fight the centaurs and the unu. And, at the end of it all...we will own everything south of Whisperwood. It will be ours."

"Father, this is madness! How can you control these men? And what is stopping magic from seeping out into the rest of the world. *The Stone* tells us about the dangers of magic. How dare you do this? Your madness has..."

"Enough, daughter!" Jethro stood from his throne. "You would do well to watch your tone. Everything I do is for you-for humanity. I am not mad; far from it. I am utterly in control."

"I want to see it." Jeric said interrupting him. Jethro sat back down in his chair and stared at him.

"You are a priest of the Holy Order, Jeric. You are also my future son. Do not ask this of me." His voice grew troubled. "The Heart of Fires is pervasive. I have used it once, and it stretched my mind, my very soul, to breaking."

"Nevertheless..." Jeric began.

53

"You may see it, Jeric," Jethro cut in, "but you cannot use it; you cannot touch it." Jethro's eyes were haunting, and his voice had a tremble in it that wasn't there a moment ago. Tendra looked at her father. It was then that she really looked at her father. His eyes were sunken in, and his clothes were wrinkled and tattered. It looked like he hadn't slept in days.

"Oh father,"

"No more, daughter." Jethro said sharply, "please leave us now. Your betrothed and I must speak."

"No." She said firmly. "I will see it as well."

"Absolutely not! The power within this stone...I could never allow you to be subjected to it."

"But, you will allow my betrothed to?" Tendra shot back. "Father, I am stronger than you think I am. I may be your daughter, but I am not a little girl. What is it with you men that makes you think I need to be protected?" She glanced over at Jeric before returning her gaze back to her father. Jethro's eyes seemed to grow even sadder.

"Very well. I have tried to spare you, daughter. I have tried to do what is best for you. But, perhaps it is necessary that you see what your kingdom will be founded upon." Jethro stood from his throne and walked down the steps to his daughter. "Come then, to the crypts, and I will show you the Heart of Fires. Take care though; it is seductive and it will draw you to it, but you must never touch it, or it will bleed your soul, as it has bled mine."

He turned without another word and walked to the pillar closest to the throne and pushed his ring into a small indentation in the rock, turning it. The stone fell back to reveal a spiral stairwell that was lit by torches descending into the depths of the earth. Jethro grabbed one of them and held it out in front of him as he led the way down after replacing the stone panel. They

54

traveled down farther and farther into the darkness until finally they emerged into the crypts.

Giant statues stood in eternal vigil over the bodies of the kings of yore. Balish the Unrelenting, Wade the Bard, Heran the Feared, Geraldean the Hero and a hundred more, each with a statue bearing their visage and holding their weapon of choice. Theron the Scholar held a book in his hands rather than a sword or stave. A cold blue light shone throughout the tomb, and at the end of the Hall of the Great sat a blue stone. It was a small obelisk about three feet tall and a foot wide in the shape of a diamond. It sparked and hummed with an inner majesty. Tendra watched as the light danced along the surface of the stone…it was beautiful. She felt her feet begin to move forward with a will of their own…drawn by the power of this luminous blue stone.

She reached her hand out. In the distance, she heard her father scream at her, but his shouts were drowned out by the hum of the stone. It was enrapturing. She could not stop staring at it. Her breath grew shallow and quick. Her eyes refused to blink, and her skin tingled like the air was filled with lightning. She reached out for the stone…closer…closer. Her fingers hovered barely over the surface. Her fingers wavered and the stone flashed. Then, she blinked and the world snapped back into focus.

She looked over and saw Jeric about to grasp the Heart of Fires, and she pulled her hand back with all her might. She cast it over to his and wrapped her arm around his and pulled. Jeric's brown eyes were glazed over in white. His arm fell back against his body, and they collapsed on the floor. Jeric's eyes slowly gained their sheen again as they laid there gasping for breath.

"What…how?" Jeric gasped as they slid along the floor away from the Heart of Fires.

"It is the Heart of Fires! Within it lies the power of all the world, I would imagine." Jethro was standing at the foot of the staircase as Jeric and Tendra stood clumsily back up. He stretched a hand out to each of them and pulled them to their feet. Tendra could feel the blood begin to seep back into her face as she reached her other hand out and found a statue upon which to help support her.

"Where did you find it?" Tendra asked. "And, how did you get it here?"

"In Thanatos." Tendra gaped at him. Thanatos was a cursed land. No one went to Thanatos. "It was brought here by a man that you both know. He was the greatest warrior I ever met, and he returned with the Heart two months ago." Jeric and Tendra gave him befuddled looks.

"Who?" Jeric urged.

"Jakob." Jethro's eyes were cast down to the floor, and he turned away from them to begin the ascent. Tendra saw the horror in Jeric's eyes and knew that it echoed her own. Her eyes were filled with tears, and her voice was choked.

"You sent Jakob to Thanatos?" Tendra breathed. She couldn't fathom it. "How could you? Why would you?" Jeric stepped over and draped an arm over her shoulders and pulled her towards him, but she pushed him away. Jethro kept walking. "Stop, curse you! Look at me! Are you so insane with lust for power that you would sacrifice us all to quench your own thirst?" She screamed, but he kept walking. He stopped right before the first curve in the stairwell. His shoulders were stooped, and he looked so old and so tired. "You killed your own son! You killed him, Jethro!" She screamed after him, as she dropped to the floor sobbing. "You killed my brother." Jeric wrapped his arms around Tendra and sat there with her until she had no tears left to cry.

Opening Gambit
Five

I woke, coughing, from my fitful sleep. The firelight flickered, creating a ballet of shadows upon the wall. Joven sat staring into the fire's depths, smoking his pipe. The smoke emerged and rose, intertwining, with that of the fire to create a menagerie of shapes that wove upward into the chimney we had crafted. It was a series of forty-nine small holes, each emitting only a small modicum of smoke that was inconspicuous enough to not be noticed. The others lay sleeping around us. I gingerly moved through the masse of bodies, arriving at his side.

"What is it?"

"Grey's still not back." I nodded.

"Where did you send him?" I asked sitting down. He offered me the pipe, but I declined.

"To see if he could find out anything about the gallowglass." I let his words sink in. The gallowglass were wild cards for all intents and purposes. No one was quite sure what they were; most believed them to be the ghosts of men. We weren't so sure. As far as we knew, they were naught but mercenaries-incredibly well trained mercenaries, but mercenaries nonetheless. They were incredibly powerful as well. Twice in the past, kings had attempted to destroy Daggerfall, their keep on the west side of Whisperwood, and both times the keep endured, and the kingdoms that marshaled against them had fallen into utter ruin. Since then, no one had tried to control the gallowglass any farther than their coin purse could endure.

Whatever they were, what we did know was that they were hunting us. We had made what preparations we could, now it was time to just sit and wait.

"Gallowglass. " Joven repeated. "Do you remember our first day?" Joven asked solemnly. I nodded. We had been freshly initiated into the world of Carin, hardly ten leagues from our emergence point when two gallowglass appeared before us. We knew of them, of course, but actually seeing them was something that we had not expected. Honestly, I had thought our quest was at an end at that moment. Instead they just spoke to us and then turned and walked away. Rikard had wanted to engage them, but I had held him back. They were too much of a mystery for us to demand a confrontation. Their words that day had been omnipresent in our minds ever since:

> *Seven you are yet you shall not ever remain*
> *Your balanced plans shall topple in fire and flame*
> *Whose heart even now burns in your hands*
> *But the Key to Souls will break your plans*

Dread will remake what you have wrought
To its knees the world will be brought
Pillars will shake and plunge to the grave
Despite the efforts of you oh so brave

Even the mightiest among you will kneel
So take heed while you still feel
For when Hope is lost and dream is shattered
Look to the songs of the unbattered.

You are the Vanguard of the Silent Kingdom
A land to which all go and none may come
You are the Heralds of the Ravishing of All
By your bleeding hands the kings will fall

I mentally played through the words of the prophecy. The gallowglass had been known to prophesy. Unfortunately, for the majority of the prophecy, we could find no information. We could find no reference to the Silent Kingdom or to the Key of Souls.

"It still haunts me. To this day, I have no idea what they were talking about. I don't enjoy the idea of playing into someone else's hands. The sevens have made our plans and now balance must shake our plans. Do you think the unu are waiting for us in Harin's Dale?"

"No." I said shaking my head, "They will enter into the game soon, but Herdmaster Jeronious will want his time with us before he allows the unu to enter into the picture. He isn't the most effective leader the centaurs have had, and bringing us in this quickly is a gesture that he won't let the unu impinge upon if he can help it." The fire flickered across Joven's face.

"Always playing the part of the wise eldest brother, eh? You're right though." He sighed and stoked the fire while he stared at his pipe. "I misjudged at Sterin's Throne, Aurum. I had not expected Kaelish to send that many ferals at us. I almost blew it. I mean, Syrn and that bull."

"You did well."

"Yes, but the world is different. There are no more carefully laid plans, no more control; we have been thrown into the sea, my friend."

"I know, but we have done everything that we possibly could to prepare. And we are always in control. Remember that."

"What do you think the response is going to be? I mean, Jethro's? We didn't consult him about this and that is going to anger him." Joven asked.

"The mere fact that we didn't talk to him gives him deniability, and besides, we agreed to keep humans out of this for as long as possible, remember? Now what's really wrong?" I asked.

"It's next week isn't it?" I nodded, but not without noticing that he had avoided the question. "Ten years since she died."

"That won't prevent me from doing my job." I replied curtly. I ran my hand over my staff which bore my long gone wife's name: Andusíl. Joven still hadn't answered my question, and my tone told him that turning the subject to my wife was not the way to do avoid it.

"I'm just worried about Grey. What are we going to do if he's killed?"

"Then you can all cry and hold a funeral. Or just go to lunch. Whichever suits your needs. But I promised Rayn my boots." A cocksure voice interrupted our fireside chat, and we turned to see Grey slide down the tunnel into our hideaway. "You know, I never hear you say that you are worried about Dorian or Rikard."

"That's because they aren't historians. They know how to take care of themselves. What have you got? And it better be good, Grey. I have smoked myself a quarter to death in one night." Joven was not amused.

"Well then, be prepared to smoke yourself three more quarters. We are now the most wanted men in Carin. Isn't that exciting? Fair maidens would swoon if we would but leave this pathetic hole in the ground." Grey put his hand to his chest and struck what I imagined he thought to be a heroic pose. Joven shook his head, but managed to crack a smile.

"Sit down. Details…give us details, Grey." Joven whispered, for the others still slept. I stroked the embers of the fire back to life, and Joven dumped the last bit of leaf from his pipe as set it down beside him. "How close are they to discovering us?"

"The gallowglass? Last time I checked," he put a pensive look on his face, "ummm… about two feet from the front door." I stared at him, and Grey shrugged his shoulders.

"Grey, that isn't funny."

"Good, because it's not a joke. Sorry, but they were already here when I returned. There are also seven centaurs with very long spears. I told them that I would happily come in and get the rest of you, provided that they swore on the grave of whatever childhood pet they owned, that they wouldn't skewer us when we emerged. Nevertheless, we might want to wake the others up in a timely and orderly fashion." Joven cursed under his breath and glared at Grey, who shrugged again. "What was I supposed to do? Fight them all? I wasn't equipped for that, and we all know it."

Joven whistled deep and hard. The reaction was immediate. The sleeping three's eyes snapped awake.

"We've been compromised. My guess is that we are to be escorted to Harin's Dale immediately. If I'm wrong, then we are just going to be attacked as we leave. There are two gallowglass and seven Kanans. Worse comes to worst, Dorian and Aurum will take the gallowglass, but make no sudden moves. Swords sheathed: knives, well, whatever you do with them, is your business." His voice shifted to a whisper. "Staffs only, you know what to do." We all nodded. We had been through this eventuality many times before. Everything to mark our being there was either buried or burned. Swords and daggers were strapped on and staffs were grasped. Five minutes later, we were prepared to emerge. We stood in our positions, and I felt the telltale pressure at my feet, and the light enveloped us as we slowly rose to the surface.

The cold air hit me, but it was the look of fear and astonishment on the faces of the centaurs that impacted me most. They truly were afraid of us. All but one. They were not the dangerous ones, though, that honor was to be bestowed upon the gallowglass.

The ghostly figures seemed to ebb and flow from shadow to shadow, lacking any tangible substance. It was like holding water, trying to watch them. They would slip and slide in and out of your field of vision. It was almost as if merely by trying to see them you missed them. It was disconcerting, but as we emerged, they seemed to come into focus for the briefest of moments before vanishing back into their shifting dance.

Seven centaurs stood surrounding us. They were tall and broad of shoulder. Their hair fell down around their shoulders and into manes around their horse torso and legs. They wore full battle garb and all had spears pointed at us. They were an impressive sight. Their helms were heavily adorned in bronze, and their armor covered their long bodies all the way to the tail. Their spears were long, and the tips shone in the moonlight. Gold and purple were their colors, and they were covered in them.

"What can we do for you gentlefolk at this entirely reasonable hour of the evening?" Joven asked pointedly. I looked from one to the next. Only one of the centaurs didn't wear a helmet. He was the same one that I had met at *Lingering Ocean,* and he eyed me with contempt.

"Are these them?" Asked a centaur, whose helmet was much more highly adorned than the others, addressing the gallowglass. One of them floated forward, and a long forked tongue snaked out and touched the shoulder of my tunic. I had to focus not to flinch in revulsion. They smelled of ammonia. Instead, I merely tilted my head.

"Indeed." Its voice was slick sounded similar to what I would imagine a snake's voice would be.

"Your payment for services rendered." The centaur said tossing a small bag to the gallowglass. "Twelve delorins." I heard Grey let out a short whistle. That was quite a sum. Whatever it was that Jeronious had to say to us must be really important, and the leader of this little band wanted us to know it.

"I feel like a high priced escort." Grey whispered. I barely heard his comment, and worked to suppress a smile. The one who had paid the gallowglass turned back to us and bowed as the gallowglass faded away into the night. The other centaurs followed suit, and we stood there dispassionately, waiting.

"Honored wizards, we bring word from Herdmaster Jeronious. He offers his sincerest thanks at ridding the world of such a scourge as the ferals. He bids thee welcome to the land of Carin and invites you to feast with him at the centaur citadel of Harin's Dale. If you accept, my men and I will gladly bear you across the length and breadth of this land." Joven, ever the statesman, bowed in return.

"And what, if I may be so bold to ask, is your name?"

"I am Lotius."

"Very well, Lotius, it would be our honor to receive the summons of your King, and we will gladly accompany you to the Dale." Lotius nodded in acknowledgement before looking over Joven's shoulder at our assembly.

"Where is the seventh?" Lotius asked.

"He won't be joining us." Joven said pointedly.

"I was told to bring all seven of you." He replied.

"And I am telling you that that is simply not possible, and that you will bring back six of us. If that is unsatisfactory, then we will wait here for you to ride back to your master and explain to him why you returned with none." I watched the conflict color Lotius' face as he grappled with this unanticipated dilemma.

"Very well," He said gesturing to his back. Joven nodded to us, and we fanned out, each one of us stepping up to the backs of one of the centaur soldiers. I stepped over to where Dane stood glaring at me

"Good evening, Dane."

"And to you, though your name I never received." He said cordially, but coldly.

"Aurum." I said. Joven and Lotius took off southward, and we fell into an echelon behind him. "I want to apologize for my conduct the other evening. We were not yet prepared to reveal ourselves. My words were merely the only way I could get rid of you without unnecessary complications."

"I understand the value of necessity, Aurum. Do not concern yourself." He grew quiet, and we rode the rest of that night in silence.

We reached Midway at nightfall the next evening, and we were all ready for a break. The centaurs had maintained a relentless pace, eager to return to the safety of Kana's borders. Out here in wild country, bands of ferals could hunt at leisure, and interference would not be welcome.

We departed at sunrise and crossed into Kana near sun fall. From there, the centaurs slowed their unyielding pace to a trot.

It was a stark difference between the lands outside of Kana and those within its borders. A definitive line could almost be drawn in the grass. Outside of Kana, the ground was unkempt prairie, whereas everything within was purposefully laid down. The northern lands of Kana were laid out in a series of farms, and the farmers were out in force. As we galloped through the land, we were greeted with stoic stares.

The countryside was beautiful. Everything felt vibrant and alive. There were no dead trees or grass here; everything was greens and yellows and oranges and reds. We had been here once or twice before, but had never made it more than a few hundred feet into the land before being 'asked' to turn back. The centaurs were not very welcoming when it came to outsiders.

As our journey progressed, Dane slowly began to open up as to his life's journey within the Herd. I discovered he was a captain in the Kanan Army. He told me how the soldier was the third phase in his cycle. He had begun as a farmer, then moved to the forges and worked as a bronze smith, and now he was a soldier. He also told me some of the history of Harin's Dale and of the great rulers of their past. Questions were asked about me and my past. I was able to politely evade most of them, revealing only the barest amount of information to avoid further offense.

After a night spent under the summer sky, we began to see the city rise up in the distance. It was a sight I had never seen before, but only heard stories told about it. I was struck by just how different it was from any other city I had ever seen.

Unlike most human, or pretty much any other city in Carin, this one was long and squat, with most buildings only a single story high, with the exception of the castle, which towered over everything at three stories high. This meant that the city

65

itself was over fourteen miles long. All the buildings were wood and thatch, except for the deep black stone of the castle. Harin's Dale was the only permanent settlement that the horsemen of Kana had besides the watchtower of Delmire.

The forges of Harin's Dale were legendary among the world. Raw ore from the Sparkling Mountains flowed freely down into Kana from the Iron Men, and finished goods were sent out into the world at common ground cities like Midway. The Iron Men worked steel and iron, but the horsemen dealt with the finer things…bronze, gold and silver. Every member of the great herd of Kana depended on each other. There was the hunting class, the trading class, the farming class, the forging class, and the soldier class. Every member of the herd was a member of each class at some point in his or her life. This kept the balance and meant that, while all were reliant on another, they could also be self-sufficient if the need arose.

The city had no wall placed around it, so travelers could come and go with ease. It was a little past midday as we worked our way across the plains leading up to the city

We entered from the north and wove between several houses before emerging into a marketplace that was bustling with activity. Joven gestured for us to dismount, which we did, walking steadily alongside the much larger centaurs. My legs were sore from the long hours riding, and they groaned in protest to the sudden forced movements. The marketplace grew quiet around us.

"They are not used to seeing humans." Lotius informed us quietly as we walked. "It is rare for any not of the Herd to enter Harin's Dale unless under great crisis."

"Well, great crisis is upon them now." Dorian muttered as we walked. The statue of Carius, the first Herdmaster, rose before us. It stood twenty-five feet tall, and Carius held his hammer above him in a two-handed grip as if preparing to smash an unseen foe. As we walked, the people's expressions slowly changed from hostility or indifference to awe and reverence as the realization of who we were rang out through the crowd.

"It's the sorcerers…"

"Five hundred..."

"No, a thousand..."

"Heart of Fires..."

"Magic..."

"…has Jethro done?"

"War..."

"War..."

"War..."

The whispers didn't bother me, but it was disconcerting being held in the reverence that we were. I realized, though, that this was the life we had made for ourselves, and our legend would only grow. At least that was the plan. We weren't anonymous anymore and never would be again. The crowd parted before us, and we strode confidently between the ranks of people as their stares followed us.

We walked up the ramp to the great stone doors. I took a deep breath. This was it.

"Your weapons and staffs, I am afraid, must be left at this point. None who are not of the Herd are allowed to bear arms within the Hall of Triumph." Joven nodded to Lotius in acquiescence and pulled his sword, Brightstar, from its sheath. The rest of us did the same. I heaved Widower's Wrath from its moorings and reluctantly handed it to Dane.

"Don't worry; it will be taken care of." I nodded my thanks to him and removed my twin daggers, Aim and Focus, and handed them to him as well, and finally, my staff. I looked over to my brothers as they too gave up their weapons. Dorian looked especially wary, as if he would never see them again. The doors were opened before us by two centaurs in full battle garb.

Joven took the lead as usual, and the rest of us fanned out behind him in our standard pyramid formation.

Dorian and I made up the second row and Rayn, Grey and Rowen the third. Lotius and Dane walked in front of us. Their footsteps clicked and clacked through the stone hall. The stone roof was ten feet above us, and the hall itself was extraordinarily long and wide to accommodate the centaur body type.

The hall spanned out before us, and at the end stood Herdmaster Jeronious. Jeronious was tall, like all his kind, but unlike most of them, he had long flowing red hair, which was deemed a sign of Supremor that he was fit to lead. In his hand, he held a scepter that ended with a ball of bloodstone, a red rock of a hue so dark it was almost black, the heavy stone was the most valuable gem in all the land. Jeronious stood amidst three other centaurs, which could only be his high generals, as they were conferring over a map of Carin.

"My Master," Lotius began, kneeling low, "I present to you the six wizards." He withdrew away from us, exposing us completely to the Herdmaster. Joven brought his right arm down low to his knee in a bow and the rest of us followed his lead. I was careful to make sure that my head stayed down until Jeronious bid me leave to rise. It was disrespectful to do anything else, and the last thing I wanted to do was anger our best hope at raising allies in this world.

"I bid you rise, and may your fields be ever green."

"May the sun shine bright and the wind blow fair for you, Herdmaster." Joven replied standing up straight.

"Do you speak for your herd?" Jeronious asked.

"I do. Joven is my name." He replied. I watched the exchange. We had practiced this encounter for a long time before this day; how we would meet with all of the leaders, each had their own unique flair. Jeronious nodded to his generals, and they pulled the table and maps away, leaving the hall now completely open.

"Where is the seventh?"

"Unfortunately, he was forced away on other business. He apologizes that he is unable to greet you in person."

"Very well. I suppose I should begin by thanking you for your service rendered. My scouts tell me that your displays of swordsmanship and sorcery were unmatched in all the land. You have done a great task."

"A task that is only just now beginning, my lord. We will not rest until every feral lies dead. Our goal is no less than extinction." This gave Jeronious a slight pause.

"And why is that? You are human, what grudge do you hold the ferals accountable for?"

"We may be human, but I can assure you that we are unlike any humans you or anyone in this entire world has ever encountered. We come from beyond The Rift." This caused a start among the horsemen and more than a few guffaws of laughter. Even Jeronious smiled.

"Beyond The Rift indeed. And how, pray tell, did you manage to cross that never-ending expanse?"

"I said we came from beyond it, not that we crossed over it. That is impossible. How we got here is not important, though. What matters is that we are here, and we want the aid of Kana."

"You seem to be doing an excellent job on your own. Why would I want to assist you? The ferals and the centaurs have maintained peace for generations." Jeronious coolly questioned. Now, it was Joven's turn to smile.

"Yet you greeted us by thanking us for our so-called service in disposing of three hundred and fifty of them. You also paid twelve delorins to bring us here, which means that you wanted to find us before Lord Kaelish did. The mere fact that you are meeting with us means that you have no intention of kill-

69

ing us, nor turning us over to Lord Kaelish. Finally, just because you are at peace doesn't mean that you have forgotten what the ferals did to your people all those many years ago."

"Indeed, you are correct." I raised an eyebrow at him. "Just because we are at peace does not mean that we have forgotten. But I ask you again, why should my people join with you against the ferals?"

"Two reasons-and then the real reason. The first is that you know what we did on the Fields of Corug in the shadow of Sterin's Throne. We came with you because we wanted an audience, not because seven of your men and a couple of gallowglass demanded us to. Also, it suited our purposes better than if we were brought before the Imperial of the Spire or Lord Kaelish." This brought about an amused chuckle from Jeronious.

"The second?"

"The second is that in the thousand years since the Dread War, you have accomplished nothing." Jeronious bristled. "You still maintain the Face Off between the watchtowers of Delmire and Marose, so you know that you can't trust the ferals. There is no peace between your two peoples, but rather a fear of mutual destruction. You know that if you go to war against the ferals, there will be no stopping until one side is utterly annihilated. What that means, however, is that the surviving race will be so weak that they will crumble under even the most tenuous of pressures. As king, you won't risk either of those possibilities. Your people have waited a thousand years for us to arrive. So now that we have, can you really afford to let us go?" Joven let the question linger in the air. Jeronious stood there for a moment pensively.

"And what of the real reason, as you put it?" I smiled, and I knew that Joven was smiling too.

"That is the most obvious reason of all. Because you must. If we destroy the ferals alone, humanity will rush in to fill the void of territory, because we are human and that is the right of the king. Humanity is scattered-divided. We have a king, but humanity is too spread out for it to react quickly to anything. Small, mostly autonomous kingdoms are what humanity is, but nothing solid. If the land east of the Heart is suddenly free, Jethro will not hesitate. And in a single day and night, humanity will again be one combined kingdom. They will control more land than anyone since the Dread."

"You did not mention a third possibility." Joven waited.

"If you were to die." Spears from the guards were leveled at us.

"Herdmaster, if you did not respect our abilities we would not be standing here. Just because you have our weapons does not make us powerless."

"That sounds like a threat." Jernious poured himself a glass of wine.

"Not a threat. A fact. We are here by your grace, but it is our ability to leave that makes us valuable to you."

"Valuable." Jeronious repeated. "What of your value to your king? Your value to Jethro? Does humanity's king have your allegiance?" Jeronious asked. Joven shook his head.

"No, but by the law of the Secondborn, the gains of any one member of the race are that of the entire race." Joven smiled. "All that land…can you afford to allow Jethro to control it? Can you allow the balance of power to topple in such a fashion? A united kingdom of humanity, under Jethro's rule…can you imagine?" Jeronious stood stoically, staring at us.

"Why would you not want Jethro to take it all?" Jeronious inquired.

"We have our reasons." Joven replied.

"Not good enough." Jeronious said.

"It will have to be." The stone cold resolve in his voice made Jeronious pause. He was used to getting whatever he wanted. This right here. This caused me to hold my breath. Jeronious needed to be pushed into allying himself with us, but this moment of direct confrontation was so dangerous. It looked like Jeronious might dismiss us for a moment. Instead, he smiled. We were amusing him with our boldness, or perhaps, he saw it as arrogance. Either way, I allowed my muscles to loosen.

"Kaelish does not stand alone; the telos stand with him, and what of humanity? Will they join in our righteous quest against the ferals?" Joven smiled.

"I cannot speak for humanity, as we are not of this world. We have no ties with the world of men. King Jethro takes no council from us. As for the telos, their alliance with the ferals extends only as long as the ferals hold them locked from the mainland of Carin. They hold no particular allegiance. If the ferals begin to falter, the telos will abandon them." Joven countered. Jeronious looked pensive, and he stayed quiet for a moment.

"You have presented an interesting case and certainly more eloquently than I would have thought a human capable of. You have traveled long and hard, and I am sure that you are weary from your journey. You will rest within my home. This evening there will be festivities in your honor, and tomorrow we will resume." I knew that we had won this fight…and quite handily. Jeronious had not expected Joven to be so aggressive.

"Will that be all, Herdmaster?" Joven asked.

"Lotius will guide you to your quarters where garments have been set out for this evening's festivities. You are dismissed."

"Thank you, Herdmaster. You are most generous." Joven said as we exited from his presence. As we retrieved our armaments a slight smile came to Joven's face. I wasn't sure if it was relief or triumph. We had faced our second test and come through with flying colors. It had been precarious bur successful.

Now the real work was about to begin.

72

Burning Bright From Shadowed Light

Six

Galeerial was restless, and the unsteady beating of his wings reflected his foul temperament. His wings still ached from when Ezekiel had slammed him into the cathedral after he had emerged from the stone cells. Skyguard healed fast, but it had only been one week since his escape and since his summoning before the High Clerics. His exile to the gate was the proof of how well that meeting had gone.

Or rather hadn't gone. He had gone to the Council of Clerics to reveal his evidence, but when he arrived they would not listen to him. Veriel had gotten to them first. Galeerial knew it. They said they knew about Galeerial's excursions down into the lowlands. They had not even heard him out. They merely sentenced him to the gates. To make matters worse, when he arrived, he found both the wine and their evidence gone. He hoped that Ezekiel was the one to snatch it and not Veriel. He didn't know if they had arrested Ezekiel as well. He hoped not.

His trial was in three weeks. Three long weeks. Galeerial didn't know why it would take them three weeks to decide something as simple as illegal rangings. Veriel had a plan, and all that mattered was figuring it out before he implemented it.

Veriel would not kill him that much was certain, because he knew things that Veriel didn't want the clerics to know. If Veriel killed him then as his soul traveled to Aeriel it would pass through the Cathedral, and his life would be on display for the clerics to see. It was called the SoulSong, and his would be his salvation from death. That did not rule out kidnapping, which was the most likely turn of events. The question was, if he would do it himself or through an intermediary-maybe the one whom he had been speaking to in the stone cells.

Who was that? Galeerial had no idea, but he felt that it was important that he found out. It didn't matter, though, because he was being watched by members Raptors of a different flight than his own. Veriel wouldn't dare try to extract Galeerial now, not while he was under watch. Veriel would wait until his punishment was enacted, and then he would make his move.

Galeerial strode to the outer terrace of the gates and scanned the skies. It was ironic that the place that had once been his refuge was now his prison. No one came to Cloud Breach or to Soaring or to Winter Crest whether by land or by sky. An outsider had not seen a Skyguard city since the Third Collective Council, four hundred years hence, and the Skyguard never ventured down the path on foot. A feeling of sadness and desolation came over him. These closed gates epitomized everything the Skyguard had lost. Now, it was naught but a prison.

Galeerial knew that he could fly away at a moment's notice, but he had too much honor for that. He was no coward. He pulled his blade from his belt and twirled it lightly in his fingers. It had belonged to his mother. The blade was a long, thin scimitar that stretched from his hand to his elbow. It was a gorgeous blade, though it had not been tested in true battle by him, but perhaps that would soon change.

He strode up and down the top of the battlements. The road from the city led straight to Deren, the northern and capital city of the giants. It was one of four such cities surrounding Whisperwood. Galeerial had flown over Deren on several occasions and could attest to the impressiveness of the size and scale of it. The cities were built from the Ithacan ash that made up the majority of the trees in Whisperwood. Every year at the fall equinox, the giants would march around Whisperwood with their axes cutting down the trees and dragging them back to their cities or filling the rivers with timber. It was an old tradition that dated back to the days of Sterin the Black, when the giants had attempted to conquer all the other races. Upon their defeat, as punishment, the secondborn children of Garen had bound the giants to the forest using magic. They had no choice but to march and keep the expansion of the forest in check, and that march was an event to be witnessed.

Galeerial's wings flapped aimlessly in the wind. How he longed to fly. It was a beautiful night. The stars were brilliant, weaving their tapestry of patterns in and out of the endless sky. The Eternal Host was flying in full guard tonight, and they were beautiful.

Up there flew the greatest members of the Skyguard: Myan Farflung, Jorian the Wise, Solom the Most High...and the names of the glorious past flew into his mind in rapid fire: Myrias, son of Myan, Tor, Bessemer, Desolious, Galeerial Risenstar: his namesake. The days of glory were as far behind as

75

the stars were away. These were the days of fear, the days of cloistered self-preservation. The days of the I, not of the We.

He longed for Ezekiel to come and meet him here, but he knew that agents of the Clerics were watching at this very moment. He was surprised that they had been so bold to do even that. They were so busy sitting in their cathedrals praying that he was shocked they even remembered to eat. Worship had its place, and Galeerial was as devout as any other, but worship with nothing else was folly. Why would they be placed here by the Divine One simply to praise him? The Eternal Host did that forever, unceasingly, why must they do it upon Carin as well?

He shook his head again, looking longingly at the land spread out before him. As a member of the Raptors, he had always been flying through the northern reaches of Carin: the ruined tower of Bastian, the Eye of the North, the Burning Waters. It was only when he felt the wind whispering through his wings that he truly felt at peace. He was a Skyguard, after all.

He moved back into the turret, and his wings folded in behind him. Galeerial ran his fingers along the heavy leather bindings of the books in the bookshelf: *Sarenatas, The Glorious History of the Shining Host, The Fall of Rendile, The Wind Walker, The Stone.* Among others, these were the rule of Cloud Breach and the rule of the Skyguard. He looked at them sadly: these were the Skyguard, the true Skyguard, not the hollow shell of beings mired in their own stagnancy and inaction that they were today.

He turned away from the books and walked to the hammock. It was long past sun fall and time for him to sleep. He reached down, pulling off his breastplate and then reached for his horn. He unhooked it from the loop on his belt: the Horn of Seventeen Sorrows. The High Clerics told him that they were making him the Guardian of the Gates. That was what they called his punishment-his imprisonment.

76

They were too afraid to even call it that. They told him that he was being temporarily reassigned, and with that assignment he had been given the Horn. He had no idea why. It would signal the Skyguard army, the Burning Host, to assemble, a clarion call to the kind of adventures that he lusted after. Upon the blowing of this horn, every Skyguard in the three cities would be bound to answer. Yet there had not been a Guardian of the Gates in two hundred years.

"What if I played you?" He muttered to the horn. "Would the entirety of the Host descend upon me in righteous fury? Would they kill me? Would they lock me away in the depths of the mountain?" He idly wondered. The ivory horn was utterly smooth without a single ridge along the entirety of its body. It was made from the horn of some long-dead beast and was entirely without blemish save for the small gold ringlets along the curve, from which hung a maroon cord. He raised the horn to his lips. The mouthpiece was just as silky as the body of the horn. Galeerial found himself holding his breath, and he quickly lowered the horn. He may be insubordinate, but he was not stupid.

"We wouldn't do that." Galeerial whirled around, his sword flying from his fingers at the previously unheard person. The scimitar flew straight and true, not a hint of fluctuation in its curve, and just as easily, was plucked from the air by the Skyguard who stood behind him

Veriel.

The Skyguard Lord Commander was almost seven feet of solid muscle with a long neck flowing out from broad shoulders. Obsidian black hair that wafted around his neck like tendrils. His hair was combed back exposing his forehead and the gold of his skin. His eyes were thin, and eyebrows heavily manicured to follow the shape of his eye. They looked as if they had been drawn in ink upon his face. The violet in his eyes had a mischievous glint. He wore no armor of any kind, just gold and white silk robes with an eagle upon the breast. The brown leather of his sandals stood out in their mundanity.

Galeerial watched Veriel's movements warily. By Supremor, he was fast. Veriel grabbed the blade in his fingers mere centimeters before his face, and now he proceeded to casually twist the blade in and out of his fingers, balancing it precisely as he entered into the guard tower.

"Nevertheless, I would not recommend blowing it; it hasn't been sounded in a millennia, and I would hate for that streak to be broken by some bored, lazy Skyguard." Veriel smirked. "No," he shook his head, spinning the sword on his fingers while walking toward Galeerial.

"What do you want, Veriel?" Galeerial growled watching him carefully, while backing up. Galeerial felt his back touch the wall. He cursed himself silently for throwing away his weapon.

"What we would do," Veriel continued, "is this." Veriel flipped the blade around so the handle was in his left palm and thrust it towards Galeerial's right wing. Galeerial tried to spin out of the way, shooting his left hand forward to intercept, but Veriel's hand seemed to grow longer as it snaked around his hand and plunged the blade into his wing.

The pain was excruciating. Galeerial barely choked off a scream as the blade tore through the layers of feathers and the membrane of his wings. Just as quickly, Veriel turned and whipped out a second scimitar, jabbing it into the other wing. The sensitive inner nerves of the wing sent blistering pain through his body as Galeerial gritted his teeth against them. Galeerial would not give Veriel the satisfaction of a scream, though he was not given that chance as Veriel's fingers closed around his throat.

"You stupid, pathetic creature." Veriel hissed, "did you think I was unaware of your actions, or your pathetic attempts to have me discredited? You disgust me with your own cowardice. I have been here for centuries, and this was all you could come up with? You should be honored I am even sullying myself with you." Veriel reached into his tunic and pulled out the folder that Ezekiel and he had compiled. Galeerial lunged out with his arms at Veriel, but he felt his nose shatter as Veriel thrust his head forward into the face of Galeerial and, with his right hand, batted away the clumsy counterattack. There was no blood. Skyguard did not bleed.

"Try that again and I swear that I will cut your hands from your arms. If you even speak, I will cut your wings from their mounts. Do not test me." Veriel held the folder over the candle. Galeerial watched it burn as his rage built. It was rage built on fear. Veriel was looking at him; no, Veriel was *examining* him. "You don't like me." His voice was condescending and cold. Entirely aloof. "You won't believe a word I say. So when I tell you that I do what I do because I must. I know you will think I am a liar. I don't care if you believe any words I say, because you believe in my actions." He gestured at the two blades embedded in the wings. "Now, you will tell me all that you know and who you have told. You will leave nothing out. Understand?" Galeerial breathed shallowly, still trying to fight off the pain. He would give this creature nothing.

"No." He spat at Veriel. Veriel looked at him.

"Tsk. Tsk. I told you not to speak." Veriel very slowly reached his right hand back and removed his great sword from his back. Galeerial gaped; it was one of the Cardinal Swords of Supremor. Ripper was its name, and the unheard screams of Galeerial revealed that it more than lived up to its moniker.

He awoke to the sound of muffled voices. Galeerial's body was numb. He couldn't feel anything below his neck, but he could hear, as if through a whistling wind that enshrouded his ears.

"What will we do with him?" It was a gruff voice, deep and coarse.

"We can't kill him," a second voice mused. Galeerial struggled to place it. It was so familiar; so close to mind, but he could not pierce the cloud that blanketed his thoughts. "So, you will bear him with you, to Amul Kon. Hide him deep; hide him dark; hide him close. Let him never feel the wind or the sun upon his face again, but whatever you do, don't let him die. The Clerics will know he is missing tomorrow when they find one of their Raptors battered and beaten near the gates. They already believe him to be rebellious, and now they will think him a deserter. The buffoons."

"Why can we not kill him? As long as he is alive, he is a threat." The first voice responded.

"The SoulSong, Terel. The SoulSong." This was a third voice, and this voice was also familiar. It was the being that Veriel had met with so many long days ago. The voice was raspy yet exacting. Galeerial heard a sigh. His head was beginning to clear, slowly but steadily, and he began to get feeling back into his arms.

He needed to find some way to free his hands and legs, which were bound in old iron chains. He began to look around his cage. It was utterly barren except for a shaft of light from the ceiling- a door, he realized. Strength was growing within his limbs. He didn't know what he could do against three opponents, but it mattered not. There was nothing here that he could use, which meant that he had to force them to kill him. His SoulSong

80

would tell the Clerics of what had occurred, what Veriel had done. They would know everything.

"Put him on spiced clover. That will keep him dull and weak. But even that will not stop the need for the Charist. I will acquire some this evening. He needs it once every seven days." This was Veriel again.

"I know that!" The third man snapped. "I can have him under the cover of Whisperwood in less than a day and Amul Kon in three. I know Whisperwood better than any."

Amul Kon? Galeerial shuddered. Amul Kon…That Which Lies Ruined. It was where the Skyguard tower of Horizon had once stood before the Dread had sacked it and brought it tumbling to the ground.

Galeerial felt a shiver of fear spread over his body. "I also need something that will enable me to drink the Charist, just in case. My deception has worked well up until now, and I am not yet ready to abandon this front. Supremor's chosen will be the ones to bring his tyrannical rule burning to the ground."

"I will see what I can devise. What about the Seven? Still non-interference?" The being called Terel asked.

"They have begun doing their job well, and will continue to do so, I trust," the unknown being answered.

"Ideally; however Terel, I need a backup plan. Just in case the wizards forget their place. You will go to the island of Parad; it is to the west of Nyx. There you will seek out a being named Frosh. Tell him that I will end his suffering if he performs his duty." This was Veriel again.

"And our agreement?" Terel replied.

"You will have your crown. Have patience for a short while longer. Now go get the Skyguard out of his hole. He should be waking up by now. If not, then wake him up and get him drugged. A drugged wandering man is far more common than an unconscious one being carried across the lowlands."

Galeerial felt fear grip him. They were coming! He tried futilely to break his chains to rise and his body failed him...too weak. He heard the creaking of the door open, and a shadowy figure dropped down. A laugh erupted behind him.

"Seems he is awake." This was the unknown figure. "Good evening little Skyguard, and welcome, welcome to hell!" That voice was like poison to Galeerial's ears, and it grew stronger as it came towards him. Galeerial couldn't see his face. "Now, say goodnight!" He looked up at his jailer.

"I'll die before I do anything for you!" Galeerial spat at him defiantly. He would not bow before this man.

"No," he shook his head, "I think not." He held out a hand, "Just breathe, just breathe little Skyguard, breathe and re-member no more." He blew, and dust leapt from his hand into Galeerial's face. He coughed as the spores flew into his mouth, and Galeerial felt the pain leave his body, and his mind begin to lose focus again.

"I...will...give...you...nothing." Galeerial said through gritted teeth as he tried to fight the blackness. He tried to scream, but all that emerged was a slight whimper. The last thing he saw before falling into darkness was the black hood of his captor standing over him.

Balance of Power
Seven

Drums beat *Thom Thom Thom!* Spears and shields crashed *Clang Clang Clang!* And the sky filled with the smoke from a hundred fires. The great pavilion was decorated in full honor décor, and the sprawling lawn on the outside of the city was covered with food, people and entertainers. The entertainment came from a dramatic retelling of the great play, *Born Anew,* by the famous bard, Clarion, with six rows of seven centaurs providing the orchestral accompaniment. I watched from a seat of honor along with my five brothers staring at the fight that was occurring before us. Smoke stung my eyes from the fire pits, and the heat from them burned my face and body.

We had cast off the simple robes which we usually wore in favor of more grandiose and ceremonial clothing that had been gifted to us by the Herdmaster himself; however we were not so foolish as to discard our light armor underneath. We were clothed in violet and silver. The knives we had kept hidden in our boots upon arrival were now safely tucked within our sleeves ready for possible treachery. I was on edge. I had been since we had arrived. I was entirely bereft of control here though the knife gave me some small bit of delusion of having a modicum of control. That is, it would, if I was prone to such foolishness. The others seemed relatively at ease. This was where Joven shone. He had taken to his diplomatic status with all the ease and confidence his training would a lot him. He had been out of the spotlight for a long time, and now was exalting in it.

Grey, was his usual mirthful self. He and Rowen had initially been enthralled by the spectacle of the feast, and while Rowen had taken to charming one of the centaur women, Grey had turned his attention to one of the centaurs in military garb. Grey had been talking the centaur general's ears off since they had sat down inquiring at all manner of centaur history, and the general seemed more than happy to regale what he no doubt believed some hapless human with tales of his glory.

Dorian was the only one who looked in the slightest bit uncomfortable, but I knew that was because of his anxiety over what was to come. He hid it well though, and it was only because I had known him my entire life that I could even tell. He wasn't even watching the performance; he was meditating. He was searching for his calm center: the serenity of a well, an eye in the center of the storm. The unu were coming, and Dorian did not know how they would react to his presence here.

Rayn took all of it in with a mixture of wonder and clinical observation. He was memorizing everything he was seeing, while also taking the time to enjoy it. As the youngest of them, he was the one that I felt most protective of. He was by no means innocent, but he had not fallen into abject cynicism either.

A horseman strode up behind where Jeronious was seated and whispered in his ear. A clarion call of horns broke out. This was not part of the performance. This was something new.

"Those are announcing trumpets." Dorian said. "The unu are here."

"You have the stage, Dorian," Joven murmured, "just like we rehearsed." Then, they were upon us.

"Herdmaster, I have the great honor of announcing Clansmaster Qel of the Thousand Hammers, for your pleasure." The horseman bowed and withdrew. Behind him strode twelve unu.

The human-like unu barbarians were monstrous in size. At between seven and eight feet tall, their shoulders were broad and their muscles corded. They wore loose fitting clothing of white silk and gold chains. Their dark blue skin shone with sweat, and their golden hair was tied back in braids…one for each year they were alive, and the braids of Qel and his followers were many indeed. Their beards were heavily manicured as well. They looked like gods, perfectly shaped and confident in their gait. They walked right up to the table where the Herdmaster sat. They had axes and hammers strapped to their backs and smaller ones at their sides. I started. I couldn't believe that they were allowed to keep their weapons.

The table was set up so that Jeronious sat at the head with his wife and sons. At two perpendiculars lay two other tables with a gap in between for the servers, and in this case, for announcements of new guests. The smell of smoked meat filled the air as they strode towards us. A wide smile of naturally-golden teeth broke out across the face of Qel. The clansmaster of the unu's face was thick without being fat. His arms were like tree trunks and his fingers nimble as they stroked his exquisitely thin gold beard that stretched down six inches from his chin. His eyes held a mischievous glint. He would as soon gut us as look at us.

"Greetings, Jeronious, Master of the Herd, and to you, the Six Sorcerers. I bid thee welcome and grant thee a triumphant return from the fields of battle. I..." His gaze froze as his eyes played over the six of us. We remained stoic, lifting our goblets to drink in unison as if nothing was occurring. My mind raced. This was one of the moments that would make or break our campaign. "By the throne of Supremor, I don't believe my eyes. Dorian, Dorian the Shamesword," With each repetition of the name the knot in my stomach twisted just a little more, "Dorian, once called Waterborne. I did not expect to see you here-or ever again for that matter."

"Clansmaster Qel." Dorian rose and bowed. "It has indeed been some time." Dorian replied.

"That is all you have to say to me?" Qel pursed his lips together. "Indeed... indeed it has. Three years, you spent in my clan, as much a son to me as my own. Then, without a trace, you vanished into the dark. Now, three years later, you return to disturb the balance. I always knew you were different, special, vagabond apart from your own people. Yet it seems like you had a clan of your own waiting in the folds. So tell me, Shamesword, deserter, where have you been, and what in the name of Garen do you think you are doing here?"

"For your first question, the answer is that I have been ranging, learning, watching, waiting. And for your second, well, I always did have a talent for changing the scales a little bit." Dorian smiled.

"You are a disruption to the Balance." Qel replied. There was no sense of amusement on his face.

"Must we begin this again, Qel? You say I am a disruption, yet I say we are an integral part of the Balance. It is a debate we have had many times in the past."

"True, but what you have done will destroy the scales."

"Then they were meant to be destroyed." Dorian replied.

"There can be no Balance without scales." Qel countered.

"Or you could say that the perfect balance has been achieved." I looked over at Jeronious who seemed content to allow the exchange to continue. He seemed somewhat confused, but at the same time amused at the turn of events. He could not have possibly predicted this reaction, but he obviously had no intention of stopping it despite the slight it was to have guests bicker in his presence at a celebratory feast. *He is weak.*

"So then is that your goal? Let the rivers run red, and the dead rot until there is none left alive in the world?"

"Of course not. That would be absurd. We merely want to destroy the feral race. It is time for a new balance. A balance the way Supremor designed it. Even if you don't agree, do you really believe that the thirteen of you could possibly defeat the thirteen hundred of us?" Dorian said, a wicked smile growing on his face. He spread his arms out gesturing at the centaurs.

"I only see six of you." Qel replied with a smile of his own.

"My brethren and I broke bread with the horseman, and by the laws of *The Stone*, they are bound to protect us unto their utter obliteration." Dorian played a dangerous game. None of us had our weapons. He did not have his sword...none of us did, and if the unu attacked we would be as dead as the animals on the spits roasting around us.

"Is this true, Jeronious? Have you shared food with these men?" Qel looked at the Herdmaster challengingly, almost daring him to say yes.

"Well," Jeronious said smiling, "to be precise, all we have shared is water and wine; no food from our coffers has passed their lips." Dorian smiled again shaking his head.

"Betrayed!" It was not an accusation as much as it was a mockery. "Nevertheless, you know what I can do, and my brethren are just as skilled as I-some more so." A blatant lie, but Dorian pulled it off, "but you didn't come here to fight. You came because you were curious. So, sit, eat, and drink with us, as you and I have many times before."

"Those days were long ago, Dorian. You have overturned the scales. You have upset the balance, something we of the clans are sworn to uphold. That is why we wander. Everything has been placed on this earth to be a piece of that balance, and you have ended many lives. You have tipped the scales away from the ferals, and you have made them less capable."

"Hundreds of ferals dead is never a bad thing." Jeronious stepped in, and cheers accompanied him. There was no love for the ferals here.

"Normally, no. But there was no counter balance. Forty-five for three hundred and fifty is not equal. Your lives will bring the scales back into balance. We came here because we were curious, but curiosity will not stay our hand."

"Do you know why you're wrong, Qel?" Dorian asked. "Because we do not exist on the cosmic scales. At least, we didn't until ten days ago. For you see, we are not from Carin at all, and your scales did not include us. We are from the great beyond...beyond the Rift." Stunned silence followed. Qel's eyes widened, and Jeronious rose to his feet along with the rest of the camp. Nobody breathed. Then Qel laughed. He was joined a moment later by the rest of the encampment.

"Absurd. It is impossible...there is nothing beyond that chasm. It extends to the end of everything." Qel exclaimed.

"Impossible as it may be, no human here can do what we can." This was Joven who rose from his seat, accompanied by the rest of us. "Some might call them tricks, tricks like this," Joven held his hand out with two fingers pointed at Qel's waist.

An instant later Qel's hand-hammer a thing of iron and one of two looped upon his belt came flying to Joven's hand. Joven bent his fingers and the hammer slowed its trajectory until it was floating above his hand.

"A clever trick, wizard." Qel replied.

"A trick indeed, but those who stood with us on the Fields of Corug in the shadow of Sterin's Throne know that tricks are not all we can accomplish. Our magic is strong, and whether you believe us or not is inconsequential. What matters is if we can help each other." Joven continued. "You want the ferals dead and the balance realigned. As do we. I think we can come to an arrangement.

"What do you have in mind?" Jeronious asked.

"Just over a millennia ago, the ferals were brought into being by the Dread. Your two races tried to destroy them, but for one reason or another, you were unable to accomplish your goal. Now, with our help, you can fulfill this quest your ancestors set out to achieve generations ago."

"The balance realigned...the ferals are now an integral piece of the scales of Carin, just as you are. Regardless of your origins, you are here now. So, why shouldn't we restore the balance? Why shouldn't we kill you Dorian...you and your blasphemous brethren?"

"Because this isn't the balance you want, Clansmaster." Joven replied.

"Mind your insolent tongue, human." I slid my knife into my hand.

"I didn't mean to presume-"

"Yes, you did." Qel cut Joven off. "You presume much, and we," he gestured to Jeronious, "have indulged you for our amusement. Weigh your next words carefully." Joven bowed his head slightly.

"The balance of Garen, had no room for the ferals. You know what I can do with a blade." Dorian said. "The world has seen our magic. Fight with us, let us return to the balance Supremor designed."

"Yet Supremor did not include you in the scales...you are a new variable, a new scale. You said so yourselves. So, what you want is to replace the ferals with yourselves. Tell me I am wrong."

"The feral race has grown weaker, and the rest of the Five Pillars have grown stronger as a result." Dorian proclaimed. "As one grows stronger, another grows weaker: this is balance. We are reaching out the hand of friendship across boundaries. We have extended it to the centaurs, and we extend it now to the unu. Will you tip the balance against the ferals? We are dangerously close to that point already. And, after the scale of the ferals is no more, the unu and the Kanans can sever their ties and the scales of Carin will realign themselves. The world is a resilient place. It tolerated our interjection into your affairs. We shift the balance with every action, Qel. Every unu knows this; we just happen to tip the balance with our actions a little more than most." Joven had grasped the hammer in his hand now, and all eyes were upon the confrontation between Dorian and Joven and Qel. The centaurs stamped impatiently. The firelight flickered on their faces, as they stared at each other. Dorian's hazel eyes against Qel's golden pupils...unblinking, they glared at each other. Then, the unthinkable happened.

Qel smiled.

"You have grown bolder in speech and action since last we met saw one another, Dorian. You should have introduced me to your clan sooner. I have a feeling we will get along very well." Buried within his words there was a glint in Qel's eye. "Very well then, I accept your offer. The clans of the unu pledge their support to you and your men, Dorian. Let us make a new balance." Eyes now turned to Jeronious who seemed acutely aware of the looks he was receiving.

"I would not have hired gallowglass to find the wizards, and bring them all the way here just to kill them. We fight." Jeronious said. Drums beat *Thom Thom Thom!* Spears and shields crashed *Clang Clang Clang!* The centaur warriors shouted their approval at their leader's words.

"Tonight though, we feast!" Jeronious gestured, and the ceremonies resumed. Qel strode to the table where we were seated as a new table was erected for the unu to sit and some centaurs were ushered away from their seats to make way for the unu.

"It is a fine weapon." Joven said as he handed Qel back his war hammer.

"Yes, it is. Thank you for taking care of her. I don't know what I would have done if anything would have happened to her. She's a sensitive lass." A golden smile grew upon Qel's face, and he smacked Joven across the back and laughed.

"Come now; let us sit and eat." The unu sat at the table across from us. The centaurs had vacated the positions where they were sitting, and we now sat with the unu facing us. It was only slightly awkward. Dorian was the only one who seemed comfortable with the whole arrangement. The rest of us glanced back and forth waiting for the moment when they would draw their weapons and slay us where we sat. For all of Dorian's blustering, we didn't stand a chance unarmed against them.

"So, tell me, my mystical friends...you said you came from beyond the Rift. What lies beyond it; what is your land? Tell me, where do you call your home?" Qel inquired as he gulped down a chalice of mead.

"Cambria." Joven said drinking deeply himself. "We come from the land of Cambria."

*   *   *

"What in Garen's name was that, Qel?" Jeronious paced back and forth in front of his throne while the unu clansmaster watched. The two of them were alone, and the hour was so deep into the night that the morning sun was even now being aroused from its slumber. "You had me find them and bring them here. Why? And don't give me that you needed them here quickly. You told me they upset your precious balance and that it needed to be restored. So, explain to me why exactly you and they are here, besides to discuss your alliance, because that is what it seemed to me like you were doing?"

"What did you expect us to do, kill them? They are doing what you never had the guts, and what we never had the resources to do. Restore the balance to what it was in Garen's day. The Dread changed a lot of things, and the ferals are one thing we can fix. This was our greatest failure-our greatest loss of balance that has gone uncorrected for too long."

"So your entire repartee with Dodran,"

"Dorian," Qel corrected.

"Whatever, was what? A test? And how did you know him?"

"He is my adopted son." Qel replied calmly. "He lived in my house for a number of years, and was wed to a member of another clan before he vanished on a hunt. We thought he was dead. I wanted to see if he was the same man I remembered him to be." Jeronious was dumbfounded.

"You adopted a human?"

"I did." Qel replied. "Though, I honestly did not expect to see him here. That was as much a surprise to me as anyone."

"So you came looking for an alliance, why involve us?"

"Because now, the ferals and the telos of the Spire know that you brought them here, and that while they were here, an

92

alliance was brokered between the unu and the wizards. So now, your people are directly in the arrow sights of the ferals and their allies. Even if you didn't already pledge your warriors to this alliance, the perception would have been there that you aided and abetted. You had no choice the moment they arrived."

"I don't like being played, Qel." Jeronious threatened.

"Yet you have been. Now, whether you wanted to join this alliance or not, you will come under fire. It's better that you joined us at the beginning. Your fragile peace with the ferals is over. They know you aided the wizards., and they know you conspired against them." Qel smiled.

"I didn't want this. I brought you here in good faith."

"When we win, your kingdom will have new lands, and will no longer have to worry about the feral threat. You didn't get what you bargained for, but I am offering you much more."

"I don't trust them." Jeronious said.

"Then, we agree on something. They are dangerous and not to be underestimated. My scouts reported to me from the battle. They cast fire from their fingers and lightning from their staffs. They know each other like only brothers can. I put you in an unenviable situation, true, but this assures your people's survival."

"How do you figure?"

"If you join us, not only will your feud with the ferals be ended through their destruction, but once we destroy the wizards, you will gain lands half again as much as what you currently have. However, if you don't...and the wizards defeat us...they will come for you next for your cowardly move at the banquet. If the wizards don't beat us and we kill them and the ferals, then we will suddenly have an influx of land and a grudge for all the needless deaths of unu that occurred." Qel's eyes gleamed. "Not only that, but we don't know what their connection is to the kingdoms of man are yet. The humans may not be the strongest or fastest or best, but there are many of them, and Jethro is cunning and his son and daughter inspiring.

"You don't believe them then...that they are from beyond the Rift?"

"Oh please! They may have spun a good tale, but neither of us is stupid. Thrones of dragon bones...a society made completely out of people like them...and greater? Nay, I believe they are something far worse. I believe they are the first of many to come. This is Jethro's doing."

"That would be an act of war! The magic of the world has been left dormant since Garen's death. If Jethro is reawakening it, the consequences for the centaurs could be disastrous. Magic was cast down from this world for a reason. We cannot make deals with them...they must be destroyed. No bargains, Qel. They must be killed, and Jethro must be dealt with immediately."

"Patience, my friend. You know as well as I do that if we act now, there will be bloodshed of a kind that the centaurs have never seen. You know how they fight. They may even be able to take down a gallowglass. They are dangerous. And, if Jethro really is at fault, then we need to know how deep his treachery lies. And, we will need to get the High Clerics of the Skyguard involved in order to reseal the Heart of Fires."

"Yes, you're right." Jeronious had been pacing back and forth, and now he stopped. "I know what you are doing, and I swear if you cross me, the twilight for the unu will come soon after that of the ferals. Mark my words!"

"We do what the balance demands. Right now, that means working with you to reconcile ancient wrongs and to correct current ones...but the scales are as fickle as a woman's heart. I will promise you nothing, but I will tell you that until the end of this current war, I will fight by your side." Qel held his blue hand over his blue chest in a sign of salute.

"You swore fealty to the wizards as well. Your word is nothing." Jeronious spit on the ground in front of him. "Get out! I don't trust you, Qel...but better the shadow you know to be following you, rather than the one you don't. The horse does not ally with the bear, yet at times the two of them may both run away from the same storm. Now leave me!" It was not a request.

"Of course, Herdmaster." A smile crept onto Qel's face, "as you wish."

Duality Breeds Distrust
Eight

Tendra stood at the front of the cathedral. She approached the doors and the guards saluted her, while opening them in front of her. She gave greeting before bowing her head in respect as she entered. When she lifted her eyes ten paces within the cathedral, she was greeted by a mighty shiftstone statue of Supremor, which towered over her.

The hall was long and there were only two windows, which caught the rays of the first light of the spring and fall equinoxes. When the shiftstone was hit by the rays of the sun, the statue morphed and shifted into a new shape, each time showing a different aspect of Supremor. Once, it would be a flower to show beauty, next it would be a fist to show strength, and next it could be a fountain to show tranquility. No one ever knew what would come from the shiftstone at the time of the equinox. Shiftstone statues were old, and there were few of them left. Tendra knew only of this one, the one in Gemport and at the Spire where the telos lived. Because it reacted to light shiftstone was notoriously difficult to craft and transport. It only reacted to sunlight though no torch could inspire its movement.

At this time the statue took the form of a father, with arms spread open to welcome his children to his fold. His face was soft and a whiff of a smile could be seen in his face like he knew that his children were not perfect but wanted to embrace them nonetheless. It was akin to when a parent saw a child sneak an extra portion at the dinner table. The smile was slightly disapproving yet amused. It was comforting in a way that Tendra could no longer find her own father. She bowed her head and approached the feet of the statue. She knelt down in front of it to pray.

"All-Father, who doth sit on high,
thy greatness none can deny.
Your arms welcome me this day,
your glory is beyond me to say.
Your forgiveness embraces all,
your mercy saves those who fall.
Protect me as I kneel before you,
save my soul from the evil I may do.
Thy greatness surpasses all earthly bounty,
may my actions bring you eternal glory.
And when I die and pass to you,
may I find peace in your arms too.
As my fathers before me and my sons beyond me,
I believe in Supremor with all I can be."

The ritual prayer flowed from her lips like water. She had said it so many times, she rarely even thought about the words anymore. It was always how she began her prayers. *The Stone* had written: *"When words escape you and all thoughts*

98

fade to naught, let these words flow from your lips. They will reach the ears of Supremor, and he will loosen your tongue to speak your peace before him" (Foundation, 17.4).

She stared at the stone of his feet. Supremor was the perfect father: one whose expectations and desires and code were laid out plainly. He was utterly virtuous. She placed her arms out, palms upward, offering herself to her celestial father.

"For fourteen days, I have come here to beg you to spare my brother's life, and I come here yet again to plead the same. I ask no blessings upon my betrothed or myself but only upon him. My father…" Her voice caught in her throat,

"…was a weak old man, who could not stand up to his son and is now paying the price." Her father's voice rang out behind her. Tendra turned around silently. He motioned to the stair where she knelt, "May I kneel with you awhile?" She nodded stiffly in response. She had not noticed but the cathedral had been emptied of everyone. Even the guards were gone. Whatever her father wanted to speak to her about was to be private.

"I know what you are thinking, Tendra. You believe that in my zealousness I sent your brother to a land forbidden to us, but I swear to you that was not what happened." Her father began quietly.

"You're in the presence of Supremor, father. Choose your words carefully and with truth." Tendra said sharply.

"The last twelve kings of my dynasty have searched for the Heart of Fires. They, and I, believed that it needed to be kept out of the hands of any one man, whether it be human, or giant, or unu, or whomever. So, they searched for it to be kept here, in Gemport. Jakob came to me about a month ago, asking for my permission to go ranging out into Thanatos, and I told him no. We don't go to Thanatos. We haven't since the land was bound, and the two watchtowers erected. But, then he brought me a man that proclaimed to have a map to the Heart of Fires. He told us that he knew why no one could find it: because it was in the one place no one would ever go."

"You said since the land was bound; what do you know of Thanatos?" Tendra asked. Her father shrugged.

"No one knows for certain, but before I allowed your brother to go, I buried myself within the deep vaults. There I found manuscripts telling of various explanations for what occurred. Those manuscripts tell of a great disaster. They say that when Garen attempted the First Binding of magic he tried to bind it within a tower with no doors and no rooms, but he failed, and the world shook with fire and storm. Yet another tale tells of a man who lives there as a prisoner. A being who sees all, and that Thanatos is his land, and none may enter save by his leave. *Shattered Dreams.*" Tendra looked at him incredulously.

"It's just a children's rhyme." Tendra said.

"Perhaps." He replied. The rhyme was a cautionary tale that parents told their children to convince them to do chores.

In a dark land, in a forbidden place
There sits a man that watches your face
He sees every action, every smile and frown
And into his book he writes it all down
So watch what you say and watch what you do
Or like all naughty children Ohm will write you down
too.

"But Jakob did. He entered. Garen help me, but he did." Tears came to her father's face. "Not a day goes by that I don't look at him and regret letting him go. He and two others went. When he returned, he did so alone and yet not alone. With him came the White and from Jakob it spread to the rest of the city, and for two weeks we dealt with that calamity. The rest, I'm sure you already know. He found the stone, and we took it to the crypts, and there it has lain for the last three weeks." Jethro fell silent for a moment. "Jakob was so strong, I felt sure that if

100

anyone…if anyone could do it, it would be him." Jethro's flowing tears littered his face. Tendra looked over at him, reached over to her father and laid a hand lightly on his shoulder. He grabbed it firmly in his own and gripped with abandon.

"I'm so sorry, daughter. Forgive me-please forgive me." He collapsed to the floor of the cathedral: sobbing. Tendra reached down with her other hand and pulled her father's head into her lap. She bent down and kissed his forehead.

"I…I don't know if I can forgive you yet. You knew. You knew all this time what had happened and said nothing. It was not until the Seven forced your hand." Tendra said, hating herself for saying so, but she couldn't just let what her father had done go by without some consequence. "You opened this door, and now you must deal with what emerges. Qel and Jeronious will come to you about the sorcerers, and so will Kaelish and Eferven. They will demand answers. You have cast heavy stones into a tranquil river. The ripples are about to ricochet back to you, and you must be prepared."

"How? How can I save our people when I can't even save my own son?"

"Did Jakob ever touch the Heart of Fires?" Tendra asked. She had set her face to a mask of impenetrability. She was tired of tears; now she needed to think.

"What?" Jethro looked up at her confused.

"Focus. Did Jakob ever touch the Heart of Fires?"

"No." Jethro shook his head. "No, I asked him, and he said that he hadn't."

"But these seven men did, right? And, so did you. Father, can you use magic?"

"No," Jethro said, "I tried, but when I touched it…nothing…nothing." Tendra's mind worked quickly.

"I am going to go meet with them, and I am going to get one of them to come here to save Jakob- while you work on saving the city." Tendra's face became a mask of resolve, as Jethro's face suddenly got a strange look on it. He looked almost scared.

"Daughter, be careful with these men. They were trained to be killers. For years, that was all they knew. They will put their mission ahead of anything, and their mission is to start a war that will ravage Carin-a war that will cause four of the enemies of humanity to fall. Whichever side wins this war, we win as well. That was the plan." Jethro told her. He stood up, and Tendra followed him.

"Yes, but they know that I am your daughter. They will have to come, if you summon them." She said questioningly.

"Perhaps, but they will claim to not know me or anything about the Heart of Fires. Or, if they do, it will be that they control it, but they should not even reveal that much to you. Daughter, the last time I allowed one of my children to go away from this city, he came back with a sickness that swept away thousands of people in my city, and my son is currently resting on his death bed. Don't come back like that. Your safety takes priority over everything. You will be accompanied by one hundred members of the city guard." Jethro proclaimed.

"Nonsense! There are twenty five thousand people in this city, and they are all looking to you and the Guard for protection. There will be a reckoning for your actions. If the rest of the world isn't too busy killing each other, they will come for you. So you have to be here to protect this city. Jeric and some of his monks will accompany me." Jethro tried to protest, but Tendra held her fingers up to his lips. "They are as skilled as any member of the gallowglass. I will be fine. It will be a ten-day journey at most and a five-day journey at the least, depending on where they are. But we must leave immediately. We know they are at Harin's Dale, meeting with the unu and the Kanans, but we don't know for how long. If I am going to go, it must be now." Jethro looked into her eyes. He ran a hand across her cheek.

"You are so beautiful, daughter...and sharp as a sword. You will make a fine queen of men one day."

"If my quest is a success, I will never have to be." Jethro stood and watched as his daughter walked away from him...no doubt to go and speak with her beloved Jeric. He would not be pleased with this development. Jethro himself was not pleased with this turn of events, but he had seen it coming a league away. Just as he knew what his daughter had told him was absolutely true. The unu, or more likely the Imperial of the Spire, would call for a Council of the Five Pillars and demand the Heart of Fires, and his daughter would ride to meet it. He pondered how she would handle the news. He shrugged. She needed to grow up, and this was one way to do it. If she could get one of the wizards to Gemport in the process then all the better.

Jethro walked as he brooded. He had no aim or goal, but eventually came to rest in the Haloed Gardens. They hung about in eleven tiers, each more brilliant than the last as one spiraled inward towards the center of the maze. The doorway to the next level was exactly opposite that of the one before, so you were forced to appreciate the beauty of the world around you. Jethro knew immediately why his feet had led him here, but he didn't resist his fate. He walked slowly through the garden's tiers.

Firebloom, clover, hollywhite, magen, horus, porus, lily, stranglevine, thornbrush, red asp, and so many more. Jethro marveled at their beauty as he made his way through the winding ways toward the center of the garden. As he wandered, he thought of his life-of the choices he had made, the manipulations, the lies, the murders, the deaths. He always grew pensive in the gardens. He did not weep very often. The tears for his son earlier had been exaggerated, though slightly genuine. The emotion when he came to the center of the garden was always real. A tear came to Jethro's eye...a tear for his beloved wife, Maria.

He stood in the center tier, and in front of him sat a simple carving of a hand...the Hand of Supremor. It reached out to grasp the souls of those still alive: for repentance and guidance, and to lead the spirits of the dead to Aeriel. His wife's grave stood lain out before him, and it was the reason for the Haloed Gardens. He knew that if he had been anyone else, he never would have made it past the fourth tier. He had a gallowglass on permanent station here to watch the final resting place for his bride. She had died two years into their marriage...only three weeks after giving birth to Jakob and Tendra. He knelt down before her.

"Well?" A fluid voice asked interrupting his reverie. Jethro didn't even look to see who it was that had followed him into his sanctuary: a devil in a place of angels.

"Vizien, I swear upon my love for my dead wife that if you ever enter these gardens again I will have your fingers cut from your hands, and you will be fed them while you rot in a cell at the bottom of Glimmerglass Bay. Do you understand?" Jethro's voice was cold and hard.

"Yes. But as I said before, how goes the plan?"

"Come now, these are not matters for the grieving and the spirits. These are matters for the living." Jethro rose from the grave of his wife and reached out to grasp the hand and offer a silent prayer to Supremor for her soul before withdrawing. He did not speak another word until they had left the Haloed Gardens. Jethro entered back into the castle proper, followed by Vizien on his heel.

"The grave of my wife is not for you to enter. It is for none-none save my family of which you are not a part. Apparently, the gallowglass did not realize this. He shall be punished for his disobedience, and as for you, you know this,

Vizien. Your predecessors had more respect." Jethro spoke quietly yet precisely.

"The stones speak and listen better, my liege, within the Haloed Gardens, where as you said, none are allowed to enter due to the presence of the gallowglass. We may speak freely."

"My daughter is on her way to bring one of the magi back here. As soon as he arrives, I want him brought to the throne room."

"I want to speak with him." Vizien said.

"You will have your chance, Inquisitor, but stay your curiosity for a few brief hours." Jethro saw the questioning look in Vizien's penetrating green eyes. "The wizard's first priority will be my son. Jeric and his band of monks can do nothing for him, and all the healers that we have brought in have fared just as poorly. The White spread across Gemport and then fled; yet it still lingers within Jakob. Perhaps with their magic, they can determine why, and possibly even cure him."

"I want to see it before he arrives." Vizien said abruptly. By this time, they had reached the throne room, and Jethro took his seat in the high throne while Vizien stood beside him. For some reason, this disturbed Jethro more than the question. Vizien saw himself as an equal to the king. He was far too bold, ambitious and intelligent. That was what happened when your story played out like Vizien's had. The boy had been born into a low family and had been sold into servitude in exchange for a low title. He had come to court as the ward to one Lord Daramont and had risen quickly thanks to his cunning. Joven had recognized it in the boy early on, and when Lord Daramont had departed, Jethro had requested Vizien stay as a student of his previous Grand Inquisitor. A Grand Inquisitor whose ship had been sacked by Damaen Longshore, the pirate. Vizien had come to court hungry, and he was hungry still, just not for bread.

"See what?

105

"Don't play coy, your majesty. The Heart. I want to see it." Vizien replied impetuously. Jethro gritted his teeth. "Come now, I would not be very good at my job if I didn't know everyone's secrets."

"There are some things that even you should not know. Know that it is in a safe place, and you may see it when I decide."

"Safe-like your throne room perhaps?" He walked down the five stairs to the main floor of the room striding to the pillar closest to the throne on the right, directly opposite the one that led down into the crypts. Jethro watched with interest as Vizien reached into the folds of his black cloak and pulled something out which he proceeded to press into the Eye-Star of the Great Eagle Throndir, and a hidden door slid back. Vizien drew his rapier as the door opened and plunged it straight through the breast of a man who had been standing at the bottom of a winding staircase: the staircase which led up to the roof of the palace. Jethro made no motion as the man let out a gurgled yell of surprise before collapsing to the ground. The metal of the blade stung the stone floor, as it landed, sending out a sharp retort.

"Even here, in your place of power, you are not free of spies." Vizien said, quietly reaching down to grab his sword. He pulled it from the body and wiped the blood from it nonchalantly on the man's corpse.

"He was one of your own men." Jethro replied. It was not a question.

"Yes, he was, and I placed him there to illustrate a point. I know everything that happens within the walls of this city and much of what occurs in the world beyond. You rule because I have not seen fit to reveal secrets of yours that would bring you down. I favor you right now, because, like me, you are never satisfied. Now, as a courtesy, I am asking you to see the Heart of Fires. I don't need your permission, but I am asking for it nonetheless."

"Only my ring can open the door to the crypts that lie beneath the city." Jethro responded.

"I made a duplicate of your ring the second day of my tenure as Grand Inquisitor. I can enter and exit those tombs at my leisure, as well as anywhere else on the castle grounds." Jethro sat upon his throne amused. For four and a half years, Vizien had been an advisor and an executor. His wisdom was sparse, but his youth and cunning made him a force to be reckoned with. He was a risk taker, something all too rare amongst stodgy old men like himself. This was a gamble on Vizien's part: an impetuous one. He rolled his tongue within his mouth, as he stared at Vizien before smiling.

"You think yourself so clever, Grand Inquisitor," Jethro's tone was equal parts condescending and amused. It was time to show Vizien who really held the keys to the kingdom, "but you know nothing. You have no power. I am king and at the snap of my fingers," Jethro snapped his index finger against his palm and three gallowglass appeared, almost from nowhere encircling Vizien. He glanced around, visibly rattled at the unexpected turn of events, "I can have you, and even the very memory of you, erased." He smiled again before waving his hand to disperse the gallowglass as they melted back into the shadows.

"Quit overcompensating for the fact that you failed. Miserably and utterly. A master of secrets and shadows, yet you had no knowledge of the seven until they revealed themselves to the entire world. And here, I thought you were good at your job." Vizien opened his mouth in protest before closing it again slowly.

"I know more than nothing." He said pointedly.

"Enlighten me."

"They have been out and about in the world for several years. We have unconfirmed reports that these are the same men that killed one of the Horrors at Lake Lefron, though there were only six then, and that one of them had been masquerading as a pirate smuggler named Damaen Longshore. Other than that, all I have is the usual battlefield drivel." Vizien said. *Longshore, that was unexpected.*

"The seven have been training under my orders for the last twenty five years, preparing for these last few days. They are the greatest warriors the world has ever seen, and I made them that way. The Heart of Fires was merely an extra layer of steel upon an already fine blade." Jethro smiled again, a wickedly curved smile of triumph. "Now, not only are they the greatest fighters in the world, men capable of taking on hundreds of enemies individually, but now they have power rivaling that of Garen himself."

"I want an hour with the one who comes back with Tendra." Vizien held up his hand to stop Jethro's refusal. "After he sees Jakob, of course. But, I want to know the next time you do something like this. As your Grand Inquisitor," he pointed a finger at Jethro, "I am here to know everything."

"You are here to know everything, but not to have power over anything."

"Knowledge is power."

"Yes, but you are a passive power behind the throne, whereas I am the active power behind the throne. Do you understand the difference, Vizien? You are ambitious and cunning, and I value those things, but you must temper that with ration and judgment. You're smart, but also young, which will be your undoing. You failed me today. Don't make a habit of it." Vizien gritted his teeth.

"I…"

"I'm not finished." Jethro said severely. "You are also proud, which is why, right now, you are trying so hard not to swallow your own tongue, because you are biting it so hard. Now, you need to understand that I am not doing this to shame you. If I wanted to do that, I would have done this in front of the court. The reason I am doing it is because you need to learn a lesson. You are young, and you have been given power, but you don't know how to use it-not yet, anyway. You have ascended the ranks at an astonishing rate, and that is to be admired. But, naked ambition will destroy you. That is my 'pearl of wisdom' if you will-from an old man to a child."

"Thank you." Vizien said, quietly bowing.

"I know you say that because you were warded in a good house." Jethro rose from his throne and took slow careful steps down to base level. "You are good at what you do, and you can have your hour with the wizard when he arrives. But, if you so much as think about going down into the crypts, there will be a knife at your throat and your blood on the ground." He whispered in Vizien's ear. Vizien paused, struggling for words.

"I will…learn, but I will continue to rise, and it may not be my blood that stains the ground." Vizien replied with his lips pursed together. Jethro chuckled lightly. "So, you have learned something, that's good. But, you have still not yet learned to mind your tongue. Now get out. I must think." Vizien didn't move for a moment. "It wasn't a request." Jethro said flatly. Vizien whirled around, his black cloak billowing out behind him as he stalked out of the room.

The Butterfly Effect
Nine

"Aurum Guilden." My eyes snapped open at the sound of my Thul. Only two people in all the worlds knew my full name. They were both dead. My eyes adjusted as a flash of nearby lightning illuminated the world around me. The entire area was white as a sheet and the bolts of red lightning cast a menacing pale over the entirety of the area surrounding me, and a human stood directly before me. The human was unlike any I had ever seen. His skin was a deep red that was in an almost perfect shade-for-shade alignment with that of the lightning flashing around us. Oddly enough, there was no thunder; that was how I knew this was a dream, but it was unlike any dream I had ever had before. With my dreams there came a sense of freedom, but here, it was like being within the waking world. There was weight to my arms and legs, and my mind was clear; I was a presence.

111

"How do you know my name?" I asked. This man was not a construct of my lower mind. He did not belong here. I played my eyes over the rest of his body as he stepped forwards. His skin was marked heavily with drawings all over of symbols that I didn't recognize. His hair was black and was cut tight around his scalp. He wore no shirt, only a loose fighting pair of breeches. And his eyes. His eyes were pure black opals of bottomless void. A shiver went down my spine as I looked into the unblinking, unmoving eyes.

"I serve the Highest Power. There is not much I do not know." The Highest Power was one of many names that the denizens of Carin gave to Supremor. I probed my memory for some information that might pertain to who this man was, but spirituality had never held much interest for me.

"Indeed. What, pray tell, does Supremor want with a pirate?" His face broke from his impassive frame into a slight curl of a smile.

"It is not with Damaen Longshore that I have business, but with Aurum Guilden." the man said.

"I seem to be at somewhat of a disadvantage. You know my name, but I have yet to be appraised of your own."

"Power comes in many forms. For example," the man twirled his right hand and a snappoppy appeared there, "this flower holds the power to be a symbol of love and affection. Yet, it also has the power to prove a point." The man began to twirl the flower between his fingers. "It is delicate, and beautiful, and," he suddenly crushed his hand while the flower was within his palm, "dead. The wrong action at the right time can make all the difference. Understanding your ability to change the world around you is yet another kind of power. It is a power that you understand, and, more importantly, wield with care."

"You did not answer my question." I replied.

112

"No, I did not. Names, these also have power. Your staff, for instance, is named for your wife; your sword for what you have transformed her memory into; your daggers because that is what they do, but it is not what they are. Unlike many, you do not know me. You do not trust me. I am going to give you a gift." I cocked an eyebrow at him. "Your knives will wield new names, and their significance will not long be lost upon you. You have been guided, and you have been groomed, and you have been tempered for the coming days. You have ignited a fuse, but it is fire that will soon spiral out of control. You need to not only be prepared; you need to have the tools with which to fight. Dream shall be the name of your left dagger, and Havoc shall anoint your other. Names have power Aurum, and these names are not given lightly." I decided to abandon my line of questioning in regards to who he was because I did not believe that he would ever answer that question. This left only a single question that mattered.

"What do you want?"

"Now?" The man shook his head. "This was merely an introduction, but soon you will be called upon to perform a task of critical importance. I know you have plans, you and your brothers have grand designs for the world of Carin, and I applaud them. This world has long been broken and wandering, but know this, by your actions today you have thrust yourselves into a larger playing field. You have just been drafted into a war of ideals. You believe you are in control, but you are just pieces on a board: kings and pawns, Champions, and Imperials. This is a time of origins and endings." I contemplated his words for a moment.

"Champions and Imperials." I murmured in response. These were both pieces in the game Crowns, which was a common war game played in Carin. Each one of seven players chose a race, and each race had a trio of pieces called the Triumvirate.

Those pieces were called The Champion, The Imperial, and The Will. "Is that all we are to the Highest Power? Pieces on a board to be manipulated?" I asked.

"Not manipulated. Merely guided." The man shuddered for a moment. "Now our time here is at an end. Seek out your new acquaintance, Dane. He is no longer enjoying the comforts of my kingdom."

"I thought time within a dream was infinite." I said.

"Well, then I suppose even one of the famed Seven can be wrong." He said. "We will meet again, Aurum, sooner than you would like, I would imagine, yet, not soon enough for another." The man turned without another word and faded into nothing. I stood there for a moment unsure of how to proceed. The lightning had slowly faded over the course of our conversation and now only a few scattered bolts remained. I closed my eyes and counted to ten. I imagined myself falling out of this world, shredding through another layer as I fell out of my lower mind and into my higher mind. At ten, I felt the familiar transition from sleep to waking.

"Well, this is an improvement." I muttered quietly to myself. The others were still sleeping, but I could see the first rays of light peeking up over the horizon bathing our room in a soft glow, and I knew that I would get no more rest this night. I wiped the sleep from my eyes and stifled a yawn before rising and hopping from one empty spot on the floor to the next, as I navigated through the mess of bodies that were my sleeping siblings.

A thought struck me as I reached for the doorknob. I reached into the folds of my cloak around my arm and pulled my daggers out. My left one had the word Havoc inscribed upon it in fiery crimson lettering, and my right had Dream burned in ice blue. *Extraordinary.* There were very few points in my life that I had experienced true terror in my life or true wonder. I felt an

114

inexplicable combination of both of them at this exact moment as I looked upon my blades. My breath shook in my lungs. Whatever that being was in my dreams, he was more powerful than I could have ever thought. I wondered briefly if I should wake the others or at least Joven. There was nothing to tell them at this point. I would wait for him to contact me again.

I pushed open the door and stepped outside. The cool morning air greeted me as I walked through the wide hallways toward the main hall. Our room was off the hall on the second story, so I had to walk down a series of ramps to reach the main level. I came out from behind the throne in the grand hall and walked outside.

I looked out over the far expanses of Kana. Harin's Dale stretched out only a few miles, but the land beyond it was full of rolling green hills. It was a beautiful land, and it pained me to think that soon it could all turn to ash.

"Quite the view, is it not?" A voice broke my reverie, and I turned to see Dane striding forward to meet me. The click-clack of his four hooves echoed across the stone platform. His long hair was tied into braids, and he wore no shirt. "Aurum."

"Dane." I nodded a greeting. "It is indeed. Do you often wake with the sun, or is this a special occasion?" I asked while stifling a yawn.

"I begin each morning with the sun and leave each evening with the sun. It is only through the passage of that bright light that we are able to establish order in our lives. Our seasons are arranged by it...our days, our weeks, our months and our years. Our harvests and hunts as well. Everything is dictated by the sun. Why should my life be any different? You, however, don't appear to be used to it at all."

"It is not that, but rather that my sleep was filled with dark dreams and even darker words." We stood in silence for a few moments watching the world come alive. "Do you believe in fate, Dane?"

"Of course!" He said without hesitation. "Everything in this world is guided by Supremor's will. All of our lives are bound to it and by it. Why do you ask?"

"Is there anyone in this land that does not believe in Supremor?"

"I had never really considered it. Belief in Supremor, is a fact of life here. Do you not believe?" I shook my head, and he stared at me puzzled.

"We are not from here. In my land, there is no god. Coming here, seeing this absolute devotion to a deity...it is completely alien to me."

"I am sorry to hear that. The embrace of Supremor provides comfort in dark times." I turned away from the rising sun to look at him.

"How old are you Dane?"

"Thirty-one." He replied slowly.

"You have no wife, no children?" Dane shook his head and sighed.

"It is a story, and a long one, at that." I gestured back towards the hall.

"They will not be rising anytime soon, and I will not fall back into dreaming. So come." I sat down upon the ground and he knelt beside me. I pulled a flask from my inner cloak and took a small sip before offering it to him. "Careful." I warned. He took it in his hands sniffing. He gingerly pulled it to his lips and took a drink. Coughs erupted from his mouth, and I couldn't help but laugh.

"Little strong, eh?"

"What was that?" He croaked.

"It is from my home, it is called tequila. This flask is the last of what we brought with us. It'll wake you up the morning." I said with a wry smile. "Now, tell me your tale."

"When I was sixteen, there was," he paused, "a terrible mistake was made. I will not go into the details, but it is enough to know that the result was that I killed almost my entire family: two sisters, a brother, my mother and father." His voice was dispassionate and cold.

"You said it was a long story." I replied. The bait was there for him to continue, but he didn't take it.

"What is it like?" He looked me in the eye for the first time that morning.

"What is what like?

"Having no past, yet having all this power. You come from a land where you are, by your own admission, no one, yet here you are gods among men. You walk where none have tread, you have cast open doors long buried. You recreated yourselves in a land not your own, while I am ever painted black by my past. Do you see this?" He pulled up his long hair that stretched down the length of his bare back to reveal a great cross burned into the flesh. It stretched from the base of his neck all the way down his back, and the cross beam was from shoulder to shoulder.

"A brand." Dane nodded.

"Indeed: the brand of the Forsaken. I am ever apart from my own people. No woman will dare touch me for fear of being tainted. Even to my own brothers-in-arms I'm an outcast."

"Then why were you among those sent to retrieve us?" I inquired.

"Whenever there has been a task where risk is involved, I am sent. My life means nothing to the Herd. I am Forsaken, and therefore I am the first that is sent to die. It is my place." I had no words to offer him, so I merely rested a hand on his shoulder.

117

"Do not offer me your comfort or your pity, Aurum, for I want none. You asked for the story."

"and you gave me the consequences, not the story itself. As for your question," I weighed my words carefully, "it hurts. But it is even worse now. We rarely used magic before our encounter with the ferals, and when we did, it was only in very small displays. Now, we've gathered our power, but it hurts every time. Magic is neither tame nor peaceful. All magic is inherently wild and chaotic. Accessing it means opening yourself to that chaos. Your mind is called to that chaos. Your mind is called away from the comfort of the world. You see in your mind's eye the sheer thrill of that world-the pure and unadulterated joys of letting go. It is truly a siren call to destruction that sounds so sweet. It is the ultimate temptation. It hurts, every time." The two of us sat there quietly watching the sun pull itself out from over the horizon.

"I am sorry for your loss, Dane. I know what it is like to lose a family. Not for nothing is my sword called Widower's Wrath. My wife and child were..." I struggled to find the words, "...taken from me. There was nothing left for me in the old world, so I came here with my brothers." This time, it was Dane's turn to place his hand on my shoulder.

"Do not offer me your comfort or your pity Dane, for I want none." I looked up at him and grinned. "So, are we even?" Dane chuckled, letting his hair fall back down upon his back.

"Yes, Aurum, I would say that we are." We sat there watching the sun peak over the mountains of the Rift, its golden rays shone down upon the land, mingling with the green of the grass and giving the world an ethereal hue.

"Tell me about the Dread." I said quietly.

"You pick the happiest subjects to talk about, Aurum." Dane said with a smile. "What do you want to know? I mean, I am sure that you have read about it. The Dread War is the most well-documented event in history."

"True! I have heard the perspective of humanity and the Skyguard, but I would like to hear it from the centaurs."

"The Skyguard perspective? How did you manage that?" He asked incredulously.

"Magic!" I said with a wave of my hand. Dane shook his head.

"Fine. Keep your secrets. You want to know about the Dread, where should I start?"

"At the beginning. Where else?" I said.

"About a thousand years ago, 867 NW, Corug the Silent, a member of the Legion of Light came down from the north where they had been ranging."

"The Legion of Light?" I knew who they were, but I wanted to hear how he described them.

"Yes, it was Geraldean the Hero's group. Geraldean was Supremor's Champion in the Dread War, but that was later. Before that, he assembled all the greatest heroes of the age: Corug, Arestephan the Farsight, Frosh the Bearer and others...too many to mention. Anyway, Corug fled south with word of a nameless shadow stretching across the land at the head of a vast army. Two weeks later, three hundred of the Iron Men arrived at the Dale. In those times, the races freely consorted with one another, and the centaurs were the Iron Men's greatest customers, as we remain today. We were good friends with them. Anyway, they fled from Dynast, their citadel, claiming that it had been sacked by armies of man-wolves, called ferals, and dozens of Horrors, including the great wolf, Rirnef. The Iron Men's leader was named Harin."

"I knew that wasn't a centaur name." I interjected.

"He met with the first Herdmaster, Carius the Magnificent. In those days, the Herd was still young, having been united only a few years earlier. Carius, in his wisdom, heard the pleas by the Iron Men and agreed to travel north to aid them. Thirty thousand centaurs left to travel north, leaving the young and the women and the sick and the old behind. By the time we arrived, the Legion of Light had been utterly annihilated. Even Geraldean had fallen in single combat against the Dread. By the time the war ended, only twenty eight centaurs came back alive."

"Wow." I breathed.

"The war took thirty-three years, but without the centaurs to hold the line, it would have been over far sooner. The Dread would have overwhelmed the world. Carius' hammer, Greenwind, struck the fatal blow to the Dread in the year 900 NW. It was not by his hand, but rather the hand of Harin, who took up the Herdmaster's hammer after he was destroyed by the Dread." I cocked an eyebrow. *Interesting.* Both the Skyguard and humanity said that the Radiance killed the Dread. The Radiance had been a group of Skyguard High Clerics, Lord Commanders and Light Monks, back when they were still a force to be reckoned with.

"After the war, Harin returned to the Dale and erected the castle in honor of his friend, Carius, who had sacrificed everything to help his people. That is why the castle is the way it is- so different from the rest of the city." Dane said with a gesture back towards the Hall of Triumph.

"How did the Dread create so great an army without anyone taking notice?"

"He created the feral race, and they breed like cockroaches. Not only that, but his army contained the likes of the Horrors and Bizin the Black Dragon, the last of dragonkind as well." The sun was now fully above the horizon line, and Dane pulled his eyes away from it. "Now, I must go about my duties." We stood up together. I turned to stare at him.

"It would be my honor to fight alongside you, Dane. I care not about your past, only your future." I reached out and clasped his hand with both of mine. "If there is anything, anything I can do for you name it, and it shall be delivered." Dane bowed.

"You have my thanks. You are like no one I have ever met before-human or centaur." At that Dane turned and trotted off down toward the gates, leaving me to brood on the steps alone. Or so I thought.

"Nice to see you making friends, Aurum. Haven't seen much of that." A pensive voice broke my reverie. I didn't know how long my youngest brother had been lurking in the background, but his presence now was unmistakable. He was sneaky, not a trait he had always possessed, but he was probably the most adaptable of all of us.

"How long have you been listening, Rayn?" His black bangs threatened to overtake his eyes as they peered out from behind them. He was without a doubt the smartest of all of us, but also the quietest.

"Just long enough. You could have picked a better time to start making attachments, Aurum." From anyone else it would have been a chastisement, but from Rayn, I knew it was merely an observation.

"He is an ally, and he is just the type of ally we can use. An outcast shunned by his own people. Yet, still a ranking official in the military caste. He will prove very beneficial to us, and when the coins are down, perhaps he will even help us destroy his own people." I smiled.

"Joven wants to meet with all of us before we meet with Qel and Jeronious. We are drawing up a war plan later today, and we all need to be on the same page." I nodded in agreement. This game of Crowns was working out quite nicely. Phase One was complete, and Phase Two was just beginning.

I turned and followed Rayn back into the hall. Yes, the plan will work. Everything will work. In the twenty minutes, in which I had been outside with Dane, the hall had become a flurry of activity. I looked at Rayn questioningly.

"We also need to discuss the raven from Kaelish, who arrived while you were outside. Kaelish is calling for a meeting of the Five Pillars of the South." I glanced at him before nodding in understanding. It was a smart move. The Five Pillars were the unofficial name of the collection of species who owned territory in the south of Caring: the unu, the centaurs, the humans, the ferals, and the telos of the Spire. Bringing all five rulers together in one place was also dangerous. Kaelish was risking much to call it, especially after we had so blatantly violated the code of conduct at Sterin's Throne.

"Will Jeronious accept?" I asked.

"Joven thinks so, hence the meeting. If the Five Pillars are called, King Sumenel will be there." I walked next to Rayn as we weaved our way through the throne room. Fires were being lit and breakfast was being prepared for Jeronious' court. The others were just finishing strapping on their weapons as we walked in. Joven had a grave look on his face, and I knew exactly why. I closed the door, and Grey secured the gaps in the frame with blankets.

"Let's not waste any time. Jeronious will accept the convening of the Five Pillars, and so will Qel, because they don't believe us."

"Maybe that's because we lied." Rowen replied. Joven shot him a warning look. Rowen responded with a shrug.

"They will try and get information out of King Sumenel, and we need to be prepared for that. It is imperative that we meet with the king prior to their gaining access to him. Rowen, you're in charge of that. Once we arrive, you're in charge of locating and opening communication with the king. Be dramatic."

"I'm good at that." Rowen replied.

"Never would have guessed." Dorian said drolly.

"Cut the chatter." Joven said. "We need to know his cover story is for us."

"The king will make contact with us, so we shouldn't worry about it. Right now, we just stick to the plan. Whatever the king's agent tells us to do, we will take into consideration, but remember, we are to keep humanity out of this as long as possible." I said chiming in quietly.

"We just have to play it smart." Joven said.

"Stating the obvious already? This meeting just started." Rowen said. His legs were kicked up and he looked bored.

"Check the humor at the door, Rowen." Joven said. The rest nodded in agreement.

"Where will the meeting take place?" Rayn asked. A knock on the door interrupted any possible answer. Joven gestured, Rowen removed the sound baffles from the door.

"I think we are about to find out." Grey muttered.

"Enter." Joven said. The door opened, and Lotius stepped in. We reciprocated his bow as he entered the room.

"The Lord of Ferals, Kaelish, has called a meeting of the Five Pillars of the South to..." he was searching for the right word, "...discuss the ramifications of your actions. We leave for Midway within the hour. You six will accompany the group as sentinels for Herdmaster Jeronious and Clansmaster Qel of the Thousand Hammers. Joven, since you speak for your group, you will be allowed into the council. We will discuss more along the way. Do you understand?" We nodded.

"Breakfast will be served in twenty minutes in the main hall if you are interested. Provisions will also be packed for the road, as it is a two day journey."

"Thank you, Lotius. We will be there shortly." Joven's words held a tone of finality. Lotius bowed again and removed himself from the room.

"Wish we would have found out about it a week ago. We could have just stopped there and waited. Seems like a horrible waste to keep backtracking." Rowen grumbled.

"Missing an important date, Rowen?"

"Always," he said with a wink.

"There are a few things that we need to consider. First, if the king doesn't make contact, do we assassinate Kaelish and Eferven? Second, what if it is a trap?" Dorian asked.

"No assassinations. Kaelish is a weak leader. He is a politician, not a general, so having him in power is beneficial to our cause. As for Eferven, all the telos are the same, so if we kill him, it won't make any difference, another clone of him will just step right up to the plate." Joven replied.

"We also already broke the honor code at the Fields of Corug. We should not do so again. There may be times in the future when it is necessary for us to use those rules to our advantage." I counseled. Joven nodded in agreement.

"All that we can do is watch and wait. We knew this would happen, and now, provided we don't get sold out-which shouldn't happen-we will continue on our present course."

"There is no reason for us to negotiate anything." I said in agreement, "the whole reason Qel and Jeronious agreed was because of the Heart of Fires, which everybody believes the king has because of us." I said. "They don't trust us."

"We don't trust them either," Rayn who had remained relatively quiet the entire conversation finally spoke up.

"Before we start worrying about anything else, we need to worry about Qel and Jeronious-especially Qel, because, have no illusions; he is the one in charge here. We need to figure out exactly when he will betray us, and then we need to kill them before they kill us." Dorian remarked.

"Don't you mean if they betray us?" Rayn asked.

"No, it is an eventuality, not a possibility." Dorian let that sink in for a moment.

"Well, as cheery a mood as this conversation is getting us into, I'm starving." Grey said, turning his back on us, shoving the door open and walking out. We watched him depart with equally bemused looks on our faces.

"I guess that concludes the meeting." Rowen remarked wryly.

One Minute From Eternity

Ten

Galeerial woke to an open field. He blinked heavily to wash the sleep from his eyes and thrust his arms into the air in an enormous yawn. The sun shone high above him at its apex in the sky, and there were not even the faintest wisps of cloud to obscure the perfectly blue sky. He sat there just looking at the world around him for some time. He felt no particular urge to do anything. He had no sense of desire: just contentment. After a time he decided that perhaps he ought to stand up. There was nothing wrong with sitting or anything better with standing. So doing so was merely a matter of whim. He rose to his feet and turned about in a circle. Everywhere he looked, he was greeted by an endless, perfectly flat expanse of perfectly green grass.

Galeerial breathed deeply, and the air perfectly filled him up and the temperature around him, despite the fact that he

127

was under the noonday sun, was utterly…perfect. A quizzical look grew upon his face. Galeerial knew something was wrong, but he couldn't bring himself to grow worried about it. In fact, the only emotion he felt was contentment: so much contentment in fact that he did not feel the need to move. So he did not. He stood there with his eyes half-closed just waiting. Waiting for what, he could not say, but just waiting was fulfilling in and of itself. As he waited, his mind drifted to and fro, without much purpose or aim. He was not bothered by this. He was not bothered by anything at all. He merely was.

After some time, he could not have guessed how much time, for the sun was in the exact same position as when he had stood up, he decided to bend his knees. There was no reason to bend his knees, no drive behind it. He simply decided to do so. He bent his knees, and thought a delightful thought about jumping.

Galeerial bent his knees and leapt into the air. He wanted to get a higher eye view of the territory. He was almost surprised when he didn't take off into the air, though at first he could not say why he expected to go any higher. He turned his head this way and that growing puzzled for he knew that he was supposed to be seeing something, and yet, nothing was there. It took Galeerial a long while to realize that the reason he could see his full back was because his wings weren't there. He ought to have wings. Galeerial knew that he should have felt something, but sadness, anger, and anguish were just words to him. The emotions were so far away; they might as well be non-existent. Someone must have borrowed them from him. He did not remember giving them to anyone in particular, but he also could not remember not giving them to anyone in particular. He wondered if he could perhaps think about it really hard. He was not sure if that would be a good idea, but after many, many long moments of deliberating about whether he should or not, he decided to try.

He concentrated hard, closed his eyes and furrowed his brow and his wings…wait. No, that wasn't right. He had no more wings. He tried as hard as he could to summon any type of emotion, anything at all. But try as he might, nothing came to him. Oddly enough, this didn't seem to bother him. Instead, he began to walk. He didn't know which way to walk, for the sun had not moved in the time that he had been awake, so he simply began walking. He didn't know why he was walking. He was just content to be walking.

Walking did not seem to get him anywhere in particular. He walked and walked and walked, but the flat grass of the prairie never gave way to any other kind of feature. There was just more grass, more sun, more blue sky. Galeerial was tenacious though, and so he kept walking despite no motivation to do so.

Eventually though, Galeerial decided to sit down. It was not uncomfortable to keep walking, and he was not dissatisfied with his walking. He just decided to sit down at random. There were no thoughts behind his actions, only random chance. He sat down and rested his chin upon his hands. Absent-mindedly, he reached down, plucked a strand of grass from the ground, and began to chew on it. If only he could remember where he was supposed to be going or what he was supposed to be doing. Somewhere very close, he could hear the faint sound of laughter.

"mmmos mer?" Galeerial seemed almost surprised at the sound of his own voice, as if he had forgotten that it even existed, much less how to use it. He tried speaking again.

"mmmos ter?" Once again the tenor sound of his voice seemed so foreign to him that he wasn't sure the noise had originated from him. He tried making more new sounds, forgetting temporary about the sound of laughter he had heard just moments before. He changed the shape of his lips and his tongue and made many wonderful sounds. He could vaguely recall that there were words that he could say that were names for the things around him, but none of the sounds he made sounded quite right.

Eventually he remembered the laughter that had prompted him to make the sounds with his mouth, and he began to casually looked around searching for the source. He could see no one, and there was nowhere for anyone to hide. The grass was only a couple of inches tall, and there were no trees or structures of any kind for someone to be watching him from.

"He-, He-, Hel-, Hi!" That sounded like a word that would be used when looking for someone. He thought perhaps it might be. He did not know for sure, and, seeing as how no one answered, he thought perhaps he was wrong. He hollered once more, and with no answer forthcoming, he shrugged his shoulders. With that, he rose and began to walk yet again.

And that was how it went, at first at least. He tried to keep track of time as it seemed like days and days were passing, but the sun never moved in the sky. He retained a pattern of sitting, walking, and making sounds trying to find the names of things. The sun was just as high in the sky now as it had been when Galeerial awoke in this perfect little land. As he walked, he could hear the laughter that always seemed just out of reach and just out of sight. But as he walked, slowly but steadily, recollections began to infiltrate Galeerial's clouded mind. He was able to form the words for the world around him.

"Soon." He frowned, glaring at the glowing orb in the sky. "Su-, Suun. Sun." He smiled, and felt for the first time elation and accomplishment. He blinked his eyes several times in the feeling of another new emotion: delight!

"Oooh." He said. He was like a child: child- a young one of me. Once again, elation flowed over him, and he began to hop up and down with delight.

The emotion was the catalyst: the stone that started the avalanche. With the emotion, came a deluge of memories that flooded back into his consciousness, carried by a torrent of curiosity, anger and despair. At first, he couldn't quite parse the memories from the emotions. The emotion was so overwhelming it almost crippled him. His breathing grew labored, and he clutched the sides of his temples as the emotion wracked his chest and head. He struggled to breathe. As the wave of emotion began to dull down, his memories took their place.

He remembered the faces of his parents. He remembered training to become a Raptor. He remembered sitting and drinking wine with Ezekiel all those times at the Dead Gates. He remembered following Veriel down into the stone cells. And with a shiver down his spine, he remembered what Veriel had done to him. He reached back to his shoulder blades and felt the bare skin.

He fell down to his knees, looking down at his empty hands blankly. His wings were gone! Even in this drug addled state, he believed himself to be without his wings. They were gone! His hands began to shake, and his breath grew ragged and shallow. He felt the slow procession of tears flowing down his cheeks become a flood. His whole body was wracked with tears of pain and anguish. He was paralyzed, lying there on the ground unable to move, unable to speak-unable to do anything but cry. His wings were gone! Never again would he soar through the air. No longer would he feel the wind in his wings. He was as a human. A chill threaded its way through his body and he shook as it hit his spine. Slowly, those tears began to dry, and he cried no more. He had no tears left to cry. He put one foot out in front of him and pushed himself unsteadily up to his feet. He closed his eyes and set his jaw.

He took a deep breath.

Then another.

And finally, a third.

When he exhaled for the third time, his eyes opened and wrath accompanied them. The time for tears was done. They would do him no more good here. He would find some way to get them back later, but now...now he needed to get out of here, and then-then he would take his vengeance.

"Veriel!" Galeerial spat the name out as he would a curse. "That shadow-spawned, thrice cursed son of a..."

"Now, now, no need for such cursing. There are, after all, others watching us." Galeerial whipped around and saw a being before him. He was shorter and stouter than Galeerial. He stood roughly five and a half feet above the ground and wore a simple black cloak. He removed his hood from where it hung over his face, and Galeerial flinched, utterly revolted.

The being that stood before him was almost skeletal. That was the only word that could Galeerial could find to describe it. The first thing that Galeerial noticed was that everything about its face was just wrong. It had no eyes, and in place of them were massive grapefruit-sized cavities within its face. It had a massive mouth that contained long teeth, and the sickly gray skin around its lack of lips was pulled gaunt so its mouth was forced into a perpetual smile. It had no nose, merely a slit down the center of its face. The rest of its head was completely and utterly smooth and gray, like a great marble. A cold shiver ran down Galeerial's spine. It was standing not ten feet from him, and Galeerial raised a hand and waved it in front of the thing's face to see how it would react.

"What are you doing?" It asked, tilting its head to the side.

"You-you can see me?" Galeerial responded still repulsed by what he saw.

"Of course." It was only then, after his initial shock and disgust had subsided, that his anger was remembered...but he held it in check. If his suspicions were correct, there was no point in attacking this creature, whatever it was, while they were still locked inside this cage.

"What are you?" Galeerial inquired. He needed information more than anything else. He knew perilously little about his current predicament and that, more than anything, scared him. The creature opened its mouth into that disturbingly huge gaping smile.

"Oh...the question game." It said with a chuckle. "I do love the question game." Galeerial took note of how much it enunciated its 'T's.

"Very well, seeing as how this conversation will go much more smoothly knowing a name by which I myself am referred, preferred, deferred to."

"The Wither." Galeerial interrupted him. The name came to him unbidden; yet once he said it a second torrent of information filled his mind. He remembered speaking to Ezekiel about the Wither, and a stupid poem about the creature. He remembered the Dread War, and Geraldean and his Legion of Light. Galeerial gritted his teeth and clutched his temples as he doubled over. Insipid laughter filled his ears. "What are you doing to me?" Galeerial screamed.

"Ah HAHAHA." Galeerial opened his eyes just enough to see the Wither leaping into the air with joyous, raucous laughter. Galeerial tried to concentrate, but his efforts were broken as he felt a boot slam into his chest, and he was thrown to the ground. More laughter. White-hot fury gripped Galeerial. He clawed his way through the mental pain of five hundred years' worth of memories being flooded into his brain in the span of a second. He lashed out with a kick knocking the Wither to the ground.

Galeerial opened his eyes, which he did not even realize he had been closing, leapt on top of the Wither and wrapped his

133

fingers around its throat. This action was met with even more laughter.

"What is so funny?" Galeerial screamed at him.

"You, of course," The Wither said through wheezing breaths. "You think you have power here," he vanished beneath Galeerial's grip only to reappear behind him, "but you don't, and you can't." The pain in Galeerial's temples subsided, and for the first time since he had awoken in this Garen-forsaken place, he could think with utter clarity. He nodded with understanding.

"You ate the root."

"Impressive, no longer repressive, yet so obsessive, but not at all dismissive."

"Spiced clover-that's what you have me drugged on. A word of advice-something that I think you would have learned in all your centuries of life: if you are going to try and break a Skyguard, then don't try it through a time-altering drug. I have been here, by my reckoning, about three hundred 'days.' That is not even a year, and by Skyguard standards that is no time at all. I could sit here for three hundred years, and it would still be as naught to me. Time holds no fear, no boundaries, for a Skyguard." Yet again this brought about a fit of impulsive laughter.

"I didn't send you here to break you, fool, stool, tool, mule. I sent you here for the journey. I couldn't have you causing trouble on the way here. Now that we have arrived, perhaps since you are so com-fort-able here, maybe you would like to rejoin your body in hell."

"Hell?"

"I know, I know, it isn't much but it is..." The world began to bleed away from Galeerial's vision. It was like coming out of a dark tunnel, except the whole world began to run like colors in a wet painting. The colors of the world faded and became muddy in his vision, and he felt his ears pop. Galeerial

134

suddenly found himself gasping for breath, as if emerging from a pool of water into the air. He gasped, feeling his lungs fill with sweet air, and he began to hyperventilate, trying to grasp as much air as he could. "...home." Galeerial's lips cracked as he gasped for air with all his might. He looked around for the first time and immediately wished that he had not been so bold while on the drugs.

Mangled and mutilated bodies greeted him all around. The dim torchlight played across two dozen headless, armless torsos, and a pile of rotting body parts lay in one corner. The stench was unbearable, and he recoiled in revulsion. He watched as The Wither stared intently at him...smiling.

"Hi. Welcome-welcome to my family." The Wither went dancing from one corpse of rotting flesh to another, greeting each one in turn while Galeerial grew more and more reviled.

Galeerial felt the cold stone against his back as he hung there, but what he didn't feel was what was most important to him. He felt the cold on his shoulder blades and directly beneath them. Galeerial's breath grew shallow. It was true! He hadn't truly believed it because his mind had blocked out the memories of what Veriel had done to him. He hadn't been able to fathom it, but now it became all too clear.

"What-what did you do?" He said slowly. His hands began to shake. "What did you do?" He screamed. "What did you do?" He screamed and jerked hard against his chains. The clinking of the metal reverberated through his bones. Tears began to well up in his eyes. "How could you do this to me? What are you? AHHHH!" He screamed and threw himself forward. The Wither merely stared at him. "I will kill you. I swear, I will kill you."

"It doesn't look like you're in much of a position to do anything, or everything, only nothing." He said. Tears flowed down Galeerial's face.

"Do you know what you did to me? Do you have any idea?" He spat at The Wither, who watched as it fell short of hitting him.

"Of course! We took what was most precious to you in all of the world. I took what made you a Skyguard. I made you human." He smiled. "You're welcome."

"Go to hell."

"Look around, you're right here with me." The Wither responded.

"You are crazy!" The Wither stopped suddenly and turned to face him. The smile on his face no longer seemed quite so mocking, and his hollowed out eyes never looked more directly at Galeerial than at that moment.

"I am not. I am not crazy." He walked slowly over to where Galeerial lay chained. "Do you hear me?" He said slowly. "I am not crazy. Do you hear me?" He screamed in Galeerial's face. "No. No. I am afraid that I am the only sane one among you all. You live in a world of illusions. Only I see through them. Would you like to see? Yes, you do." He began to laugh once again. "You will see, and when I am through with you, being wingless will be the least of your worries, hurries, yessirees." Galeerial watched as he picked up a small knife made of rusted iron.

"Let's start simple. How about the brain?" The Wither shook his head as he wandered about the poorly lit room. Galeerial needed to do something or this creature was going to lobotomize him. Screaming wasn't helping. He needed a different tactic.

Galeerial breathed slowly. The adrenaline slowly began to seep from his body. His flaming anger began to die slowly, down from an inferno to smoldering coals, ready to spring back to life at a moment's notice. He would keep them burning. "Where are we?"

"Did I say you could speak?" He screamed at Galeerial. "Did I? Did I? You will learn. Yes, yes you will. You will learn what it feels like to live," he leaned in close to Galeerial's face. His breath was cold as ice and smelled like death, "like..." he stuck his tongue out and reached it out almost to Galeerial's face, "...me." The Wither had a worm in his hand, and he reached up and put it in his mouth. It crawled out a hole in the side of his cheek and down his skin. "Are you ready?" He lifted up a torch and tilted his head back towards Galeerial. "It's play time."

"I have a great idea." The Wither said suddenly reverting back to his jubilant state. "How about the question game? You were so fond of it earlier. How about another go? Every question you ask, I get to make a cut." The creature ran his hand over a short black knife. "Anywhere I want. Deal?" Galeerial pondered his offer for a moment. He stared into the hollow eye sockets of his captor. Galeerial knew that whatever torments this creature would perform would be done regardless. He nodded.

"Ask your first question, Skyguard-I'm sorry, human."

"State your origin." Galeerial said.

"Cheat!" The Wither screamed. "How dare you?"

"You asked a question, so now I can cut you. Untie me!" Galeerial commanded. It was ridiculous to be sure, but this creature was mad, and the only defense against madness was madness.

"Those are not the rules, and since you cannot behave, I am going to have to discipline you." Galeerial felt two blocks of stone placed against his temples slowly begin to contract inward. At first the pain was excruciating, and then it really began to hurt. Hot needles of black fire exploded in his mind, and Galeerial screamed.

"Yes, yes, scream for me. No one can hear you but I, and I feed on your screams, little forsaken human." Galeerial's head felt like it was about to burst inward when suddenly the pain

137

subsided. "Now, let us try this again. You ask a question, I cut. Or else we can just jump straight to the really fun stuff. You see, I have not had a live one in, well, a long time. So, I have all sorts of projects I have been working on that I just can't wait to show to someone. We are going to be best friends!" Galeerial grew quiet, thinking. There were the obvious ones to ask, but he wanted information, so while he spoke with The Wither, he would have to be canny. The Wither walked up to him and tilted his head right in front of Galeerial and jutted it in his face.

"Well, fell, sell me on your cleverness."

"What is Veriel?" The Wither shook his head.

"You disappoint me...I thought you had something truly clever to ask me. 'What is Veriel?' Veriel is a freak. He is an anomaly, an outcast. Just like me. Just like our friends, the seven sorcerers, he is beyond the rest of you, the rest of Garen's pathetic brood. He is the greatest enemy that your god has ever faced. He will bring destruction like this world has never known. Should be fun. I've been lingering in the shadows for a long time. So long I can barely remember the time before all of this. There is a great light coming. You can see it on the horizon. If you really squint."

"You mean, has not known since the Dread?" Galeerial responded.

"No. Never known, period. When he is finished, no one who was supports the throne of god will be left alive. Isn't that great, fate, hate? Now, two questions equals two cuts. MATH!" The Wither pulled the knife up to his mouth and rubbed it across his massive teeth. Galeerial shuddered. The Wither sliced downward, carving a slow deep slash into his left breast right atop the heart. He made two slashes creating two sides of a triangle. Galeerial gritted his teeth, but refused to cry out in pain or give any hint of his discomfort. It hurt. By Supremor, it hurt.

"How do I know that anything you tell me is true?"

138

"Nothing is true; everything is permitted. You have not learned this? But you will, I assure you, you will. For you must, everything we do, we do for you. You will see that. Oh yes, you will see that." He dug the knife into Galeerial's skin and drew it upwards from the tip of one of the lines. Galeerial felt a shiver run through his body, and he offered a silent prayer for strength to Supremor. The pain was nigh unbearable. He gritted his teeth together, grinding them against each other. Anything to keep from screaming.

"What is Veriel's plan?"

"Better." The Wither acknowledged. "But still not good enough. Veriel's plan is to free you all from the shackles of your god. You think you know what he is. You will have a very exquisite surprise coming. His agents are already in play, in fact. The Twilight of Ages has begun. Your friend Ezekiel was smart, a little too smart for his own good, but he will get what is coming to him."

"If you touch him, I will rend you limb from limb. You have my word on that." Galeerial spat.

"You still think that you have some power here? You have none. You will, but now? No, you have nothing. You are nothing beyond what I make you. And if you survive, and you will survive, you will be stronger than ever before." Galeerial swallowed and braced himself. The Wither walked right up to him. His breath was hot on Galeerial's face. He took the knife and carved a horizontal slash across the point that he had already cut before.

Galeerial refused to scream. He closed his eyes and breathed deeply. The pain filled his entire being. The blackness under his eyes was so inviting, so tempting to succumb, but rationale took over.

He will cut me anyway. He thought. *Two more, and then I will fall...two more.* He grew pensive, as The Wither clicked his tongue in anticipation.

"You speak as if you know me. How?" Galeerial asked.

"You are the greatest of all Carin, but no one knows it yet. It is you who will make all the difference. Without you, it all falls apart." The Wither grew angry. "Now come, you were making progress, and now you have regressed back to yourself. I know everything, so ask. Ask me something that proves yourself to me." Galeerial thought hard, pulling his mind away while the Wither made his downward slash connecting the disparate parts.

"What is the greatest secret of Carin?"

"Victory! Do you see this? Do you understand what just happened to you? And so much faster than my other patients. You moved beyond yourself. You have moved from yourself to your people. Now, you did go back to yourself, but it wasn't about yourself now. It was your future-your destiny. Now, though, now you are concerned about the future of the world. I have made you." He made sweeping gestures with his hands as, Galeerial watched him dispassionately.

"Aren't you proud of me?" The Wither asked. "The greatest secret of Carin," he snickered, "here is a secret that no one knows. No one but my master and eye." He said pointing at his own left eye. He leaned in close again, putting his mouth right next to Galeerial's ear. "I...wrote...*The Stone.*"

"HAHA, HAHAHA!" Galeerial burst out into a fit of halted laughter that caused his chest to burn. "I knew you were lying to me from the start, but I didn't realize just how crazy you really were." Galeerial was almost crying in tears of laughter. It was not a laughter of amusement. It was the combination of the absurdity of the statement and to keep him from weeping in pain. The Wither pulled his face back from Galeerial's, tilted his head

140

to the side and rolled his tongue around on the inside of his mouth. Then he started to laugh along with Galeerial.

"I am not crazy!" He suddenly screamed grabbing Galeerial by the face. The mirth was gone, and there were just those hollow eyes staring at him. "No. What is even more funny, is that you don't believe me," the Wither said laughing all the way to the door. Twenty seconds later, the torches went out all around Galeerial. The darkness flowed through the room, seeping into every nook and cranny. *Supremor save me, he didn't even cut me.* Galeerial's last thought before he fell away from this world into an even blacker blackness.

He didn't even cut me...
He didn't even cut me...

Guilt By Association

Eleven

Ezekiel approached the altar with his head bowed. The Cathedral of Light rose high around him. The stone carvings had been handcrafted in the days when the world was young and full of promise. The cathedral rose hundreds of feet into the air, with each piece intricately crafted by Ceridian the Builder. Glass burned into many colors shone with the light of the midday sun, and the whistle of the winds through the rocky crags made harmonious music that filtered down into the lowest floors of the cathedral. There it resounded and rebounded back and forth, building upon itself into a crescendo before dying back down again into the faintest of lulls. Ezekiel doubted that his people would ever make something so beautiful again.

Ezekiel raised his eyes slightly to behold the five High Clerics standing in a semi-circle in front of the altar up on the pulpit watching him as he approached. They were dressed in crimson, white and gold-the holy colors: crimson for sacrifice, white for purity, and gold for glory. Their flowing robes pooled around their feet and their wings were folded in close behind them. They looked every bit the part they were born to play in this world: that of the rulers of the Shining Host.

Ezekiel's footsteps were long and confidant strides as he made his way to the pulpit. His head was bowed in respect and deference to the holy men who stood before him, yet his eyes roved free. All around him the cathedral floor was empty.

Ezekiel caught the eyes of the Clerics. Their gaze was unflinching and unblinking, a constant burning that burrowed into his very soul. He quickly looked back down to the ground.

Ezekiel halted his approach not three feet from the pulpit where the clerics stood. He kept his head bowed and his hands folded in front of his body. Ezekiel swallowed. He was resolute in his purpose; this needed to be done. He stood there silently, waiting to be spoken to. Yet the clerics said nothing.

The red carpet was exquisite beneath his feet; it contained not the slightest of blemish. He had never been so aware of his surroundings as he was now. Seconds passed into minutes and minutes passed into more minutes as he waited. Ezekiel did not know what they were waiting for, but he was about to break the silence when it was broken for him. The sound of wings and broken air currents resounded through the cathedral. Ezekiel looked up, and from the height of the cathedral, through one of the gateways, a shape emerged and floated downward.

Veriel, Lord Commander of the Shining Host, descended down to the floor, and Ezekiel stared at him dispassionately.

The Skyguard was massive. His smooth face was resoundingly handsome, and the Lord Commander had many suitors; yet he had never taken a wife. His black hair, a rarity among the Skyguard, flowed around his two foot wide shoulders. His corded muscles shone through even the loose robes that the Lord Commander wore. He was the image of a perfect Skyguard, like something from a painting made real.

"I apologize for my tardiness, Holy Ones. I was deep in my studies of *The Stone*. Supremor has been opening marvelous doors within me." He bowed low to the ground. "Now, what is this concerning?" Veriel played the role of innocent well.

"You stand accused yet again, Lord Commander. It seems that Galeerial Strongwind was not alone in his musings. This is Raptor Ezekiel Gracefall, Galeerial's flight brother, and he shares Galeerial's concerns and accuses you of not only the same charges as Galeerial but of kidnapping that self-same Raptor." High Cleric Remiel responded.

"Yes, I had heard that the coward had fled his post late last evening. Apparently he gravely injured one of his guards as well."

"Indeed he did."

"Honored Holy Ones, I must protest. I came to you in confidence. By revealing me to him," Ezekiel said gesturing to Veriel, "you have sealed my fate, just as you did Galeerial's."

"Galeerial is not dead; his SoulSong never rang through the walls of the Cathedral of Light." Cleric Remiel responded.

"Then let me go and search for him." Ezekiel protested.

"Absolutely not. You are also under suspicion of the same treasonous activities as your flight brother. You are forbidden to leave Cloud Breach. Please continue, Clerics." Veriel replied.

"Thank you, Lord Commander. Now, what evidence do you have that the Lord Commander perpetrated this act?" High Cleric Saria asked.

"No, I will not let that go. You forbid my own ranging, because I am under investigation. I will accept that. But even before all this it took the blessing of three of you and that of the Lord Veriel in order to leave the city. It was practically impossible. How is a Skyguard supposed to live with his feet perpetually on the ground?"

145

"Where are you going with this, Ezekiel?" High Cleric Benien asked. Ezekiel pointed a finger at Veriel.

"Before his arrival two hundred and fifty years ago, we were allowed to free roam throughout Carin. What changed? He came." Ezekiel looked back to the Clerics. "Slowly but surely, we lost our freedoms. Now, we linger in stagnation. You handed away the keys to the kingdom to him not a half a century after his arrival, why? There are all these questions, and they all lead to him. To Veriel. Galeerial knew the truth; he witnessed Veriel meeting with enemies of the Host. He came to you, you ignored him, and now he's gone. I have observed the Lord Commander for the last eight years, almost as long as Galeerial himself, and there are discrepancies in his actions."

"Such as?" Veriel inquired.

"Andrel, Michael and Kirel, three Skyguard who supposedly committed suicide, after a long series of disagreements with the Lord Commander. They opposed his appointment for years."

"Their SoulSongs attested to their murders by their own hands. They all drank from the same poisoned cup; there was no foul play about it." High Cleric Saria said.

"Yet Veriel was there and did not drink. How is that suicide?"

"They willingly drank from the cup that gave their own demise; Veriel saw the effects of the poison and cast it aside. He is blameless in this; no Skyguard would ever kill another. It is forbidden."

"So is suicide." Ezekiel shot back.

"They had fallen far from their purpose in life. They had grown aimless. Do not follow their path, Ezekiel. Let this go." High Cleric Benien said. Ezekiel gritted his teeth. *They aren't listening.*

"Why is he here?" Ezekiel asked pointing at Veriel.

146

"The Lord Commander has a right to know what he is accused of and by whom. His guidance has been invaluable over the last two hundred years."

"And therein lies the problem. Clerics, I beseech you. Never in my five hundred and seventy-two years of life have I ever asked you for anything, but I ask you now, please. Use the Five Eye."

"You presume much, with little to no evidence of wrongdoing. You have accused one among us of horrible crimes, including outright deceptions within the cathedral itself, as well as kidnapping and treason. *The Stone* says not to test the power of Supremor." High Cleric Saria said.

"It also says *'Be not a fool trusting in those in shining coats of mail and bearing great gifts. But rather look into the soul for richness.'*"

"You have given us nothing, Ezekiel. Give us proof." Cleric Remiel said.

"Why are we not allowed to range?"

"The world is growing dangerous. Supremor demands our attention. We have grown lax in our worship. He demands better of us. There is no time for random rangings." High Cleric Benien chimed in.

"He demands more praise?" Ezekiel asked incredulously. "Why?"

"It is not our place to question Supremor, but to have faith in what he tells us is truth. Faith, Ezekiel. You must have faith." Ezekiel shook his head growing angry.

"Oh I have faith. But not in you. Any of you. The time of prophecy is upon us. The second Pillar, us, has been strangled by itself. We are ineffective; we are useless in this world. We will pass into the night; the Ravishing of the World is upon us, and he," Ezekiel pointed to Veriel, "is its agent. What happened to us? Galeerial always looked for the glory of the Skyguard. He

147

wanted a return to the old days. He loved our people more than anything in the world. And now he is gone, after investigating the Lord Commander on suspicion of treason. We saw that Veriel does not drink the Charist." Veriel's face grew slightly pale, and Ezekiel smiled in satisfaction. The Clerics stared at each other confusedly.

"What are you talking about, Ezekiel?" Saria asked cautiously.

"Galeerial and I followed him after the Gathering on Sunday. He did not swallow the Charist." Ezekiel smiled triumphantly.

"That is ridiculous, Cleric Benien; you have served me the Tears of Supremor for two hundred and fifty years. Surely you do not believe these preposterous claims." Veriel said incredulously. The Clerics looked back and forth from one to the other.

"Where were you yesterday, Ezekiel?" High Cleric Ty asked him suddenly.

"What?" Ezekiel asked. He was thrown off balance by the abrupt change in questioning.

"Where were you yesterday? It is a simple enough question." Cleric Ty repeated.

"I was doing menial tasks in the storerooms. A task far below my station, yet I was assigned it anyway." Ezekiel responded.

"Did you see Galeerial after he was sentenced to the Dead Gates?"

"Yes. I watched him from afar, but I was prohibited from interacting with him by none other than the Lord Veriel."

"I see." Benien replied pointedly. "On the day of his escape, you were conveniently assigned to the storerooms: the exact location where the Finger who was assaulted was stationed to watch over Galeerial."

"You think I did this?" Now, it was Ezekiel's turn to be incredulous.

"We said no such thing." High Cleric Benien said coolly. This was a losing battle. The Skyguard were being led by blind fools. Ezekiel despaired.

"I want my friend back. I want to know what you are doing to save him. I want to know why Veriel is so far above reproach."

"Since Galeerial fell, we have been working diligently to discover what caused his poor soul to fall away from the path that Supremor set for him," High Cleric Benien said blithely. "But now that he is gone, there is no more need for concern. He has abandoned his brothers in the Skyguard; he is fallen now. Nothing more can be done for him." Ezekiel blinked several times, and he felt his wings tense up behind him. Astonishment came over his entire face, and his jaw went slack. Ezekiel looked at Veriel who smiled back.

"That's it? Have we sunk that far? Is his poison that deep? I will not accept this." Ezekiel cried, through gritted teeth. "*The Sarenatas* themselves say that no member of the Ethereal Host is so lost as to never find his way back."

"You will not leave this city." Veriel cut in. His voice was stern. There was an aura of menace about him that was almost palpable. Ezekiel glared back into the eyes of the Lord Commander. He was huge. Ezekiel had never quite realized just how physically daunting the Lord Commander was. He stood a foot taller than Ezekiel, and he was garbed in golden plate armor with his crest, that of two crossed wings in red with a sword between them displayed prominently on his breastplate.

"You cannot stop me, Veriel."

"You are bound by the laws of the Skyguard and by those of Supremor himself. You may have no respect for me, but if you forsake the laws of your people than your soul will never

149

find its way to the Eternal Host." Veriel replied with a mocking tone.

"Forsake them? Forsake them? How dare you? All of you. You are the ones who have lost your way. Test him. Just look at him once with the Five Eye, or make him look in the pool of Supremor's Tears or drink from them if you want something to show me that you are not as foolish as I believe you all to be."

"How dare you!" Veriel said. His voice was menacingly low, and the threat was apparent.

"Choose your words carefully; you are riding unstable winds, Ezekiel." Cleric Remiel lowered his brow and stared at him cautiously.

"This is ridiculous. I do not know what this ploy is supposed to prove," Veriel replied. "But if that is what is demanded, then I will be happy to end this ridiculous procession." High Cleric Tamiel moved to the fountain at the center of the pulpit, from this fountain flowed the Charist.

"If I am wrong, then may my wings be sheared, and may I be condemned to darkness." Ezekiel proclaimed. Veriel glared at him.

"Give me the cup." Veriel grabbed it from Tamiel and raised it to his lips. Ezekiel saw him wince right before he drank and drank and drank, until the cup was dry. He then opened his mouth for all to see. It was empty. He smirked at Ezekiel, whose face contained equal parts shock and horror.

"No, no, I have seen it. No!" He shook his head in disbelief.

"Your accusations have proven pointless and unfounded. Know your word will be kept to the letter. Your wings will be sheared, and you will live out your days beneath a stone sky." Veriel smiled a wicked smile that was slightly tainted red. Ezekiel shook his head.

"No, I will reveal the truth. I will find Galeerial. I will open your eyes!" Ezekiel crouched low and leapt into the air, wings spreading out behind him pounding the air around him. Veriel lunged upward to grab him, but he grasped empty air.

"Guardians, subdue him!" Remiel shouted, but Ezekiel was already gone. He beat his wings behind him as he hurled skyward within the cathedral towards one of the windows. The gateways were too low, and he needed open sky and strong air currents to flee. He hurtled upward, weaving in and out of the platforms and stone carvings of the Cathedral of Light.

He spied a blue and green burned glass window and threw his arms in front of him right before he hit the window. He spread his wings out straight behind him as he flew through the narrow gap. He grimaced in pain as the glass broke around him and cut deep into his arms and wings. Ezekiel felt the open air blast him in the face as he exited. The air felt smooth beneath him, and he found an air current upon which to ride. He oriented himself south towards Whisperwood. Ezekiel knew he had the best chance of losing any pursuit in that tangled mess of a forest, where the murmurs of the ghosts and the shadowed brush made tracking nigh impossible. Ezekiel hurtled forward but glanced back at the direction of Cloud Breach and saw Veriel in pursuit. A snarl lit up Ezekiel's face as he pounded his wings in the air.

Ezekiel tapped his finger to his gauntlets and released his scimitars, Talon and Torrent, from their sheaths within his gauntlets. He didn't know what possessed him to bring them with him to the Cathedral today, but he was glad he had them. He glanced back again and saw Veriel. He was shouting something, but Ezekiel couldn't hear anything, all he could see was the look of determination and gleeful jubilation at being proven right.

Ezekiel spread his wings, stretched them harder and further than he ever had before. He had to figure out what was go-

ing on with his people-what was going on with the world-and the
only way to do that was to escape. Curse the Clerics; curse their
eyes. A growl behind him alerted Ezekiel to the fact that his time
was up. Ezekiel narrowed his body and swooped down, lowering
his elevation flying hard towards Whisperwood. He was at least
a two thousand meters up and about ten thousand meters away.

"Ezekiel!" Veriel yelled. The wind whipped Ezekiel's
long brown hair into his face, and his robes spread out behind
him were fluttering in the wind. Ezekiel pulled his blades up to
his shoulders and cut the robes away. He heard a snarl.

Oh Garen, he's right behind me. Ezekiel whipped his
wings out and flew hard straight up in a tight loop. He watched
as Veriel overshot and then impossibly he watched, as Veriel
seemed to slow immediately to a stop and reverse direction,
coming right at him. Ezekiel barely had time to react, and then
Veriel was upon him. Veriel grabbed for the throat, but his hands
were ignored as Ezekiel threw himself forward into Veriel's
body, bringing his short swords around and embedding them
within Veriel's shoulder blades. Veriel shrieked, and Ezekiel saw
Veriel's head change shape before his very eyes. Veriel grew a
long scaly black snout and giant fangs for a brief instant, and
before becoming Veriel again just as quickly. Ezekiel gaped,
astonished at the horror he had just witnessed, and Veriel took
advantage of it. His hands wrapped around Ezekiel's throat, cutting off all oxygen. He pulled himself in close.

"Your wings will be hewn and you will live in darkness!
Utter darkness!" Veriel screamed spitting blood into Ezekiel's
face. They plunged earthward in a spinning freefall. Ezekiel
looked down as the forest rose before them. It took a moment,
but Ezekiel saw his future, and he knew what must be done. He
had absolute conviction in his purpose; there was no more doubt
in his mind. This creature wasn't a Skyguard, and it needed to be
put down.

Ezekiel blinked heavily as the wind shear caused tears to stream from his eyes as they plunged earthward. He tried to focus his eyes on the ground rising up to meet them, but couldn't. His SoulSong would tell his tale, and the Clerics would no longer be able to ignore the world around them.

Ezekiel grabbed the corners of the golden breastplate of Veriel and pulled him close while at the same time folding his wings around their bodies. Veriel's eyes widened in shock and surprise, and he struggled to disengage, but there was no turning back. The ground flashed forward to meet them like a mother's arms.

Ezekiel felt the bone and cartilage in his nose shatter and break as Veriel head butted him, and Ezekiel's grip loosened. Veriel broke free and tried to fly away but his wings had been pinned to his back by the daggers. Ezekiel smiled one final smile as he grabbed Veriel by the chest. Ezekiel offered one final prayer to Supremor for forgiveness for the sin he was about to commit, but to allow this monster to survive would be a far worse transgression. His final thought before they hit the ground as he pushed Veriel's body beneath him was for his beautiful Jariah. A smile rose to his lips as they plunged through the trees and into the unforgiving ground beneath.

Divine Interference
Twelve

"They what?" Tendra's voice rang out across the flat plains.

"Dreadspawn!" Jeric cursed. They had just met with a herd of centaurs at the borders who said that Jeronious' court had already moved out to Midway, and that Qel, clansmaster of the unu, and the seven wizards were all accompanying him.

"Well, Jethro did say that Kaelish would call the Five Pillars together." Jeric said.

"You will leave our land immediately." The centaur leader proclaimed to Tendra, Jeric, and the three Light Monks, Faren, Zechariah and Na, as they wheeled their horses about and took off northward.

"He didn't say anything to me about it." Tendra said pointedly as they rode.

"Yes...well, maybe he didn't expect it to happen so soon. Nevertheless, we need to get moving if we are going to meet up with them in time to be Jethro's representatives at the meeting." Tendra sighed and gritted her teeth.

Why wouldn't he tell me these things? Tendra rode hard across the plains of Kana and looked angrily over at her 'escorts.' Whenever anyone entered the land of Kana, they were escorted wherever they went. The Kanans weren't the biggest supporters of non-centaurs. In fact, they were downright hostile until they had found out who she was, and then they merely became stoic. Now, they wouldn't catch up with the wizards until they reached Midway.

The two-and-a-half day ride passed quickly. They rode northwest for a day and then slept at the watchtower of Delmire, where the centaurs left them. The following morning, they continued on to Midway along the Golden Road. It was the road from Gemport to King's Port, and it was always well traveled.

They met up with a caravan of bards on their way up to King's Port. Sefat and the Glorious Wanderers was their name, and they provided welcome entertainment along the road to Midway. They arrived half a day behind the other members of the council, late in the evening.

Midway was a traveler's town. It was a massive marketplace with a few houses interspersed among the shops. It was a place where few people lived and many passed through. The landlords were the wealth-bearers here, and they would rent out property to the merchants who traveled there to sell their wares. As they approached, rain began to pour down upon them. Thunder boomed moments after lightning lit up the sky behind them. The fires from the guard towers guided their way to the gates. As water poured down his hood, Jeric stepped forward and pounded hardily on the wooden gate.

"State yer business." The call rang out as a small opening revealed a man with a lantern hung from a long pole.

"I am Jeric Tybius, Visionary of the Order of the Light Monks, and I travel with Princess Tendra Sumenel, daughter of Jethro, King of Humanity. We are here to attend the Council of the Five Pillars."

"Ah, ah course, we've been expectin' someone from Gemport, just not quite so late 'n da evening. Please enter." He closed the window and slammed on the gate three times for the cranks to be turned. The gate was opened slowly before them, and they led the horses in slowly. The gatekeepers hurried down to ground level as they entered and fell to their knees.

"Rise!" Tendra said impatiently as the three of them hurriedly tried to get up in the slippery mud of the road. She pulled her hood from her face so they could see that she was, in fact, whom Jeric had proclaimed.

"Ah course...Ah course, Den 'ere 'ill escort ye to da castle. De 'ave everythin' that you be needen prepared an' ready for ye. And if ye need anythin' else me lady, da name's Potter," He said with another bow. Tendra was beyond weary and could barely understand the man's prattling, but it seemed that the man's name was Potter.

"Thank you, Potter, but I would just like to be dry and find a bed."

"Ah course. Den!" He shouted, gesturing wildly toward Tendra. She found his accent irritating and hoped that everyone didn't speak in this manner. "Git on wit ye. Da lady is needen to be in da castle hours ago. Go on, git. 'N don't forget ye manners." The man called Den looked irritated to be bothered by Potter and derided in such a way, but nevertheless bowed low and politely asked for the reins of her horse before guiding it quickly up through the winding roads of the town. The castle

157

could barely be seen in the distance, and it was a modest affair-nothing extravagant.

The dirty roads were absolutely barren, with the sole exception of a man scurrying through the rain, desperately trying to keep his papers dry. The streets meandered through the town, even though Den tried his best to keep them on a straight path to the castle. They arrived at the stables to the castle about fifteen minutes after they left the gate.

"Thank you, Den." Tendra said courteously. He bowed in response before turning and leaving without a word. Out of the corner of her eye, she saw Jeric flip him a coin. She smiled as Faren stepped forward to open the gates to the stables and led their horses in.

"Naw, Naw, Naw. Ah don't t'ink so." A tall and very flustered man walked up to them as they entered. "What do ye t'ink yer doin? Who are ye? An, what are ye tinkin' at this time in the evenin', arrivin' 'ere?"

Tendra stepped down from her horse, exhausted, and again she threw her hood from her face. Jeric, Faren, Zechariah, and Na followed suit silently behind her.

"I am Tendra Sumenel, daughter of his majesty King Jethro Sumenel, and if it is pleasing to you," she said pointedly, "I would like to lodge my poor horses here for the evening. If it isn't too much trouble, of course." His hand flew to his agape mouth.

"I offer me 'umbelest o' apologies. Me name be Den," Tendra exchanged looks with Jeric who merely shrugged, "and I be de most 'umblest of stable keepers 'ere at de castle. Please...please leave yer horses. I'll see dat dey receive only de best o' care. I swear on da grave o' me father."

"Thank you. Now where can I..."

"Lady Tendra, my most sincere apologies. I was not aware that you would be arriving until tomorrow." Tendra turned around to see a man rushing down the stairwell. The fact that this man used an accent that was actually understandable was a relief to her. He was a large man, and he hurried forward as quickly as he could on his squat legs, to greet her. She watched his robes billowed out behind him while he waddled down the stairs. "Magistrate Genis at your service, my lady." He and his three attendants bowed low to the ground, and Genis took her hand and kissed it lightly. Tendra bit her tongue...she had to remain cordial.

"Thank you, Magistrate Genis. It pleases me to be here. My companions and I are weary from our travels. We are eager for a good night's sleep and warm clothes."

"Of course. Of course, now if you would please just follow me, and we will take care of you. Rooms have been prepared for you in the turrets of the tower. We had fresh clothes sewn for Your Excellency, especially when we heard that you would be traveling light and fast to arrive here so promptly." Tendra cocked her head.

"My father sent birds to herald our arrival?"

"Yes, of course. He explained his own absence with his deepest regrets, followed by instructions for your arrival, though he said that you would not be arriving until tomorrow morning."

"We were eager to finish our journey. The prospect of sleeping in the comfort of Midway was a proposition that is scarcely refused and only to the traveler's detriment." They strode together through the wide halls of Farifax Castle. As they walked, Genis filled Tendra's ears with the tales of the other members of the council and, most especially, of the wizards.

"There are six of them. Each one has a foul look about him. I don't trust them, but the children of the city love them. They arrived with the centaurs and unu two days hence. They traveled with the official party. They have been causing quite the stir. The priests of Supremor have not been happy with them, not

159

in the slightest, and I don't trust them either." He repeated, mopping his forehead with a handkerchief. "They are all tall and dark, and they carry their weapons everywhere they go with no regard to the laws. But, they have put on a marvelous show for the children. Fire fountains they call them, and they are marvelous to behold."

"Fire fountains?" Jeric asked. He had been listening to the conversation as they had walked, but this was the first time he had spoken. It caught Genis off guard.

"Yes, they send fire up into the heavens, and it explodes into a brilliance that I have never before beheld."

"Those were the strange lights we saw last night, then," Jeric said, and Tendra nodded.

"Is there any way that we could meet with them this evening?" Tendra asked, as they arrived at their rooms.

"I will go to the rooms of the sorcerers myself. If they answer, I will tell them that you wish to speak with them. But, my lady, it is long past the apex of the moon, and it is likely they are asleep."

"Of course, you are correct, Magistrate," The Magistrate beamed at Tendra's words, "and thank you again. But, though I said it politely, it was not a request."

"Yes, of course, my lady." He bowed again. "And I will see you in the morning. Hot food and wine is already in your rooms, as well as hot water for a bath. I take my leave from you." He bowed again and scurried off, leaving them standing amidst a rotunda of five rooms.

"Was that really necessary?" Jeric asked, staring at her. She shrugged and smiled as the other three Light Monks excused themselves from the hallway. She moved up behind him and rubbed his shoulders. "Eat with me?"

"We should get dry and changed first, just in case the wizards actually do show up."

"Oh, please. It is far too late in the evening. But, I suppose you're right," she said reluctantly letting go of his shoulders. "Hurry up though, I don't want to speak with them alone, if," she said with emphasis, "they do show up. And if not, I am hungry, and we should eat together."

"Nothing would please me more." He turned around and faced her, smiling. He reached his hands out and locked fingers with her. She looked at him, and he stared squarely into her eyes. That was one of the things that she loved about him: he would always look deep into her eyes. She had yet to meet another man who would do that. There were no secrets between them, for they were always peering into each other's souls. "I will return momentarily, my lady." He said.

"You'd better." She backed up to her door and turned the handle. "Don't forget to knock." He gave her a look, not just a look, but *the look*, and she smiled mischievously.

"See you soon." He leaned down and kissed her lightly across the lips. Just as quickly as it began, the sensation was gone, and he was walking backwards away from her. She shook her head and pulled him back in for another kiss. This one lasted longer, but it still wasn't long enough. He pulled away from her again. She clicked her tongue in disapproval, but this time he wouldn't let her pull him back. He slipped free and walked away, with a goofy grin, to his room.

She watched him back away from her, hands on her hips and leaning against the doorframe. She blew a kiss at him as he vanished from view behind his own door. She turned away and closed the door behind her with a sigh.

"Two more years," she sighed. It was an eternity beyond the forever that she had already suffered, and still the time until Jeric achieved Blazer status in the Light Monk order. That was two ranks higher than where he currently was ranked. Then they

161

could marry. But, that was the price that had to be paid, and it was a price that she had accepted four years hence.

She slipped out of her wet clothes and into the hot water of the bath. She instantly felt the needles of pain in her legs and up her torso as she sank deeper and deeper into the hot bath. She sighed as the aching cold was flushed from her bones. She took in a deep breath and plunged her head under the water...feeling the warmth eradicate the last bastions of iciness in her body. She remained under for as long as she could hold her breath before silently re-emerging into the cool night air. A fire was roaring in the mantle, and she pulled on a series of clothes that had been laid out for her on the large and well-adorned bed. This was either the Magistrate's own chambers, or perhaps a local earl's, judging by the furnished gold trimmings and the mirror.

Tendra marveled at the mirror. She loved them...she loved seeing the reflections of things within them. This mirror stretched as tall as her body, and she stared in it as she dressed for the evening. A soft knock at her door interrupted her musings.

"Who is it?" She called out softly.

"My name is Rowen, and I speak for the Seven." A cold knot twisted itself into being within her stomach. She had honestly not expected any of them to appear this night, but now that one was actually here, she found herself at a bit of a loss.

"One moment." She replied. She took three deep breathe to calm herself. She quickly ran a brush through her hair to smooth it before checking her appearance once more in the mirror. Her evening gown was neither flashy nor impressive, but it would have to do. She walked over to the door and opened it.

Her breath caught in her throat as before her was a…a god in human form. The man named Rowen had black flowing locks that hung across his shoulders and had a face made from pearl. The moment she opened the door his face was solid and kept; yet once he saw her, he broke into a lopsided smile. He slightly declined his head in more of a nod of respect than a full-on bow.

"You called, my lady?" He said, still maintaining that smile while at the same time cocking his eyebrows up.

"Yes, please come in." She said slightly flustered. She had, of course, seen handsome men before, but this man was leagues beyond any of the others. It wasn't just his looks but his presence. As soon as she had opened the door, the room had been flooded with it. She found herself almost needing air because she was being drowned; it was so pervasive.

"It would be impolite of me to enter a lady's chambers at this hour of the evening." He replied, smiling again. Tendra tried but couldn't quite bring herself to become angry at him.

"I have no patience for this; I am tired and hungry and if you wish to remain in the hallway that is perfectly fine with me." She turned away and smiled in satisfaction as he stepped gingerly into the room, shutting the door behind him. "You will scarcely enter my room; yet you close the door behind you."

"I understand the need for secrecy, just as you probably understand the need for discretion when inviting men into your chambers." She smiled again, but recomposed her face before sitting down at her small table and gesturing for him to do the same.

"Are you hungry, or do sorcerers not eat?"

"Oh, we eat, just not typically at three in the morning...and I never said that we were sorcerers." He replied.

"Yet you use magic."

"I would say that makes us magicians, not sorcerers."

"There's a difference?" She asked, pouring herself and him a cup of tea. He accepted the warm cup gratefully as he sank into his chair. He looked completely at ease but still formal. She was not quite sure how he accomplished that feat.

"Well, yes. Of course, or else why would there be two words for it? Like pretty and beautiful, both of which apply, but one is much more befitting." He said staring at her. She met his gaze and was surprised when he held it as well. She knew that she had a very pointed stare, and thus most people wouldn't meet it. He did.

"Nevertheless, it is irrelevant." she dropped her voice low. "My father told me everything. There is no need for this façade."

"There is always the need for a façade. And, in our case, image is everything...especially the fake ones. But, you say that your father told you everything? Well, that is all good, but I've never met your father, or you, unfortunately, before today."

"My father told me about you, but not what your cover was. I need to know what your story is. How you have magic, and how you can use it."

"Our story? Hmmm, it is three in the morning, and we have nowhere near enough time or tea for that. What I will tell you is that we come from a land on the other side of the Rift to the west. We arrived seven years, seven months and fifteen days ago. Our world is called Cambria, and in it there is a hierarchy of wizards, my brothers and I are mid-level wizards in a branch called the Tower of Water. We have been sent here to wash away the sins of this world." Tendra was equal parts amused and incredulous.

"People actually believe that?" She asked.

"I'm afraid that I don't follow." Rowen said with a completely straight face, and Tendra rolled her eyes.

"Your story. I expected something outlandish, but crossing the Rift? That's a little far-fetched don't you think?"

"You are saying you don't believe me?" Rowen asked.

"Of course not. Like I said, my father told me all about you."

164

"Apparently not." Rowen replied. "What exactly did your father tell us?" A sinking feeling began to grow in the pit of Tendra's stomach. She was not exactly sure why, but she suddenly felt uneasy about revealing too much to this man. *Change the subject.*

"It doesn't matter. The real reason I asked for you, was because I need your help. I need one of your number to return with me to Gemport at the conclusion of the Council."

"Why?" Rowen asked, finishing his tea. Tendra felt his eyes upon her as she slowly ate a slice of bread. She took a breath.

"My brother, Prince Jakob, is dying, and I need one of you to come and heal him."

"Like I said, why?" Rowen asked pointedly.

"Why?" Tendra grew angry. "What do you mean why? This is my brother we are talking about, the crown prince of the human kingdom."

"Yes, I got that the first time. What I mean is that our mission is of paramount importance," Rowen began.

"Not to me."She interrupted him. "Not to me." Tendra repeated. Now, she was angry. Rowen looked regretful.

"My lady, I…" he was interrupted by a knock on the door. Tendra rose to go and unbolt the door to let Jeric in. Rowen reached out and grabbed her wrist. "Wait! I must speak with my brothers, but everything depends upon the results of tomorrow's council." He hesitated. "I'll see what I can do."

"Tendra?" Jeric called out.

"I'll see you tomorrow." He let her hand go with a wink, and she watched as he walked over to the window and leapt out.

"Tendra?" Jeric's voice grew more urgent in the background, but she could barely hear him. She stood there, gaping at what had just transpired, before running over to the window and staring out. The rain had stopped, but the few

165

torches that had been relit upon the banisters of the castle did a poor job of illuminating the night sky. She saw nothing.

"Tendra!" Jeric yelled outside the door. "I'm coming in!"

"No!" She called. "I'm coming." She walked over to the door and pulled it open.

"What happened?" He asked storming into the room, sword brandished.

"I'm fine. One of the magicians was here."

"What? Where is he?" He paced agitatedly around the room, looking in every nook and cranny.

"He jumped. He jumped out that window." Tendra pointed to the balcony watching as Jeric's face conformed into a mask of disbelief. "He's gone, and if tomorrow's council goes well, then he will come back with us to Gemport."

"I don't like that he was here with you alone." Jeric said.

"I can handle myself, Jeric. I don't need you always watching over me." She chastised. Jeric held up his hands in defeat.

"Very well. So did this sorcerer have a name?"

"Magician." Tendra replied.

"I'm sorry?" Jeric asked confused.

"They're magicians...not sorcerers."

Crisis Counseling
Thirteen

Tendra was puzzled. She knew that there should be some
kind of excitement, an electricity in the air, but all she could feel
was the cold pit in her stomach. The Council of the Five Pillars
of the South was not something lightly brought together. In fact,
such a gathering had never even occurred. The last great council
was the Third Collective Council half a millennium ago, and
now a new council convened. The difference being that neither
the Skyguard nor the giants would be attending. This was just the
Pillars of the south. It certainly made things easier as far as
accommodations, but it only further reinforced the animosity that
had grown between the seven races of Carin.

Tendra looked around the manor gardens. A thousand
and more hues assailed her vision and as many, if not more,

smells coalesced into a single fragrance of life that filled her nostrils. The smell made her comfortable, and she shook her head to clear her senses. She needed to be sharp for the coming meeting.

Tendra sat in one of four chairs that ringed a large circular stone table in the center of the gardens. She had made sure that she was the first to arrive. When Supremor had destroyed the old world and remade it; the only two survivors were Garen and Meren. They were both human. Over the course of the first hundred years of the world, Garen and Meren were transformed into each of the other races by Supremor. That was why mankind was referred to as the template, and how every race had humanlike features. As such, humanity always served as the arbiter of such proceedings as this, and, in this case, her species served as a balance point between the two opposing factions. She also knew that the Heart of Fires would come up, and all animosity would turn toward her. She would be ready.

Unbidden, her thoughts turned to the magician. After he had left last evening, he had remained at the crest of her mind. He had not been afraid of her. He had treated her as one would any person meeting them on the street, not like royalty. There was none of the usual posturing for good graces or hushed tones that she usually received. He had been cavalier with her, had been-she couldn't quite come up with a word to explain him.

The rustling of branches caused her to turn her head to the left to watch the approach of Jeronious, the centaur king, and Qel of the Thousand Hammers, head of the unu clans. Both towered over her both in height and weight. They were massive beings. All thoughts of Rowen were purged from her thoughts. She couldn't afford to be distracted. Tendra rose at the entrance of the two- no, three beings. Tendra paused as she saw what had to be one of the wizards in between them. Tendra was not able to linger on him as the other two rulers strode in and took their seats at the table.

To Tendra's immediate left sat Kaelish, Lord of Fangs. He was diminutive when compared to the other races. Even Tendra stood at just above eye level with him. Tendra had extensive dealings with the ferals before. She had never treated with Lord Kaelish directly, but her father had on multiple occasions. His golden brown fur had been pristinely groomed, and Kaelish wore simple robes as his attire: nothing exotic or fancy.

Eferven, the telos Imperial, on the other hand, was the epitome of splendor. He flowed as he moved over to his chair. His luxuriously long white robes pooled around his feet and swept out behind him while he walked. The nine foot tall telos stood above the other races, but their slim features belayed none of the strength of them. The telos had silky smooth, bluish-white skin and incredibly long limbs, which gave the impression that they were more akin to a work of art than a living creature. Eferven's long face and lack of a nose made looking at him slightly uncomfortable. A shiver went down her spine as his stark white pupils and glowing green corneas stared at her. She had only seen a telos twice before in her life. Neither had been particularly positive occasions and as such she did not have a particularly strong positive association with their species.

She turned her gaze quickly away to observe Qel fix himself into his chair, which was more of a couch than a throne. The unu was massive in proportions. His tight muscles bulged even through his loose fitting ceremonial red robes. She had to withhold the distaste in her mouth as she looked at him. The unu had muscles that looked like they were about to tear out of his skin. It was almost disgusting to look at, if it weren't so fascinating. The large bundle of golden ropes of hair was a testament to Qel's skill in battle as a commander. His golden eyes shone as he studied the assembly, much as she was doing. She thought about what she knew of him. He was incredibly ambitious and even stronger willed. He did what he wanted and was smart enough to get the clans out of any situation. Her father had once told her that Qel was the most dangerous being alive.

Then, there was the wizard. This man looked rather plain when compared to the myriad of beings assembled, as well as compared to Rowen. He wore a simple brown cloak and had his hair cut close to his skull. He had a noble face, like an old lord from long-ago times. His composure was pristine; he knew what he was doing. It was a plainer version of what she imagined that Jeric would look like one day. As the leader of the Seven, he was not at all what she expected, and that made her all the more unsettled by him. He turned and stared at her, his green eyes piercing directly into hers. *What was it about these men that they were so bold?* She broke his gaze and looked at the next and final member of the council whom was seated at her right hand.

Jeronious, Herdmaster of the centaurs of Kana. He was tall and broad of shoulder, and his flowing red mane complemented the reddish-brown of the hair on the lower half of his body, which was finely groomed. His face was cleanly cut, and his eyes were quite shifty. She had spoken at length with her teachers about the other kings of the world and knew that not all of the centaurs truly believed in Jeronious' ability to lead. He had been chosen in a most unorthodox fashion. He had been handpicked by the last Herdmaster, Deneb. His rule had never been put to a vote, which was how it had been done for thousands of years. It was something that Jeronious had been struggling with over the last eight years of his rule.

"I bid thee welcome, Lords of the Five Pillars of the South. I am Princess Tendra Sumenel, daughter of the High King of Humanity, Jethro Sumenel the Just, Forty-Second in his line. I speak on his behalf. I trust we all know each other. You have been called together to discuss the fate of this world. In Gemport, we have heard news of what has transpired, but a firsthand account of the crimes of the Seven will be required. Judgment will be passed down, and this conflict will be brought to an end."

"How are we supposed to discuss the execution of the Seven, when one of those creatures is here at the very heart of power itself?" Kaelish demanded, jabbing a finger at the wizard.

"Joven is here, because he represents the group that is on trial. He is here, because he represents a group of immense power in the south. He is here, because he is our ally." Qel answered him cordially. Joven. Finally, a name. Her father had given her nothing to work off of.

"Ally? Ally?" Kaelish repeated in outrage.

"Kaelish, you bring your grievances here. Let them be stated for the council to hear and judged upon." Tendra tried to regain control of the conversation.

"You are going to allow this-this beast to sit at our table? One act of war and suddenly one is elevated to the very halls of power itself? Let them go kill a few Skyguard and perhaps they will be invited to dine in Acheron itself," Kaelish spat. "I refuse to speak, as long as that sorcerer is here."

"The wizard is here as a witness for the actions of the Seven, who have committed crimes against an entire kingdom. Therefore, the representative of the Seven will be given limited representation at this council. He will be allowed no voice beyond giving a direct account of their actions. If the conclusion is reached that they are to be executed for war crimes, then you will be able to execute him very promptly. Qel, you will keep the wizard on his leash. Is that understood?" She said firmly.

"Of course, my lady." Qel replied. Eferven folded his fingers together.

"Tell me, child." His words were hisses that came from a pursed mouth. "Where is your father? Presumably, the only reason any of us came here, besides to see the death of the wizards, was to demand that he turn over the Heart of Fires, and for the council to pass judgment upon him for his crimes against the world. He has acted in direct defiance of the Third Collective Council. What say you?"

"My father is too weak to travel, and my brother lies upon his deathbed. I was sent in his stead, and any questions that you would have asked him may be asked of me as if I were him." Tendra said sharply. She braced herself for the coming assault.

"Very well then, you heard what Eferven has said. These humans, your people, Lady Sumenel, clearly used magic against my people. If your father has the Heart of Fires, then his usage of it is an act of war against all of Carin." Kaelish said. After the War of the Breaking, three hundred years ago, the feral and telos kingdoms signed a mutual protection pact. So, any war between the unu and the ferals would bring the telos into the fold. And with the apparent combination of forces between the centaurs and the unu, it seemed like the whole south would soon be at war.

"Then, I am afraid you will have to find the missing page of *The Stone*. I am sorry you wasted your time in coming." Tendra replied.

"Don't play games with us, child." Eferven warned. "The mere existence of the Seven proves that Jethro has Garen's Tomb, or at least a piece of it.

"I wouldn't dare waste the council's time, or play games with them. I have never seen this man in my entire life, and as for the Heart of Fires, I will say again: Gemport does not have it." Tendra said flatly. The hostility being radiated toward her was not unnoticed. *Time to change the subject.*

172

"You may have come here chasing fairy tales, Eferven, but I came here to stop a war. A war of the south will accomplish nothing."

"I beg to differ, my lady. For two thousand years, we have suffered these cosmic abominations," Qel pointed at Kaelish, "to disrupt the balance. No more! We will return this world to the way it was, a pure world-a world of balance between the firstborn races."

"Your incessant prattling grew wearisome centuries ago." Kaelish replied. "We allied ourselves with the Dread a thousand years ago, and we were horribly punished for it. Let it go, Qel. We are as much Garen's children as you are." Qel shot to his feet.

"Heresy!" He spat. "How dare you? I will cut out your blasphemous tongue."

"You may cling to your antiquated notions from centuries past all you want, Qel, but I am concerned with the present," Kaelish growled. "Those humans killed three hundred and fifty of my people, and I will not let that go. So, I will make it simple. As simple as it can be. Give us the Seven, all of them; no questions asked. If you do this, there will be no war. But, if you continue to aid them, to provide them shelter, then we will break your bodies across our swords and rend your bones with our teeth. The Kingdom of Fangs is not so named for nothing."

"Your threat is hollow! Three hundred and fifty of you were slaughtered by seven, not even seven gallowglass, seven humans." Qel mocked. "Do you truly believe that you can stand against the combined might of the centaurs and the unu? Your cities will be but rubble before the arrival of winter's first chill."

"Kaelish does not stand alone, Keeper of the Balance," Eferven said, "and do not mistake your people's respect for the balance of the universe with your own ambitions." Qel bristled at this. "And you, Master of the Herd, what have you to say? It was

173

your people who first brought the Seven into the fold, if I am not mistaken. Is the Unu of a Thousand Hammers your keeper? I thought that it was the sorcerer who was supposed to be kept on a leash, not one as eminent as you."

"Wizard or magician, actually." Joven chimed in.

"I am sorry?" Eferven looked almost confused, if such a thing were possible on the inscrutable face of the telos.

"We are not sorcerers, or necromancers, or witches, or anything like that. We are magicians or wizards, if you want to stretch the definition, and I am highly offended that you would call us by anything other than what we are. It would be unto me calling you a Skyguard. It just isn't right." Joven said.

"Jeronious, keep your magician, or wizard, or whatever he is, quiet! He will speak when spoken to and not a moment before." Tendra said harshly.

"He is not my property, any more than I am Qel's, and I am insulted that you have insinuated as much." Jeronious said. "For centuries, we have been forced to maintain not just the Face Off, but constant security around our borders from feral invaders, thieves, and brigands."

"Rebels." Kaelish said dismissively.

"Your people." Jeronious accused. "Since the Third Collective Council, a formal ceasefire has existed between our people. That is not peace. My forefathers had neither the strength nor the will to campaign against you. That is no longer the case. You have taken advantage of our clemency for far too long."

"What are you talking about?" Kaelish asked incredulously. "You would send your people to war for what? Bandits? The unu I understand. They are zealots." Tendra glanced at Qel, who shrugged in apparent agreement with the feral. "We can fix this." Kaelish pleaded. "If the positions were reversed, there would be no call for war right now. I would be here to present their heads to you on a platter. Give my people justice."

"Justice for what crime exactly?" Qel asked.

"Murder." Kaelish replied.

"You sent three hundred soldiers against them. Against seven humans. Why?" Jeronious asked. "You're afraid. Your people are weak, and you know it."

"Come against us, and you will see our weakness first hand." Kaelish threatened.

"There is no need for any of this!" Tendra cut in. "There is no need for war."

"Need?" Qel asked. "Perhaps not. Desire? Absolutely. The winds of change are in the air. I did not come here to relinquish a tactical advantage. I came to tell Kaelish that his rule will end in blood and the burning of Long Fang."

"Why? Why are you doing this, Qel?" Kaelish asked. He seemed scared now.

"The Balance." No one believed Qel's words.

"There is no balance to your ambition." Kaelish replied bitterly.

"And you, child," Eferven turned to face her. "Pray tell, what is your father's position on this? Will he support the Lord of Fangs in his lawful dispute or will he side with the supposed World Balance?"

"I see no lawful dispute. I see a military action that failed. There is no crime here. My father's position is quite clear. If you wish to kill yourselves over something so foolish as a few humans, albeit obviously very well trained humans, but humans nonetheless, my father will not interfere. We claim no side."

"So, the humans, who started this bloody affair, will watch us tear at each other like mad dogs. Your father must be pleased that his plan is working," Kaelish said.

"My father would be pleased that you credit him with the ability to conjure seven magicians from thin air. A useful skill. Perhaps he can conjure up seventy...or seven hundred...or seven thousand? And, if we really had the Heart of Fires, do you honestly think that we would have only seven? No, and again, if we had the Heart of Fires, the entirety of Carin would know about it. A secret such as that is not easily kept. These wizards will tell you the same."

"I have never seen Her Ladyship in my entire life until this day, and I have never seen the Heart of Fires either. I give my word." Joven said.

"Your word is as hollow as Qel's promises. You have no honor. Need I remind you what you did to my people at Sterin's Throne a mere handful of days ago?" Kaelish spat back at him dispassionately.

"My brothers and I began our war with the ferals to prevent a tragedy. In our world, the ferals have been hunted to nigh-extinction for the crimes they perpetrated against humans, but even that is not enough. We were sent here, as thousands of our brothers were sent across the Rift in every direction. Across every land, we will hunt them down until there is not a single feral left in this entire patchwork world."

"We had nothing to do with whatever occurred in your world. We merely wish to live in peace." Kaelish responded.

"Peace! Peace? Ferals have been raiding our lands for as long as we can remember, and Qel and his clans fight with the ferals at every turn," Jeronious angrily shot back.

"I have done my best to keep my people within the bounds of our kingdom, but you can ask the Princess Sumenel how easy it is keeping tabs on every little faction of your people. Not all the ferals are of the same herd, Jeronious."

176

"That is no excuse. We have suffered your attacks on our people long enough, and now we will fight. We are no longer the prey, but the predators."

"You don't know the meaning of the word," Kaelish snarled. Quiet descended upon the council. Kaelish turned to her. "If you will not offer up the Heart of Fires to the council for the use of all, the feral army will take it by force. It is too great a power to be in the hands of any one race."

"If the feral army makes a move toward Gemport, the unu will stand opposed to them. The unu stand with Jeronious and the Seven against the feral kingdom, and any act against Jethro will be an act of open war." Qel tossed back.

"The Wielders of the Fire have already committed an act of war, and so have the two of you by allying yourself with them," Eferven coolly replied.

"Congratulations, Princess Sumenel." Kaelish bitterly said. "Tell your father that the fools of the west are playing right into his hands. This meeting was a waste of time. I had hoped to talk sense into all of you-to see that our true enemy was Jethro and his machinations, but you all are too stupid to see through this charade. When they betray you, you will find no allies in my kingdom." Kaelish said bitterly to Jeronious, rising from the table.

"Your kingdom will be burned to the ground by winter's eve." Qel said with a smile. Tendra's head was spinning. *How had everything spiraled out of control so quickly?* She struggled to recover.

"Perhaps we should adjourn and return once we have all calmed down." She said. Kaelish laughed.

"There is no recovery from this, Princess. There is nothing left to do now but fight." Kaelish said.

"He will not stand alone." Eferven said, standing from his chair and placing a hand on the feral's shoulder. "If it is war, then the telos will fight with their brothers."

"You don't have to do that, Eferven." Qel said. "Fight with us. Spare your people fighting a war in which they have no stake." Eferven's long thin tongue snaked out in an involuntary hiss of disgust.

"Unlike you, I am not so quick to abandon my friends."

"So that's it then?" Tendra asked. "Just a small catalyst was all it takes for the world to ignite?" She shook her head. "Humanity will play no part in this conflict. All parties will have safe conduct to return to their respective kingdoms. After that, may Supremor have mercy upon your souls." Tendra said.

"You will regret this...all of you. Your race will fall, burning in oil and flame, into the abyss. The wolves will feast upon horseflesh in the coming weeks." Kaelish turned and whispered, "you will know darkness," as he exited from the council. Eferven bowed and smiled, his black tongue playing across his long perfectly white teeth as he did so.

"My lords, my lady, wizard... I expect that this will be the last time I will ever see any of you alive. It has been my utmost pleasure. Enjoy your late-night congregations with the wizards." He turned and walked out, to Tendra's speechless expression. She turned back to Jeronious and Qel.

"We have a war council to marshal. We must be prepared for Kaelish's attacks." Qel said rising from his chair.

"Do you honestly believe him to be arrogant enough to go on the offensive?" Jeronious asked.

"No, but I do think he is desperate enough to try the unexpected. My lady." Qel said bowing.

"You bloody fools. The south will burn for this. What you have begun, will not end until one side is utterly obliterated." Tendra said.

"I know," Qel smiled, "a good thing then, that I have a thousand hammers by my side." Tendra was not amused. She shook her head. "And, now that we are alone, tell us about the Heart of Fires. Your pet..." Qel never finished his sentence. He was hurled across the garden. He slammed into the thirty foot oak with enough force to make the mighty tree shake and buckle under the force of it. He slumped to the ground dazed.

"I am no one's pet. You would do well to remember that." Joven said, gesturing at Qel, who had just risen unsteadily to his feet.

Qel stared at Joven. His face was contorted for an instant in a gross caricature twisted with anger and rage before quickly returning to the blank unreadable gaze that he had maintained before.

"That was most unwise, magician. Most unwise," he said as he walked by Joven and out of the room.

"You should not test him so." Jeronious said to Joven. *Fractures already?* Tendra thought. "Joven, we leave for Harin's Dale in two hours. We must prepare." Jeronious said; his voice bowed with the weight of his decisions. And then there were two.

Tendra stared at Joven, and he back at her. They said nothing. They merely stood there staring into each other's eyes.

"I..." She began, but Joven silenced her with a motion of his hand. He made a series of hand gestures telling her that talking here was not a good idea, and she nodded her agreement.

"I apologize, my lady, but I cannot speak right now. I must prepare for our imminent departure." He stepped up right next to her, leaned in, and kissed her on the cheek while whispering, "ten minutes, lower kitchens," before stepping back. "It has been my pleasure." He said, bowing low before turning and walking out of the room, leaving Tendra alone, staring at the three chairs before her. Her father would be pleased.

179

Four of the Five Pillars of the South were at war. *How long before humanity was drawn in as well?* She took a breath and began to move out of the garden towards the kitchens. The stone corridors of the castle folded in around her as she walked. The scurry of people in the castle flowed around her like she was a rock amongst a river of people. Those who recognized her would stop and bow before continuing along their way. She couldn't believe what had just happened. This had never been a negotiation. This had always been a declaration of war. Nothing more. They had been in there less than an hour.

She was greeted by a cacophony of noise from the kitchens long before she arrived. The sound of chefs screaming, knives chopping, the cackling of fires, and the pounding of pots and pans surrounded her. It was midday and lunch was being prepared. The roar of fires, and the smells of smoke, burning flesh and fresh vegetables filled her nostrils as she breathed in deeply. She realized her hands were shaking, and she forced them to stop. She took several deep breaths.

Tendra saw three men standing in one corner near a roaring furnace, and she made her way towards them, avoiding two chickens running around the kitchen and a cook chasing after them with a cleaver. Before her stood three men: Rowen, Joven, and a third, who was older than both of them and almost as handsome as Rowen but in a different way.

The third man had a hard face and was the first to bow. His hair had been cut short like Joven's and unlike the other two, was a dusty brown color. He had the face of a warrior. He looked like a man who had seen terrible things and survived them but with an immeasurable cost tolled upon his soul. He was shorter than the other two. He had plain brown eyes that watched her as she approached. He had the hint of scruff on his face, like he was used to shaving, but had not done so today.

180

"My lady, my name is Aurum. You have already met my brothers." the man said. "I apologize for the location, but secrecy is paramount here. The noise of the kitchen will drown out anyone listening. I understand that you want to take Rowen with you to Gemport?" she nodded. "Your brother-what kind of illness does he have?"

"We call it the White. It passed through our city two months past. Everyone who contracted it has died, but it has not affected him nearly as strongly. He lingers."

"What are his symptoms?" Aurum asked.

How interesting. Tendra thought. Joven was the spokesperson for the Seven; yet it seemed like the true power behind them was in this man.

"He is always tired, and he can barely speak. He is often completely incoherent, and he mumbles incomprehensibly. His skin is white as newly fallen snow. And, his hair is falling out."

"Anything else?" Tendra struggled for a moment

"He cries-he cries tears of blood." At the mention of that, Aurum's face jerked up, and he stared at her. He took a deep breath, and Tendra saw the furtive glance that he shot at his companions.

"His eyes grow milky and white when he cries." It was not a question.

"Yes." Tendra replied cautiously. The three of them looked at each other.

"Please excuse us for a moment." Tendra nodded. They stepped back by where a man was chopping up carrots. Tendra strained to hear as they spoke quietly together but gave up when they came back a minute later.

"Rowen can treat him. But, he will need time with your brother and supplies." Aurum said.

"Supplies? What about your magic?"

181

"This is not a problem for magic to solve. It is a problem for a doctor to solve. We have seen this before. Rowen will heal your brother, but more than that, he will be our representative to Jethro. Through him, we will speak to you, to your father, and to your people. Do you understand?"

"Yes," she said without hesitation.

"Good, because you will be responsible for him in the same way that he will be responsible for you and your father."

"I'm not sure I understand that part," Tendra said quizzically.

"Qel doesn't trust us, and your stunt today basically told him that we are working for your father." Joven said.

"What are you talking about?"

"You are a good speaker, but you are not a diplomat. You shamed us at every opportunity. You tried too hard. Now everyone suspects that you were covering for us. Rowen will go with you, but you have to leave now. We will win the war of the south in no time at all. Our strength is too great for Kaelish to stand against, but after that, Qel will come for you. We will try to stop him, but the only guarantee we can offer you is Rowen," Joven told her. Rowen grinned.

"Now, you need to leave quickly. Rowen will heal your brother, and he will help train your soldiers. We want to keep humanity out of this for as long as we can, but Qel's zealousness is going to force us to accelerate our plans. Rowen, you have two hours; gather what you need, and the rest you will have to find along the way. I will help you make a list. My Lady." Tendra glared at him pointedly.

"I want reports every eight days, and your word that you will keep Qel in line with the Rules of Warfare as laid down..."

"I can give you no such word, because I will keep no such word. The race of ferals will become extinct by year's end and the telos possibly with them, depending on the course

Eferven chooses to pursue. Kaelish is too weak a leader, and the telos have barely enough numbers to sit in their libraries. Now is the twilight of their ages, and they will fall into the night. Now, if you will excuse us, we have a war to win." Aurum turned and walked away from her without so much as a word of courtesy. Joven did the same, leaving Rowen and her facing each other.

"Well, my lady," he said with a smile, "shall we?" He asked stepping forward and putting out his arm.

"We shall indeed," she replied, brushing coldly past his arm.

Wake Up and Smell the Decay
Fourteen

I woke to a red face peering closely at me in an ocean of green. I groaned.

"Is it inconceivable that I perhaps get a full night of rest?" I demanded. I rubbed the sleep out of my eyes and looked into the void of the red man's eyes. He again held a snappoppy in his hands, though this one was blood red, which now contrasted with the ocean around us.

"No. But we have much to discuss. Have a seat." I turned around, and there was a simple wooden rocking chair behind me.

"I like the new design."

"The design reflects your temperament. Right now you are calm; before, you were anxious. Everything is going as planned. But it will not continue for long." I cocked an eyebrow at him.

"A new player has entered the field, and it foretells badly for your campaign." The man placed the flower into his belt, and then pressed his right thumb to his left forefinger and the same on the opposite side, creating a box, and a picture was formed within it of a man chained to a large stone. A hooded, cloaked man was cutting into his chest with a ragged looking knife. The man pulled his fingers apart steadily from one another, slowly but surely making the picture bigger. I watched as they spoke, and the cloaked figure slowly but steadily carved into the flesh of the other man with the knife.

"This is occurring right now, and it is a situation that needs to be remedied immediately. You may not realize it, but you do not have as much time as you may believe. Events are progressing at a faster rate than you can imagine. There are people who will take advantage of what you have done. There are greater consequences to your actions than you realize."

"What consequences?"

"I could explain them to you, but in your ignorance, my words would mean nothing. These beings are who you need to focus on. The balance will shift for or against you based on their actions."

"Who are they?" I asked, still entranced by the picture.

"The one being flayed up like a dead rabbit is named Galeerial. He is a person of interest."

"Not to me." I replied.

"Not yet, but if you do not rescue him he will cause the death of all of you." I peered closer and saw gaunt features stretched thin onto a decrepit body. It looked like he had not eaten in a month. His skin was an ashen gray color. "The other is an old player in this new game. He is dangerous-far more so than any other foe you have faced. Even the Horror that you and your

186

brothers fought three years ago at Lake Lefron is nothing compared to this creature. Tread carefully and in the light." He watched me intently, as I stared at the man dangling from the ceiling in chains.

"How do I save him?" The man sighed.

"Take the Light Monk Jeric with you, and leave immediately for the ruins. Leave your longsword with your horses. Be quick. When you are no longer in doubt, go to the left, but do not overstay your welcome."

"I do not know what that means."

"You will." With that, the man turned around. He had a large red eye painted on his back in intricate detail, and beneath it, an eagle. I watched as he slowly vanished yet again. I sighed and closed my eyes.

The next time I opened them, the soft light of my window was a much more welcome sight than that of the Red Man's stony face. I leapt out of bed and dressed quickly. I strapped my daggers to my belt and Widower's Wrath to my back. I grabbed my staff and pulled open the door in time to see Grey holding his fist up in preparation of a knock.

"I could be wrong, but I think you're supposed to open the door after I knock on it. Would you like to try it again?"

"Not now, Grey." He instantly sobered up at my tone, as I pushed by him and began to walk down the hall.

"Did you see him again?" He asked, keeping stride with me. I nodded.

"How many times do I have to tell you, these late night meetings between you two...he's only going to break your heart." Grey said, trying to get a smile out of me. I shot him another look. "Alright, fine. What did he say?"

"I'm leaving."

187

"Wait. He said that he was leaving, or you are leaving?" he asked. We turned the corner, and I strode to Joven's door, knocking twice upon it.

"I am leaving. Jeric and I have to go to Amul Kon."

"One second!" Came the call from inside the room.

"You're che-" Grey stopped his sentence abruptly at my stern look. "-cking out Amul Kon? Why? That place is nothing but shadows and rock. Not even cool rocks."

"The Red Man told me that I had to go there and to take only Jeric with me."

"Jeric? You mean that stuck-up jerk who is always following Ms. Gorgeous around and looks like he wants to murder you if you so much as throw her a glance?"

"He's the one."

"Wait, I'm confused. Why does scary red painted man hate you again?"

"Hehe." I said in mock laughter. The door opened before us as I saw Joven still trying to wipe the sleep from his eyes and smooth out his ragged mess of hair.

"How long will you be gone?" he asked, beckoning for us to come in. I entered first, followed by Grey. There were clothes scattered around the room. It was most unlike Joven. I cocked an eyebrow at him.

"We won't meet again until you arrive at the Face Off. I'll be there for that battle, but from now until then, don't count on me for anything."

"Close the door." Joven said, and I did so slowly.

"Aurum, you put me in charge of this operation, and I can't have you doing things like this. Now, I don't know what is going on with you or who this freak is that you're having dreams about, but you need to get this figured out now. Do you understand me? We're messing with fate enough as it is. There is no sense in tempting it beyond what necessity demands. This is your one shot; now, are you sure that we can trust this guy?" I shook my head.

"No, but we can't afford not to. If he's playing us crooked, then I'm capable of defending myself. If he's playing us straight; however, and we ignore him, then we're in trouble." Joven nodded in agreement. "Not only that, but look at this." I pulled my knives from his cloak and handed them to Joven. Joven peered over the lettering on the blades.

"Nice handwriting." Joven said.

"The first time I saw the Red Man, I woke up and found that inscribed in my blades. Whatever he is, he can do things that we don't understand. He can invade my dreams and impact the physical world, albeit in what appears to be a limited manner. I really don't think we want to make him angry." Joven handed me back my knives, and they disappeared back into their sheaths. He paced back and forth pensively before me.

"Alright, do what you need to do. I can run things at Harin's Dale without you. Are you taking Dane?"

"No. He said nothing about Dane or anyone else: only Jeric." Joven shifted his eyes back and forth in thought as he moved around the room cleaning up.

"You're trying my patience, Aurum." I bristled. "You need to keep working on him. I have a feeling that he could be the difference between victory and defeat. After Long Fang, we will need him as a spy anyway. I need that to be a priority." I nodded.

"If that's it, I am going to go find Jeric and see if he's up for a working vacation. Grey, can you get two horses prepped with a week's worth of supplies and a field kit? Thanks," I said without waiting for a reply. "Joven, I'll see you in a few days."

"Remember, you're uncaged at the Face Off. I can't guarantee that we'll be there in time, so don't be afraid to break the bars." I nodded before turning around with a wave to my brothers and stepping out of the room.

"No problem, Aurum. I'll get right on that." Grey called out to me. I tossed him another wave over my shoulder as I kept on walking. Tendra's chambers were in the south turret. I walked through the barracks where we had been housed and out into the day's light. I quickly walked through the courtyard toward the castle proper. The stone pathway meandered carefully through the pristinely kept grass. I made my way toward the gates and watched the guard's heads follow me as I wove toward them.

I passed by the guards at the front of the castle with a nod before entering. For such a major town, the castle was quite small in comparison to even the ones at Mesnir and Bicoln. This was a trading town and the Magistrate's cut of the profits obviously didn't go toward the castle's opulence, which made me wonder exactly where it did go. I dodged two screaming children as they ran out the door, and I chuckled as their mother came running out the door after them a moment later, begging my pardon.

The castle was abuzz, as people were already awake and going about their daily activities. I almost chuckled at the sheer dullness of it all. These simpletons had scant idea of what was to occur in the months ahead. Their entire world was going to be splintered into a thousand fragments and transformed into something marvelous. Yet here they went about their daily lives as if everything were the same.

I remembered how it was years ago, when I had still thought that an everyday life was to be my life. Unbidden thoughts of my wife and daughter came to mind just as quickly. I shook those memories from my head. I was not the same man I was before. I was better now.

I approached the spiral staircase that lead up to the south turret and began to climb. My leg was still a little bit sore, and I felt it twinge slightly as I climbed.

I reached the top of the staircase and heard raised voices. I moved quietly forward, careful to keep my staff from bumping anything.

"Why does it matter if he has gone north?" this was the princess.

"Because he didn't go west. The Light Monks across the world are on watch, because of what happened with the Seven. We don't know what is going to happen, and so we are investigating every possible lead. If Kaelish is going north for some reason other than taking the scenic route home, we need to know why." I knocked on the door, and the conversation inside immediately stopped.

"Who is it?" a voice called out.

"Aurum of the Seven." silence followed for a moment before the door was opened by Jeric. I had seen him before but only from a distance, but this close I could see that he was a mountain of a man. His face, like his demeanor, was hard as stone.

"What do you want?" he said curtly.

"A pleasure to meet you too, sir." I said, bowing. It would be best not to start off on the wrong foot, despite his best efforts to the contrary. I raised my eyes and saw him doing the same begrudgingly. "Aurum."

"Jeric. Would you like to come in?" he said coolly.

"Thank you." I stepped into the room and saw the princess sitting at the small table on the south side of the room sipping something. "My lady," I said, bowing again. Jeric closed the door behind me with an audible click. I leaned my staff up against the frame of the door.

"Please sit." She said gesturing to the chair sitting opposite her. Jeric took up residence behind her left shoulder. He was like an attack dog, poised to strike. "Now, what brings you here?"

"I am here for your escort." I said, nodding to Jeric. He cocked his head to the side slightly. "My lady, what I am about to tell you none but my own brothers know, and I am telling you and your betrothed this in the strictest of confidence." I was going to lie. Again.

"I thank you for your trust." She said. "Tea?" She asked holding out a cup.

"Thank you." I said bringing it up to my lips. It tasted of honey and licorice. The heat of it burned my throat as it descended to my stomach. It sent a slight shiver down my spine. I set the cup down but kept my hands wrapped around the cup, feeling the heat warm my hands.

"As you well know, my brothers and I are well attuned to phenomena outside of the physical sense. Included in this is the gift of knowledge divined from sources, outside of the commonly available realms. Most recently, these phenomena have manifested themselves in the form of a man who comes to me in my dreams." Jeric remained stone-faced, but I could see the doubt in his eyes.

"And this man, what does he do?" Tendra asked. I could sense the slight bit of doubt and mockery in her words.

"He provides me with information, in exchange for, well things that really don't concern you. But, he tells me things that no one else knows, things that no one else can know."

"Such as?" Jeric inquired.

"Matters of fate: of death, of war, and of secrets. Last night, he came to me and told me that I needed to go to the ruins. Now, the only ruins of any import are Bastian and Amul Kon. I sincerely doubt that he would send me to Bastian, so that leaves only Amul Kon." I saw Tendra shoot Jeric a furtive but nigh-imperceptible glance. She was so inexperienced still. She was intelligent, but not wise, in the ways of deception and politics. "He also said that I was to go with Jeric."

"Why me?" Jeric asked.

"He didn't say. All he said was that it needed to be you who came with me."

"Why do you have to go there?" Tendra inquired.

"There is a man imprisoned there. He is being tortured by an unknown figure. My source said that he has universal relevance. I can't afford not to investigate this, your majesty. So, with your permission, I would like to take your bodyguard with me to Amul Kon. My brother, Rowen, is traveling south with you, and I assure you that he can protect you against whatever forces may accost you."

"Jeric is not my bodyguard; he is my betrothed." I let no emotion play across my face, but inwardly I grimaced. So this was Rowen's competition for the princess's affection. Rowen was playing a dangerous game here. He needed to keep himself under control long enough to subtly eliminate the man. I just prayed that Rowen could contain himself for that long. Rowen was smart, but he could be impatient. He had tempered it over the years, but he was still too much of a romantic for my tastes.

"I apologize for my error. Nonetheless, my question still stands." I looked Tendra right in the eyes.

"If you will give us a moment to confer?" She asked.

"Of course." I rose from my chair and bowed before turning and walking to the door. *Interesting*. She had requested it rather than ordered it. She saw us as above the usual rabble. She wasn't stupid; that was something at least.

I grabbed my staff and took it with me as I pulled open the door to the piercing stares of the three Light Monks who were standing right in front of the door. Each one had their hands on their rapiers.

"Good morning," I said in greeting. They wore the star with a single stripe above it, which indicated that they were all members of the Brightness Level within the Order of the Light Monks. Jeric was a Visionary, which was the ninth level, and he had a star with two stripes beneath it. The patch was worn on the left shoulder, and I knew that they had a tattoo of six straight lines in their skin above their hearts. The highest level was Radiance, which was held by a single woman, Anhelo, who dwelt in the city of Illuvium. The name Anhelo was more of a title than an actual name. Every ruler of the Order held that name. It created continuity among the ranks. The first Radiance Anhelo created the Ke, the fighting style of the Light Monks, which consisted of lightning-fast strikes done with thin swords. It was actually very similar to that of the telos: all about sliding blocks and elegance rather than brute strength or killer instinct.

"Enter." The call rang out, and I turned from the unblinking stares of the three monks. I opened the door to find them in the exact same positions as when I had left. I again laid my staff to rest at the doorway. People found it uncomfortable when a wizard had his staff. It was like they expected to be turned into a frog at a moment's notice.

"Well?" I asked looking from one to the other.

"Jeric will explain why to you on the way. You are to leave immediately. You will go to Amul Kon and rescue this man. You will find out who his tormentor is and, if necessary, eliminate him. You will then meet back up with Rowen, Zechariah, and me at the Face Off." I maintained a stoic glance. Her demeanor had changed dramatically. This was a princess talking, not a woman.

"What of the other two Light Monks?"

"They have missions of their own that are of no concern to you." She replied curtly. I smiled. She was learning.

"Fair enough. As long as they don't go to Amul Kon I am satisfied."

"Excellent." Tendra said

"My brother has already prepared two horses with a week's worth of supplies for us. I will await you there." I said, and with one final bow, I withdrew from the room. I grabbed my staff and began the descent.

"Aurum!" I turned around and saw Jeric striding forward to the staircase. "Let us walk together."

"Why did the princess agree for you to come?" I asked.

"She wants information about you." I looked at him surprised.

"I did not expect you to be so…honest."

"You already knew that to be the answer, so there was no point in keeping any kind of false pretense." Jeric replied. I nodded.

"Nice to see we aren't under any kind of false pretenses then."

"Indeed." Jeric said. "That being said, I would rather not have this take too long." The trip to the stables passed quickly. I pushed the door open and saw Grey pulling the feed bag from a black stallion while a stable boy looked on.

"Grey, Jeric. Jeric, Grey." Jeric nodded in greeting.

"Charmed. I got you the two best horses I could find. This one is Bane of My Existence, and that one over there is Death to All Over Five Feet Tall," he said gesturing to a gray colored horse impatiently pawing the ground. "They're all stocked up and ready to go." I clasped Grey on the shoulder.

"Excellent. I'll see you in a couple weeks. It's your job to make sure Rayn doesn't kiss up to Joven too much." I smiled as I pulled Widower's Wrath from my back and stuck it onto the saddle.

"You always give me the best jobs, Aurum. Thank you so much," Grey said sarcastically. "First, I get to arrange for your horses, and then I get to keep our youngest brother from his natural state of being. Are you sure you don't want to send me to The Eye of the North? It would be easier to survive there."

"Oh please, you would barely be an appetizer for the creatures up there. Now quit complaining. You got to do all the fun stuff for the last seven years; now, you get to do a little bit of the dredge work. Enjoy it." I said with a grin. "Open the doors." I told the stable hand.

"What's her real name?"

"Beauty."

"Cute." I replied as I climbed on top of her.

"And mine?" Jeric asked pulling himself up.

"Windfall." Jeric gently stroked her mane as he whispered to her. Grey shot me a funny look, and I shrugged.

"You ready?" I asked Jeric, as he brought his horse up next to mine. He nodded. Grey handed me the reigns.

"Heeyah!" I spurred my horse, and we trotted out into the city proper. The city was bustling from the harvest as new farmers flooded into the city with their crops. We took care to avoid the crowds as best we could. When we rode down into the town proper, people would stop and stare at us as we passed. These town folk didn't know us, but they knew my staff. The day before the princess and her escorts had arrived, we had put on quite a spectacular light fountain show.

People were watching as we rode, but they were crowding around us. I didn't have time for this. I raised my staff and shot a lightning bolt into the sky. The crack of thunder in the cool morning air resonated through the marketplace and the people cheered, but more importantly, they immediately made way for Jeric and me. He gave me a disapproving glance, to which I didn't respond. *Who was he to judge me?* We made it to the city gates in record time and passed through with the slightest of nods to the guards.

The open road beckoned to us, and we took off across the plains. We urged our horses into a fast trot. It was a three-day journey to Amul Kon. No sense in having exhausted steeds by the time we arrived.

"Why did you do that?" Jeric asked me as we rode. It was a gorgeous day with nary a cloud in the sky as the sun shone above us.

"Do what?"

"Use your powers for personal gain. When we were in the city, you fired off that thunderbolt to make the people move out of the way. Why?"

"It would have taken us an hour to get through that crowd. I don't know how much time our man has to live. I was shown him, and he looked like he was standing on death's doorway. He was gaunt with hunger, and his skin was ashen. If he really is as important as I have been lead to believe, then I have to use every means available to make sure that he stays alive." Jeric pondered this as we rode. There was a wind at our backs, which made the journey go by even faster.

We broke for lunch about six hours into the journey at a small brook that we stumbled upon. There wasn't much out here except for farmland and the occasional small community and tavern. No big cities, just a whole lot of nothing. We ate some dry bread and fruit that Grey had procured for us and were back riding within the hour. The horses had been good choices. They were strong. As we rode, we spoke of the world and of our families. I didn't tell him about my wife and daughter.

197

We made our way across the plains in good time. Three hours after dusk, we brought our horses to a halt near a giant tree that dominated the otherwise flat landscape.

"This is the Tree of the Bronze Children." Jeric commented. I nodded. "Interesting that we rest here for the night."

"Hopefully, the results of our quest are more fruitful than those of the Bronze Children," I replied. Jeric smiled. We scavenged some wood from the base of the tree, careful not to touch any of the branches. The Bronze Children were said to still dwell within the higher boughs of the trees, and it was not wise to bring them down from their perch.

Jeric sat down across from me as we ate on the cool ground. The grass was perfectly cut beneath the tree, and there was a single burned-out pit where we built a fire. The Children were used to guests. It was tradition to leave them an offering. I honestly didn't know if it was just superstition or if there really was some group of creatures that lived in the tree. This wasn't the time to find out. The smell of smoke and burning meat entertained my nostrils, as we made small talk for a while before Jeric finally broke through the ice into deep water.

"May I be perfectly candid with you, Aurum?" Jeric said, pointedly. I thought about it for a second before nodding.

"Be my guest." I said sweeping my hand out. I had my staff laid across my lap, and I was rubbing an oiled cloth across it while we ate.

"I'm worried about your brother."

"Which one?" I said with a smile.

"The one who is accompanying my betrothed to Gemport: Rowen. He is very cavalier." I couldn't help but laugh, which elicited a disapproving glance from Jeric.

"Yes, he is, but he is also a professional. He will do his job. He has a mission, a duty to perform, and he won't jeopardize that."

"And, what exactly is that mission?" Jeric asked.

"To protect Lady Tendra and prepare Gemport to withstand the coming assault. The floodgates are about to be opened, and Gemport can't afford to be swept away. The Unyielding Throne cannot pass into inhuman hands." Jeric nodded.

"I agree with you on that. You will forgive me if I don't entirely believe you though."

"I would be disappointed in you if you did."

"Disappointed?" Jeric asked.

"You are the betrothed of a princess. If you trusted that easily, your future station would be very difficult for you." Jeric chuckled at this.

"Thank you. You have put my soul at ease with your words." Jeric said. He seemed earnest in speech, but his demeanor was still as rigid as ever. He spoke, but he did not really believe.

"You're welcome. Now come, much sleep is needed for the coming days. I will take the first of the night watches." Jeric nodded in agreement and wiped the juice running down his chin with his mess cloth. I watched as he settled in for the evening. And I stood watch as branches of the tree shook and a bleeding moon rose in the distance.

*   *   *

Before the Dread War, Amul Kon had been a tower that stretched over a thousand feet high. It had been a nexus point for the world. The forest had not been quite so close back then, now the edges of Whisperwood almost totally enshrined the ruins.

The Skyguard had owned the tower, and it was a center for art and culture. The Dread led his army through Whisperwood and launched a surprise assault on the city. The city was far away from the frontlines and believed itself safe. The Dread and his army punished them for their arrogance by shattering the tower completely destroying it. The tower was abandoned after that. Now, it was a labyrinth of moss-covered stones and dirt.

I had never been here before. There had never really been reason to. We had considered placing one of our supply stations here, but it was too far away from really anything to be of use to us. I didn't think of any of that right now.

The moon was bright in the sky. It wasn't quite full. Jeric and I had arrived early in the afternoon but had waited about eight miles from the ruins until nightfall. We rode quietly up to the entrance. Jeric was obviously uneasy. We didn't really have any kind of plan. We really couldn't. Neither of us had been in the ruins. We didn't know the layout, the players involved, or the escape routes. I didn't like it. I was a planner. This scenario didn't sit well with me, but we had no options. We kept it simple.

Get in, get out, and don't get caught.

We entered silently into the darkened ruins of Amul Kon, stealthily making our way through the stone maze. The rocks were worn smooth by years of fierce winds during fierce winters. Jeric followed behind me. The moon lent us the advantage of being able to see while robbing us of much of our cover. We stuck to the shadows as best as we could. It still wasn't nearly enough. I felt a cold feeling in my stomach. It wasn't fear. It was uncertainty. There were too many variables. I could hear Jeric breathing heavily behind me.

The walls were oppressively close. There were still a dozen levels in various states of decay. It could take all night to search and then well into tomorrow. I hoped it wouldn't take that long.

It didn't. The thought had barely crossed my mind when a moment later I peered we came to a fork in the road. I peered down the left pathway. In the flickering a blue torch I saw a man in chains stretched upon a massive boulder. I recognized him from my dream as the man we had been sent to find: Galeerial. I gestured to Jeric, and he took a look. From the other branch, I heard the sound of laughter erupt. It sent a chill down my spine. I pulled Jeric in close.

"Can you pick a lock?" I asked. Jeric nodded, and I pushed the tools into his hands. Grey had put them in my saddlebag back in Gemport. "Get Galeerial down and back to the horses. I'm going to keep his captor occupied, or kill him if I can." Jeric nodded once again.

"I'll be quick." He slipped around the corner and moved swiftly towards where Galeerial was chained. I went the other way. The corridor narrowed briefly before opening into a wide plaza. There were two flickering torches placed on either side of a broken piece of rubble that now served as a seat for the creature the Red Man had shown me in my dreams. A feral lay drowning in white chalky blood on the floor. As my eyes adjusted to the light, I silently cursed. It was Kaelish. That was bad. Kaelish was perfect for our purposes...weak and ineffectual. I didn't dwell on the repercussions. *What was he doing here?* My sense of unease grew.

"You may come out of the shadow if you wish, fish, dish." The creature's defined "T" reminded me of something, or someone, but I couldn't quite pin it down. I stepped into the light.

"What are you?" I asked. I could just barely see his shoulders shrug in the dim light.

"I know why you are here. You've seen him, and I really can't let you leave here alive with that knowledge." I drew my daggers from my belt and waited left foot forward and arms raised across my chest. I had left Widower's Wrath with the horses, despite Jeric's protests and my own uneasiness regarding the proposition. I didn't know what to expect, but I would be ready. I still couldn't see his face, but I knew by his body build that he was at least humanoid. Most likely he was one of The Horrors still dwelling within the world, and fortunately, I had killed one of those creatures before.

"You are brave, but I am the leech that saps your soul." I blinked, and he was gone. A hard fist to the jaw sent me reeling. Then, a swift kick to the leg in the other direction almost shattered my knee, but I was able to angle it away at the last moment. The creature suddenly appeared right in front of me and, for a brief moment, I saw his fleshless face snarling at me before throwing myself to the left in a roll to avoid an uppercut, though I still received a glancing blow to the shoulder that sent me spinning.

"You're fast, but I am speed incarnate." He snarled, hitting me three times in the back and then vanishing as I plunged my dagger backwards. This pattern. I had seen it before. I hung my hands taut at my sides ready to strike out at the moment's provocation. I saw a slight blur on the left and whirled around stabbing furiously, but all I hit was unforgiving stone. My blade slid right into the stone, like butter, but my arm felt the shock as the hilt struck the rock, and I winced slightly with pain.

"You're strong, but I wither strength to ash with a touch." His appearance above me was the final confirmation. He dropped down and landed on my shoulders, causing me to go into a crouch, but I was able to snap my neck forward to avoid a club to the face. He was following the Horizon Arc, albeit in a different form.

It was an old technique...really old. I remembered seeing it at the Book Castle of Mesnir a few years ago. It was an enormously effective series but one that had been abandoned long ago. He appeared to my right again and launched a savage kick into my stomach, but not before I flexed to cushion the blow. I stumbled backwards into a stone pillar. *Enough!*

"You're smart, but I am the darkness that swallows all brilliance." I cursed. He knew that I was aware of what he was doing. In the Arc, he was supposed to appear in front of me. *When you are no longer in doubt, go to the left.* The Red Man had told me that. I whipped to the left and plunged my dagger into his suddenly appearing heart.

"And you are as predictable as the tides." I growled, ripping my dagger out of his chest and with my other hand smoothly sheathed Havoc and whisked my staff from my back, pressing the tip of it into his stomach

"Strike!" I called. A flash of lightning burned out of the tip of my staff.

The creature shuddered momentarily, and I saw the arcs of electricity course through his body. His clothes caught fire, and I saw a glimpse of his skeletal face before he went flying across the room. His corpse slammed into the crumbled stone of the broken wall with a crunch. I breathed a sigh of relief. Whatever that creature was, it was dead now.

"Jeric, are you done?" I hollered.

"Ten seconds!" He shouted back. I turned from the throne and began to walk towards the entrance, when I heard a sound. I froze before slowly looking back over my shoulder. My blood chilled as I saw the creature rising up from the ground. It was wreathed in the flame of his burning tatters of clothing. My brain couldn't process what my eyes were seeing. I looked down. There was no blood on my blade, and the smoking hole in the creature's chest seemed to have little effect on it. My blood froze.

"We need to go now!" I yelled and fled. I didn't know what that thing was, but it had just taken a bolt of lightning without even a second's hesitation.

"Is that all?" He whispered. "You're weak, and I am the boot that crushes. Your fear is delicious. We will meet again, but the next time, your heart will be colored by rage rather than by valiance." I could hear his voice all around me. I looked back and saw him still standing there. I turned, and I ran.

These Broken Chains...

Fifteen

Galeerial awoke screaming. His world was alight with fire, and his vision was a cornucopia of dazzling brilliance that made his stomach heave. Tears flooded down his eyes, and his nose was beyond the point of irritability as the smoke filled it. He felt his limbs stretching behind him, and he could barely find the strength to look up and see that he was hanging by his arms and legs from the ceiling.

But that was not what woke him. The Wither was standing beneath him holding a torch up to his chest and snaking it back and forth along his cuts, burning them into scars. Sweat poured from his body, and the salty wetness only made the cuts

205

sting worse. The smell of burning meat filled his nostrils. He didn't cry out in pain anymore. His screams had died along with his prayers to his deaf god. Now, he just suffered.

"Good, good you're awake." The Wither smiled up at him. "I was getting lonely. That and we are running out of time. You see, the game has begun and the opening gambits have been made, and now-now the swords are starting to clash. In fact, the first volley was fired yesterday, and one team doesn't even know about it, but he'll find out right about now." He looked around quizzically. He turned around. "Helloooo?"

Galeerial tried to speak, but nothing came out but a low guttural growl. His cracked lips bled.

"Shhh, no talking, no talking." He turned back to me. He pulled a knife from his cloak. "You make a sound, I slit your throat." Galeerial laughed at him, before spitting in his face.

"If that is the case, then I will scream louder than all these nights that you have tortured me." Galeerial said weakly pouring all the defiance he could into his voice.

"Why do you want to die? Your people are a broken shadow even in the strongest of lights. Your romantic illusions of the past are just that: illusions." Galeerial tried to think…tried to imagine a world before the endless pain and darkness. He could vaguely remember books. He remembered his hate for this disgusting creature, but even that was merely hazy embers.

"I'm going to kill you, Wither." Galeerial said weakly. He had said it over and over to himself, but he no longer believed it. The Wither looked at him with what Galeerial suspected to be confusion.

"Why do you insist on calling me that?" Now it was Galeerial's turn to be confused. He laughed. "When did you come to that name?" Galeerial struggled to think back, it was so long ago, back before…all of this. When he had been drugged. Galeerial suddenly grew very afraid. The Wither laughed at

Galeerial. "Foolish Skyguard. The Wither. Haha. I don't know how you could be so naïve. Could it be that I am not who you believe me to be? That I am, in fact, that which the world most fears?"

No, no. I don't believe that. The Dread was dead, killed a thousand years ago.

"Now, you will be silent. I believe that you misunderstood me before. I said I would slit your throat, not that I would let you die. I will leave you here bleeding, pleading, needing but unable to speak more than a few gurgles worth of blood. So you will remain quiet."

He stepped onto the table and reached up and pulled Galeerial's head back and forced a small vial fupl of liquid into his mouth. Galeerial felt the pain in his throat subside. He tried to speak and instantly his throat swelled up, and he could barely wheeze out the slightest of breaths.

"There we go, all better." His disgusting face twisted into a haunting facsimile of a grin before turning and skipping off the table. A moment later, Galeerial heard a raspy and raw voice: a feral's voice.

"My Lord?" The voice called out

"I am not pleased with you, not pleased with you at all. In fact, you could almost say I am disappointed in you." There was a pause.

"War has been achieved, My Lord."

"Through diplomacy. You were too afraid to take the initiative, so tell me, Kaelish, what good are you if you aren't strong enough to protect your people? Perhaps we chose wrong in you, Kaelish. Your general, Fashnar, appears to be a much more worthy specimen." Galeerial heard a snarl.

"Fashnar is an animal. The ferals would never follow him."

"But they will follow you?" The Wither asked.

207

"To the ends of the earth. Ferals are loyal to the head of the pack."

"Like dogs." Another snarl.

"The feral race is key to my plans; however, before they can be unleashed, they must die. As must you." The feral stepped into the dim torchlight. It was perhaps the first feral Galeerial had ever seen. It hurt so much to remember. Its head was that of a wolf with a longer snout, deep brown fur, and longer teeth. It stood slightly taller than the Wither and had slightly longer arms than legs.

"What would you have me do, My Lord Dread?" Galeerial went numb.

"Your people will fall before the onslaught of the unu, the centaurs and the Seven, but not all of them. My army is almost prepared. There are only a few more preparations to be made to usher in the end. I am going to kill you for a short while, Kaelish. Then you are going to lead your people once more."

"Our bargain?" The feral asked.

"In order for your heart's desire to be fulfilled, you must do this." The feral hesitated.

"Very well then." The Wither laughed that horrible laugh of his.

"Then die you will." The Wither passed a finger over the neck of Kaelish, and blood began to torrent out where the incision was made: white, chalky, disgusting blood.

The Wither sighed.

"You did well." He said, reaching up and patting Galeerial on the face. He couldn't even muster the energy to recoil from the touch.

"Shhhh, don't be afraid. I am going to leave you now, but just for a while. Will you be okay?" Galeerial tried to respond, but he still couldn't speak. "Just nod." Galeerial did nothing.

208

"Excellent. Our time here is almost done. You have been a good friend." The Wither smiled, and then grabbed the arm of the feral and walked out. A bloody smear followed them out, and the torches went out with them, but just for a moment before one reappeared. The changing light gave Galeerial a headache and rendered him temporarily blind. Galeerial's gaunt body was so weak. How long had he been here? The days had stretched longer and longer.

"Don't make a sound." A whisper from his right caused Galeerial to jerk his head over in the direction of the sound. He could still see nothing. The effect of the fires had stripped him of his night vision temporarily, and it was just beginning to manifest.

"My name is Jeric, and I will get you out of here, but you need to be as quiet as possible. We don't want that thing coming back anytime soon." He spoke softly and with a sense of urgency.

"Kkkk-kill me." He whispered out to him. Galeerial's throat was aflame, and his voice was pathetically weak, but that was all the strength that he could muster. But the human…Jeric…it was so hard to think; he didn't kill him. Instead, Galeerial watched as he stood on the table beneath him and carefully began to pick the locks of his chains.

Galeerial could only listen as there was a slight click and the binding on his right foot loosened, and he felt his leg swing down towards the table. The second clasp came undone, and Galeerial's whole body sagged downward.

"Ten seconds." The human yelled. Galeerial didn't know who the man was talking to. Galeerial screamed silently at the pain as both shoulders dislocated, and he hung limply by his two arms. Burning thorns of pain threaded throughout his entire body. He hung there paralyzed by lack of food and strength. He

209

heard the human whisper something, but he was already fading into blackness.

"Kill... me." The chain on his right wrist detached itself, and he swung downward, cascading around the room as his weight shifted, and he hung like a rag doll from the cord. Galeerial's vision grew colored in spots, and then his entire body became cold. The five slash marks burned into his chest screamed in pain at him as he lay there shivering, his naked body huddled on the floor. The cold stone caused him to start shivering. He curled up into a ball as his teeth clacked together.

"C'mon, stay awake." He heard whispered to him. Galeerial felt himself get propped up and pulled from the cold stone floor. He was thrown over the human's shoulder He raised his head up as they moved through the ruined castle. He saw the Wither standing there in the flickering light of a small candle.

"We need to go now!" Galeerial heard a voice scream out and saw a man running towards them.

Galeerial's eyes opened wide, and he tried to warn the human, but his voice was lost.

"I told you our time was almost up." The Wither whispered softly. The human didn't appear to hear it as he continued to move stealthily from shadow to shadow.

Galeerial blacked out and next he knew a warm breeze was greeting them as they emerged into the night sky. The light of the stars fell lightly upon them as the human broke into a run. He ran for what felt like an eternity before finally he felt darkness take him.

He awoke to the jostling of the ground. Galeerial looked down and saw a horse beneath him. He was riding it. Large, gloved hands held the reigns, and Galeerial sat there numbly as the rocking motion of the horse went up and down, up and down. Galeerial felt himself gag, but he had nothing to throw up.

"Hold on, we will stop up ahead, get you some food and water and let you sleep. Just hold on."

Once again blackness eclipsed him, and the next thing Galeerial knew was the cold taste of water upon his lips. He took a small sip and then coughed it back up fitfully.

"Easy, easy. Just a little bit. You need to drink. By Supremor, how long did that thing have you there?" Galeerial sipped some more water. "What is your name?" Galeerial looked up at him blankly, "your name." The human pointed at him from across the fire. He hadn't noticed that there was a fire, or that he was now wrapped in a blanket. He couldn't remember.

"Your name?" The man said once again. "Jeric," the human said pointing to himself. Galeerial took another sip of water. "It's okay, don't try to speak. You can tell your story when we get to Delmire, or, even better, to Gemport. The world is about to ignite, and we don't want to be here when that happens." Galeerial tried to stand. He began to rise to his feet, but his legs couldn't support him, and he crashed to the ground. Jeric quickly picked him back up from the ground.

"You have to listen to me; you are in no shape to do anything right now. You barely have any meat on your bones; your muscles have corroded to almost nothing. You're lucky to be alive. You need to rest; in a few weeks you will be as good as new. Right now, however, I will knock you out if I have to. We're safe. We are in the shadow of Beth's Bridge; none that are unwelcome may remain here. The Watchers Black are eternally vigilant, and my status as a Light Monk and the fact that I am the Princess Tendra's suitor have helped to smooth things over quite nicely with them. We will be at the Face Off in two days. There we will meet my lady." He said. "Sleep. We leave an hour after first light. We have a lot of ground to cover."

"Kill me." Galeerial wheezed. "Kill me."

211

"No. You're safe; there is no need to die. Not anymore. You're safe." Galeerial's strength left him, and he collapsed onto his back and lay there looking up at the stars. They were not quite as bright as he remembered them being. Some of their luster had been lost since he had been taken from his home.

*   *   *

Galeerial woke to burning. The sunlight upon his eyes was unto fire being stabbed within him. But the pain did not bother him, what did was the realization that he was dying. The burning sensation came from his very bones. His rescuer held him tight against his body as they rode hard and fast. The human kept up a relentless pace as they went along. He was being eaten away from the inside out. He looked down through skeletal eyes.

"You look like death itself, my friend." A man said. Galeerial turned and looked at him. His eyes burned from the sun, and he had to squint in order to see. He still felt the smoldering pain. The man looked at him, and then leaned in to look closer. Galeerial could only stare back blankly. He tried to speak, but his throat burned, though not as much as it did before.

"By Supremor." The man said. It was not the same man who had saved him.

"What? What is it?"

"Let me see his shoulder blades." The man said quickly.

"Why?"

"Just do it." Galeerial felt himself get rotated around.

"That's no man. It's a Skyguard." The man on the other horse breathed, "but his eyes...they're blue. Skyguard have violet eyes."

"What does that mean?" Jeric asked.

"I don't know. I don't know."

212

When Hope is Found

Sixteen

"How about a song for the road, My Lady?" Rowen asked. They had been traveling slowly for the majority of the day toward the Face Off. It was four days since the Council of the Five Pillars. He and the one remaining Light Monk, Zechariah, were now escorting Tendra southward to Delmire one of the two cities that made up the Face Off. Delmire was a centaur fortress, and Marose was the centaur fortress. They were separated by a quarter mile. There they would meet up with Jeric and Aurum, before continuing on to Gemport.

"I would love one." Tendra replied with a smile. Rowen sat there for a moment, staring at her from his horse.

"Well, I was actually hoping that you would sing one for me, but I suppose I rode right into that. Very well. I had hoped to spare our present company the torment of this, but nevertheless, at your insistence." He began to hum softly before beginning. At first, his voice was so low that Tendra had to lean in to hear him, but his voice slowly grew stronger and more hypnotic.

"I walk these roads every night
Under the moon and stars so bright
Every rock and every flower
The shadow of home beneath the tower

I walk these roads, these roads of home
I walk these roads, these roads of home
Every night I walk alone
Through these roads
I am home

Trumpets sound and banners call
And every man, large and small
March along those very roads
But they are not home
But they are not home

I walked those roads, those roads of home
I walked those roads, those roads of home
Every night I walked alone
Through these roads
I am not home

The roads are long and hearts are heavy
Oh where, oh where, oh where is home?
Bellies burn and death draws nearer,
The call rings out have no fear.
Blackness comes and hands are glowing,
'Time to go home', the crows are crowing.

I walk these roads, these roads of home
I walk these roads, these roads of home
Every night I walk alone
Through these roads
I am home."

Tendra clapped. "A bit morbid, but good nonetheless." Rowen hopped off his horse and went into an exaggerated bow low to the ground.

"In the future, I will attempt to tailor my musical untalents more to My Lady's incredibly specific standards." He said, coming up with a grin. Tendra looked back from a few yards ahead. She hadn't stopped. "Hmmm. Oh, I see how it is." He said, mounting back up. "You have your image to maintain." He rode up right next to her, leaned in close, and whispered in her ear, "Don't worry; I won't tell."

"Please step away from Her Highness." Zechariah said.

"It is fine, Zechariah. He means me no harm." Tendra said, bemused.

"It is improper for any to speak in so cavalier a manner to a woman betrothed. It is dishonorable." A look of mock horror rose upon Rowen's face.

"My most sincerest and utterest of apologies, My Lady. Please accept my mostest humblest of apologies." Tendra rolled her eyes.

"Keep speaking like that and I will let Zechariah gag you."

"He would be welcome to try." Tendra caught a cocky sparkle in his eye.

"Well, who knows what the future will hold? Perhaps you will get your challenge, wizard." Rowen raised an eyebrow at her wicked grin.

215

"My Lady!" Zechariah's voice called out. She turned to stare ahead into the valley as they crested the hill. A pillar of smoke rose before them, and the cause was plain for all to see. "Stay back." He warned.

"Not a chance!" She said, kicking her horse into a run. She heard Rowen and Zechariah behind her as they charged down towards the blazing ruins of the homestead. She knew that it made more sense for her to stay behind, but that had never been her style.

She reared her horse as she got near the fire and leapt off lithely, followed quickly by Rowen and Zechariah, who quickly drew their swords and flanked her.

"I'm going in." Rowen called out. Zechariah grabbed Tendra's hand before she could even offer to enter as well. She could only gaze fruitlessly into the tongues of licking flame as they waited for Rowen to re-emerge. Tendra circled around the house with Zechariah searching for tracks, anything that might indicate who had done this. But there was nothing beyond the well-worn path out to a well and the road that led out of the valley. The barn on the far side of the house from where they had emerged was still intact, and a quick search revealed no one inside.

Tendra turned quickly around and ran back toward the rear of the house at the sound of haggard coughing.

"Rowen!" she cried out. She rounded the corner and saw Zechariah emerging from the other way. Rowen was on the ground hacking, his face black with soot and his robes covered in minor fires. She ran closer and saw that he had a young girl, no more than twelve years old, lying on the ground.

"Come on! Come on!" He said. He lowered his mouth to hers and exhaled, breathing air back into her lungs. He did this several times before pressing down upon her chest. Tendra watched, fascinated. She had never seen anything like this before. He moved back to her mouth and breathed into her lips.

The girl convulsed into a coughing fit, and a smile of relief filled Rowen's face. Tendra found herself echoing that same broad smile.

"Water, I need some water." Rowen's voice snapped her into action as she turned and ran to the saddlebags to retrieve a water skin. She hustled back and handed it to Rowen, who had propped up the girl. He took the skin from her and held it up to the girl's lips, gently pouring water down into her throat. She coughed again, spitting the water back up, and Rowen gently gave her another drink, which the girl managed to keep down. Zechariah came around behind her.

"We need to find out what happened, and fast, My Lady. This blaze was just set and whoever did this may still be near. We need to get you and the girl to safety." Tendra nodded.

"What is your name?" Rowen asked.

"Hope." The girl said quietly and hoarsely. Tendra saw Rowen's startled look quickly transform back into his mask of concern.

"Okay, Hope, my name is Rowen. I am going to get you out of here. You're safe now." Rowen lifted her up easily into his arms and carried her over to the horses. He handed her to Zechariah, stepped up onto his horse and reached out for her. Zechariah handed her up to him, and Tendra mounted her own horse.

They rode long that day, but they were unable to reach Delmire before evenfall. Rowen didn't want to risk the girl's safety by pressing too hard; so they made camp about three hours away from the Face Off. The girl, Hope, sat staring into the fire wrapped in Rowen's blankets. Rowen was speaking quietly with Zechariah, so Tendra made her way over to where Hope was sitting and sat down beside her.

217

"Do you remember what happened?" The girl's eyes never left the flickering of the fire's tongues, but she nodded in acknowledgement. "Will you tell me what happened?" Once again the girl nodded.

"He came and my Da went wit 'im, 'e said it was to keep us safe, dat we would never have to worry about the wolves again. Dat Ma would be laid to rest. Dey took 'er a while ago, and she never came back. Den 'e left, said 'e would be back soon. But 'e didn't. Aye waited for 'im. But 'e never did. But aye wouldn't let the wolves take me. So aye set a'fire to the 'ouse. And then 'e came back."

"Who?" Tendra asked. Hope turned her head slowly to look directly into Rowen's eyes. Tendra watched him freeze and then break off his conversation with Zechariah and walk purposefully towards where they were sitting.

"We...uh...we're leaving early in the morning. We need to get to the safety of Delmire as soon as possible."

"Rowen, we are on the Golden Road; no one would dare attack us here." Tendra said barely keeping the absurdity from her voice.

"Princess, with all due respect, you are not traveling with your royal entourage. There are four of us out here, and your sharp tongue is no good against sharp steel." Tendra's jaw dropped. She quickly closed her mouth into a hardened look of determination.

"Is that what you think I am? Some pretty little princess who needs to be protected at all times by the gallant knight from the big bad wolves." Rowen looked to be mulling it over for a moment.

"Yeah, pretty much." He said with a shrug, raising his eyebrow. Tendra stood quickly from her place on the ground and stalked over to her horse. She pulled her saber from her saddle and turned around to see Rowen standing with a dagger in hand.

"Now, now My Lady, you really don't want to do that," Tendra saw Zechariah stealthily make his way up behind Rowen, "and you really don't want to be doing that my friend."

"Why not? I am, after all, just a princess to be saved. It isn't like I actually know," she said striding towards him, "how to use it." She lunged forward thrusting straight at Rowen's chest. He easily sidestepped it, and she brought it back around to the left trying to catch him on the backstroke, but he bent over backwards, his head almost touching the ground, and then pulled himself back to a standing position.

"It isn't me that I am worried about. It is Zechariah accidentally stabbing you, which would inevitably result in Jeric stabbing me, which would result in unhappy endings for the lot of us." Rowen said dodging another one of her slashes and blocking one of Zechariah's with his dagger. "C'mon, can't we all be calm, rational and..." Tendra watched as he dropped a second dagger from his right sleeve and blocked her swing behind him and Zechariah's in the front, "...discuss this like ladies and gentlemen?" He spun away from her, and she moved forward in a series of slashes. No more games...

She came at him with a flourish of six moves strung together gracefully attacking him from all angles. Zechariah leapt in beside her; yet still this infuriating man just wouldn't back down.

"Fine then," Rowen said shrugging. He twirled his daggers around in his hands causing one to disappear and then leapt forward right at Zechariah dodging her cut. He blocked Zechariah's attempt to stop his advance with his knife and then swung his left elbow around into Zechariah's face. Tendra heard bone shatter and saw faint droplets of blood spurt out in the dim light of the fire's glow. They had maneuvered away from their camp, and she saw Hope just sitting and staring at them. Zechariah stumbled backwards and Rowen followed up with a kick to his stomach that sent him flying backwards and onto the ground.

Tendra swept low trying to take out his other leg, but he leapt into the air twisting to avoid her blade and landed lithely on his left foot, which he pivoted around on so he was facing her. He feinted forward, and she pretended to bite so when he came left she was ready, bringing her blade around quickly seeking to bisect him at the waist. Impossibly, he leapt into the air and twisted around into a midair roll avoiding the blade's bite by mere inches before resuming his approach.

He grabbed her wrist and twisted it. Tendra felt pain shoot up her arm, and she was forced to drop her sword to ground. He twisted her arm around and behind her back, and she felt his hot breath on her neck. His breathing was barely above the normal rate whereas she was breathing heavily.

"Well, that was fun." He said cheerfully.

"No, but you are lucky that my brother needs you or else you would be dead the moment you entered into my father's realms." Tendra said through gritted teeth.

"Please, My Lady..." he twisted her around and let her arm go and bowed, "...you never really wanted to kill me. You were angry at being slighted, and for this, I apologize. My comments were rash. However, as a lady and, perhaps more importantly, as a warrior, you need to know your own limitations. In combat, I am as far beyond you as the stars. Take care when challenging your betters. I knew that I could defeat you and all four of your companions within five minutes of first meeting you. The way you moved, the way you talked, the way you lifted things, the way you rode. All of these things told me what I needed to know. Take care to observe your opponent before engaging him. It will do wonders for your life expectancy. Now, why don't you tell me what is really bothering you? And, for the love of Supremor, tell Zechariah that if he tries to stab me with

220

that little tooth picker, I will slit his throat." Zechariah froze behind him with his knife raised. Tendra sighed, and then shook her head.

"At peace Zechariah. Wash your face and leave me with Rowen for a moment if you would." The look on Zechariah's face showed her that there was nothing that he would rather do less, yet he still obeyed. "Walk with me, Rowen." She led the way over to where a tree had fallen a short ways away from the campfire.

"Who is Hope?" She looked over and saw the confused look on Rowen's face.

"Umm, well she is the girl that we rescued earlier today..." Rowen began before Tendra cut him off.

"Don't." She said. "Don't play games with me. Just give me a real answer, an honest answer." She looked him in the eye, and for the first time, Rowen turned away from her gaze. He folded his hands between his legs and looked at them, as if seeking some wisdom within their sphere of influence, yet finding none.

"Aurum isn't going to like this." Rowen mused.

"Why?" She interrupted.

"Because you aren't one of us. You're a bystander, and I am only supposed to tell you certain things. I am pretty certain this isn't one of them, but here we go anyways. When we emerged into this world, my brothers and I, we were confronted by two gallowglass. They spoke a prophesy to us about how we were the Heralds of the Ravishing of the World and all this crazy fate stuff that I am sure Rayn will tell you all about being the book boy that he is. However, there was one verse of the crazy foretelling that wasn't like the others. It said, '*When Hope is lost and Dream is shattered, look to the song of the unbattered.*' Now, for the longest time, we had no idea what that meant, but just at random we find a girl named Hope? That one of us finds a

221

girl named Hope. That's not chance." Tendra considered this for a moment.

"You think Supremor..." She began.

"We don't really believe in your god." Tendra gaped at him.

"What?" was all she could manage. Rowen gave an exasperated smile.

"Yeah, we get that a lot. So now you know. If you get any ideas, give me the head's up will you? Thank you My Lady, and good night."

"Good night." She said. With that Rowen rose from where they had sat, and Tendra watched as he walked back toward the fire. She took a deep breath, rose and followed him back and soon after followed him into the deep recesses of sleep.

*　　　　　*　　　　　*

Tendra awoke to the sensation of being shaken. She snapped awake and saw Rowen kneeling beside her.

"Wha...what is it?" She asked still disoriented from being awoken.

"It's Hope...she's gone. Not only that but so is every shred of evidence that she was ever here. My blanket is folded and placed inside my saddlebag, and my water is replenished. Everything!" Tendra saw Zechariah finishing his morning prayers, and Rowen strode over to him. She heard hushed voices and so meandered her way over to the fire pit where she could just barely make out their voices. Tendra began to stoke up a fire to boil water for tea, while still straining to hear. It was obviously a conversation that they wanted kept from her, but she wasn't going to stand for that.

"Why?" Zechariah asked.

"To see if it was ever there." Tendra saw a queer look cross his face.

"Alright, but I don't want to hear from Princess Sumenel that you tried anything…" Tendra started. *Try anything? He wouldn't dare.*

"I am insulted that you even feel the need to say that."

"Then, perhaps your shame may stay you when your honor fails." Rowen looked like he had been slapped. Zechariah turned away from him and mounted his horse, rearing the black stallion around and galloped off. Tendra watched as Rowen just stood there for a moment and then walked toward her.

"What was that all about?" Tendra asked innocently.

"I sent him to check and see if the burned homestead is still there." Now, it was Tendra's turn to have a queer look about her.

"Why wouldn't it be?"

"Aurum isn't going to like this either. Since the moment we began our crusade, it has felt like someone has been pulling our strings. That all of…" Rowen gestured around, "…this, is carefully controlled. I mean, our experience with that girl…her name…and Aurum has been having these dreams and…well, it matters not." Rowen looked up into the crisp blue sky. "It is a beautiful day, and you are a beautiful woman, let us have some beautiful breakfast." Rowen smiled, but Tendra could tell that it was forced.

"Rowen, about last night…" Tendra began as Rowen pulled some bread and dried fruit from his pack.

"I already apologized for insulting you."

"It isn't about that. The girl, Hope, she told me that you took her father with you to fight the ferals." At that Rowen stopped. "Is it true?" He shrugged.

"To be honest, I couldn't tell you. Most of the men who fought with us, we knew less than a week. We told them that this would be their chance to get back at the ferals who had killed their loved ones, pillaged their farms, and stole their animals and belongings. We never got to know them though." Tendra chewed on her lip for a moment.

"Did you plan for them to die?" Rowen handed her some food, and she poured them both a cup of tea. For the second time, Rowen would not meet her eyes when he spoke to her.

"They did," was all he said.

Interception At Point Providence
Seventeen

We rode through the night, pushing the horses to the brink of death in an attempt to put as much distance between us and Amul Kon as possible. When we finally stopped to rest, it was dawn. The horses were exhausted and so were we. Galeerial had yet to awake, and it was beginning to worry me.

"You said he spoke to you?" I asked Jeric as we ate. He nodded. We had not exchanged many words last night, we had merely fled. I still had no idea what that creature was, but it looked similar to the man they now carried as a passenger: the very visage of death.

Jeric held Galeerial's head up as he forced some water through the man's parched lips. He had cuts and burn marks all over his body, including several deep cuts in the shape of a star upon his left breast. I shuddered, as I looked at him. It was disgustingly brutal.

"What is in this field pack of yours?" He asked me, in an attempt to avoid answering the question.

"I'll get it." I pushed myself up to my feet and walked over to the saddles. The horses were grazing nearby, enjoying the respite. I pulled the small brown bag from its holding place and tossed it to Jeric. He opened it up and carefully examined each thing within. There was a knife; a thread and needle; a flask of Hogen, which was strong enough to knock you out with but a sip; and a burn salve made from some unusual plants, among various other items. Rowen was the doctor who had concocted these strange remedies. I just had to know what each thing did, not where it came from. Jeric carefully arranged each thing and then went about applying them to Galeerial where he could.

"What did he say?"

"He begged me to kill him. What about you, what happened?"

"I fought death itself. It was unlike anything I have ever faced before. Not even the Horror was like this thing." Jeric raised an eyebrow at that. "This creature, whatever it was, it was fast. I barely survived."

"Even with your magic? You have no spells of protection?" Jeric asked as he applied the salve to Galeerial's body and forced some liquid into his mouth.

"Like I told Lady Tendra, magic is destructive in nature, it cannot heal, only destroy." I stared at Galeerial's gray body. "How long do you think he was there?"

"Well over a month, I suspect. Look at the discoloration of his skin. It hasn't seen sunlight in a long while and the amount of body mass loss is astounding, to say the least. I mean, by Garen, I can't imagine what was done to him down there. Look here." He gestured for me to look at Galeerial's back. His back had long marks from what looked like claws raking across it, with chunks of flesh missing. It was like a map had been carved with mountains and valleys of flesh and rivers of blood. A shiver went through my spine.

"We need to go." I said quickly looking away and scanning the horizon. "We need to get to Delmire as soon as possible, and then we need to get him to Gemport, where he will be safe." Jeric nodded and began to pack up the medicines as I gathered the horses together and saddled them.

"Do you really believe that Gemport is safe?" Jeric asked as he mounted up, and I lifted Galeerial's nigh-lifeless body up to him.

"I know that it is far safer than the Face Off. That is where this whole situation will erupt. Gemport will be safe from this fight for at least a little while. And none of the other factions except the telos have anything approaching a navy; so you will be well supplied on that front. I do not fear for Gemport, but I do fear for his life." I said nodding to Galeerial. I climbed aboard my own horse and urged him forward.

As we rode on, we discussed the war and magic and swordsmanship. He taught me about the Light Monks, and I taught him about magicians, and our made up land of Cambria with its magical hierarchy. Jeric listened to everything. Every word he soaked up. I silently reminded myself to thank Rayn for making such an airtight creation for us.

We switched off and on carrying Galeerial in front of us. He felt brittle, as if I could snap him in half with the slightest of pressures. Dusk was fast approaching, and Galeerial sat in front of Jeric when I saw him stir.

"Jeric!" I murmured and he looked down as Galeerial swung his head over to look at me. "You look like death itself, my friend." I winced, thinking back to what I had said that morning about The Wither. As I looked at his face, I caught the glint of his eyes, and it startled me.

"By Supremor." I whispered so softly that my voice was almost lost to the pounding of the hooves.

"What? What is it?" Jeric asked bewildered at my expression, which was one of shock and dismay.

"Let me see his shoulder blades." I said quickly.

"Why?" Jeric replied confusedly.

"Just do it." Jeric ripped down the brown cloak that clothed Galeerial, revealing the man's back. His shoulder blades stuck out from his body, and there were heavy scars lining the skin beneath them. I cursed myself for not seeing it before.

"By Supremor." I murmured. "That's no man...it's a Skyguard. But his eyes...they're blue."

"What does that mean?" Jeric asked.

"I don't know...I don't know."

"It would explain why he looks the way he does. He hasn't had the Charist." I breathed out slowly, rubbing my face with my hands.

"We can afford no more delays. We ride straight for...Dread." I cursed. How could they do this? They were still over a day away from Delmire and three days from Soaring. A Skyguard could not last more than a week without the life-giving Charist. "We ride for Delmire. Then, to Soaring. The Seven have friends there."

"You do?" Jeric asked. He sounded impressed.

"Yes. It's a long story, but let's just say that the Skyguard owe us a favor or two, so we must hurry. We must save him."

"Save the Skyguard...save the world?" Jeric asked.

"Precisely. Now less talk...more ride." I kicked my horse, and we shot forward. Galeerial had fallen back into his sleep, and we rode on through the night. The stars above us shown down, and the nigh full moon illuminated our way. I looked up at the stars and saw the Jade Pirate with his one eye hovering over the Treasure Chest. I saw the Coin and the Stave. I saw the Flask and the Clover and the Stag and the Flower. These markers guided our way through the blackness of the night. I was surprised that we were not accosted as we rode through the farmland. The rampant feral tribes must have been recalled to defend the heartland. The night was their time...the predator's time, and to them all humans were prey.

At dawn's light, we both rode on slumped exhaustedly in our saddles. It was going on three days without sleep and in a saddle. The bruises that The Wither had inflicted on me made most of my body sore, and all day and night spent riding took care of the rest. We began to see signs of activity in the form of bands of centaurs ranging up The Heart. The first group paid us no heed, but the head of the second group rode right up to us without even so much as a greeting as the other members of his detail circled around us. What arrogance.

"Halt and be recognized! State your name and purpose in these lands."

"These are human lands...we may go wherever we wish." Jeric replied, and the centaur commander eyed him warily. I almost laughed. Here were two bone-weary men and a Skyguard on the edge of death, and Jeric was harassing a group of warriors.

"My name is Aurum, and I am one of the Seven. This is my companion, Jeric Tybius, a Visionary in the Order of the Light Monks and betrothed to Her Majesty, the Lady Tendra Sumenel. And our...indisposed companion is a Skyguard. Now let us pass." The centaurs exchanged glances and a few of them even began to laugh.

"I am sorry, but those are rather outlandish claims. I will require a crest of office to substantiate them." Jeric tossed him an annoyed glance and began to search through his saddlebag.

"You want some proof?" I pulled my staff from my back and aimed it right above his head and let loose with a lightning bolt. The boom of the thunder almost knocked them over. The lightning bolt caused the leader to rear up so high that he fell over, which undoubtedly would have caused a fit of laughter if the others hadn't been scared stupid. The air sizzled with electricity. "Now, you will let us pass!" I growled. The circle broke apart, and we led our horses out of it. I looked at our pathetically weary horses and inspiration struck.

"You two." I said stopping suddenly and pointing to two of the centaurs. They looked at each other furtively.

"Us?" One of them asked questioningly.

"Yes...you two with the stupid looks on your faces. You will bear us as fast as you are able to the Face Off. And you..." I said pointing at a third one, "...you will leave this detail and follow us with our steeds, but at a slow pace for they have been through much in the last few. You will arrive no later than tomorrow's dawn...do you understand?" By this time, the leader had righted himself, and he looked indignant. The three centaurs nodded as Jeric and I pulled ourselves off of our saddles. My legs ached as I stepped onto the ground. The pain was far out of proportion for the severity of the action, I thought. I helped Galeerial down from his horse, and Jeric positioned him in front of me on my centaur.

"Do you have a problem with my orders?" I asked the captain darkly.

"Yes I do. These men are here by order of Herdmaster Jeronious himself. You have no authority to commission them for your own purposes."

230

"On the contrary, I have every right! You will continue on whatever designated mission the Herdmaster has set you on. When he arrives at Delmire, and if you still have a problem, you have my permission to take it up with him personally. I am sure that he would love to hear how you accosted one of the Seven and prevented him from salvaging this campaign. He will be overjoyed to hear such a tale...I am sure." The captain paused for a moment.

"Very well, carry on." He said slowly and carefully.

"You heard him didn't you?" I asked my mount who still stood still.

"Yes sir!" He replied skittishly.

"Then, why aren't we moving?" I demanded.

"I am sorry, sir."

"No, you aren't. Don't apologize...just correct it. That means move." The centaur finally leapt forward into a gallop. I shook my head, and Jeric cracked half a smile at my frustrations. We were both just tired, and the rest of the trip proceeded in a blur. My mind clicked back into focus as the towering visage of the Face Off shown before us. Twin towers, each directly across from the other, with the Golden Road passing in between. I saw a flurry of activity along the tower of Marose, the feral tower, as we galloped in, but no arrows rained down upon us. We were too far out of range. The towers were positioned so that even the strongest archer's arrow would, at best, hit the walls. I knew that the ferals wouldn't be so stupid as to waste a ballista bolt or catapult ammunition on two centaurs.

The sun was high in the sky as we passed through the north gate of the city. As we entered into the courtyard, a flurry of activity surrounded us. I paid little heed to the bombardment of questions; I merely stumbled wearily off of my mount and pulled Galeerial down with me. Three figures pushed through the mass of the centaurs and moved quickly toward us.

Lady Tendra moved first to embrace Jeric, and I nodded to Rowen and the Light Monks.

"You look terrible." Rowen said.

"Thanks" I tiredly admitted.

"I wasn't talking about you." He said bending down to examine Galeerial. "Let's get him out of this. He needs serious help." He pulled him from my arms then turned and nodded to the Light Monks who quickly moved to make a path through the swirling herd of centaur flesh. I walked forward, exhausted, and heard Jeric following me, whispering to Tendra. We made our way up one of the ramp ways and into a barracks of long tall rooms. We entered, and Rowen laid Galeerial down upon the bed.

"There is no help that you can give him Rowen...he's a Skyguard." Rowen let out an exasperated sigh.

"Alright, I'll take him to Gabriel. We can get him some Charist from him."

"No, I'll do it." I mumbled. "You need to stay with Tendra.

"Aurum, you can barely stand. Jeric and the Light Monks can take care of Tendra for three days. Don't worry, I'll save him." He laid something on the table. "Here's a key to this room. There is food on the table as well as water and wine. Get some sleep. That's an order, from your doctor. I'll take care of the Skyguard." He asked. "We need you rested. Dane is in charge of operations here. You need to keep working on him, and you need to coordinate the defense of Delmire until Qel and the unu can get here. Understand?" I yawned heavily.

"Now sleep." I stumbled over to the makeshift bed that had been made up for us by the centaurs and collapsed upon it, knowing no more until the next day.

*   *   *

I awoke to the first fragments of purple and pink sunlight creeping through the clouds. I shook my head to clear the cobwebs and rubbed the sleep from my eyes. I let out a yawn, rolled over and did a series of push-ups and some simple stretches to wake my body up from its slumber and relieve its soreness.

I leapt up from my back to my feet and walked over to inspect the food that had been brought in. The centaurs were mostly vegetarians, though on special occasions, like the banquet when we first arrived at Harin's Dale, they did eat meat. My plate was a mixture of fruits, cheeses and vegetables. I reached first for the flagon of water and drank deeply. The coolness of it flowed down through my throat and into my stomach. I changed clothes as I ate. Rowen left me some fresh robes, for which I was grateful. I pulled my boots on, which I hadn't remembered taking off and then grabbed the plate and key and headed out.

The tower was a flurry of activity, and I watched as centaurs rushed about. I moved purposefully, but carefully through the menagerie of activity. There were no humans, but I did see a few unu...the first of many to come, I imagined. I saw a very familiar centaur atop the battlements giving orders to a group of lieutenants. I cautiously made my way up the staggered ramp to carefully avoid the rushing traffic as centaurs galloped up and down them.

I finished my breakfast and fitted the crescent moon shaped platter into the interior fold of my robes. Dane saw me approaching and waved me over.

"Excellent, you're awake. I was afraid that I would have to send the trumpeters in to wake you." He joked.

"Not hardly," I replied with a grin. "What's going on?" I said tossing my head down to all the activity.

"A scouting party just reported in. The ferals are burning all the bridges across The Heart both north and south of here." I rubbed my head. Of course they were. Hadn't Joven warned them of this? That was the first thing that Kaelish's replacement was going to do. That would force them to trek all the way back north to Beth's Bridge, all the way south to Gemport, or else build their own bridge. It would take weeks in all those cases.

"How far out are the unu from Ornus?"

"Reports say that they will be here by nightfall. They have been harassed all the way by bands of telos and ferals, otherwise they would have been here yesterday. Walk with me."

"What do you need from me?"

"Funny, I was just about to ask for your advice." We strolled across the battlements as we spoke amidst the cacophony of activity. I thought hard as we walked. My index and middle fingers rubbed my thumb on my right hand as we walked.

"How many soldiers do you have here?"

"Six thousand," he replied.

"You need to get out there." I said quietly. "You need to take all of them and go. How far north have they burned?" I asked.

"Up to the Bulge, our troops are holding the bridge at the Inway, but I don't know for how long. I'm sending two flights out to deal with it now."

"That's not good enough. They are moving fast."

"You have no idea." I cocked an eyebrow at Dane. "Harin's Dale was burned the same day as the Council." I breathed out deeply.

"We need that bridge Dane."

"I know." He replied. I stared out grimly across the expanse before Delmire over to Marose.

"When will Qel and Jeronious arrive with their troops?" I asked.

234

"The Hammer will arrive in two days' time." I raised an eyebrow to him, and he shrugged in response. "It's what they are calling the coalition between the centaurs and the unu."

"I can do it."

"What?" Dane said looking at me.

"I can hold Delmire until the unu arrive from Ornus. Everyone here needs to be gone within the hour." I turned and began to walk away.

"You must be joking." I turned to face him; my expression was one of complete sobriety. "You are serious." He rushed to catch up to me and leaned in close. "Aurum, I can't leave our most valued fortress in the hands of a human. The centaurs wouldn't stand for it. No matter how powerful you are, I cannot simply abandon Delmire to go and save a single bridge."

"If you don't hold that bridge, we will fight this war in the throes of winter. Neither the centaurs nor the unu are equipped for that. This war needs to be quick and decisive or else it will drag on and on and on. I can guarantee you that if we lose that bridge, the slaughter at Long Fang will be unparalleled. The ferals will only have to defend one side of their city and a torrent of arrows and stones will cascade upon our army until we are washed away in a river of blood." Dane sighed and began to walk again.

"Be honest with me, Aurum. Can you hold Delmire alone?" I began to answer yes, when he held out his hand. "You will need to hold it for twelve hours. By that time the unu will be here. No feral has ever set foot inside. I do not want today to be the day to break that tradition." I nodded.

"I can hold it." I said, with as much confidence as I could muster. I felt a knot of fear well up in my stomach and part of me hoped that he said no, simply because I wasn't positive that I actually could. I could see him mulling it over. His face was solemn.

"Very well, and may Supremor smile upon you." He turned away from me to face his troops. "Centaurs of the Herd!" He shouted, and all those below halted their activities to stare at him. "Prepare for battle! We make for the Inway with all haste. The feral cowards seek to burn the bridges leading into their lands. Our valiant comrades stand strong against them, but they will not be able to hold out for long. Every man here will be ready to depart Delmire within the hour. They are to be armed and ready for battle. We have no time to waste. For glory and victory!" The centaurs didn't react for a moment, but a wave of cheers broke upon us a moment later. These centaurs had been stationed here for years without any action. Now they would get some. I couldn't help but notice that there were several centaurs who had not partaken in the clarion call. The army below took off again, back to their newly assigned duties. A group of centaurs rode quickly up to approach Dane and me.

"Dane..." I cocked an eyebrow at the utter lack of respect from the lead centaur; yet Dane remained stoic, "...you can't possibly be considering abandoning the Face Off, not with the unu and the Herd already so close." One of them asked.

"Of course not Chopan, the magi will stay and hold the Tower." The astonished looks on their faces made me smile.

"May I speak with you alone?" Chopan asked.

"No..." Dane replied, "...as your commander and the centaur in charge of the forward vanguard against the ferals, I will make whatever decisions I see fit for the good of this campaign. And you will follow my orders." Chopan gritted his teeth at the rebuke.

"But, you can't seriously be considering handing over this fortress to a single being, much less a human." He spat out the last word.

"No..." Chopan looked confused for a moment, "...I am no longer considering it. My decision has been made and my orders have already been explained in as exacting of detail as I would have you know. Now, unless you want to be beheaded for treachery, and your family stricken from the Book of Names, I would advise you to stand down." Dane said firmly. "That goes for all of you." His eyes shifted to the rest of the dissenters. "Now, prepare to depart. We have a battle to win." The six centaurs turned around without even the slightest of courtesies.

"You should not have let them live, the way they disrespect you so." I said quietly as we made our way around and into the barracks.

"I am Forsworn, and despite the position that I have been placed in, I will always be so. Forget about them. What do you need to prepare?" I scratched my head.

"I need twelve men and all the crossbows that you can spare. With the accompanying bolts of course. And rope...lots of rope." I watched as he pulled his sword band across his chest and latched it.

"Done. Anything else?" I shook my head.

"I'll only need them for an hour to set up, and then you can take them with you." He nodded.

"So, why are you still here?" He eyed me. "Go!" He urged. I bowed and ran. I needed to get to the cellar first. That would take the longest amount of preparation. As I ran, I called out to centaurs in my path, yelling at them to follow me. Rikard had been the one to infiltrate Delmire and place the supplies here. I had no idea how he had done it, but hopefully he came through. I silently rebuked myself. Of course he had come through. He was Rikard.

We made our way through the kitchens and down the long hallway of the cellar surrounded by cool stone and crates of vegetables and fruits until we came to the wall in the back.

"Give me your hammer." I said to one of the centaurs who eyed me suspiciously. "Give it to me." I reiterated. I didn't have time for such hesitation. I gripped it with both hands, raising it above my head and slammed it into the wall. The wall buckled, but didn't fall, and I gritted my teeth before raising it once again. This time there was no grinding jolt into my arm, as the entire wall crashed to the ground. The fake wall revealed a massive stack of barrels stacked five high up to the ceiling. Thirty in all. The centaurs stared in astonishment.

"Alright, I need all of these tied up to the battlements as soon as possible, hanging so that I can cut them loose and have them fall upon the enemy. Understand?"

"What's in them?" One of them asked.

"It doesn't matter, all that matters is that you don't break them open and don't ask questions. Just do as you're told. You'll live longer that way. Now, let's go...we have little to no time." While they hauled the barrels up to the wall, I headed to the munitions room with four centaurs and gathered up as many crossbows as we could carry. We brought them up to the top of the wall, laid them at regular two-foot intervals all the way across the top and loaded them up with bolts. I would only get one shot.

The two groups finished their task just as Dane was gathering up the herd to leave. I nodded my blessing for them to go, and they left gratefully. Dane gathered the entire garrison in the main courtyard in front of the gates. I stood above the gates on the wall and looked down upon them. He offered me a deep salute, and the rest of the soldiers did the same, so I reciprocated. Dane raised his horn to his lips, sounding the call, and the gates were opened as the Herd surged forward and out of the gates. The stream went on and on until the last of the centaurs was gone, and I ran down the ramp to close the gates behind them.

I could only imagine what the feral commander was thinking as he watched this mass exodus. His advisors were either telling him to go for it or that it was a trap. I hoped that the voices of the latter would ring out louder than those of the former, but I did not think it would be so. I quickly began placing my barricades on the tower gates. It was back-breaking work, and I was forced to run up to the battlements every few minutes to make sure that no ferals were attempting to storm the city. My body was slick with sweat when I had finished. I picked up my abandoned robe and made my way up to the top to observe Marose, while I worked on threading the crossbows.

I carefully attached and cocked each one, and then wired them ten at a time to a single trigger. When I finished, I ate some dinner while watching the opposing fortress. I couldn't imagine living here every day, seeing your hated enemy so close, yet never doing anything about it. It was idiocy wrapped in an air of brilliance. The day had stretched on, and there was still no sign of the unu reinforcements. As the sun finished its daily traversal through the sky, I began to grow worried. Nightfall would embolden the ferals in a way that the day had discouraged. I had no more preparations to make. I had done everything that I could and if the ferals wanted to come, then they would come.

I dropped to a seated position and was watching the sun make its final descent into the Rift Mountains, when a centaur rider came galloping up to the city gates and began to pound upon them. I rose quickly and made my way over to the gates.

"State your name and purpose." I called down.

"My name is Geoff, and I bring word of the unu assault force from Ornus. Who are you? Where is Dane?"

"I am Aurum of the Seven, and I am in charge of this garrison now. Now, tell me of the unu. Where are they?"

"You are in charge of Delmire?" He asked aghast.

"Yes, now speak and be quick about it." I said.

"The unu will arrive just after nightfall."

"Tell them to delay their coming." I shouted down.

"What?" The centaur asked questioningly. I sighed.

"Wait right there." I turned away from the befuddled centaur and grabbed the length of coiled rope that I had gathered earlier in the day. I wrapped it around my waste and tied it off on the stone wall. I backed up to the edge and rappelled down to Geoffry.

"Now listen, and listen very carefully. If you do exactly what I say, then perhaps, just perhaps, not a single soldier will die taking the Face Off."

I, Of The Storm
Eighteen

The fall of darkness brought with it the sound of thunder and the black moon: the scent of death. They were coming, and I would meet them.

Alone.

A storm was brewing around me-a storm of swords, a maelstrom of metal, and a rain of red. The feral army tried to be stealthy, but in the dark stillness of the night, there was no mistaking their advances. It was the sound of death approaching. I was gambling again. I had found myself doing it more and more in these unpredictable times. I didn't like it. I like certainties. I knew myself, and I knew my enemy. I was not afraid. I knew I wouldn't make mistakes. That was not my way. I needed to be flawless. I was not a man of faith, yet at that moment, I sincerely wished that I did believe in some god. Not a benevolent god such

241

as the men here believe in, but a god of blood and death who would smite my enemies before me.

A god of war.

Yet I did not. This night, I would survive the onslaught alone. My circle of torches cast out flickering shadows into the night sky. There was a black moon, and the stars provided scant illumination. I could not see them, but I heard them. I heard the thunder in the cloudless sky. I could smell them. I knew it was time for the reign of blood.

I took a deep breath.

I rose smoothly up from my cross-legged pose and strode to the end of the wall where the turret was. I cut loose the first of the barrels and watched as it fell to the ground with a crash. The whole of the barrels' contents began to pour out in a mass of smoke. I pulled my helmet onto my head, so the cloth would filter out the noxious haze.

I moved to the next and the next and the next, until the ground beneath me was naught but a swirling mass of fog. The smoke was merely the effect of the real threat, which would cause the death knell of the ferals.

"See through it!" I said simply. My vision grew clear through the smoky haze, and I saw the army massed against me.

My blood grew cold as I saw thousands of ferals rushing towards Delmire. The thick black fluid ran along the ground. The ferals began to slip in it, but they continued their march. I saw a group holding ladders move forward and entrench the feet of them into the ground.

I took a deep breath.

I began to move back and forth, firing off each of the twelve series of crossbow bolts, one at a time. Howls of pain began what I knew would become a glorious crescendo of confusion amidst the twangs of the crossbow bolts and the cackles of the fire.

I took a deep breath.

The loud scrape as the first ladder impacted against the wall moved me into action. I ran forward and quickly pulled up the twin claws that anchored it to the ledge and cast it back. I grabbed my bow and arrow and pressed it against the torch, firing the flaming dart through the air.

"C'mon." The world in front of me suddenly flew ablaze as the flame touched the black liquid. Suddenly, the plains in front of Delmire erupted into a carpet of flame, and the howls of burning ferals and the absence of ladders meant that I was protected for the moment. The whole of the castle was now an island amidst a sea of flame. The flames would hold the ferals back for a short while. This was a fire that would not be extinguished by water.

But it would not be enough. It burned too fast and would only provide me refuge for so long. I leapt down and onto a ramp and ran down to the courtyard. I ran over to the catapult that I had stashed there and ignited the pitch. I slammed the lever down, and the flaming projectile went hurling through the night sky.

I cranked it back, rotating it about ten degrees, before pushing the next rock onto the arm. I set it off once more, before running back up to the top of the battlements. Before me, I beheld not the chaos that I had hoped for, but rather the patient orderly lines of the feral army waiting beyond the flames. I grabbed my bow and began firing toward them.

The fire would burn for an hour at the most. Hopefully, I could kill enough of them with arrows in that time that they would just leave. To my dismay, they simply turned and began to march out of range. They knew that the element of surprise was over; now they would simply overwhelm me.

I took a deep breath.

I walked over to the one barrel that I hadn't cut loose, the one that I had hoped wouldn't have to be cut. I cut the rope on the last barrel and then ran. There was a coiled rope that I reached down and scooped up as I ran.

I leapt.

I soared downwards and held the rope hard, waiting for the jerk. I soared over the field of fire, and I saw the thick black smoke pour out of the barrel, coating everything in blackness. My shoulder screamed in pain as the rope yanked me backwards, and suddenly I found myself falling earthward. I let go, as I swung backwards about ten yards from the fire and fell twenty feet to the ground. I cushioned the impact with my knees and rolled forward twice before springing up to my feet.

I saw the ferals still maintaining their calm lines even as the inky smoke poured over them. There was a huge army, and I saw it now moving to encircle the fortress. I cursed. This was an all-out assault. I pulled my daggers from my hips and began to run. The smokescreen would only last so long. I needed to sow maximum confusion in the least amount of time. I reached the vanguard of the detachment that was peeling west, and I ran right through their center. They couldn't see anything because of the smoke, but I could see perfectly. I lashed out as precisely as I could; cutting a bloody swath in the ranks ten deep before they knew that I was even there.

Then, the screams began.

"Someone's here!"

"Behind you!"

"Help!"

"Where?"

It was chaos then, as they realized that something was out there. I ran through them, my daggers a blur as I cut, not even to kill, just to wound, anything that would cause confusion or put them out of commission: a cut to the neck, a slice to the back, one in the head, one in the leg. The ferals began to swing about wildly as I zigzagged through their ranks. I dove over a sword strike, which killed two other ferals. I was invincible. I was dripping in blood when I made it to the other side. I looked back and saw a swath of stumbling ferals swinging their swords desperately trying to hit something.

I smiled, but just as quickly, that grin was knocked off my face as a hammer came around and sent me flying backwards. I moaned from the impact to the chest and rose unsteadily to my feet.

"Here!" The feral screamed. "I got one!"

I had two cards left to play. I ripped my helmet off. It was stifling, and the smoke had cleared anyway. There was no way that I could hold my own against this kind of force. So, I wouldn't. The fire was close. I needed to get my back to it. I sheathed my bloody knives and ran forward murmuring magic words as I ran throwing my hands out. Before me, a wave of force spread out throwing the nearest ferals into the air and pushing farther ones back. I sprinted forwards. I just had to reach the flames. I leapt into the air, vaulting a top a final feral who stood in my way reaching the wall of fire. It seared my back as I turned to face the ferals.

They came at me in masse, and I threw them backwards just as quickly. I had backed myself against the fire, and no feral could come within twenty feat of me without being thrown back. They fired their arrows at me, but I stopped them in mid-air and threw them back from whence they came. Soon, they just waited.

No feral approached me. So, I began to move toward them. I had to try and kill as many as I could before the fires burned down, and the blaze was already growing lower by the minute.

They backed away, giving me a wide circle to stand within. I took off running. The ferals scrambled to run away, but

245

they were not fast enough, and I began to throw them into the flames.

"Fight us, wizard!" came a call from the ferals that stopped me in my tracks. A smile grew upon my face. *Perfect*!

"I would fight you, but it seems like all you are good for is being slaughtered." I said with a laugh. *That's it, provoke them.*

"You use magic," came another voice.

"And, you use your teeth and claws. Who leads this rabble?" I asked.

"I do!" A feral made his way forward. He was larger than the majority of ferals and wore a ten-link chain: a general. "I am General Tosh. So this is one of the Seven Wizards." He said.

"I am indeed, and you are finally someone worth killing." I whispered, licking my lips.

"I have heard of you: whispers and legends."

"I am no legend. I am flesh and blood, and I have an offer for you, General." He approached me cautiously. "I can continue to kill your men, and eventually, yes, you will kill me. But I can guarantee you that it will take thousands of your men to kill me, or you can take me prisoner and leave Delmire alone." He laughed. I unsheathed my knives. I wasn't sure what was going to happen.

"You are almost defeated as it is. Your wall of flame burns low. Soon we will own Delmire, and you will be dead. Why would we accede to your demands?"

"Like I said, I will take ten thousand of your men with me to my grave. And, that's not even considering all the men who will die from the spells I've laid carefully within. Also, there is the matter of the protection spell that I have laid across several of the doorways, such that if one was to walk through it, the entire fortress will be reduced to rubble." I said confidently, staring into Tosh's eyes.

A second feral walked up next to him. This feral had one of its arms missing, and his fur was made up of motley patches. He looked familiar, and the hate in his eyes as he glared at me reminded me exactly where I had seen him. This was the same feral I had fought at Sterin's Throne- the captain who got away.

"We meet again." I said, bowing in mock grace. He walked towards me. I held out a blade stopping him. He looked me in the eyes, and I casually returned his glare.

"He's lying." The feral snarled.

"Is that a chance you can afford to take?" I asked. "I don't want a destroyed fortress any more than you do. Instead, you can fight a good clean battle against the Hammer when they arrive, and it will be a fair fight." I mulled this over for a second, "Well, fairer."

"Or, we just kill you now, and then take our chances with the fortress."

"But that would defeat the whole purpose of this fight. You came out here because you wanted to take the fortress and surprise the Hammer when they inevitably arrive here to kill all of you, am I close? And I swear to you, if you go into that fortress, it will not still be standing by morning." The feral captain turned and strode back to the general. By now, the fires had burned down to almost nothing. The next two minutes would be critical.

"Why would we not just kill you?"

I snorted. "Because I am far more valuable alive, and you will need all the bargaining chips you can muster in the coming days." I replied.

"What are you talking about?" Tosh asked, staring at me.

"I'm talking about the war that is at your doorstep." I sheathed my daggers. Tosh regarded me coolly. I knew he was calculating the losses, and if it was truly worth it for them to try and kill me.

"Very well." The general murmured. The snarls of anger erupted from the army. "Silence!" He roared. The cries grew still as the night. "I need your word, under the eyes of Supremor, that you will not use magic while within our keeping and that you will not attempt to escape." I moved my jaw back and forth in thought.

"Very well." I strode forward and handed my daggers to Tosh. "Take good care of those. They're better made than any that you have ever seen or touched."

He bared his teeth at me, and I stared back into his eyes. A feral moved forward and bound my hands behind me, and the wounded feral captain came up behind me.

"You will pay for every ounce of blood that you took from me at Sterin's Throne." He snarled in my ear. "I will make your every waking moment a torment and your every sleeping one a nightmare." I didn't respond, but I had to suppress a soft smile.

"We take the fortress at dawn, when we can see every one of these traps the wizard has prepared for us." the general announced. "And every feral that dies from one will be another cut into the wizard's flesh!" he bellowed. Cheers arose as the mass of ferals moved in around me as we walked toward Marose. The two fortresses were almost mirror images of each other. The night air had cooled considerably now that the fire had burned out, and I felt a shiver go down my spine as I prayed that my plan would work. We marched silently through the night. It was black as fireglass, and I could barely see where I was walking.

We arrived at the gates. Tosh strode forward and slammed his mailed fist against the door. I waited patiently as the doors opened. I was still sweating from my exertion and steam was rising off of me. The doors slowly crept open to the silent interior. Tosh marched straight ahead confidently into the courtyard.

"Bys?" He called out. "Light a torch. I can barely see my own feet." The procession of ferals continued to flood into the courtyard, and I smiled.

"General Tosh." The General turned to look at me as I spoke. "I regret to inform you that the Hammer is now in control of this fortress. I am giving you this one chance to order all of your troops to lay down their weapons, or they will all be slaughtered. This is your only chance." I stressed. He appeared taken aback before breaking into laughter.

"You think I am a fool. Bys!" He hollered.

"I do now. Thunderbolt!" I shouted. Instantly, a torch sprang to light followed quickly by hundreds more, revealing six thousand unu with bows strung, drawn and aimed at the feral army below. I savored the look on Tosh's face. It was a mixture of astonishment and defeat. "Now, if you would please cut my bonds, we can get on to the pleasantries." Tosh nodded to the one-armed feral, who moved behind me and began to slice through the rope.

"This isn't over. Not today." I turned around to face him.

"Yes, it is." I turned my back on him and began walking toward Tosh. "Now, if you would be so kind as to order your men to place their weapons on the ground, it would be appreciated." I walked past him, taking my daggers from his belt.

"Thank you," I said and walked up the stairs to the top of the battlements where the unu archers stood. A single unu pushed his way towards me. He was obviously the commander judging by the intricacy of his hair. I nodded to him, and he returned my greeting in kind.

"Do it!" Tosh called. There was a clang of steel on stone as thousands of weapons were dropped to the ground. The feral army shifted nervously. "You seem to be in command, sorcerer. What would you have us do now?" I shook my head in disgust.

"We are not sorcerers." I whispered, exasperated. "That feral, there." I said pointing to the one-armed captain. "Come here!" The feral pushed his way through the throngs of ferals to the base of the stairs and began to slowly walk up them. He stood before me, defiantly staring at me with hate. "This is a fine blade," I said twirling Havoc in my hand. "It has drunk deeply of your blood before." I twisted it around in my hand and grasped the palm firmly in my palm, slamming it into the neck of the feral.

"Strike!" I hollered, and a volley of golden arrows struck like lightning down upon the gathered ferals. "And it does again." I ripped my blade from the dead captain and kicked his corpse down the staircase before making my way up the rest of the stairs. The screams and the sounds of ferals, desperately trying to flee, fell upon deaf ears. Well, not quite deaf ears. I managed to smile as I walked around the battlements to above the gate where the ferals loped out and away from the battle. I saw the dark wraiths of centaurs flash by, covered in soot, killing all who attempted to flee. Not a single feral would escape. The unu commander approached me while I watched the carnage below.

"Excellent work, wizard. Gorn of the White Pike is my name." I regarded the unu with indifference. I didn't really care what his name was. What I did care about was that I had won the battle of the Face Off, and I had done it without losing a single soldier.

I smiled.

What a glorious night.

Don't Put Your Life in Fragile Hands

Nineteen

Galeerial awoke to silence, but more than that, he awoke to strength. He lifted his arm by his own power, and saw the fingers move as he willed them. He felt the scarred skin on his wrists that wasn't black and blue with bruises from months spent in chains, but was a soft pink. It was almost beyond comprehension. He didn't believe what his eyes were seeing. He didn't believe that the flesh was white and fully covered his bones. He licked his lips. They were not cracked , but smooth. It was at this moment that he despaired.

It would have been easy to die as the pathetic, miserable thing that he was within the Wither's lair, but now- now when he felt his strong body beneath him? When he could feel all of his toes and see color in his skin? *How can I possibly do what must be done?* And Galeerial wept.

He felt the twitching of his shoulder blades where his wings had once been, and he wept more. Tears flowed down his face unabashedly, and his shirt grew damp with their moisture. He reached his hands up, grabbed his clean white shirt, and tore it off only to see the massive star still carved into his skin. And he wept more.

He ran his hands over his back and felt the divots where his flesh had been ripped from his body: the long thin lines from the whips, and the deep ravines that were the knives. His body was a landscape made from the valleys of scars, the rivers of cuts, and the mountains of broken bone. He felt his arms with a shudder. He reached up and ran a hand through his motley hair. What had been a flowing mane once long ago was now a scattered plot of hair mixed with bald flesh. The Wither had ripped his eyebrows and eyelashes out. He looked at his hands: they were rough, but white.

Finally, after an eternity of salty tears, the wells dried. Galeerial sat there staring blankly at his hands for ages before glancing up at his surroundings. It was bright. The sunlight filtered in through a myriad of windows, and there was a bookshelf in one corner of the room. There was a plant arrangement under the window, and right next to the door there was a chair. And seated in that chair was a human.

Galeerial sized him up carefully. He didn't recognize him. He hadn't heard the human come in, so he must have been watching him the entire time. Galeerial took several shallow breaths before speaking. He honestly did not know what his own voice would sound like.

"Who are you?" Galeerial asked slowly. The sound of his own voice was a noise he never thought he would hear again. It was beautiful and sad all at once. "Where am I?"

252

"My name is Rowen, and I am one of the Seven. You are in the west tower of the royal castle in Gemport. Do you know what that is?" Galeerial thought for a moment. His memories were an exhausted jumble of pieces like shattered glass that had been forged back together with some of the old cracks left behind.

"It's a human city, in the far south," Galeerial replied. He looked carefully at Rowen who nodded.

"That's correct." He was a handsome man with long brown hair that reached just past his shoulders, not unlike how Galeerial's hair used to fall. His face was very familiar, as if he had seen it somewhere long ago in a dream.

"What happened?"

"You got beat up pretty badly, but my brother, Aurum, was able to get you out before you landed yourself in a shallow grave. Do you remember your name?" *My name?* Galeerial had to think before it came to him, and he sampled it before allowing it to emerge from his mouth. It had been so long since that name had been formed by his lips. It was like a long-forgotten delicacy that is rediscovered after an eternity of absence.

"Galeerial." He said hesitantly as if reluctant to release it to the world. Rowen nodded.

"It is good to finally know just who exactly my patient is. I'm going to ask you some questions. Is that permissible?" Galeerial nodded. "Who is Veriel?" Galeerial froze at the mention of the word. That word, that name brought a sense of dread into his heart. "Galeerial?" A shiver crawled up his spine and wrapped its claws around his neck.

"Veriel." The name caught in his throat and corrupted his tongue. It coated his mouth black, but slowly that blackness began to burn red: the red of fire that fused the rest of his memories back into place. "Veriel." Galeerial felt his eyes ignite. "How do you know that name?"

253

"You were muttering it in your sleep: over and over again." For the first time, Galeerial became acutely aware of the two knives hanging loosely from the man's belt. He also glimpsed a bowl of steaming water sitting by his bedside. He slowly swung his legs over the bed. "Was he the one who did this to you?"

"You said you were one of seven. The seven what?" Galeerial asked slowly.

"Wizards." That was all Galeerial needed to hear. He knew there was something about this human. He had seen the flicker of deception in his eyes about Veriel. He would have to be quick. Galeerial grabbed the basin of water and hurled the contents in the man's face before vaulting across the room and in two swift motions had the sorcerer pinned. A moment later, Galeerial slammed the wizard's head against the wall. He breathed in exhilaration; he didn't know how he had done that, but it didn't matter. Strength was coursing through his bones. For the first time in a very long time, he felt strong. He felt in control.

"Speak, and speak quickly. If I don't like what I hear, I won't hesitate to kill you." Galeerial said through gritted teeth.

"What do you want to know?" The wizard said calmly.

"Why are you here?"

"I saved your life. I wanted to make sure that I did a good job of it." He threw his head to the left and whipped his right forearm into Galeerial's wrist to break the lock. Galeerial didn't move. He felt the pain echo up his body, but it held no dominance over him. "Apparently I did."

"That is not what I want to know, and you know it. What does Veriel want with humanity? Where is he?"

"I don't know what you're talking about." The calmness the wizard exhibited was unnerving.

"Don't lie to me!" Galeerial screamed.

"I'm not. I swear the only thing I know about Veriel is the name. You were screaming it so loud three nights ago that we had to drug you." Galeerial pulled Rowen's head back and slammed it into the wall again. He saw blood spurt out. There was no fear in this man's voice. It was as if he was playing a game. As if he was the one in control.

"The Charist, you have some?" Galeerial asked. Rowen pointed to a canteen sitting on a corner table. Galeerial grabbed it wrapping the leather cord around his neck. He dared not check to be sure, he would have to hope the man hadn't lied to him. He wouldn't make it to Soaring without it.

"Walk." Galeerial ordered. He angled him towards the door. "Open it." Galeerial said.

"You have to let go of my wrist first." Galeerial thought for a moment. He couldn't release the wizard's hand. Galeerial knew that despite what this man said, he would be dead a second after he made that mistake. "Where are you going to go, Galeerial? Without a horse and food, you won't get five miles. War is breaking out all over the south of Carin. If the centaurs and unu don't get you, the lack of supplies will."

"Quiet!" He couldn't linger. The wizard was trying to poison his mind. Galeerial turned the man's head and smashed it into the wall again, this time the man didn't stay awake. Instead, he slumped to the ground. *That takes care of one problem.* Galeerial pulled open the door and stealthily peered out. It was empty. There was a staircase that led down and up. He chose to go down. He didn't have wings anymore; going up would do him no good. Galeerial carefully made his way down the stairwell wary of any sign of life.

He had never been in a human castle before, or any kind of castle for that matter. All Skyguard buildings were built with verticality in mind, but who knew what human architects would conceive for their limited species. Galeerial came to the bottom

255

of the winding stairwell a moment later. There was an archway but no doors. Two human sentries stood there. Galeerial took a deep breath. He had three options. He could either go back to the unconscious wizard or go forward casually. Galeerial became very aware at his lack of a shirt and of the intricate designs that had been carved into his skin. There was no way he could blend in, which left the third option.

Run.

Galeerial leapt through the archway, sprinting for all he was worth down the corridors. The stunned guards let out shouts of astonishment and bewilderment, but he was already moving. His breath soon became shallow, and he gasped as he glanced back at the pursuing soldiers. He came upon a right passage and ducked into it before taking a sharp left. He followed the hallway only to round a corner and discover a stairwell.

"No." Galeerial grimaced. He heard armored feet clanking behind him.

"Here" a soft, yet commanding voice rang out. Galeerial turned to see what he had initially believed to be a tapestry turn out to be a door. The clamor of footsteps grew louder, and Galeerial raced to the doorway. "Hurry! Close the door behind you. It wouldn't be a very good secret passageway if everyone knew about it." Galeerial pulled the door closed, enveloping them in darkness. Galeerial's breath caught his throat at the darkness surrounding him. the air was close in here. The voice seemed to be coming from a long way down the tunnel. The ignition of a torch illuminated the world around him, and more importantly, under him. Before him was a ladder that descended into the bowels of the earth. "Come."

Galeerial stepped down tentatively onto the ladder. The rungs were slick with moisture from the caves, but the metal felt solid beneath his feet. The old fear rose in him. The same fear he had felt when he had descended into the stone cells. He felt the icy cold grip his muscles, but he was desperate. He needed something to focus on. He counted every rung as he descended: twenty nine. The torch hadn't moved the entire time that he had spent descending until his feet touched the floor, and he saw it held in the hands of a human garbed wholly in black.

"Follow me." He turned on his boot heel and began a brisk pace. As they walked, Galeerial studied the man in front of him. He was a man of power, that much he could see, yet his gait and mannerisms were quite different from the wizards. They passed a number of wooden doors as they moved, and Galeerial had no idea if the man was actually leading him where he needed to go or simply into a trap. But, it didn't matter because this was Galeerial's best chance at getting out of here, and he couldn't afford not to take it. They had been moving in silence for about five minutes when Galeerial started as the man abruptly stopped.

"Here," he said simply.

"How do you know?" Galeerial inquired.

"You need to be at the stables, and this door leads to the stables. We are on the west end of the castle, and, if you walk thirty paces straight out this door, you will arrive at them. In the third stall there is a black horse that is saddled and supplied."

"Who are you?"

The man ignored his question. "You will walk the horse through the city roads. You will carry the reigns in your left hand, and for the love of Supremor, stop walking with such perfect posture. Slump your shoulders, put your chin down and don't always be looking straight ahead. You are a commoner now, not a Skyguard. Act like one. The city gates remain open until eight o'clock this evening. Right now it is four thirty; you should be out of the city in twenty minutes maximum, so this will not be a problem, but don't dally. You will walk straight south in order to arrive at the city gates. Do you understand all of those instructions?"

257

"You didn't answer my question." Galeerial said darkly. The man was unfazed.

"I can only do so much to help you. Names have power, and mine is unimportant at this point in time."

"I find that extremely doubtful considering where we are and what you are able to provide." Galeerial said firmly. The man seemed to consider this, but remained silent."Why are you helping me?"

"Because the world is about to ignite. The war is just beginning, and the ferals are merely the appetizer. The Skyguard will be dragged into this war one way or another, and all I ask is that your people land on humanity's side."

"And you believe that I can accomplish that feat?"

"Probably not, but I before today I had never meet a Skyguard. If I didn't take this opportunity I would be fool."

"I will do what is necessary to protect my people." Galeerial said simply.

"Then you and I share a similar goal. Vizien is my name." The man offered his hand out to Galeerial.

"You are an honorable man. I will not forget this." Galeerial said. He stepped forward and grasped the man's hand. Galeerial ripped it forward, throwing the man off balance and grabbed the back of his head with Galeerial's left hand thrusting his knee upwards. He felt the man's nose shatter. "But no matter your intentions, I can take no chances."

He allowed the body to slide onto the ground before pushing the door open cautiously. Just as the man in black had promised, the stables lay before him. If everything else happened as he had said, soon Galeerial would be in Soaring, and then onto Cloud Breach. He had to make it in time. Supremor would not spare him from death at the hands of the Wither only to watch his people burn at the hands of Veriel. He would not let that happen.

For the sake of his sanity, he couldn't.

The Price of Life
Twenty

For the first time in far too long, Tendra was able to look at her brother's face without tears springing to her eyes. Color had returned to his face, and he was in a jovial mood. He was still bed-ridden and would be for two or three more days, but at least he would live. She couldn't hardly believe it had been almost two months since the Face Off. Rowen had departed the watchtowers with the Skyguard for Soaring after leaving her with medicine to give to Jakob. She had ordered him to continue with her to Gemport, but he would not be dissuaded. When he had finally arrived in Gemport, he had brought the Skyguard with him looking none the better. Since then, Rowen's time had been split in three between Jakob, the Skyguard, and working with the city guard to transform them into a standing army. Humanity had a strong naval force, but when it came to land battles for the most part it relied up the calling of the bannermen. City guards were more accustomed to breaking up bar brawls than open warfare though many of them were veterans of the Hunter Rebellion that her father and uncle had put down when she was still an infant She didn't know what all the wizard had done to help Jakob, but whatever it was, it had worked. *And not a moment too soon.*

After the initial victory at the Face Off by the Hammer, the campaign against the ferals had moved quickly. She had barely been able to keep up with the flurry of hawks with messages from the constantly advancing front. Her father had sent out falconers to trail the battle and make reports on movements. After the ferals initial attempt to completely isolate themselves through the burning of the bridges all up and down the Heart and Rope Rivers had failed, they had begun consolidating their population into cities to eliminate the centaur's cavalry advantage. On the backs of the unu's siege towers and the wizard's magic, the feral cities were falling quickly. That wasn't to say there were no casualties on the Hammer side. By all accounts, the Diving Spear clan had been virtually exterminated in a failed sneak attack at Charon, and the centaurs had suffered heavily losses in the close confines of the cities. Tendra stifled her mind from all that war talk. There was more than enough of that in her father's war councils. They were preparing for the inevitable turn of the Hammer away from the ferals to humanity. Right now though, the focus was on her brother seated before her. Her healthy brother.

"Hello, brother." She said, standing in the doorway with a smile. She walked forward and saw a smile creep across his face as he looked up from the book he was reading. He removed his spectacles and set the book down on the bed in front of him.

"Hello there, sister!" He replied with a smile. "Long time, no see." He said teasingly. She had hardly left his side in the last few days as his recovery quickened. When she wasn't here, she was with her father overseeing battle preparations or sleeping. She walked over to the window and threw open the blinds to let in the sunlight.

"Honestly Jakob, it is no wonder you need those things, reading in the dim light." He shrugged. "What have you got there anyway?" She asked.

"Ah, this would be the work of my physician. *The Undying Knight* is called. He is quite the jack-of-all-trades, our new wizard. A doctor, a writer, a wizard, a soldier, honestly, I'm beginning to feel rather inadequate."

"You shouldn't." Tendra replied. "Has father been to see you today?" Jakob nodded before coughing heavily into his arm.

"Yes, he is quite pleased with my recovery. He is hoping for me to sit in on the council tomorrow. One of them at least. I have had nothing but time, and time brings about lots of ideas. I've been writing them down." Jakob gestured to the left at a scroll of parchment. Tendra extended her hand to grab it, but she was waved off. "No peeking!" Tendra looked at him crossly. "Did you hear about the Skyguard?" Jakob asked.

"What about him?" Tendra asked taken aback. Jakob grinned mischievously.

"How is it that I hear the palace gossip before you do, and I can't even leave the room?" Jakob pondered. "It seems that he is no longer on the castle grounds, and apparently he gave your new suitor quite a beating during his escape." Tendra just sat there for a moment, unsure of whether or not he was kidding, and which thing to address first.

"Suitor?" She said with a cocked eyebrow.

"Oh yes, it has been the talk of the castle. Much to Jeric's chagrin, I would imagine. The princess and the wizard. Sounds like a title of a book to me." Jakob said with a wink.

"It's nothing. He is one of the Seven, and he is your doctor; nothing more." She grew quiet for a moment. "Do you really think that it is going to happen? That the war is going to come here? All this preparation we are doing. Is there no chance that it will stay in the north?" Jakob shook his head solemnly.

"It will come here. Qel is too ambitious to do anything else. Nice change of subject by the way, but next time let the pause last longer. It gives a more dramatic effect." Tendra rolled her eyes. "Father has been playing with fire, quite literally, and our whole house will burn down around us if we aren't careful."

"What are you saying?" Tendra inquired.

"I'm saying is that we need to keep careful watch over everyone here. We need a cabal of people that we can trust. Start with Jeric and Rowen, but make sure that you can trust the wizard first. Then, move out from there. It is no surprise that our family has enemies, and this situation that Father got us in is untenable. From what I hear, the Elders are furious about the matter, but they are scared. Scared of how quickly the Hammer is sweeping through the feral army. I am too. I just don't know. If war comes to Gemport, a coup attempt is not only likely but almost assured. We need to be prepared for that eventuality."

"Terrance Greenhorn," she said flatly.

"Yes, among others." Tendra cocked an eyebrow quizzically. "I don't have anything definite yet, but I am working on it. I'll let you know. Now, get out of here." Tendra started as a pillow hit her in the face. "I want to finish my book in peace and between Rowen, Father, and you, not to mention the endless array of well-wishers, I scarcely have a moment's peace. Now off with you!" He said with a smirk.

"Hey, be nice," Tendra said, before shaking her head and rising to her feet. She leaned down and gave him a kiss on his forehead, before turning to the door. A second flying pillow caused her to stop and stare at Jakob, who merely laughed in response.

She wandered aimlessly through the castle. She really had nothing to do this afternoon until the Council meeting this evening with her father, Rowen, Retren, the royal accountant, and Wesley, the captain of the guard. Jeric had cast off a week ago to meet with Magistrate Viscus in King's Port to rally the banners to march south. Father was busy coordinating the stockpiling of resources for the possible upcoming siege with Retren.

She found herself watching the soldiers drilling in the west courtyard. There was a battalion of the city guard out practicing with a very familiar instructor at the helm. She watched as they broke into groups of three or four who then proceeded to circle around a fifth. The goal seemed to be to survive for as long as you could before being dealt a fatal blow by the wooden practice swords. They fought in full armor and the silver sheen of the steel shone with the sunlight

She let out a small chuckle of laughter as Rowen marched furiously up to a group of them and corrected the one in the middle on how to fight.

"Magnificent, isn't he?" Tendra refused to jump at the sound of the voice right behind her. She hated it when he did that. She angled her head back around to see Vizien. The Grand Inquisitor was dressed in his typical black and gray leather armor and his cape was held in place by a silver chain.

"You should know better, Inquisitor, than to sneak up on a lady. She might get the wrong idea. As for your question, yes, they are magnificent."

265

"Ah, but that was not what I asked, now was it?" He stood next to her with his arms leaning against the balcony.

"He does his job, and you sound almost envious, Vizien. Not an emotion I often see from you." Tendra replied curtly.

"There is much to be admired in him."

"Feeling threatened?" Tendra asked.

"Not in the slightest. Popularity doesn't well suit someone whose job is to stay in the shadows." Vizien said with a smile. A short period of silence formed between them as they watched the soldiers fight back and forth. Rowen was almost comical as he marched from circle to circle correcting inconsistencies. "Your brother seems to be doing quite well. It seems like Rowen is the magician that he claimed to be after all."

"If what you've heard about at Sterin's Throne is true, then you haven't seen anything yet, I'd imagine."

"And you? Have you seen some of his magic?"

"A little bit. Nothing spectacular." She lied, remembering his disappearing act in Midway. She watched as Rowen turned away from his troops and grabbed a bow and arrow. She observed confusedly as he did something hidden from view with the arrow, nocked it, and raised it towards her. She opened her mouth in astonishment.

"Get down!" She yelled, grabbing Vizien and pulling him down beneath the balcony. The arrow flew over their heads and stuck into the wooden door right behind where Vizien's head had been a moment before. They rose up and looked down at Rowen, who was merely staring at them. She turned and saw a small piece of paper wrapped around the arrow and tied neatly. She untied the knot and pulled the paper off. *Join the fun.* She looked back down at Rowen, who was smiling widely.

"Well, he certainly knows how to keep an audiences' attention."

"And invite participation," she said handing him the note.

"Hmm," was all Vizien could say.

"Well?" She said looking at him expectedly.

"Well what?"

"Your princess demands that you accept his invitation." She had to work to keep from laughing at Vizien's face, which was wholly devoid of amusement.

"You must be joking."

"Absolutely not; now off with you." She said, a smile finally breaking through her face.

"As My Lady commands," he said without an inch of amusement, but instead with a bow he then turned on his heel and walked away. Tendra turned back to the courtyard and saw Rowen's confused expression and merely smiled. Rowen shrugged and continued his duties, and a few moments later he shot her a look as Vizien came into view, his long black cloak waving in behind him.

Tendra laughed. When they first arrived in Gemport, the two had met, and Rowen had taken an instant dislike to the man that had only grown more acute after the interrogation that Vizien had put him through. Rowen told her how he had walked out, after one of Vizien's more inane questions, as Rowen measured it, but she knew better. Vizien didn't do anything without a reason.

She watched with interest as Vizien marched straight up to Rowen, and they began to talk. Vizien pulled his saber from his sheath, and Rowen did the same from his back. It was almost comical how ridiculously Rowen's huge broadsword dwarfed Vizien's saber.

Tendra watched as the guardsmen cleared out into a wide circle around the two of them. She watched as a dialogue went on between them. Rowen went over to one of the guardsmen, saying something to him, and then the two were off. Their blades were a whirlwind of swordsmanship as she watched them go back and forth. She watched them go through a particularly complicated series of maneuvers before Rowen released his sword with his left hand, lashing out, and knocking Vizien back into the crowd. The circle quickly moved around them, obscuring her vision. She moved around the balcony trying to see, but still all she saw was the throngs of the crowd until they suddenly broke apart. Vizien and Rowen both rose up with nocked bows and fired twin arrows that landed on either side of her. This time she didn't flinch, or at least not as much.

Once again each arrow had a note attached to it. The first read *Very funny* and the next read *Nice Try.* She shook her head at them and turned away from the laughing riot of soldiers. She was less than amused. She wandered the hallways, desperately trying to devise some devious plan but eventually gave up. She would ask Jakob about it later. He had always been better at pranks than she was anyway. She finally found herself in the library. She loved the library.

When she had first journeyed to the Book Castle of Mesnir, she found herself mesmerized by the endless stacks of books. She trailed her fingers along the new, old, and older leather as she browsed for something to read. She finally found her way to the spirit section. It was her favorite section of the library. This section revolved around the myths of the world. Her hand came to rest on two titles. One was entitled *Endless*. It was a book she had read long ago about seven immortals. The other, though, was a compendium of children's rhymes called *Songs of the Children.* She pulled both books off the shelf and opened to the first page of the children's book. The first rhyme was entitled *Unknown to Storms.*

The world of a child is joy and glee,
Pleasure in all, their world is a sea

The oceans smooth and winds fair,
They glide across even waters of air.
They know not the sharks and the sharp of stone
They are unbattered in heart, mind or bone
They waft along from port to sea
The world of a child is joy and glee.

On the opposite page was a poem entitled *Shattered Dreams.* Tendra stared at the pages. There was something about them that made her not turn the page. Her eyes kept returning to the word 'unbattered' on the page. She had heard that word, not exactly recently, but recently enough that it triggered something in her head. It took her almost five minutes before she realized what it was. Rowen had said it to her. The words that the gallowglass had spoken to them. Tendra couldn't believe it. She looked upwards towards Supremor and shook her head with a smile.

"Mysterious ways indeed," She murmured. She took the rhyme book, along with *Endless,* with her to a chair in the back and drowned away the hours. She wished she could have more days like this, but she was afraid that these simple days wouldn't last for much longer. Tomorrow was the Council of Elders, and she was determined to attend. She knew, if nothing else, it would be highly entertaining watching them attempt to complain about her father with her being there.

The day passed by, and finally the sun began to dip below the horizon as she threw her arms up in a yawn.

"Come now, my lady, surely you cannot be so tired already. The night has barely begun." Tendra looked up from her reading and saw Rowen standing in front of her.

"Are you intentionally following me around? I believe that such an act is worthy of the city guard being called down upon you." He grabbed a chair, twisted it around, and sat down facing her.

"Yes, well, I actually came to invite you to dinner with your father and me." She eyed him carefully.

"Oh did you now? And why, pray tell, would I do that?"

"Well, for a myriad of reasons," he said perching his chin on his hands, which rested on the back of the chair. "For starters, I know that you rarely get to see your father when it is not business-related, and I know how much you enjoy spending time with me. What other reasons do you need?" She stared at him for a moment, aghast.

"Two is hardly a myriad." She chastised. "Tell me something, Rowen, do you have to try to be that full of yourself, or were you born over-stuffed?"

"I am one hundred percent natural," he said with a lop-sided smile. "Though what can I say, you bring out the best in me."

"You think you're the first? The first man to come in with charming words and a pretty face? You're just another in a long line. I love Jeric, and we are already betrothed, so whatever you are thinking, you may as well give it up now. It is never going to happen." Rowen started to speak, and she smiled in triumph.

"See, the sad thing is that you think I'm serious. If I was really trying, we would be sitting at Rainbow Falls sipping Hoy's Fourth," he said with a smile. "However..." he said rising back up, "...if my lady would not like to join her father and me for a pleasant evening, then I will acquiesce." He bowed, turned, and began to walk away. He turned over his shoulder. "Oh, and the request was your father's, not mine." Tendra sighed.

"Rowen." The man stopped walking at the sound of his name. "What if I told you I have solved your riddle-your gallow-glass prophecy?" A sly smile came to her face as she said the words. She was enjoying this.

270

"I would say that you just became actually attractive to me. Then I would give you a gold star because even Aurum had no idea what that crazy verse was about."

"Why is everything compared to Aurum?" Tendra asked. Rowen shrugged before returning to his chair.

"He's the gold standard. He's Aurum." There was a momentary pause. "Are you going to share or am I going to have to guess?"

"Wait; just give me a moment to savor this feeling of supremacy over you." She took a deep breath. "Alright." Tendra spun the children's book around so that *Shattered Dreams* faced him. She watched his eyes as he read it.

In a dark land, in a forbidden place
There sits a man that watches your face
He sees every action, every smile and frown
And into his book he writes it all down
So watch what you say and watch what you do
Or like all naughty children Ohm will write you down too.

"What's an Ohm?" Rowen asked.

"It's a person, I think. This poem was written to scare children about Thanatos."

"Woah. You are telling me that I have to go to Thanatos? Are you insane? I don't know if you have seen that place, but it's not very nice. And there are no pretty girls. I'd be lost." He grinned. She rolled her eyes before slamming the book shut.

"It's just a theory, and it is more than you had before anyways."

"True, but you want to know something?"

"What?"

"I deal with theories better on a full stomach, and dinner is getting cold."

"Fine." She picked up her books, yawning once again, as Rowen watched. "No offers to help?" He shook his head.

"Nope, I made dinner; you can do the clean-up."

"You made dinner?" she asked as she picked up the last of her things.

"Why do you sound so surprised?"

"Because you are a man, and an influential one at that." Rowen looked at her expectedly, as she walked towards him.

"And?"

"And, that is just not something that people like you do."

"I enjoy it! It is like medicine, just something fun that I do. Am I not allowed to have hobbies?" They walked together through the castle, and Tendra thought back to what Jakob had said that morning, before quickly brushing those thoughts from her head.

"Of course, you can do whatever you like."

"Well, obviously not whatever I like." He said looking at her with a gleam in his eye.

"You are insufferable, Rowen, and honestly, if you were not so important to my father's plans, I would have absolutely nothing to do with you." He grew quiet at that, and they walked the remainder of the way-not the dining hall, as she had expected- but rather the throne room, where a table had been set up, and the food was sitting there along with her father and two other chairs. Rowen moved forward to pull the chair out for Tendra to be seated and then moved to his own chair.

"Where did you find her?" Jethro asked.

"The library, reading children's books." Rowen replied. Jethro looked at her disapprovingly.

"I was studying history." She said back. *Technically.* Rowen winked at her as he took his seat.

"My daughter, always has her head in the clouds of the past." Jethro said shaking his head. Laid out before her was a bowl of dark and boiling stew along with a basket of bread still warm from the fire. There was no dining ware to be seen.

"By studying the past, one can gain valuable insight on the future. You taught me that, father." Tendra reminded him. "Where are the utensils?"

Rowen merely smiled and reached out, breaking off a piece of bread and dipped it into the broth eating it with his hands. She stared at him. That was not a fitting way for a lady to eat at the dining table. She looked over to her father who merely shrugged before following Rowen's lead.

"His meal, far be it for me to tell a chef how to eat it." Jethro said.

"Come now, princess. Try it, you may even find that you like it. Perish the thought." Tendra carefully broke off a piece of bread, dipped it into the stew before consuming it. As she took a bite, her senses were assailed with a cornucopia of flavors. The bread was soft and warm, and the broth of the stew was rich and heavy. She tasted ingredients she couldn't readily identify, but they complimented each other well. She looked up and saw Rowen eyeing her carefully.

"It is very good," she acquiesced, and Rowen beamed in satisfaction before going back to eating. They finished their broth, and Rowen rose quickly to bring out the next course leaving her father and her alone in the room.

"Not a bad cook, our wizard," her father said. "So, what do you think of him?" He asked, staring at her intently. In the torchlight his face seemed to flicker and dance with light.

"I like him well enough, I suppose," she said carefully. "He is cocky, borderline narcissistic, and self-centered, perseverant, smart, and well-trained. He knows what he is doing."

"The men like him." Jethro commented, and Tendra nodded in agreement. "But do you like him?" He asked pointedly.

273

"What are you asking?" Tendra said sharply, a cold feeling sinking into her stomach. Before Jethro could answer, Rowen returned with a platter full of food.

"I apologize; I only had time to make three courses, though hopefully you will find this one fulfilling." She looked at it and saw a mountain of chicken mixed with vegetables of all colors atop a base of rice. The chicken looked as if it had been soaked in something and then fried, because it had a crisp outer layer to it that made the meat look very well done. "And, this time..." he said reaching out his hand to her, "...you get a fork."

"Thank you," she said politely before digging in. Despite the savory nature of the food her father's words sat like a rock in the bottom of her stomach. She ate, but her appetite was stymied.

"Rowen, the entirety of Gemport has become fascinated with you. You have earned a fair amount of fame. How are you coping with it?"

"To be honest, your majesty, I have thrown myself into my work, into trying to make all the preparations necessary for what is to come. I haven't been able to get out among the people nearly as often as I would like."

"Yes, well, in the weeks that you have been here, I have heard nothing but praise. In these times of shadow before the darkness comes, you have been a much needed ray of sunshine to illuminate the lives of this city, so thank you." Rowen half-smiled in actual embarrassment. It was the first time that she had ever seen him exhibit anything even approaching shame.

"I am only doing what I can to help. If I can save a single life, then all of my time and effort will be worth it."

Jethro smiled as if that had been exactly what he wanted to hear. "Now, let us get on to the real reason why I asked you both here."

"The real reason was because I have a very difficult task for the two of you-something that can only be accomplished by the two of you together and requires your absolute dedication to the kingdom of humanity. Do you have that dedication?"

"Of course," Tendra said immediately and stared at Rowen when he didn't do the same.

"I do." He said carefully.

"Excellent. Now, this will be hard on you. Harder than anything you have ever endured, but I swear to you that it is for a purpose and that it is for the best."

"Father, it sounds as if you are shipping us to Bastion or something." Tendra said, attempting to make light of the sudden tone of sobriety the conversation had taken.

"What I want, and what needs to happen for the good of the kingdom, and for the good of you two is..." Tendra only had time for a single thought to run through her mind, *oh no, he can't*, "...for you, Rowen, to take my daughter's hand in marriage."

Stranger Inside Than Out

Twenty-One

Galeerial looked up at the gates to the city of Soaring.
They were exactly the same as the gates in which Ezekiel and he
had spent so much time; yet he seemed so small in comparison to
how large they were. He had never bothered to stand at ground
level when he had wings, never stopped to appreciate the
massiveness of scale that the Skyguard had achieved in their
architecture. He had watched the Cathedral of Eternity grow
larger and larger as he had moved in concentric circles around
the mountain of Darrow's Peak. It had been almost four days
since he had departed from Gemport. He was finally here.

Darrow had been a Skyguard, born in the second
generation of Skyguard, and he had been the one to discover how
to burn glass with pictures and colors. He used this knowledge to

design the cathedrals that still stood to this very day. Before his death, this mountain had been called Peregrine's Nest.

Galeerial was at a loss as to what to do now. The gates were shut, and there was no reason for any Skyguard to be down by the gates. Nevertheless, he had to hope that someone had noticed his ascent.

"Hello!" he called out. "Hello!" he shouted again.

"There is no need to shout, I have been watching your approach for the last twenty five minutes." Galeerial whirled around as a Skyguard lightly descend down to the ground. Galeerial felt tension rising in his throat and tears start to form in his eyes. For a second he didn't know why, then he realized it was the wings. As he stared at the Skyguard's wings, he had to fight back tears. They were beautiful. His shoulder blades ached from the loss of his own wings. He blinked quickly and wiped his eyes. "We don't get visitors here, much less human ones." The Skyguard said.

"Who, who are you?" Galeerial asked.

"What good is knowing my name?" The Skyguard replied.

"Who are you?" Galeerial repeated as he swallowed heavily. He slowly let go of the reins of his horse and assumed a defensive posture. This Skyguard could be one of Veriel's spies.

"Talkative fellow. Gabriel is my name, and yours is…" the Skyguard offered out his hand. Galeerial stared at it without taking it.

"Galeerial." he said with a pointed glare. He thought he saw something that looked like recognition on the Skyguard's face, but he couldn't be sure.

"That is not the name of a human." Gabriel commented.

"That is because I am a Skyguard." Galeerial replied.

"Of course you are." Gabriel's wings started to flap. "Be on your way, human. We want nothing to do with your kind."

278

"Wait!" Galeerial called out. His breath caught in his chest. He could not come this far for nothing. "Wait." Gabriel hovered in the air. "I can prove it." Gabriel didn't move. Galeerial grasped the bottom of his shirt and pulled it up and off revealing his myriad scars.

"By Supremor..." Gabriel whispered. Galeerial turned around to reveal the cauterized stumps at the ends of his shoulder blades where his wings had been.

"I told you. I am a Skyguard." Galeerial reached in his saddle bag and threw the canteen of Charist to the Skyguard who caught it. Gabriel opened it, and smelled the liquid within.

"And one with quite a story no doubt." Gabriel murmured.

"One that I need to tell to the High Clerics. Immediately."

"Why? Why would I allow you in to see them?" Galeerial seethed.

"Because I have no wings, and the creature who did this," Galeerial gestured to his chest, "and the being he follows are a danger to the entirety of our race. Every hour that I delay more could die."

"Who is this creature?" Gabriel asked. Galeerial looked around.

"How do I know that I can trust you?"

"Simply put, you do not. But the real question is, can you afford not to?" Gabriel said, staring into Galeerial's eyes. "Why not come inside, my friend? I have a feeling that your story is about to cause some very big changes around here." Gabriel descended to the ground, reached out his hands yet again. Galeerial pulled his shirt back on, and warily reached one hand out. With his other, he clutched the small dagger he had found in his saddlebag. Gabriel beat his wings heavily to get them both aloft. Galeerial's breath caught in his throat, and he felt the wind whip through his face as they made their way to the top of the gates. It was nothing like flying on his own; yet the sensation… it was like going home.

Galeerial closed his eyes and finally felt the air fade away as his feet touched the ground. They landed on the other side of the gates and began to walk toward the towering Cathedral of Eternity.

"How do you know the wizard?" Galeerial asked cautiously.

"Wizard?" Gabriel asked.

"The one who brought me here some time ago. I don't remember much from the journey, but I remembered some of the climb."

"What makes you think that I have ever seen you before or this wizard?"

"The fact that you were expecting me and that this is only one place the wizard could have gotten the Charist." Gabriel mulled this over for a second.

"Fair enough. Actually, I know all seven. I first met them about four and a half years ago. One of our Rangers, by the name of Samuel, was sent by the Clerics to investigate some mysterious happenings within Thanatos. Well, the wizards brought him back here forty-five days later. We had no idea what exactly happened to him, except that he had died on day thirty-six. The Clerics never said what he uncovered within that demented place. Nevertheless, the Seven brought his body here for us to burn, so that he could fully join the ranks of the Eternal Host. His wings had turned black and had shriveled to almost nothing. His face was burned, his body was covered with boils, and he was missing a leg. It was one of the most horrifying things I have ever witnessed. After that, well, what can I say, one thing led to another and soon enough we just started meeting.

They give me information about what is going on with the lowlands, and in return I give them history lessons."

"What have you told them?" Galeerial asked sharply.

"Why does it matter? It is the past." Gabriel asked, fixing him with an odd look.

"The past holds great power over the present." Galeerial said darkly.

"Maybe so, but the reward is far greater than the risk," Gabriel replied.

"How can you possibly know that? How can you possibly see all futures? You can't. There is always something that you will miss."

"You are correct. I cannot. But I know those men."

"How well?"

"'Well enough', would be the most appropriate answer. They are good men, honorable, and excellent warriors. Though Rowen is probably the least of them-then again, maybe Rayn is worse. In truth, a bad one of them is still the equal to apparently a few hundred ferals."

"Do you trust them?"

Gabriel hesitated for a moment, before nodding sincerely. "Yes, I do."

"Why? They wield unbound magic. They have desecrated the tomb of Garen."

"I have known them for many years. They are good men, a testament to their race. They believe in honor, truth and justice."

"How do you know that?"

"Because I have followed them, and I have watched them right wrongs over the entire breadth of Carin. They are like what the Skyguard used to be. Do you remember the Tolomin?" Galeerial shook his head. The name sounded familiar, but he couldn't place it.

"Long ago, before The Dread, and even for a couple hundred years after him, there was a group called the Tolomin that existed within the Skyguard. They were what we all had hoped the Light Monks would become before they became pacified. They wandered the world as arbiters of justice to all races. Every being recognized their authority. They were the best of us, and they brought their wisdom to the rest of the world. That is what the wizards are. As for the Heart of Fires, do you ever believe that perhaps magic should not have been bound to Garen's tomb?" Gabriel said quietly. Galeerial turned to stare at him. This was heresy. Gabriel began to laugh.

"I have seen that look before."

"No, I have never doubted the wisdom of the Secondborn. They were told by Supremor himself to do what they did."

"Why do you believe that?"

"Because I have faith." Galeerial replied. Gabriel stared at him sadly.

"So you do; so you do." Silence accompanied them as they made their way upwards. They had reached the bounds of the city by now, and Galeerial stared as dispassionately as he could at the buildings, yet at every turn he was reminded of Cloud Breach. It made his heart ache in a way that The Wither never could. He could see Skyguard flying about their aeries not really paying them any mind. Occasionally, he would see one pause in his activities to take notice of the human who had entered their city, but for the most part they were ignored. They continued their journey towards the cathedral at the center of the city.

"Tell me about Veriel." Gabriel said. Galeerial eyed him.

"What about him?"

"You spoke in your delirium, saying over and over again that you would kill him." Gabriel replied.

"He cut my wings off and cast me into hell, where I spent an eternity being tortured by the devil." Galeerial turned away from Gabriel and shrugged the other's hand off his shoulder.

"I'm sorry."

"It is past. All that matters is the future. Cloud Breach must be warned."

Gabriel nodded. "The past holds great power over the present." Gabriel said softly. Galeerial glared at him. They had arrived at the doors to the cathedral. Galeerial's breath was taken away by the sheer size of it. It was so much bigger than he remembered. He was dumb-struck. "Galeerial?" Gabriel began.

"What?" Galeerial was shook from his reverie. Gabriel was now standing in between him and the doors.

"Maybe you should let me do it. Tell me your story, and I will tell the Clerics."

"No." He shook his head. "They must hear it from my lips-see the truth in my eyes. It has to be me and no other."

"Galeerial," Gabriel grabbed his arm and looked into Galeerial's eyes. "I beg you, let me tell this story. Leave this place. Leave now. Forget this quest for vengeance, and let the burden pass to me. I will be a good steward of your pain. Leave now and find somewhere far away, where you will never be found, and let me take care of this." Galeerial looked at him disbelievingly. He pulled his face right up next to Gabriel's.

"No! What are you trying to do, Gabriel?"

"I am trying to help you."

"Then open the doors." Galeerial said. His voice was bound in hard edges. The two large wooden doors of the cathedral stood before them. Gabriel raised a fist and pounded on the doors three times. Nothing happened. Galeerial waited for what seemed like an eternity before reaching up and grabbing the two bronze loops on the doors himself and pulling with all his might, ripping them open.

The two sentries looked startled, as Galeerial pushed his way past them into the bottom floor of the cathedral. The cathedral rose high into the sky, and Galeerial heard the wind organ playing as the breeze whipped through it deep in the cathedral heights. The five clerics were statues watching his approach, and Galeerial obliged them. He marched straight forward to the pulpit and then bent down to a knee. Everything came back to him in a rush. It had been so long since he had stood in a cathedral not unlike this, in front of clerics not unlike these. That had been half a world away, and an entire lifetime ago.

"High Clerics, my name is Galeerial Strongwind, and I am a Skyguard."

"We know of you, Galeerial. Your name has been whispered in the halls of power. We understood you to be a deserter, though it appears as though there is more to your story." one of the clerics said. "My name is Benjamin, and I will serve as the voice of the clerics in this." His voice was cold and distant.

"I beg of you to hear my words. I have come a great distance to be heard." Galeerial began. "On a matter of the very survival of our race." the clerics looked back and forth amongst one another.

"You have our attention, Galeerial." The cleric who spoke before said. He gestured to one of the benches in the cathedral. "Sit, speak, and we will listen." Ordinarily, Galeerial would have stood, but he knew his story would take some time. He entwined his fingers together.

Galeerial began at the beginning, starting fourteen years ago, when he had first begun to believe that Veriel was not all that he appeared to be. He told them of Ezekiel and the evidence they had gathered. He told them of the meeting in the stone cells and of the mysterious being, Terel, who had been sent to find the

284

being named Frosh. He told them of his imprisonment and torture. Throughout it all, he kept his composure. Every word was calm and measured, and his voice never cracked: not once. When he finally finished, the sun had crossed its apex and was well into the afternoon.

"Your tale carries a disturbing familiarity to us, Galeerial" High Cleric Benjamin said to him. "Veriel did much the same here in Soaring. However, by end of his tenure, he was cast out. He was ambitious and persuasive. It caused a great schism within the Host, resulting in an almost complete breakdown of society after Veriel was excommunicated. Yet, the clerics were able to restore order and righteousness. I believe that I speak for all the clerics, when I confess my sorrow over all that has happened to you. I cannot possibly imagine what all you have been through. We are grateful that you have managed to reach us with this information, and impressed at the remarkable amount of detail you can recall." Galeerial nodded.

"Thank you." He said, humbly.

"Now, we must decide a course of action on addressing Veriel." one of the other clerics said.

"Take me to Cloud Breach and help me assassinate Veriel." Galeerial cut in.

"We do not assassinate members of the Skyguard. Surely there is some other way." the same cleric said.

"Have you heard nothing?" Galeerial reached up and tore his tunic off. His body still held the star-shaped scar that was carved into him by The Wither, and he bared it all for them to see. The clerics regarded his scars with the same level of clinical interest as they had his entire story.

"Galeerial, we require time to confer." High Cleric Benjamin said.

"There is no time!" Galeerial cried out. "Veriel will burn the Skyguard to the ground." He felt a hand on his shoulder and turned to see Gabriel behind him.

"Galeerial, give us a moment." Gabriel said. It was not a request. Galeerial suddenly felt drained of energy. He had never told anyone everything before, and the adrenaline he had gained in weaving his story was gone now. He slumped in his pew.

The Clerics exchanged glances and then removed themselves to confer. Gabriel strode up to the altar and spoke with them. After several long minutes, the five Clerics and Gabriel broke their circle. He prayed they were wiser than the Clerics in Cloud Breach.

"Please, he will destroy everything." Galeerial whispered.

"Not if we can stop him." Benjamin said. Galeerial sagged in relief. He bit his lip to hold back tears of relief and joy. "And you, Galeerial, will be given a new name, no longer are you Galeerial Strongwind, you now stand as Galeerial Starheart. We will send Gabriel and a contingent of Skyguard to Cloud Breach to treat with the clerics against Veriel and his machinations."

"I will be one of those Skyguard." Galeerial said.

"No." The word was like a slap to Galeerial's face. He slowly rose from the bench he was seated on.

"It wasn't a request." He replied.

"Nevertheless, it is denied." A second cleric said. He had not spoken before. "I am Eliel, and you will not accompany the party to Cloud Breach." he said.

"Why?"

The clerics looked at each other uneasily, and Galeerial felt nothing but dread.

"The reason is…" Cleric Benjamin looked at the other four clerics with a sad look on his face, "…is because you are no longer a Skyguard." Galeerial looked at them incredulously before laughing.

"What are you talking about? Because I lost my wings?" He asked, his tone a mix between hurt and anger. Cleric Benjamin closed his eyes and exhaled.

"You no longer have the Aer."

"Then, how was I able to drink the Charist that Gabriel gave to the wizard? If I had lost the Aer, then I would have perished instantly in ash and water."

"Because, I gave you no Charist." Gabriel said from behind.

"What?"

"I never gave you any Charist. I treated your wounds and helped nurse you back to health. But, I gave you none of the Tears of Supremor. The canteen you gave me was weak rum. That's why I sent you back with the wizard. We are not your people, Galeerial."

"How?" Galeerial said through choked words. He couldn't stop the tears now. "How?" He repeated.

"To be honest, Galeerial, we don't know what is happening. This has only ever happened twice before in the history of the Skyguard. You no longer have the Aer. If you were to be cut, you would bleed. You are truly human. I am sorry." Cleric Benjamin said. The look of pity on his face stoked the fires in Galeerial's heart.

"No!" Galeerial sprinted up the dais, pushing past one of the Clerics and gazed into the fountain of Charist and saw...nothing. He had no reflection in the pool of Supremor's tears. He fell to his knees.

"I am truly sorry, Galeerial." Galeerial felt a hand on his shoulder. "I tried to spare you from this. But, there is nothing more that you or anyone else can do."

"How could you do this to me?" Galeerial whispered.

"What?" Gabriel asked.

"How could you take this from me?" Galeerial looked up at the shiftstone statue of Supremor. It was in the guise of a father, but all Galeerial saw was a monster. "How could you take this from me?" he screamed. He pulled the knife from his sleeve and hurled it at the statue. The knife plunged into the forehead of the statue and stuck there.

"Blasphemy!" Cleric Eliel cried, and Galeerial grabbed him by the robes. Cleric Eliel's wings spread out beyond him. How Galeerial hated those wings.

"Say it again," Galeerial growled. His face was pressed against Cleric Eliel's and the smell of fear filled Galeerial's nostrils. Cleric Eliel's face radiated terror. Galeerial shoved him backwards and the cleric stumbled, falling to the ground. "I hate you!" Galeerial said turning back to the statue. "I gave you everything, and you betrayed me. I…hate…you." Galeerial turned and saw the clerics backing away from him.

"Galeerial, you do not mean that." Gabriel said. He held his hands out trying to calm Galeerial down.

"Oh, yes I do. Now, I'm leaving. You refuse to help me..." he said glaring at the Clerics, "...you are all lost. I will shed no tears when Veriel kills you all. But, he won't kill me. No, he won't get the chance." Galeerial shoved past Gabriel as he pushed the doors open and sprinted outside into the sunlight. The city was a blur as he ran through it. He could barely make out the roads as he ran. It was only when he finally reached the edge of the city and the sheer cliff face before him that he stopped.

He stared down the stone of the mountain and to the plains far below even that.

Darrow's Peak was not quite as tall as Frost Fall, but it was still a mountain, and it was a long way down. He watched the twirl of the clouds in the wind.

"Galeerial, I tried to warn you." Gabriel's voice rang out behind him. Galeerial didn't answer. "I am so sorry. That is why I didn't want you to speak with the clerics, because then you would discover what had happened to you. I am so sorry. I will fly you wherever you want to go." Galeerial turned to him. He was standing just half a pace away. The cold air whipped through his closely cut hair. Galeerial balled his hands into a fist and slammed his left one into Gabriel's face. Gabriel fell to the ground with a shocked look on his face.

"I'll fly wherever I want to go." Galeerial said turning back around. He took off running and leapt off of the cliff.

Treachery Most Foul
Twenty-Two

The stunned silence filled the air around the table.

"Are you insane?" Tendra cried out.

"Well, I can't say I'm not pleased. I just thought that I'd have to kill a few people to get to this point," Rowen said with a chuckle.

"Shut up, Rowen!" Tendra shot up to her feet. Her chair went crashing to the floor. "Father, are you crazy?"

"Perhaps." He said simply.

"Perhaps? I have been with Jeric for four years, and you have never said a word beyond expressing your happiness. You arranged the marriage. How dare you?"

"Tendra, you are a princess, and Jeric, well, Jeric is a monk-a monk in an order that lost all purpose and meaning long ago. Not only that, but he does not have the respect and love of our people. Rowen has captured more than just their hearts; he has captured their imagination."

"But, for how long?" She glared at Rowen, who sat quietly watching her. "Sure, everyone loves him now, but what about when this war is over, when his magic is good for nothing. Will they still love him then?"

"I'm sitting right here," Rowen murmured. She glared at him.

"Try to understand, Tendra..." Jethro began.

"No, I won't 'try to understand' anything. You may have known Rowen all his life, but I met him only a few weeks ago. I am in love with Jeric. I will not tolerate your interference in this matter."

"I am your father!" Jethro said firmly, rising slowly from the table. "You will do as you are told."

"No!" Tendra saw Rowen's eyebrows rise in surprise.

"What?" Jethro leaned forward. "What did you just say to me?" His voice was low and threatening.

"I said, no! I will follow your orders as king, because I am a loyal subject. But understand this: if you force this decision upon me, I will hate you for the rest of your life." Tendra turned on her heel and walked out. She shook her head as she walked away in disbelief. Her mind was awash with anger all through the halls. She eventually found her way back to the library and sat down amidst the endless shelves of books.

She had always found comfort in the library. It was a place of knowledge, a place of learning, a place of isolation. She loved her family more than anything; yet it was here that she found solace in silence.

She loved the smell of the books, the old ink and even older parchment, the smell of worn leather. She loved the texture of the binding upon her hands and the smooth flow of the writing upon every page.

She thought about what her father had asked of her. *Lunacy*! She thought back to when she had found out that her father had promised her to Jeric. Jeric's father, Cohl, was an incredibly influential member of the council, and their marriage was a peace offering, even though Jeric had already entered into the Order of the Light Monks. Upon hearing word of her betrothal, she remembered not speaking to him for two weeks.

Although she had known who Jeric was, she had not known him well. He had been the epitome of a monk, never saying more than four words to anyone. He was always aloof and away from people. In the four years hence, Cohl had fallen from grace, and hence that political necessity was no longer there. Now, Rowen was the man of the hour, and her father sought to sell her like so many cattle.

She wouldn't have it. She would never marry that insufferable, intolerable man. Yes, he had his charms, but he was…Tendra found herself unable to even think that thought. He wasn't like any other man. He was bold: reckless, even. He had a fire about him. Something that Jeric, for all of his nuances, all of his soft touches, never had…and she doubted he ever would.

"You know what something is that you never forget? Shame." Tendra whipped her head around and saw Sir Terrance Greenhorn walking slowly towards her. She sighed. She did not need this right now.

"Sir Terrance, if you know what is good for you, you will turn right around and walk back to whatever hole you were spawned in and die in it. I swear, if you continue to speak with me now, you will end up unable to move." Terrance simply smirked, as she glared at him darkly.

293

"You know, they said we should wait. Until after the unu came. Honestly, I knew we couldn't wait nearly that long. Your family started this whole war, and it is going to bring humanity to its knees." He put his hand down on the table and vaulted over it, landing directly in front of her. His hand cut off her quick shriek of surprise and she pushed off the floor, kicking her chair as it crashed to the ground. To no avail, she scrambled to get out of it, but his grip was simply too strong.

"You humiliated me in front of my men. You shouldn't have done that." He whispered. She felt his hot breath on her neck. A shiver of fear went up her spine, as she felt the cool steel of the flat of his knife slide across her throat. "The others, they wanted me to kill your brother, but I volunteered to come for you."

"You will never leave this room alive if you so much as leave a scratch on me." She heard a snicker of laughter.

"See now that is where you are wrong." She heard him breathe in. She elbowed him in the stomach, but hit only chain mail. Her heart was racing.

"So you kill my family, then what?" She whispered. His hand closed on his throat.

"Then we fix this, and ensure humanity's survival." He grinned. "And I get a dukedom out of it." Tendra swallowed heavily.

"You have four seconds to remove your hands from her or else I will remove them from your arms, just before I remove your face from your skull." Tendra felt the knife press back against her throat, as she was turned around again. Rowen was standing directly in front of her.

"Back off sorcerer, or I'll gut her like fish!"

"One..." Rowen replied.

"I'll do it. You think I won't, but I'll do it, and then I'll kill you. I've seen you fight, and you're nothing special." Tendra focused on Rowen, waiting for his signal. He had something planned. He must.

"Two..."

"Walk away now or I kill her. I'm not going to say it again." Terrance called out.

"Three!" Tendra saw his wrist flick, and she threw her head back into his face. As he fell crashing to the ground with a cry of pain, the knife nicked the edge of her leg, and she winced in pain. She dove forward out of his reach, and Rowen strode toward him in a flash, pulling his broadsword from his back. He held the blade up to Terrance's throat.

"You said I had four seconds," he spat out grimacing. His hand clutched his leg as blood spilled out from it. She saw only the hilt of the dagger and the end of the blade sticking out the other side.

"I lied." Rowen said dispassionately.

"Do you want to do it?" Rowen asked turning to face her. He gestured with his eyes towards Terrance.

"Yes..." she said forcing calm into her voice despite her racing pulse, "...but not here, not now. Let him rot in the dungeons, and then the whole city will see what we do with people like him," she said.

"As you wish. Your leg..." A look of concern broke onto his face.

"Just a scratch." She said. Her legs were shaking.

"Get up!" Rowen kicked Terrance in the stomach, and Terrance slowly rose to his feet with the blade to his throat. "Walk!" Rowen said, pulling the sword back and pressing it into his back. Terrance gimped forward, trying desperately to stay off his leg.

"This isn't the end, wench." Terrance called out, "I was careless. I'm just one of many." He laughed, and Rowen kicked him in the left knee as he hobbled along. Terrance fell howling with equal parts laughter and pain to the ground.

"Guards!" Rowen shouted. Two armed soldiers appeared a few moments later.

"Yes, sir?" They said in unison.

"Take this piece of trash to the dungeons. Lock him deep. But, whatever you do, don't let him die."

"Yes sir!" They repeated, though this time not as a question but an affirmation. The guards moved forward and lifted Terrance from the ground.

"Wait!" Rowen walked forward, grabbing his knife and ripped it out of his leg as the Greenhorn howled in pain. Tendra watched and took a deep breath, before sinking to the floor. Her hands began to shake. She felt an arm wrap around her.

" It's okay, you're safe. I've got you." They sat there on the hard stone floor in silence for several long minutes that stretched longer and longer. Tendra finally felt her heart stop ringing in her ears, and her hands slowly began to fall still.

"Do you want to tell me what happened?" Rowen finally said breaking the silence.

"He, he..." she took a breath, "...he came after I stormed out from dinner." She said slowly. "He said that it was payback for humiliating him. He said-" Tendra's heart skipped a beat. "Jakob!" She swallowed hard, before bolting to her feet and took off running through the halls.

"Wait!" Rowen called out after her, but she didn't stop. She sprinted through the hallways, cursing that she was so far away and praying for his safety in the same breath. She heard the footfalls of Rowen behind her, but it didn't matter. All that mattered was getting to Jakob. She took the stairs two at a time up to his turreted room. The heavy wooden door was wide open, and there was no guard as she approached.

"No!" she leapt up the last four stairs and ran into the room. Inside, she saw Domini kneeling by his side and two guards standing at the foot of his bed. Domini's eyes widened when he saw her, and he gestured franticly at the guards. "Get away from him!" She shrieked as the guards moved forward to restrain her. "Get off of me!" she screamed. Rowen burst into the room behind her. "What did you do to him?" she screamed. Tears were running down her face. Rowen stood there unsure of what to do.

"My lady, my lady!" Domini called out, approaching her slowly. "Calm yourself." She kicked out at him, and he backed off. Rowen grabbed her face with his hands.

"Tendra, Tendra! Calm down." She glared at him, but quieted herself. "Calm down!" He said firmly. He turned away from her.

"If you want to lose your arms, leave them where they are." She hissed at the guard who had his arms wrapped around her waist, and he immediately released them

"Now, what is going on here?" Rowen demanded. "And, I had better be convinced or else I am giving her one of my knives." Domini fidgeted nervously.

"About an hour ago, I was called here by one of the guards. He said that the prince…that his fingers had turned black, and he wasn't moving." Tendra pushed past Rowen and Domini and went to her brother's side.

"Jakob?" She whispered. "Jakob?" She wrapped her hand in his.

"I came immediately. It seems, like his lordship was poisoned. He…He's gone." Tendra felt her tears flow hot and free down her face.

"No, no." She felt a hand on her shoulder. "Rowen, fix this!" she demanded. "Fix this!" she screamed, burying her face into the bed at Jakob's side.

"I'm...sorry," he said haltingly. "I'm a wizard, not a god." His voice was pained, but Tendra could barely hear him. Her body was wracked with sobs. "I'm sorry. I'm so sorry." She felt his arms reach across her shoulders.

"Daughter." Tendra heard her father's voice ring out, and she looked up.

"Father, Jakob...he's," she couldn't finish her sentence.

"Yes, Tendra, I know...I know." His face looked so old and forlorn, as if the weight of a thousand years of pain and suffering had suddenly been released. "They came for me too. Get out. All of you." The guards fell back, and she watched as Domini bowed before leaving. Rowen lifted his arms from her shoulders. "Rowen."

"Yes, my lord?" Rowen asked. His voice held none of his usual bravado. Tendra wiped the tears from her eyes, but they just kept coming.

"Your dagger." She heard the steel slide from the sheath, while she turned back to stare at Jakob's pale face. His eyes were empty.

She saw her father kneel down beside her, and he laid his hand on Jakob's face. She could hear him murmuring Death's Prayer. It sent a shiver down her spine as the words danced in her head.

Jethro bent down and kissed both of Jakob's eyes, and then Jeric stood up and tore his robes open, revealing his chest. His lean body had never looked so old and withered to Tendra, who could only watch as tears streamed down her father's face. Jethro took the knife and carved a slash into his own chest, right below the scar from another. Her father winced in pain, but he did not cry out. He pulled his right hand up from his side and pressed his ring to the flowing blood. He held it there; his body wracked by grief, before finally pulling it away and pushing the seal onto his son's forehead.

"I am so sorry, daughter." He turned and looked at her forlornly. "I never meant for this to happen." He fell to his knees, and Tendra crawled across the floor to where her father was, and they held each other, alone and together in their grief...whispering prayers to a god whom she could find nowhere in her heart.

Twilight of Dreams
Twenty-Three

Not a single candle burned in a home that night. Not even the guard's lanterns were lit. The entire world was in darkness but for the high tower of the castle, where, atop the uppermost turret, three flames burned.

Tendra wore a long black robe emblazoned with a gold viper upon the chest, just like the other two who stood surrounding Jakob. It was the crest of her family. The first person to approach Jakob's pyre was her cousin, Jonathon. He was a Brilliance in the Order of the Light Monks and had a mess of a beard upon his face. His eyes were downtrodden, and his posture bent, but there were no tears to catch the moonlight upon his face. He shuffled forward solemnly and laid a hand upon Jakob's eyes.

His murmurs were lost to the biting wind that swirled around her. Her uncle was the Magistrate of King's Port and was aiding Jeric in raising the banners. Her father was behind her. It was only the three of them.

Jonathon finished speaking and stepped back. She watched the flames flicker across his eyes and face as the tongues licked at his skin. The red made his eyes glow with an inner fire. Tendra closed her eyes and sighed, desperately searching for some manner of calm. She scoured the depths of her soul, searching for something to say, anything to say. But all words escaped her as all thoughts faded to naught. Then, without warning, words began to flow from her lips.

"All-Father, who doth sit on high..." she began, "...thy greatness none can deny." She spoke haltingly as she looked down upon Jakob's lifeless body. It was so rigid-as if made of stone rather than flesh. "Your arms welcome me this day...your glory is beyond me to say." She brought a hand up to her face, and a chill went down her spine.

"Your forgiveness embraces all-" She heard Jonathon say behind her, "-your mercy saves those who fall." There was a pause, but she said nothing. "Protect me as I kneel before you, save my soul from the evil I may do," Jonathon continued.

"Thy greatness surpasses all earthly bounty...may my actions bring you eternal glory," Tendra said quietly. "And..." Tendra felt a tear began to well up in her right eye, "...and when I die and pass on to you, may I find peace in your loving arms too."

"As my fathers before me and my sons beyond me, I believe in Supremor with all I can be." Her father's words were so soft that Tendra could barely hear them over the wind.

She shifted her torch into her left hand and placed her index finger at the edge of the crest of blood that was on Jakob's forehead. She traced the circle of dried blood around his skin.

"And the circle will be complete. I will see you again brother, at the end of all days." She closed her eyes and opened them one final time to stare into her brother's eyes. She leaned down and placed a kiss on his forehead. "Why did you have to leave me?" She whispered. Tears flowed down her cheeks. "Why did you have to go? I can't do this without you. It should have been me. I'm not strong enough for this. I'm not ready. I'm not ready for you to go. I'm not ready for you to go." She pulled herself back from the wood-and-thatch throne that he lay upon. Now, it was Jethro's turn.

He walked up to where his son lay and traced his right hand from the tips of his toes to the top of his head. He leaned down and placed a kiss on his forehead, where his blood had stained the skin. Tendra saw him stand rigidly up and toss his torch upon Jakob's chest without a word, then turn and walk away.

Tendra laid her torch down into the thatch as his clothes caught fire. The hay began to burn and proceeded to feed the wood of Jakob's final throne. The flames were hungry and ate at the wood ravenously before moving up to his flesh. As the flames moved to his body, Tendra could watch no longer. She turned away from the pyre, and Jonathon wrapped his arm around her.

"Get some rest, now. I'll collect the ashes." He said squeezing her into a hug. Tendra struggled with her tears. She had already cried too much.

"Thank you. Thank you for coming." She said. Jonathon nodded.

"Anything, anything you need." He replied. "Family first." she held him close for one more second before releasing his arms. She turned and walked away, back towards the stairs, following her father. She paused at the doorway, staring one final time at the burning pyre, before collapsing to the ground.

"Tendra? Tendra!" She heard Jonathon's voice, but it was so far away and everything was so dark. She slowly began to realize that another voice was speaking to her.

"Tendra Sumenel. Open your eyes." Tendra snapped her eyes open. Everything around her was dreary and dull. There was no landscape at all. A man sat before her in a chair with a flower in his hand. he wore a long white robe. "I apologize for the abruptness of the actions, but I have urgent business with you that simply cannot wait."

"What are you? Where am I?" She asked. "What have you done to me?"

"None of those questions matter. All that matters is that there is a man in the stables preparing to leave." His voice was monotone, and as Tendra approached him, she saw that his eyes were completely black and his skin was red marble.

"Rowen?"

"Please, do not interrupt...but yes. Now, it is in your best interest, and the interests of your people and your family to stop him from leaving."

"Why are you telling me this? Please, whoever you are, leave me in peace. Please." She begged.

"Your grief and your feelings are not my concern. What is my concern is the departure of Rowen. That cannot be allowed to happen. So, what you are going to do is shut your eyes and count to three. Then, you are going to walk down the stairs from Jakob's funeral..."

"Don't you dare say his name!" She cried out.

"...And go down to the stables, where you will convince Rowen to not depart for Long Fang to aid his brothers against the ferals."

"Why? Why would I do anything you want? Just leave me alone." Tendra sunk to her knees as tears finally erupted from her eyes.

"You may know nothing about me, but you would be surprised how much I know about you, Tendra Sumenel. We have been watching you for quite some time. You are one of the key players in this story. And your actions this night will determine the ultimate ending of this tale. Do you understand?"

"Go away." She said wearily. "Just go away."

"Close your eyes. Count to three. And then move. You have one chance to save a life."

"Whose life?" Tendra watched as the man rose from his chair, turned and began to walk away. "Whose life?" she called, running after him, as he turned away from her and walked into the darkness, but no matter how fast she ran, he kept growing smaller and smaller until he vanished all together. She closed her eyes and began to count. A cold draft of air wafted across her skin and she awoke with a shiver.

"Tendra?" Jonathon sat cradling her head on the ground. "Are you okay?" Tendra looked up into his eyes and blinked heavily.

"I'm...I'm fine." She tried to push herself up from the ground.

"No, no you're not. You've been out cold for five minutes."

"I said, I'm fine, Jonathon. But, there is something I have to do." She rolled over, out of his lap, and pushed herself up from the ground. She felt the blackness encroach upon her vision, but she fought it off and ran down the stairs.

She pushed the hood of the robe back from her face, as she ran. After an what seemed like an eternity of running, she found herself once again at the door to Jakob's room. *The hidden passageways. They would be quicker.* She paused before entering into the room. Everything was cold and dark, with only the faintest shimmer of moonlight to illuminate the room. She took one step forward, haltingly, and then a second. She thought back to

305

when she and Jakob and Jonathon had first discovered them. They had spent days exploring all of them...together.

Tendra forced herself to come back from her memories, grabbed the handles of the wardrobe in the corner of the room, and ripped the doors open. She scrambled to the floor, running her hands over the smooth wood before finding the small bronze ring. She pulled the cover off and slipped down onto the ladder. She didn't even bother pulling the cover behind her as she worked her way down the rungs as quickly as she could. She took off, sprinting through the stone corridors. As she went, she counted doors. At the eighteenth door, she slowed down to catch her breath. It took her a few moments to bring her breathing under control. She couldn't risk Rowen fleeing before she spoke with him.

She quietly pushed the door open and crept out into the darkness. The moon was just a sliver in the night sky and it shone down with scarcely any light at all. She made sure to close the door behind her, and she moved stealthily over to the stables, which were just as dark as the night.

"Easy, easy girl," a voice whispered, Rowen's voice. Tendra slipped into the stables and made her way towards him. He had pulled one of the horses out of her stall and was saddling her up. He had his staff and sword slung across his back. "Shhhh," he said, running a hand along the horse's mane.

"What are you doing?" She asked. Her voice was shaky and hoarse. Rowen whirled around.

"Your brother?" He asked.

"He is within Supremor's embrace now."

Rowen nodded. "My brothers are preparing their final assault, and I was readying my horse. I have to leave tonight if I am to make it there in time."

"Why are you leaving? The people need you. You give them hope. You cannot leave. You were just going to leave in the middle of the night. the middle of tonight?" She whispered. She felt Rowen's arms wrap around her in an embrace.

"I'm sorry. But I have to be there or else my brothers will die." Tendra thought about the red man and what he had said before swallowing and pushing him away.

"You can't," she said.

"I have to," he replied. "If I stay I'm putting my whole family at risk."

"What about my family?" she shot back. Rowen looked at her. "What if they try again? Who will protect me then?" Rowen placed one foot on the stirrup and swung himself up onto the horse. He pulled one of his daggers and its sheath from his belt and held it out for her. The briefest of sparks ran between her skin and his when they touched. Tendra felt the energy pass through him into her.

"You don't need me to protect you. You're stronger than you know. I'll be back. I won't leave you alone. I promise."

"What's her name?" She asked.

"Heart..." he said simply, "...and it belongs to you." Rowen's eyes gleamed, and he kicked the horse and rode out of the open stable doors into the night. Tendra watched him go, and when she could no longer see him, she closed her eyes and listened to the clacking of the hooves on the cobblestones of the road all the way down to the gate.

"Then go." She whispered. "Go, save your family. I will still be here when you get back." The city was silent that night, and all she could hear was a knight leaving her alone in the darkness.

On The Precipice of Chaos
Twenty-Four

"This campaign could not be going any better," Qel said with a hearty laugh. "Our forces in the south have reported that Gnashcon is all but sacked. Charon has been deserted and Feram, well, Feram will fall in due time. But now we can attack Long Fang directly." He was right. It had been a whirlwind since the Face Off. I could scarcely believe it had been almost two months since then. After the centaurs had prevented the destruction of the bridges across the Rope River, the centaur army had been able to march in to the Kingdom of Fangs from the west while the Hammer attacked from the south and west. The feral army had been on the run since the very first day, and now they were cornered. Only two cities remained of the once large kingdom.

But these two cities would be devastating to sack. I sighed in frustration. He just wasn't listening.

"You may have swept through the Kingdom of Fangs easily enough, but Feram and Long Fang won't fall so simply. They are the largest strongholds in the nation, and whoever is now in charge knows this. He's smart...he knows that he can't beat us in the open field, so he retreated to where he has the advantage: in his cities. The cost to take either of them will be catastrophic."

"But they must be taken," Qel replied.

"I agree," Jeronious chimed in. The leaders of the two races and their war advisors, as well as Joven and I, were all standing around a table with a map of Carin laid out before us. It was a Crown's map, and we had set up the forces of the unu, centaurs and ferals as best we could estimate. "We lost three thousand centaurs at the Battle of Yumon alone. That is unacceptable."

"And we lost twelve hundred unu at the ford." Gorn of the White Pike Clan, one of Qel's warmasters chimed in.

"You will lose ten times that taking Long Fang." I replied. "If you are fortunate." I said.

"There have been loses on all sides," Joven said, stepping in, "nevertheless, we are making good progress. What about hostages? Jeronious? Your men, sweeping down from Gnashcon, must have picked off some stragglers...women, children, the old or sick?" Joven asked, fishing. Jeronious shook his head.

"No. I gave orders that every feral was to be eradicated on sight...no quarter given." Jeronious replied.

Wow, he used a word with more than two syllables...impressive, I thought dryly.

"So, what now?" Joven asked. "Do we just storm the gates? Throw enough bodies at the city walls and pray they come down?"

310

"We were hoping that the wizards would have something that they could use to help us get into the city." Qel said, looking back and forth between Joven and me. Joven looked at me, and I nodded.

"Yes," Joven said. Joven turned back to the rest of the assembled members of our council. "We have something that can open the gates for you. We will need a few days to prepare."

"You have four. That is when the rest of our forces will arrive here at Long Fang. After we take the citadel, we will move on to Feram. It will be an easy conquest after their spirit has been broken," Qel said with a smile.

"The centaur forces from the north will maintain an interdiction around Feram to prevent any attempt to escape." Jeronious said.

"Excellent. Is there nothing else?" Joven asked. When nothing was immediately forthcoming, Joven and I bowed and walked out.

"This is happening fast, Joven," I muttered as we walked through the myriad of tents. "Too fast. The ferals are barely putting up a fight. Why? What is going on?"

"I don't know." Joven said curtly. "But I suspect that we are being played, in more ways than one."

"I sense the same. Has Rowen arrived?" Joven shook his head.

"He'll be here in three days. Jakob's funeral is today, and he'll leave soon after." I cursed silently to myself.

"That's ahead of schedule." I said quietly.

"I know. Someone beat us to it."

"Vizien?" I asked.

"Most likely. We knew he'd be a problem, just not this much of a problem this soon." I mulled this over, as we walked. "We'll have Rowen kill him upon his return." Joven said.

"Do we need Rowen here?" I asked. "Can he remain in Gemport? Rowen working on Tendra is important, very important. Can we spare him?"

"Not if we are going to use Disparity. We don't have anything else that will bring down the gates. And the Shatterpoint is close. I'd feel a lot more comfortable if we had him here. Six targets are better than five." We walked through the barrage of tents, each bearing the crest of the clan or family to which they belonged. The rows of tents extended out seemingly forever, and I smiled at just how well our plan had worked thus far. Three months, and look what we had accomplished.

"Alright, call Rowen in." I said, brooding. "It isn't ideal, but we will have to make do. We just have to make sure that he is back there quick." Joven nodded. I pushed my way into our tent and saw the others look up.

"Gentlemen." I said.

"Gentlemen? Does that mean your meeting went poorly?" Rayn asked.

"It went fine." Joven said. "Rayn, I need you and Dorian to go and get the materials for Disparity." Dorian nodded, and Rayn immediately stood up. "And, I shouldn't have to tell you this, but do whatever you must to make sure you aren't followed-full liberties." Dorian nodded, looking up from his whetstone, which he was rubbing across his blade.

"As you wish." Dorian rose from his chair and followed Rayn out of the tent.

"Aurum, how are things progressing with Dane?"

"He's fully on our side. When the Shatterpoint comes, he'll stand with us." I replied.

"Excellent! Grey, Disparity is your area of expertise, so you're on point. Whatever you need from us, you have it."

"Finally, I get to do something. Aurum's been stealing the spotlight. We might as well just be background characters in his grand ballad," Grey said, punching me on the shoulder playfully.

"Well, I can't help it if you guys are just too lazy to make it out to the fun," I replied with a smile.

"Alright, Aurum, thank you so much for volunteering yourself. We wouldn't want you to get too lazy after all. You'd lose that muscular stone-wall figure that women just find so attractive" Grey said mockingly. "So, come on," He lifted a bow and arrow and held them up. He pushed himself by Joven and me.

"I'll be along in a minute, Grey. I need to speak with Joven."

"Whatever," Grey called out flippantly over his shoulder.

"Have you heard from Rikard?" I asked.

"He is in position and made contact with Breva in Ornus three week after he left us. Since then, he says that he continues his preparations. The Feast of Bejor is in just over a month, and he says he'll be ready." I nodded in satisfaction. Outside of a few minor hitches, the plan was going perfectly. Dorian's wife Breva would keep Rikard safe until we could make our move in Ornus. This would work.

"Alright, I'll go help Grey with his measurements. It shouldn't take too long." I pushed the flap of our tent back open and walked out along the encampment.

I saw Grey out on the fields between our encampment and Long Fang. There were some forty thousand troops, with another ten thousand on the other side of The Heart ready to attack Long Fang. The city sat at the crux of three rivers: The Rope, The Heart and The Rope. Another ten thousand unu were on their way from the south. This battle would be a bloodbath. I knew that at least half of them would be killed. Fifteen percent of that, before we even made it to the gates, from catapults and arrow barrages. Ferals used nasty barb arrows that were dipped in poison, so even the smallest of wounds would lead to death. They were getting desperate and with good reason.

We made our way closer and closer to Long Fang, until we were almost within arrow distance. The ferals wouldn't waste a ballista bolt or catapult ammunition on two random humans. Grey handed me the bow and arrow.

"Fire this at the gate to see how close you can get." I shrugged, nocked an arrow to the string, raised the bow, and fired. We watched as the arrow went sailing forward and landed about thirty feet before the gate. Grey nodded approvingly. "Good Enough! Now, turn ninety degrees to your right and fire it again. Same pull, same angle." I nodded and once again, I raised the bow, pulling back to my cheek and fired. "Don't move or I'll stab you in the throat." Grey said.

"Fair enough. Seems a little excessive," I muttered, standing still. Grey walked up to me and began making long sweeping strides toward where the second arrow had landed. I stood there watching him take his measurements. I knew that it was necessary, but it was still funny to watch him work nevertheless.

"Are you laughing at me?" Grey suddenly said, whirling around in mid-stride.

"Yes."

"By Supremor, he truly has developed a sense of humor. Supremor be praised!"

"Just keep walking. You're keeping me from dinner."

"Perish the thought," he called out. He arrived at the arrow, picked it up, and walked back to me. "Alright, I got this one, now you go get that one." He said, tossing his head toward Long Fang.

"Very funny. What's the damage?"

"We are going to have to be within arrow range to make this work."

"Dreadspawn," I cursed. "How far?"

"Well," he said scratching his head, "about forty-five, fifty feet."

"We'll be wounded deer. We'll be slaughtered. There is no way they will allow us to come that close and cast. They will empty coffers of arrows if it means killing us."

"Isn't that great?"

"Go mark our spot, and I'll think of something to keep them off our backs while we cast."

"Oh, thanks! I always wanted to get shot full of arrows. It's just what I always wanted. You're so kind to me on my birthday."

"Wait. It's your birthday?" I asked, taken aback.

"No, I just wanted to make you feel extra bad," he said with a smile. I picked up a stone and threw it at him. It missed right, and Grey watched it go by. "Remind me not to recommend to Joven that you provide range support." He turned and kept pacing towards the city. He made it about forty feet when the first arrows began to sail towards him.

"Hurry up, Grey," I called. He took four more steps. "Grey!" He didn't speed up though. He merely kept stepping. I saw black lines in the sky as arrows rained down. Grey stabbed his marker into the ground, turned, and started sprinting back. An arrow caught him in the back, but it bounced harmlessly off the mail. Grey had his hands held up to cover his head. A last arrow came flying down towards him and hit him in the calf Just as he made it back to me. The impact caused him to stumble, but I grabbed him and held him up.

"Don't move!" I told him. I bent down and looked at his leg. There was a hole in the robe, but the mail had done its job. I breathed a sigh of relief.

"Alright, you're fine."

"You could have just asked." Grey replied. "Now, we wait for Rayn and Dorian so I can make the alignments." We began to walk back towards the tent.

"That's it?" I asked.

"Yeah, why?"

"I just thought we had more setup that needed to be done."

"Like I said, not until Rayn and Dorian get back." Grey responded. "Until then, we just have to figure out how we can stay under cover until we are ready to cast." As we passed by, the centaurs bowed to us. It was still slightly disconcerting, but it brought with it a feeling of elation and power. It caused me to stand a little bit straighter and hold my head up just a little bit higher.

"Are you practicing your hero's walk or what?" Grey asked me, chuckling. I didn't reply, but tried to think. As we moved through the camp toward where the fires were roasting meat for the evening meal, I felt a shadow pass over me. I looked to my right and saw the answer to our problem.

"Well, that was easier than I thought it would be."

*   *   *

"This is bloody brilliant," Dorian muttered under his breath.

"Quiet," Joven said. The six of us stood within the shadow of the siege tower. The unu stood watching us in a mixture of confusion and awe. We stood in a semicircle with Grey at the focal point. Before us rested a glass ball upon a staff, and I took a deep breath. We had never tried anything this big, and Grey had been working tirelessly the last two days to make sure that everything was precisely right. We had very few spells designed

316

for this kind of work. It had actually been Grey's idea to have some really big ones. He was the historian after all, and he knew the value of breaking a siege quickly.

"You all know the words. We have only one shot at this, so make sure you get it right."

"On my mark, begin to move the siege tower." Grey called out to the unu.

"As you wish," Tyr, the head of the unu manning the siege tower, replied. We all had our staffs in hand and were ready to go.

"Mark!" Grey said calmly. There was none of the usual playfulness in his tone: this was all business. The siege tower that blocked our view of the gates of Long Fang began to slowly pull away. The early morning sunlight began to play across our faces, Rowen first, then Grey, followed by myself, Joven, Dorian, and Rayn.

"One." We raised our staffs straight up into the air.

"Two." I blinked and let out one last breath.

"Three."

"Seamonish Seolasticira," we chanted, "Terfim Yzneckronon. Hogun. Viv Ia." As the last word left our lips, we brought our staffs down parallel to the ground and pointed straight into the crystal ball. Beams of light flew from the tops of our staffs, and the ball glowed with a red fire as the six beams coalesced into one, and it shot forward into the gates. The stone of the gates glowed and began to smoke as the stone turned to air and the light from our staffs extinguished. Where once had stood solid stone, now stood a massive hole at the bottom of the gates. The entire world grew silent. The stench of fear was everywhere, on both sides of the battlefield.

"Go!" A voice screamed out. I found myself being pulled from the ground by a centaur while arrows rained down and was whisked away to one of the siege towers as they

creaked, groaned and were pushed forward. A stone from a catapult shattered the tower to our right sending debris cascading
down behind us.

"Are you okay?" Dane asked as we arrived behind the
cover of our siege tower. "Are you okay?" he asked me again.
He helped me down onto the ground where I collapsed.

"Yes, yes, I am alright. I just…need to catch my breath."
I replied, taking a deep breath. Joven and his mount arrived right
next to us.

"That-that was incredible, Aurum." Dane said. I paid no
attention to him; I merely looked over at Joven. His face was one
of relief. I looked up as I heard the impacts of flaming arrows
upon our tower.

"Are we going up?" I asked. Joven nodded. "At the
front?"

"How big of a death wish do you have, Aurum?" Joven
asked. I started laughing and couldn't stop. Dane stared at me
with a concerned expression on his face.

"Aurum?" he asked questioningly. "Are you okay?" I
looked up at him. Then, I looked over and saw our army of centaurs sprinting forwards toward our new entrance. Beyond them,
I saw eighteen siege towers being pushed forward along with a
stream of hundreds of unu behind, waiting to rush up the stairs
and into battle. I reached up my hand, and Dane pulled me to my
feet.

"It's perfect." I replied. "Let's go!" I pulled myself onto
Dane's back and we took our place behind the siege tower, walking slowly as it advanced. The pounding hooves sent a shiver
down my spine.

"Are you ready for this?" Dane asked.

"It's a good day to die," I said, "but an even better day to
live."

Angles of Angels

Twenty-Five

The feel of the wind streaming through his face sent a chill down Galeerial's spine. The exhilaration...it was a drug to his system. He had never felt more alive. He smiled at the irony. Galeerial spread his body out behind him in an arrow and just let himself fall down.

Down.

Down.

He knew that he had about twelve seconds left to live. He tried to take a breath, but the air flying past him made it difficult. Instead, he just relaxed his body and waited for the inevitable. He looked down and saw the ground approaching beneath him through tears eyes. He took a deep breath.

This was it.

The force impacted his body in a direction that he had not anticipated: horizontally. The force of the collision expelled the rest of the air in his lungs, and he felt his chest constrict as his ribs cracked. The sharp pain barely registered to Galeerial.

Galeerial felt himself be lifted into the air and then flatten out while Gabriel shed momentum. But, it wasn't enough and they crashed into the earth. Galeerial landed hard on his right shoulder. The pain of impact ran up his arm, but he ignored it. He twisted to avoid landing on his head as he bounced off the ground.

"Are you insane?" Gabriel screamed.

"Perhaps..." Galeerial simply replied, dusting himself off and rising to his feet, "...perhaps that is why all of this is happening. Maybe I am crazy."

"But, still Galeerial, do you want to be damned? You know what *The Stone* says about suicide. You may have lost the Aer, but you have not lost your soul. But if you kill yourself, you will. This is not the answer. This is not an escape."

"How dare you!" Galeerial walked towards him and grabbed him by the collar with both hands. "How dare you? I know *The Stone*-every verse and every line. I have lived The Word for over half a millennium. Tell me what kind of god would do this? He sent me to hell and then tempted me with salvation-let me taste it before snatching it away. I have lost everything. What sane man could endure the things that I have endured? Why should I not despair? I have lost everything," He bellowed. "There is nothing left of me," Galeerial said wearily.

"If you truly wanted to die, you would have waited until I wasn't there to catch you." Galeerial threw his head forward and slammed it into Gabriel's face letting his hands go simultaneously. Gabriel stumbled backward and fell to the ground, and Galeerial pounced on top of him. His hands were

320

balled so tightly the nails dug into the flesh of his palms. He ached with so much pain and sorrow.

"Get off of me, Galeerial," Gabriel said. There was an edge to his voice that made Galeerial pause. It felt like he was taking his first breath since the fall. Slowly, Galeerial rose off the man, and faced the dying sunlight.

"What happened to me?" Galeerial asked.

"The Wither did something to you. We do not know what he did, but your Aer was gone by the time I reached you. I am sorry. I tried to stop you from speaking to the Clerics because I did not want you to find out."

"Don't you think that I would have found out when I drank from the Charist in a few days' time? Oh yes, then I would have found out as my body shriveled to dust."

"You are right, I did not think it through. I knew you would despair. But there is something that you should know-something that may give you comfort."

"What could possibly do that?" Galeerial asked, staring blankly at the horizon. Twilight was descending upon the world. The sun glowed brilliantly as it fell beyond the Rift Mountains. The sky was enthroned in a cascade of gold, bronze, and crimson. A crown of clouds erupted into a brilliance of maroon when the rays hit it just right. It was beautiful.

"Galeerial, the last Skyguard who lost the Aer...you know his name well."

"And, what would that name be, Galeerial Risenstar perhaps? My namesake? Or, perhaps Gabriel, the firstborn Skyguard, your own namesake? I'm tired of your lies." He asked bitterly.

"No, it was neither of those, but rather a name enshrined in human history that really belongs in Skyguard. Geraldean the Hero." Galeerial let out a sharp bark of laughter. "Think,

321

Galeerial. How else could he withstand the entire army of The Dread? Why else would he wield the sword Shineheart?"

"And, why would that give me comfort?"

"Because Geraldean's name is revered in the history books. And yours can be too. But, even more than that, there is a chance that your name will surpass his. There is a way for you to get your Aer back." Galeerial turned slowly around.

"Speak, Galeerial said quietly.

"It is the secret of the Skyguard, and I will not utter it here. Not in this unprotected place. Just know that you must go back to Cloud Breach."

"The High Clerics will imprison me before I get ten paces into the city. I will rot in the stone cells as a Forsworn before anyone will hear me out."

"They will listen because you will carry this." Galeerial heard the sound of metal on metal and he turned around to Gabriel, who stood holding a blue blade before him. The blade shone in the waning sunlight and radiated the color back out in a holy sheen that showered over Galeerial's face.

"Behold, Eon, the Sword of Time. It is yours now." Galeerial stared at him as Gabriel rotated the sword in his hands, extending the hilt to him.

"HAHAHA!" Galeerial burst out laughing. "You must be joking."

"Galeerial, I have never been more serious in my entire life." Their eyes met, and Galeerial grew somber.

"The last Skyguard who wielded one of the Cardinal Swords hewed my wings with it. Why do you have it, Gabriel? You aren't a Lord Commander." Galeerial slowly began to circle around Gabriel.

"You can answer that yourself." Gabriel said. Galeerial stared at him.

"No..." Galeerial said, shaking his head. "...this is just some twisted trick, and I won't have it." Pieces coalesced in his mind. There was no reason Gabriel should have been allowed to stay, much less confer with the clerics. Not if he was just some Ranger like his clothing suggested. The Skyguard had a hierarchy. There were the common Skyguard, then Lord Commanders, then clerics, and above all the clerics there was one: a Supreme Cleric. The identity of the Supreme Cleric was kept secret to the common Skyguard and known only to the clerics except in times of great crisis. At any time the mantle could be passed. The Supreme Cleric had the right to carry a Cardinal Sword, and he also carried the Five Eye. The Five Eye which could sense a beings true nature.

"This is no trick, Galeerial. No more lies. Doubt has seeped into your mind. Its claws have dug deep into your soul. Do not-do not let it destroy you. You are a good man, Galeerial. Be strong." Galeerial turned away from Gabriel.

"You're wrong ,Gabriel-wrong about it all. I have only my vengeance. If giving me that sword will give me vengeance, then that is all I ask." Galeerial began to hear muttering and his blood-blood he never had before-grew cold.

"Karo nise feonasira, tero ben jemonisira, sibenodin uvielel."

"No!" Galeerial turned and leapt at Gabriel, who flipped the blade around and hit him with the flat of the blade.

"By the Writ of Madian, you are now bound to the Skyguard. Your life is no longer your own. By the rule of Supremor, you are now chained to your duty. Your duty as Supreme Cleric."

"You can't do that!" Galeerial shouted. "Only the Supreme Cleric can do that!" Gabriel sighed. He reached up to his right breast and undid the right side of his tunic and pulled back the cover. He reinserted Eon back into its sheath on his back and pulled open the interior clothe. Galeerial's eyes were drawn immediately to the blue gem that hung around his neck.

"The Five Eye," Galeerial breathed. He had seen it once before. When he had been only a hundred years old.

"Yes. Now do you understand? Do you comprehend all that you now are?"

"What have you done?"

"I have given you purpose; I have given you focus. Your vengeance is nothing. Your life is no longer your own. You belong to the Skyguard." Gabriel swept his hand in front of him. "That path leads to damnation. I have done all I can for you, Galeerial. Your path now lies to the north." Gabriel reached his hands behind his neck and unfastened the gem. "This now belongs to you...as does this." Gabriel pulled the sheath and the sword from his back and stretched them out to Galeerial.

"I didn't want this." Galeerial said.

"I know." Gabriel said, nodding, "but your reluctance will give you restraint."

"I'm no longer a Skyguard."

"And, that is why you have the potential to be the greatest Supreme Cleric that has ever been. You have something to live for, and you are unbound by the limitations of our race," Gabriel said.

"Why are you doing this to me?" Galeerial asked.

"Because, just as *The Sarenatas* say, no Skyguard is beyond saving. There is redemption for you at Cloud Breach. But, go for justice, not for vengeance."

"I don't know how to use this blade." Galeerial grasped for excuses and questions to hurl against Gabriel like a starving man groped for food. Gabriel pondered this for a moment.

"You have one month. In one month we will bring Veriel to justice. During that time, we will investigate the Lord

Commander. We will send word to Cloud Breach and keep Veriel under surveillance."

"What should I do until then? Sit here at Soaring, waiting?" Galeerial asked. Gabriel shook his head.

"You will find no peace here. Only resentment," Gabriel said.

"What then?" Galeerial asked. Gabriel considered this.

"Go north. Seek the Seven."

"The Seven? Why?" Galeerial responded.

"Control. Serenity. Acceptance. They will help you get through this, and they can teach you how to use the blade."

"Shineheart was lost a thousand years ago."

"Then you must find it." Gabriel replied, simply.

"Where can I find them?"

"Long Fang. But, I believe that you will need this." Gabriel whistled loudly. Galeerial looked around. "Just wait." Within moments, Galeerial saw a horse trotting toward them. It was the horse that he had ridden here from Gemport. "I had a feeling that you might need something like this. Go to the wizards now. Veriel is powerful, and you will need powerful allies to defeat him., Seek out Aurum. He is the leader, despite what Joven says. He will help you, as will the others. Tell him that the king is now in his court. He will understand what that means, but if you cannot reach him, then it is because his destiny lies in Arestephan's hands. And whatever happens, do not be afraid."

"I don't know what that means." Galeerial said. At that Gabriel finally smiled.

"Supremor is watching all of this. It is not by accident that we met, nor is it purely by fate." Gabriel replied. "Great change is upon you. You can become something great, Galeerial."

"I am not a warrior, but I will learn to kill a thousand if it means that I can kill one." Galeerial said looking at the blade.

"Do not kill for vengeance. Kill for justice." Gabriel replied.

"I cannot promise you anything."

"No man is perfect; all I ask is that you try."

Galeerial stepped forward and began to run his hands along the horse's neck and down to its saddle, which held two curved scimitars. He pulled them from their sheaths and found them to be exactly equal in length from his elbow to his hand. He replaced them into their sheaths.

"Why won't you tell me what I must do?" Galeerial said, swinging himself unsteadily up onto the horse.

"Because the path of faith is something all beings must find for themselves. The doubting heart will be your end. Now ride," Gabriel paused. "My Lord." He said before going down upon one knee.

"Rise! I don't do this for you." Galeerial said simply. Gabriel nodded in reply.

"Not yet...now ride!" Gabriel called, and the horse sprang forward. Galeerial held on tightly to the reigns as he felt the horse's body ebb and flow and buck and weave.

He rode through the night, and the horse kept up a relentless pace. Galeerial still felt slightly uncomfortable riding on the horse-the way he was buoyed about by something completely out of his own power, like flying through a hurricane. He saw bands of unu marching southward, and he flew by them without a second thought. They cast arrows at him, yet not a single one touched the horse. It was as if there was an aura of protection around him. Nothing would keep him from Long Fang.

His eyes began to grow weary as the night pressed on and on. He finally succumbed to their temptation when the first rays of daylight peeked over the horizon.

Galeerial unfolded the blanket that had been packed in the saddle, ate some of the bread and cold meat that was wrapped in it, and then fell into a dreamless sleep that he awoke from a few hours later, just as the sun hit its apex in the sky.

Galeerial emitted a yawn before rising. His legs were sore and chafed from the horse, but he merely stepped back up onto the horse and urged it on. Pain held no chains for him anymore. The afternoon stretched on, and Galeerial began to see the form of a castle taking shape in the distance.

Galeerial squinted. He was no longer blessed with the perfect vision of the Skyguard; he had human eyes now, and they were a poor replacement. At first, it appeared that the sun's rays were being bounced back and forth, but Galeerial slowly realized with horror what was occurring. Long Fang was burning.

"NO!" He screamed. He urged the horse on as all thoughts of sleep were driven from his mind. He was too late. No, he wasn't too late. He would make it.

He had to make it.

Surge
Twenty-Six

Blood sprayed into my vision, and I reached my hand up and wiped it from my eyes. The sparse stone city of Long Fang spread out before me. It was the third day of the battle, and it was the first time that we had managed to gain a staging ground in the city. The first two days resulted in massive losses, as we tried to flood into the city using Qel's siege towers. Twice we had been completely repulsed and had been forced to pull the towers back rather than risk them being toppled onto our troops. A thick strip of blood dripped down off of Widower's Wrath, as I ripped it free from the gullet of a feral soldier. They just kept on coming. It was deathly hot.

Bonfires of bodies littered the top of the battlements-feral, unu, and centaur alike. On the first day, Dorian had been

329

hit with a ballista bolt off a ricochet that had collapsed his armor, yet even that had not put him out of commission. However, the arrow that ripped through the flimsy centaur replacement armor did. He was healing in the tents of the unu. Joven didn't like that at all. We would be making our move soon, and we couldn't afford to have any of us wounded when that confrontation arose.

I saw Rayn firing lightning bolts at a series of archers that had been harassing us all morning. I caught an arrow in my leg, but my mail managed to blunt the majority of the damage.

"Aurum!" Qel bellowed. I whipped my head around and saw him and his elite guard, the unum, fighting toward the castle, down the main causeway of the town. I shook my head.

"Idiot," I muttered. "Joven!" I shouted, gesturing wildly towards the rooftops on either side of Qel. He nodded. I backed up against the outer edge of the wall, took off running, and hurled myself to the rooftops, just as three ferals arrived atop the wall to engage me. An explosion greeted them and it helped propel me the fifteen feet to the neighboring building.

I landed hard, dropping quickly into a roll, and took off running. Feral archers gathered on the rooftops and were busily focused on raining down arrows on the unu soldiers...and doing a good job of it. Qel and his men were pinned down, but not for long.

I watched as Joven mirrored his movements to mine. We were silver streaks in our mail across the rooftops, cutting down feral after feral as we leapt from building to building. I jumped again and landed on the last building in the row before the city turned upward to the citadel. Six ferals greeted me with swords drawn. I merely kept running. I threw my hand out murmuring my word-weapons, and all six of them went flying off of the rooftop from the force of the magic to land twenty-five feet below, where the centaurs and unu could finish them off.

330

I checked to make sure Joven was keeping pace. The ferals were not the best warriors, but their numbers were staggering. Even after the battles that we fought at the Face Off, the Ford, across the Kingdom, and the three days of fighting that they had endured here, their numbers were still beyond count. The next gap was too far for me to jump, so I began to climb carefully down the side of the stone building to the surface.

I wound my way carefully down the vertical surface, until I was about ten feet up and dropped to the ground. As I landed on the ground, a boulder hurtled over my head and crashed into the building that I had just vacated. Stone crashed around me, and I leapt out of the way, barely avoiding being crushed. *What was that?* I ran out of the alley way to see Qel and his warriors breaking in the doors and entering into the houses one by one. Stones continued to fly over our head.

"What in Garen's name are you doing, Qel?"

"What are you talking about?" he said calmly.

"Why are the catapults firing at us? They know that we're in here," I yelled back at him.

"Those aren't ours." I opened my mouth and then closed it again. The ferals were bombing their own city.

"The centaurs are on their way to the castle. A charge went by just before you gave us higher ground support. About seventy of them went," Qel informed me. "We're searching every building. We don't want a Jamon's Victory." I shook my head. "We're going to make sure every one of these beasts is dead."

"Joven and I are going up to the palace...are you coming?" I asked. Qel looked at his guard.

"Yes, I want to be there to see Fashnar beg." Fashnar was the new leader of the ferals. None of us had seen him, but he had sent an emissary the first day the Hammer had set up camp outside the city. He spoke quietly to his own men while I watched the outside. This was it. We were so close to victory.

"Qel!" I barked. He turned back to me. "Let's go!" I ventured out from the store without even looking back for him. Joven caught my intent and started his own sprint up the street. We rounded the corner to the final stretch up to the palace, and I saw carnage before me. Everything was alight with fires that the centaurs had ignited on their desperate charge for the palace, and the massacred bodies of ferals and centaurs alike littered the streets. The street was slick with blood-not just slick, but a veritable river was flowing down from the palace, where the slaughtered bodies of ferals and centaurs lay. This was impossible. *How could there be this much blood?* I scanned up near the palace and saw giant vats with spigots on the front. They had been collecting blood. I swallowed. To the end of my days I knew that I would never forget that sight.

I hit the blood-filled street head on, and my feet immediately slid out from under me, and I crashed to the ground. I was barely able to get my sword out of the way or else I would have been impaled. I spat out some blood that had found its way into my mouth and moved my way over to the side of the street. This was the only way to the city gates. There were no more side streets, no more alleyways; just a single road and a single solid stretch of buildings. I grasped the doorframe of the first building, using it to hold myself up on the slick road. I slowly began to climb my way up the street. I looked back at Qel, who has looking at me incredulously.

"The only other way is to climb twenty-five feet straight up and then straight back down at the end." He grimaced.

"This will be one to tell the children, eh, Aurum?" Joven called to me. That was the code phrase. *The time was approaching.* This was bad. Dorian was still injured. If Joven was saying this now, it meant that he thought we could take the capital today.

"Indeed, they will never in a thousand years believe it." I shouted back across the street to him. An arrow flew by my face, and I looked back to see a group of feral archers desperately firing arrows at us as we ascended

"I got them!" Joven hollered. I watched as he pulled both feet up to the stone wall and pushed off the wall into the middle of the street. He slid on his back down the bloody road like he was on a snow slope. He thrust his dagger out to slow him, causing sparks to shoot out in his wake, and came up running at the bottom of the blood river. *And he called me crazy.*

I pulled myself up the last stretch of the way onto dry ground and helped Qel and his three remaining unum the rest of the way. I moved forward cautiously. The doors had been cast open, but that didn't mean anything. I peered within and saw a prototypical castle. The throne room was directly ahead, and off of it led several corridors. Sitting in a throne amidst the surrounding cacophony of battle was a massive feral who had to be Fashnar. There were corpses all around him: ally and enemy alike.

"Go, go, go!" I said, as I threw my hand out and went flying across the room toward one of the pillars where two centaurs were under attack by twelve ferals. Qel and his unum moved into the killing fields. There were seven centaurs left fighting and they were quickly being overwhelmed. One went down with a spear thrust to the chest. The feral on the other end of that spear was the first one of the group to die: I hurled one of my daggers forward, and it stuck in its gullet.

"Run!" I shouted quickly, and the centaur wheeled about and leapt out of the way. "Frostbite!" I screamed, throwing my hand forward. The air exploded in a fountain of gas as a blast of cold air hit me, and the entire group was engulfed in ice. One sweep of my newly unsheathed blade was enough to shatter them into a flurry of ice shards. The lone surviving centaur, to my surprise, was Dane.

"Impeccable timing," he said with a smile. I reached down and grabbed my dagger. It was ice cold and almost burned my hand as I quickly sheathed it.

"Mage!" I turned and saw the massive feral twist the head off an unu, and watched the body fall to the ground as the feral leader raised the head to his snout and drank the blood dripping off of it. The voice was deep, guttural and intimidating: pretty much the opposite of Kaelish. "I am Fashnar, and I am your end." I gaped. *This was Fashnar?*

The emissaries from Fashnar had told of his size. He was a berserker, a genetic offshoot of the ferals that sprouted up periodically throughout history only to have the genes recess. As far as we knew, Fashnar was the only one of his kind at the moment, but often one was the herald of many. This was the third of Kaelish's generals. He wore two spiked gauntlets on his hands and carried a trident in his right hand. On his head, he wore a helm with three horns: one to the front, and one to each of the sides. He stepped down onto the floor, and he made even Qel look small.

"You want a fight? I'll give you a war." I said. There was a flash of hair and flesh and the blur of the room, before I came crashing back down to earth. I sat up in a daze the world spinning around me. I saw Qel smash Fashnar with both of his hammers, but the monstrous feral merely shrugged them off and proceeded to pummel into Qel. I saw the red blood as the spiked gauntlets tore holes into Qel's flesh. Dane worked his hand and a half sword into its back before it turned with its trident and fended him off into a retreat.

"Alright, let's do this." I replaced Widower's Wrath and ripped a strip of cloth from the clothes of one of the dead ferals at my feet, wrapping it around my hand before pulling Dream and Havoc from their moorings. I could feel the numbing cold even through the cloth. I ran forward to where Qel and Fashnar were dueling. I dropped to the ground and slid beneath Fashnar's legs, reaching out and slicing his feet as I did. He howled in pain. The blood, all over my mail, made me smooth enough to keep on sliding. I leapt up to my feet and spun around. I sprinted forward and jumped up onto his back, digging my daggers deep into the flesh. I tried to pull myself up to his head, but a large clawed hand reached back and plucked me off.

Once again, I found myself flying across the room, though this time it was a stone wall that halted my trajectory. I collapsed to the ground in pain. My mail had absorbed much of the blow, but my ears were ringing, and my back felt like someone had been dropping boulders upon it. I rose unsteadily to my feet.

Fashnar reached back to pull one of the knives from his back and hurled it at me. I dove to the ground and landed lightly on my hands. I heard a shattering sound, and shrapnel rained down around me. I pushed myself back up to my feet and looked around. Pieces of metal lay strewn about me. I saw a shard of metal on the ground with blue lettering. I reached down to pick it up, ignoring Qel's screams for help. It was Dream!

I let out a halted laugh. *Was it really that simple?* I shook my head in disbelief.

"Aurum!" Qel bellowed at me. I turned back and saw the unu being lifted from the ground, held by his two arms, his face contorted into a mask of horror. Dane moved in again, and I saw Fashnar whip Qel around and slam him into the centaur.

I ripped Widower's Wrath from my back and sprinted forward. I needed Qel alive for a little while longer. I had to be the one to kill him. *Great.* I was looking forward to another round with this thing.

335

Qel screamed as Fashnar ripped the unu's right arm off. *By Supremor*! My breath caught in my throat. The unu fell heavily to the floor, blood spilling to the ground. I ran forward and slashed at Fashnar's left arm before disengaging. His snarling face turned to me, and I saw his eyes glowing blood red. I cursed as it gnashed its teeth at me, and I rolled away. He cast the arm to the side and charged at me, claws at fully extended. I took off running toward one of the walls. I raised my right hand, dragging Widower's Wrath on the ground, causing sparks to fly in my wake.

I sprinted forward and flew up the wall about ten feet off of the ground. I still had to leap to make it over Fashnar's lowered head. I pushed off with my legs and flew over him. I pulled my left hand together with my right and slammed the blade forward into the back of the beast's head, as it slammed into the stone walls of the castle.

"Push!" I screamed, and the blade leapt forward from my grip slicing right through the beast's open mouth and embedding itself in the stone. I landed hard and fell into a roll. I sprang backwards into a flip back to my feet. I saw Qel lying in a pile near the throne and Dane bleeding about twenty-five feet away. I looked back and saw Fashnar's body stuck to the wall like a tapestry. White, chalky blood flowed from its skull where I had stabbed it. The rest of the room was a massacre of flesh and fur. I sighed, and my shoulders sagged as the adrenaline seeped out.

We had won.

I could barely believe it. After only two and a half months of fighting we were about to completely annihilate the feral race. A flash of movement caught the corner of my eye, and I saw Dane rise to his feet. His legs wobbled with the effort.

"Are you okay?" I asked, moving over towards him. He nodded, but I saw him holding his shoulder, which had a ragged hole in it from the trident.

I turned back to the still-hanging corpse of Fashnar and slowly began to climb up the body. The muscles of the beast were still tensed up and enabled me to use his legs as foot holds and then pull myself wearily back up to his head.

"Why am I always climbing on top of massive, disgusting creatures?" I pondered aloud, thinking back to The Horror at Lake Lefron.

"It is either a gift or poor taste in women," a voice from behind me rang out. I didn't even have to look to know that it was Grey's. I finished hauling myself up. I ripped Havoc out as I climbed and inserted it back into my belt.

"You need to catch me when I fall this time." I told him.

"Are you kidding me? Look at you, you weigh two hundred…"

"Just do it."

"Alright, alright, jeez, a guy tries to help, and he ends up being the apple boy," he muttered.

"No one knows what that means, Grey."

"It doesn't matter. People like non sequiturs." I grinned, as I braced myself against wall. The sword had gone right through the creature's mouth and embedded itself in the stone. I pressed my feet against the wall and began to pull, slowly at first, but increasing the pressure. I began to feel the strain in my legs, not just from pulling on the wall, but also the week's fatigue. I backed off the pressure, readjusted my grip and pushed outward, wrenching the blade free from its moorings.

I flew backwards through the air holding tight to Widower's Wrath and saw Fashnar's body slowly slump down to the ground. I felt myself hit Grey, and we both crashed to the ground in a heap.

"Nice," I said, picking myself up. I heard Dane snickering as he walked toward us.

"You got blood on my new armor," Grey said with mock disgust. I ignored him as I looked to Dane.

"You sure you're alright?" I asked Dane.

"I'll live." He said curtly.

"You'd better. You're a hero, my young friend. You will sit at a place of honor among the unu for the rest of your days," Qel said to Dane, approaching them. He clutched the ragged hole where his arm had been. Blood was coursing down his side.

"Report" I said to Grey. I had no interest in Qel's hollow honors.

"We are breaking down doors as we speak and clearing out any last means of resistance. Jeronious wants us to head to the wall, now that we have taken the castle." I gestured for him to lead the way. Grey nodded, and the four of us walked out of the castle.

It was a world in flames. The blood had dried up on the street, and we made our way through the myriad of bodies. We passed through the main boulevard, where we saw a dozen unu enter into a store and begin ransacking it. Dead bodies lay strewn in the street. A feral body fell from the roof in front of us with an arrow through its gullet as we walked.

We arrived at the wall and walked up the staircase to the top to where Jeronious stood waiting for us. He nodded to us in greeting. Qel moved up to one of the bonfires, pulled a shield out, and pressed it to the wound. Qel hissed in pain as the wound was cauterized.

"By Supremor, Qel, get to a medic." Jeronious said.

"Not till I see the city burn." Qel replied.

"Dane, we have set up a bandage station down the wall." He pointed to a spot around two hundred yards away. "Go get your wound taken care of. Send someone for Qel."

"I can still fight."

"It was not a request."

"Yes, Herdmaster," Dane bowed and trotted off.

"Grey, round up the others," I told him. He nodded and took off in search of our brothers. His face betrayed no emotion. He just went. I breathed. This was the end. Qel was far too dangerous to be allowed to live past the sacking of this city. His ambition was boundless, and he would turn the Hammer against humanity. That couldn't be allowed. The ferals had been taken care of, now it was time for the rest of them.

I pulled a piece of clothing from a body lying near Jeronious and used it to wipe the blood from my sword. I turned to Qel, who stood looking out onto the fields before Long Fang. I silently pulled Havoc from its moorings. I felt a slight sense of remorse. It was supposed to be Dorian doing this. After all, Dorian was his adopted son. I shrugged it off. I did what needed to be done. I always had.

"So, what happens now?" I asked him as I approached from behind him.

"Now, I believe our relationship is at an end." Qel said as I pressed the dagger to his throat.

"Yes, I believe it is." I replied. It suddenly grew very hard to breathe, and I felt an overwhelming wave of pain flow through my body. I heard a whisper.

"You humiliated me. You did what I couldn't. That was a grave mistake." Jeronious hissed. I looked down and saw the cold steel of a sword sticking through my stomach. "The centaurs are mine."

"You arrogant, pretentious human." Qel said turning to look at me. "Did you really think that you could turn on me, and I wouldn't see it coming? You thought you were the smartest beings in the world." He looked me in the eyes as I sank to my knees. He reached out and grabbed me by the neck. His gold eyes gleamed in the twilight. "You made the last mistake you ever will. You underestimated me." He grinned maliciously.

"And the last thing you will see is me laughing as you drown in your own blood."

Rendezvous with Death

Twenty-Seven

A massive hole in the gates provided the perfect entrance for Galeerial, and he raced into the city. He didn't know how he was supposed to find any of the Seven in a city this big. He urged his horse into the chaos and immediately was forced to duck to avoid being hit by a wayward arrow. He looked around at the bloodbath in front of him.

Slaughter littered the ground around him, and his brain had difficulty processing it. There was so much blood and so many corpses. Feral and unu and centaur and telos alike...all screaming in pain that mounted into crescendo of horror.

He raced through the city, urging his horse through the winding ways. Galeerial's eyes widened as he saw a spear come hurtling toward his chest. He yanked on the reigns, and the horse reared up, taking the spear in the chest. Galeerial tumbled off the back of the horse, crashing to the ground. He put his left arm out and managed to deflect the blow from his neck. He watched the horse, which was still stumbling on two legs, fall back towards him, and he rolled out of the way before it crashed to the ground where he had lain only a moment before.

Galeerial stood up and rolled over the horse's back to grab his scimitars from the saddle. The feral was sprinting towards him, and he rose to his feet, head bowed, scimitars held in a reverse grip stretching back to his elbows. He remembered all the practice he and Ezekiel had been subjected to when they had first joined the Raptors. The feral was ten feet away.

Galeerial flinched as an arrow flew through the temple of the feral, and it crashed to the ground with the shaft still sticking from his skull at his feet. He turned and saw a human staring at him quizzically, before turning and chasing a group of three ferals that were desperately retreating.

"Wait!" he called out, but the human kept running.

He saw another human running across the rooftops and he shouted up at him.

"Wizard!" he hollered and the man turned down and looked at him. It was the same one that he had met in Gemport.

"Skyguard?" He called down, confusion coloring his face.

"I must speak with you!" Galeerial shouted.

"What?" he yelled back. A feral stabbed at Galeerial, but he blocked the blow before deftly stepping forward and slicing open the feral's stomach. Its organs spilled out onto the ground, as it collapsed. Galeerial looked down at his hands. He had never killed anyone before. He felt cold as he looked down at his blades. It had been just a half second of movement, and he had killed a man.

"Hold on!" Rowen called down. Galeerial was shook from his introspection. His hands were shaking, and he didn't know why. Rowen ran forward, dropped down into an alleyway and appeared a moment later on the ground. Galeerial allowed himself to marvel for a moment, the human had dropped four stories and had emerged without a scratch.

"What are you doing here?" he asked, shouting, even though Galeerial was right in front of him. Galeerial began to speak, but Rowen cut him off. "You can't be here right now. I don't know what is going on with you, but you have to listen. You need to turn around right now and get out of here. It is not safe to be near us right now."

"I'm not leaving without you. All of you," Galeerial insisted. Rowen breathed out exasperatedly.

"I don't have time for this. Fine. It doesn't matter. If you aren't going to get out, then get to Aurum. Last I saw, he was up on the wall."

"Thank you." As Galeerial turned away, he saw two humans, one of which had to be Aurum, speaking with an unu and two centaurs atop the battlements.

"Hey, be careful or be dead. Those are your only options; don't be the second." Rowen called out to him as he took off.

He moved cautiously but quickly back the way he came. He arrived at the wall and had to run about eight hundred yards before he could find a staircase that lead to the top. He took the stairs three at a time, sprinting up them. Time was of the essence. Some of the fiercest fighting was still occurring, and Galeerial shook his head as he reached the top. He would have to fight his way to Aurum.

He moved forward, twirling his scimitars about. It had been far too long since he had wielded such weapons, but all those hours training with Ezekiel flew back into him in a rush. He deflected an axe blow from one feral and a sword strike from another, each with a different hand, before rolling forward and stabbing both ferals through the stomach.

He pulled his blades out and kept moving. Nothing would stop him from his goal. He danced a ballad of death while he moved across the top of the battlements. A feral made a desperate strike at him from behind, and its blade cut into Galeerial's back, but he did not even wince in pain. He merely turned around and looked the terrified feral in the eye before sending his sword through it. Galeerial looked up and saw that he was only about a hundred yards away.

He watched, as one of the two centaurs and a man departed nigh-simultaneously. Galeerial's heart stopped for a brief moment in time, as he watched the centaur walk up behind the wizard and thrust his blade through the human's stomach.

"NO!" Galeerial screamed. Galeerial sprinted forward, his curved blades that he had been given by Gabriel stretching out from his hands back to his elbows as he ran. He whipped across the heights of the wall, slicing through unu, feral and centaur alike as he ran. Blood flowed from his shotos. The wizard was twenty yards away.

Galeerial saw a huge unu with one arm step away from the wizard's body. The sword went clean through his chest, and the centaur stepped back releasing the saber from his hands. He went for the unu first.

He sprinted forward, leapt into the air and punched out with both of his feet, kicking the surprised unu in the face. He stumbled backward, losing his balance and fell from the wall. Galeerial stood back up and strode towards the centaur, with murder in his eyes. With every step he took the centaur took one backwards.

"Who-who are you?" he asked. There was fear in his eyes and horror in his face. Galeerial said nothing, but stalked forward. Malice and wrath were borne in his eyes. The centaur stared at him for a moment and then wheeled about and ran. Galeerial took a breath and turned around to the human who still stood staring down at the blade stuck in his stomach in shock. Galeerial knelt beside him, as the human fell to his knees. Galeerial wrapped his hands around the blade.

"No!" a ragged voice said. It sounded like he was rubbing two pieces of shiftstone together. He gritted his teeth. "Stops...blood." Galeerial nodded. He looked up and saw a centaur charging forward. The centaur that was running away ran right by him, and Galeerial saw the first centaur stop suddenly as the second one rode by. Galeerial rose to his feet and drew his swords again. He stood blades crossed ready to fight. The centaur rode up and threw his hands into the air.

"Wait, wait. I'm a friend. I can get you two out of here." Galeerial didn't move his guard. "My name is Dane. Please, let me help my friend." He begged. Galeerial didn't move, but he looked behind him and saw a swarm of centaurs racing towards them. "Please!"

"Hope lost, dream...shattered. Tell them, Dane, tell them." His face had gone white. At the mention of the centaur's name, Galeerial stuffed his blades into his belt and gestured forward.

"Alright, let's go." The centaur moved up next to him, and Galeerial reached down and carefully picked up Aurum, who was wheezing as blood spilled slowly from his wound. He pushed him to the back, turned him around and climbed onto the centaur facing him. The sword was only halfway through him and Galeerial grimaced before pushing it further in so that he could climb aboard.

"Go!" he yelled, clenching his legs tightly onto the centaurs back and holding onto Aurum. The centaur leapt forward and took off along the pathway. The centaur jumped down the stairs and Galeerial saw his future crash into a burning pyre.

One of the wizards took three arrows to the chest and fell from the terrace of a building into the river, which ran through the center of the city and got swept away by the current. Another he saw leap from the top of the wall, outward away from the city. A third he saw fighting four centaurs and two unu. A fourth he saw sprinting across the rooftops while being chased by several enemies.

Galeerial refocused on his own predicament, as the centaur leapt down the stairs several at a time. Galeerial held on tight as he felt himself get tossed about. They reached the ground level and the centaur pulled a sword from his back. Galeerial watched as the centaur cut through his own comrades as they hurtled through the courtyard to the gate. Five centaurs dead in the space of the ten seconds it took to reach the gate, and then they were free.

"Where are we going?" the centaur shouted out to him. Galeerial paused. The nearest city was at The Split, but there was the possibility that it was occupied by centaurs despite it being a human city.

"To The Split, then on to Winter Crest." Galeerial said. He had to chance it. He couldn't let Aurum die. As they rode, Galeerial did his best to slow the bleeding, but he was no doctor. He had never even seen blood until that day. As they exited they city, they were met by a second human on horseback. Dane brought them alongside the human without losing any speed.

"Dane?" the human asked. "By Supremor, Aurum."

"He needs help, Grey. Fast," Dane replied. *Another wizard?*

"Let's get him away from here. Then I'll do what I can." The human said. "Who is he?"

"I thought he was with you." Dane replied. "He kept Qel from finishing Aurum off."

"I'm Galeerial." Galeerial cut in. Grey looked at him.

346

"Did not see that coming." Grey replied. "Dane, he's good. Seems like fate has a sense of irony after all."

Epilogue One
Revelations

Tendra stepped off of *Blur* amidst a rainfall of stone and snow. She clutched her shawl close to her shoulders as she watched her breath emerge in a cloud of steam. Her father had sent her to Bicoln to speak with Magistrate Kay after Rowen left and Jakob died...and now this. Not three weeks since Long Fang had fallen, and The Hammer was already here. They wanted the Heart of Fires. As she was sailing into port, the Hammer had been launching boulders at Gemport and into the Bay of Pearls to destroy any incoming ships. Humanity was the only species, other than the telos, with a naval fleet, and thus it gave them an enormous advantage. The unu could throw boulders, but they could never completely barricade them from the sea.

"My lady?" Captain Renaul asked, breaking her north-ward gaze.

"I'll be fine. Unload the shipments. I can make my own way to the castle." He gave her an uneasy look, but obeyed none-theless.

She walked along the dock, slipping in and out of the paths of soldiers unloading shipments of supplies: arrows, meat, bread, wine. Water wasn't a problem for The Heart flowed through the city, before entering the bay.

The soldiers looked scared. She could imagine why, even though their fears were for naught. Gemport would not fall. It could get an almost endless supply of reinforcements from sea, and they were already well supplied for winter. They were bring-ing in the last of the food shipments as she arrived. In addition, the wizards should, even now, be fighting to get back here to aid them.

Yet their faces were grim. She wished Rowen were here. He always had the right words for the situation, something to make her smile. But there was nothing here to smile about. An army stood upon Gemport's doorstep, and mankind's army would not arrive for another couple of weeks. They were mar-shaling now at Mesnir by Jeric's hand. The north was on the war march by land and, in the south, Bicoln and Terakeen were send-ing troops and supplies by the legions to aid Gemport by sea.

She walked quickly down the line of piers, and then made her way into the heart of the city. The castle was on the bluff at the far west of the city. She had to enter into the city proper and go up the King's Road to reach the palace. Tendra found herself quickly in the town square and glanced at the shops. Something was wrong. She didn't know what, but since she stepped off the boat a feeling of dread had been building in her stomach.

Tendra ran through the streets towards the palace...she needed to see her father. She heard a crash above her and she felt herself get slammed forward, as rubble descended onto the street where she had been only moments before. She sat there, dazed for a moment.

"...alright, Ma'am?" She missed the question in the haze of confusion.

"What?" she said, seeing her savior for the first time. He was a boy, no more than sixteen years old, and she saw the astonishment in his eyes when he finally saw her face. He instantly dropped to a knee...annoyingly, though, he did not repeat the question. "Get up," She admonished, and the boy hastily rose to his feet. "This is war. Courtesy is meaningless. I need to get to the castle." The youth nodded.

"This way...it is along the back roads, but it will get you there faster than the King's Road," he said pulling her hand to help her to her feet. "Follow me." He took off running, his sword swinging behind him. Tendra cast off her shawl and sprinted after him.

"What's happening?" she shouted ahead to him.

"The Hammer arrived two days ago. Yesterday, they started the catapults. They have launched seven bombardments since then...each one longer than the last. Lord Vizien says that they will begin their true assault soon. Siege towers and troops continue to flood in daily from the northern front." They zigzagged through the back alleyways of the city. Tendra had never seen any of these roads before, but they were soon enough at the palace gates, which, to Tendra's surprise, had been cast open.

"Thank you, I can take it from here. Return to your post Sir..."

"Hallen, but I'm just a bookkeeper's apprentice."

Hagen this war is over, find me, and I'll see that you are elevated beyond your family's wildest hopes."

351

"Thank you, thank you my lady." In his eagerness, his helmet, which was obviously oversized, fell down and covered his eyes. He sheepishly grinned. Tendra turned back and looked up at the palace. "My lady, one more thing..."

"Yes." She said urgently.

"It's about the wizards," he said haltingly, "we have been hearing reports for the last day or so, that-that they were killed in the Battle of Long Fang." Tendra stopped in her tracks. A shiver went up her spine that was not caused by the overcast day or the harsh winds. Her heart skipped a beat.

"How reliable are these reports?" She said slowly.

"We have had three scouts come back from the battle, two of them have sworn that they saw the wizard who was here, Rowen. They saw him fall into The Heart with twelve arrows in his back, surrounded by dozens of foes." His voice grew staggered, as she felt a rush of emotion pass into her face. She shook her head.

No...No! She turned and took off running to the palace. She had to hear it from her father himself. It couldn't be true. Rowen and the wizards were more than mortal men. They couldn't die, they were humanity's hope. She sprinted up the final stairs and into the greeting chambers. She took a sharp right and entered the throne room. She was greeted with silence. Where were the guards? The entire throne room was empty. There had been no guards in the courtyard either, and, now that she thought about it, something was very, very wrong.

She saw a large pile lying between the throne and the pillar that held the entrance to the crypts. As she warily approached, she felt herself grow weak. It was no pile...it was a body.

"No...not you, too!" She ran to the body and turned it over. Glazed eyes and a pale face that echoed none of her father's warmth stared back at her. Her breath began to grow shallow and quicken. Tears flowed from her eyes. "Don't leave me alone father. You can't leave me alone." A sound shook her out of her mourning, and she whirled around. The hidden entrance to the crypts was open. She looked down and saw her father's ring gone.

"The Heart of Fires!" she whispered. She glanced furtively around and then sprinted up to the throne. She reached up and pulled down the sword that hung along the back of the chair. Valiant was its name, and it was the sword of her house. The handle was of a black fist with a red star adorned atop it. She turned and ran to the crypts.

She offered a silent prayer to Supremor and then crept downward. She would have to be silent and swift. There was a good chance that whoever was down here had already touched it, which meant that the enemy now had a magician of their own. She slowly shuffled down the stairs. She heard a muffled sound, but couldn't quite tell what it was. She reached the bottom, and the flickering light of the torches was accentuated by the blue glow of the Heart of Fires. She peered around the corner and saw an unu collapsed dead before it.

She crept forward, all senses wary. She saw a flicker of shadow near the Heart of Fires. Someone else was here. She felt the magnetism of the Heart pull her forwards. Just beyond it she saw the silhouette of a man, a man dressed completely in black.

"Vizien?" his dark eyes stared back at her. His hand rested upon the Heart of Fires. Her eyes grew wide with fear. He was a mage.

"Come closer," he said. Tendra felt the pull as she stepped carefully over the dead unu. "Come closer." He whispered again. Tendra reached her hand out. She couldn't help herself. The Heart of Fires pulled her hand closer...closer. She resisted. She couldn't touch it. She fought the pull, but a hand grabbed her by the wrist and pulled her fingers onto the glowing stone.

Tendra felt shock pass through her body, but not from the Heart of Fires. Her surprise came from the fact that nothing happened. Her mouth dropped open. Vizien's face glowed from the ambient light. She felt confusion arise. *There should be something.*

"It doesn't work," he hissed at her "It's not real. The Hear of Fires is a fake."

Epilogue Two
Ascension

"Will he live?" Galeerial asked. The stark white body of the wizard, Aurum, lay beneath him. He wheezed with every breath, and his chest struggled to raise each time air slipped through his lips. The wizard, Grey, stood next to him in the halls of Winter Crest atop the mountain called Lightwatch.

"I don't know," Geralt, the physician said. "We have not served humans in ages, and sword wounds are nearly as rare. He is fighting with every breath...fighting to return to the land of the living. Though whether he will survive the path through that silent kingdom, I know not."

"Is there anything more that can be done for him?" Grey asked.

"You can pray and hope that Supremor hears your pleas," Geralt replied. The old doctor removed himself from the chambers, and his beating wings carried him away. Grey turned back to Galeerial.

"Thank you. Thank you for everything that you have done," Grey said, and Galeerial nodded.

"I'm not doing this for you."

"I don't care why you're doing it. Al I care about is that you are doing it," Dane broke in from behind them. It had been with incredible difficulty that they had brought Dane up into the aerie, but there were no ground level barracks. Other races never came to the three cities anymore.

"If he dies, will you aid me?" Galeerial asked him.

"Aid you in what?" Grey responded.

"I need to learn to use it." Galeerial gestured to the Eon, which was laid out across the table.

"Why?"

"I need to kill a demon."

Grey raised an eyebrow questioningly, but nodded. Their conversation was interrupted by a sound that sent a chill through Galeerial's hardened heart. It echoed through his bones and resounded in his mind. It was a clarion call. The Horn of Seventeen Sorrows, which had once- an age ago-hung from his belt as he had stood within the Dead Gates, rang clear through the air. It was as if it had been blown right next to him, yet Galeerial knew that it was being blown hundreds of miles north, in Cloud Breach.

"Are you okay? You look a little...not okay," Grey asked. Galeerial shook his head as the sound of the Horn faded from his ears.

"You didn't hear that?" Galeerial asked. Grey shook his head. Dread filled Galeerial. *This can't be happening. It's too soon.* "He's coming." Galeerial whispered. "He's coming."

"Who?" Dane asked. Galeerial turned from the doorway back to Aurum. Unbidden, Gabriel's words came to his mind, *if you cannot reach him, then it is because his destiny lies in Arestephan's hands.* Aurum had been muttering words the entire trip to Winter Crest. Words he had no business knowing. Galeerial walked to the bookshelf in the aerie. Every Skyguard had a copy of the Books of Arestephan, and Galeerial found the verses he was looking for quickly. Galeerial turned back to Aurum.

"Aurum, I know you can hear me, wherever you are, listen to my words.

> *Go where angels fear to tread,*
> *And souls are alighted yet bound.*
> *Where eyes from above watched,*
> *And the beginning was found.*

> *Truth spawns from lies,*
> *The doubting heart dies*

> *The Key to all souls will be given,*
> *The door to the Book will unlock.*
> *The willing heart will bleed water*
> *And Ruin will emerge from the rock."*

Nobody moved for a moment as everyone's eyes flickered between Galeerial and Aurum. "Come on, Aurum," Galeerial whispered. "What does it mean?" Galeerial watched as Aurum's eyes opened to reveal a royal violet light.

"Ohm." His eyes flashed shut again, and the light vanished with his consciousness.

"I don't understand. What does it mean? And who is coming?" Dane's confused voice echoed his face.

"As soon as he is well, take him to Thanatos." Galeerial stepped back and up from the bed where Aurum lay. "As for

357

who is coming," one word emerged from Galeerial's lips. It was
a word of hatred:

"Veriel."

Epilogue Three
Shatterpoint

Two figures met in the shadow of the forest, in the dead of night. The whispers of the dead called to them, begged them and tempted them, offering them anything they wanted in exchange for release. This was Whisperwood.

"So that's it? We're all that is left?" Joven asked. Rayn nodded.

"I saw Dane carry Aurum and another one of us out of the city. I couldn't see who it was. Aurum, he-he had a sword sticking through his chest." Rayn said haltingly. Joven stared into the night sky.

"They should have been here by now. The solstice is tomorrow." He murmured. "It all has happened so fast. "

"What are we going to do?" Rayn asked.

"What are we going to do?" Joven repeated. "I don't know!" He yelled, grabbing Rayn by the tunic. "I don't know. I have no more plans. I have...nothing." He growled. Rayn looked unnerved into Joven's eyes.

"But, you always have a plan." He said, searching in Joven's face for something...anything. Joven released his hands and turned away from Rayn. He walked five steps away and stopped.

"We ride south, to Gemport. That is where the Hammer will fall. Qel is going after the Heart of Fires, and we aren't going to let him have it," resolve crept back into Joven's voice.

"What about the plan? There are only two of us." Rayn asked.

"Then two of us will have to be good enough. We started this all together, and we are going finish it. The others will make their presence known if they survived. We know that Rikard is in position. Qel wouldn't have killed Dorian. He will take him to Ornus for the feast, and they will connect there." Joven let his voice trail off. Rikard would do his duty. Of that he was certain. Rikard didn't fail.

"Do you hear them?" Rayn asked. Joven turned around and saw Rayn staring into the depths of the forest. "They are so sad."

"Stay focused, Rayn, and let the dead lie dead. Our alliance is shattered, and now we have to pick up the pieces. Leave the dead behind. We can't waste time on them now." Joven blinked heavily and swallowed. He opened his eyes and a fire burned within them. "We have no more time to waste." Joven stepped up onto his horse, and Rayn followed suit.

Neither man saw the shadow move silently towards Amul Kon, but they heard the winter wind howl after them, and the night go searching for another savior.

360

Now, a look at what's next in:

Dawn of Darkness

Four Months Ago
One

The spray of the sea stung Rikard Karandash's eyes. The large man felt his sinewy muscles twitch in anticipation. He watched as *The Nydian* tossed and turned beneath his steady feet towards the large gray monoliths that were the Devil's Teeth. Rikard had sailed from Seraph and was now rounding the edge of the world. The golden city of Ornus stood tall before him on the cliffs in the distance, and the Rift Mountains hung ominously in the haze behind him. Rikard narrowed his eyes as he carefully ran his thumbs along his two daggers: Bleed and Burn. The edges were sharp-real sharp: just how he liked them. They would need to be for what he was about to attempt. The cold arkaline metal of the blades was far sharper than any steel and could cut through solid stone. *The Nydian* rocked against the turbulent waters, and the sky was as dark above him as the tempestuous water below him. He carefully strapped the hilts to his hands and bound them tight. He couldn't afford to lose them.

Rikard licked his salty lips. This would be fun. The ship's captain knew him only as a friend of Damaen Longshore, the infamous pirate and reaver, captain of the *Finality*. Damaen had served as his brother Aurum's alias over the last few years. As such the captain was scared to death of Rikard, just the way Rikard liked it. It was better to be feared than questioned. Aurum had gathered quite the reputation as a pirate in the seven years' worth of ranging they had done prior to their emergence upon the world, and he had built up quite the system of favors; now one of them was being called in to Captain Ferion.

"Get us closer!" Rikard called down to him. Rikard stood at the bow of the ship and watched the massive stones grow closer as the crew wrestled against the sea for control of the boat. Beyond the Devil's Teeth lay Ornus, the capital-and only-city of the unu. The city was a fortress, unassailable by land and impossible to reach by water; nevertheless, it was his target. What he was about to attempt was suicide.

Rikard smiled. It would be a good death, dying at the hands of the gods who ruled the sea, the gods of chance, stone, and pain. Let them come. Let them break themselves upon his iron resolve and callous disregard for their seemingly infallible dominion over this expanse.

The boulders grew closer still.

"Captain!" Rikard called out. Ferion came scurrying towards him. Ferion was a mouse of a man: a trader and a businessman, not a sailor. He was no more a captain than Rikard was a king, but he called himself that nonetheless. "Your services are no longer required, and your debt to Captain Longshore has been paid in full."

"Thank you, thank you, sir." Ferion said quickly. His face betrayed his relief. "Is there anything…"

"Just die." Rikard didn't even wait for the confusion to register on the man's face; he simply took three steps back so as to arrive at the aft railing of the ship. The first stone was about three hundred yards away, and that was his starting point. He took a deep breath, "Boom!" He called before taking off running down the length of the ship. It took four steps before he took the six stair drop in stride, never letting up his pace.

Crewmen leapt out of his way as he ran, and explosions began to rock the ship behind him. The shock wave from the explosives he had placed on the ship would give him that much more of a starting edge. He would need every advantage he could get if he wanted to survive this. Rikard flew by the last sailor who was scrambling to jump off the ship as it exploded into shrapnel behind him. He hurtled onto the bowsprit. His ridged shoes cut into the wood, providing him adequate traction as he rushed forward. He hit the bow, braced his left foot, and leapt.

The shock wave of the final explosion hurled him forward. Rikard flew through the air and watched the first stone pillar grow closer. He knew that he was going to be nowhere close, but he had counted on that. He reached up and undid the clasp that let all of his clothes fall away from him. They would only weigh him down. He didn't want to make it too easy. That was his last thought before the cold water slammed into his arms and face. The shock of the water burst through his body, and his muscles threatened to immediately seize up. Rikard overcame nature by sheer strength of will.

He surfaced immediately and began swimming. It would be a long day, and he needed a hard start. He forced his arms to do his bidding, pushing stroke after stroke through the bitter, cold water. Rikard gasped for breath at every six count. He broke through wave after wave as he made a slow, beleaguered march toward the awaiting gauntlet. The waves were unpredictable and thrashed about like a creature in the throes of death. Rikard felt the ice-cold water flow across his entire body at every stroke threatening to seep in and drown him. It made him feel alive. The elongated shoes that he wore enabled him to swim faster and pierce through the water easier. As Rikard grew to within twenty meters of his objective monolith, he glanced back, searching for the wave he needed to ride. He couldn't just swim up to the stone; the waves would batter him to pieces before he would be able to make it high enough to get out of the barrage. Instead, he needed to ride a wave up to the stone pillar.

He gave one surge, pushing himself forward and to the left, toward his wave. He thrust his arms before him, and his legs were a flurry of motion as he finally arrived at his wave. It was a monster, at least thirty feet tall and was heading straight towards him. Rikard wheeled around and began to swim with the swell. He rode the wave up higher and higher until he was at the crest as it carried him towards the stone. The wave battered against the rock, and Rikard felt the blow rattle his jaw. He gasped for breath as he felt a rib crack from the impact of the unforgiving rock. He slammed his daggers forward into the stone while his feet scrambled for some kind of foothold on the slippery rock. The hard granite resisted the cold metal's sting, but the daggers were still able to slide into the stone.

Slowly and steadily, he made his way up the length of the pillar. His arms burned, and he could find no footholds on the treacherous stone, forcing him to make the entire labored climb one hand over the other. In a single motion, he kicked his shoes free; they would be useless now. The burn of his muscles working combined with the freezing water filled Rikard with adrenaline.

Rikard shivered from the biting cold but gritted his teeth and kept climbing. Failure was not an option: right, left, right, left. His arms worked furiously, allowing no time for rest. He grinned in grim satisfaction and pulled his eyes away from the stone to look upwards as his hand found nothing to gain purchase on but empty air. He carefully mounted the pinnacle of the pillar before looking out to behold the challenge that was laid out before him. There were about eight hundred meters worth of stone and sea spread out before him. The large stone pillars rose eighty feet out of the water, and the next closest one was spaced thirty feet to his right.

The top of the stone column in which he stood was about ten feet across; so he had some room to maneuver. Rikard moved back to the edge of the stone pillar and took off running once again. At the last instant, Rikard pushed off and went sailing through the air towards the second column. Rikard braced for the impact he knew would come but still felt it reverberate through his body, rattling his bones, as he forced his daggers once again into the stone. Rikard felt the unrelenting battering ram of the water cast him into the pillar again and again as he struggled to the top.

Rikard looked forward, charting his path to the shore. The outlying columns were farther away from each other, and he saw that as he moved closer to shore the stone pillars grew denser. Rikard smiled. He would do this. Not he could, but he would.

Rikard leapfrogged his way forward, repeating the cycle again and again. His arms began to grow leaden, and his entire body ached from the constant battering of the stone and the water, but he was making progress. He felt his rib go from cracked to thoroughly broken, and every intake of breath placed pressure on his ribcage, forcing a grimace to cross his face and a rasp to escape from his lips.

The shore was still a hundred meters away when he felt a sharp pain in his foot, followed by numbness. Rikard looked down and saw a small lizard glaring up at him curiously. He reached down and stabbed it through the back. It made a short cry as black blood oozed from the wound. He shook his head and prepared for his next jump. The pillar was close enough that Rikard knew that he could make it to the top. The trick was not sliding off. Rikard took a deep breath and felt a second nip at his foot. A second lizard had appeared right beside the first one, and his foot was now bleeding from the chunks of flesh that had been pulled from his foot.

Rikard reached down and picked the lizard up by its neck and looked at it. It was approximately a foot long, including the tail, and had a thin membrane between its arms and legs. It was gray with black stripes and blended in well with the stone. Its three-toed feet ended in long, curved claws that looked particularly vicious. It snapped at his face, and he was able to see the full set of teeth that the lizards possessed. Rikard held it over the side of the stone pillar and dropped it into the sea.

He watched it fall about thirty feet before its arms spread out, allowing it to glide over to a nearby pillar. Rikard then watched, fascinated, as the lizard climbed up to the top of its pillar before pushing off to return to its previous position below Rikard and begun to climb up once again. Rikard couldn't believe his eyes as he watched the lizard ascend. Rikard marveled at the lizard but thought no more of it as he prepared for his next jump. They were inconsequential and deserved to be treated as such. He gathered up and was about to start running when he caught something out of the corner of his eye.

He watched as the pillar to his left suddenly began to move. It began to ebb and flow, and Rikard watched in astonishment as well over a hundred of the lizards leapt off and glided over to his pillar.

"Oh Dread." He cursed. He took off running and leapt to the next pillar. He slid onto the top of it, and the combination of his wet body on the wet stone caused him to slide towards the edge, but he was able to get his knives dug in before slipping off. He looked back and watched as the lizards on his former pillar pushed off and glided over to where he was. Rikard cursed again and leapt to his feet. No more playing around. He crashed onto the next pillar and scrambled to move to the next one. The columns before him were very close now. He turned to look back and saw a lizard flying right at his face. He whipped his arm up, and the reptile's torso slid right onto it. The animal didn't stop snapping at him though, and Rikard threw it off and into the sea. He grimaced as one bit into his leg, and he kicked it off.

They were flying from pillar to pillar towards him by the hundreds now. "Dreadspawn," he muttered as he started to run. He leapt from one pillar to the next, letting his momentum carry him as he tried to stay ahead of the beasts chasing him. He had no idea how he was supposed to climb up to the top of the bluff and into Ornus with all of these things following him; he would be torn to shreds. The cliff face was just a short ways away, and anger clouded into his eyes. These Dread-forsaken beasts were screwing up his plan, and now he would get to kill them all. Rikard made his way to the last pillar before the cliff face. The cliff was about twelve feet away, and it stretched upward about two hundred meters before transforming into the golden hue of the city walls. Rikard turned to face the army of demon lizards following him.

"C'mon!" He screamed at them. "C'mon!" He screamed. "You want war? I'll give you war!" The creatures had stopped one pillar short of where he was standing. A single lizard propelled itself forward, and Rikard watched its trajectory. He prepared to slice it clean in half with one of his blades when a massive shadow swept in front of him. He watched as what looked like a bat with an eight-foot wingspan curved around his pillar snapping the lizard up in a single bite before flying back into one of the many holes in the cliff face.

A moment later, Rikard heard the sound of death screaming towards him. Instinct seized him, and he dropped flat to the ground as hundreds of the bat creatures exploded from the bluff. The lizards scuttled down the side of the pillar and leapt away as the demon bats plucked them from the air. Rikard shook his head as he watched nature's checks and balances. When it appeared like the last of the creatures had emerged from the cave behind of him, Rikard ran forward and leapt across the final chasm. He had planned on camping in one of these crevasses, but that no longer seemed like such a good idea.

The sky was awash with the creatures, and Rikard didn't want to attract any unnecessary attention away from their hunting towards him. He moved to the side of the cave to begin his climb up. He unlashed his daggers from his palms and tied them to his wrists. The rock here was not as weathered and smooth as it had been out in the bay. Here it was black and craggy and rife with hand-and footholds.

He was tired, his arms and legs ached, and his right leg ached worse than the other because of the stupid lizards. Yet upwards he climbed. He had work to do, and he would need every minute of every day to prepare. He couldn't afford weakness. That was one vice in which he did not partake. The stone was sharp, and he had to take care with every step to avoid being sliced to ribbons.

His right arm began to cramp about halfway up the side of the cliff, and he wedged himself into a small opening between rocks to rest and stretch. He looked out and saw the bat creatures finally begin their migration back towards the caves. Rikard slowly undid the bindings on Burn. He kept himself as still as possible. He didn't want to attract any attention, but, if one happened to come near him, he would be ready. It was awe-inspiring to watch these hunters move back into their dens until the next time they would emerge to hunt. They were beautiful.

Rikard's eyes were a flurry of motion as he tracked the hundreds of creatures move through the air. Many of them dove into caves below where he was now situated, about a hundred feet up the cliff. He watched the cascade of flesh slowly begin to work its way up the cliff, and he made himself small in the nook. He wasn't afraid, but he didn't want to draw himself into a fight that he couldn't hope to win.

He felt the rush of air as the beasts began to zoom by him up to their lairs. So far none had noticed him, but he held his breath anyway. There were hundreds of them. Rikard hadn't realized just how many of them there were. Finally, the mass of flesh began to thin out, and eventually it disappeared entirely. Rikard re-bound his blade, pulled himself out of the crevasse, and continued his climb. It had been a couple of hours since he had begun, and Rikard could feel his body screaming out despite the small respite that he had provided it.

He kept climbing. The smooth stone of the city walls grew closer and closer. Rikard finally arrived at the top of the bluff and felt smooth grass instead of stone. In one final monumental effort, he heaved himself upward and rolled onto the ground. His arms were bloody from the cuts on his hands, and his feet were far worse. But Rikard felt none of that; all he felt was satisfaction. He wanted to scream in triumph, but he held his passion in check. He still had a job to do, and this was only the end of the first round.

The walls on this end of the fortress were purely for show. The front walls were towering two hundred foot affairs, but back here they were maybe fifty feet high. The ground the city was built upon was heavily sloped, so the height of the walls was even all the way around. He stared up at them. He would wait until nightfall before climbing them. It wouldn't do for a nearly naked human to be seen running through the streets of Ornus.

Rikard felt the adrenaline slowly seep from his body, and he once again collapsed to the ground. His muscles tensed up from the cold and the exertion. He began shivering, and his teeth clacked together. He had trained for this, but it was too much. He curled up into a ball to try to keep warm. It was still summer and the air was warm despite the gray sky, but he felt none of the heat.

He slowly began to massage his muscles: first his right arm and then his left. He dug his hands hard into them working through the biting pain. The effort pulled some of the pain out and warmed his muscles at the same time. He moved on to his chest taking extra time to rub it. He wished that he would have kept one of those lizards to eat, for he was ravenous, but he quickly pushed the thought out of his mind. He couldn't afford to dwell on the past.

He moved down to his legs and finished by launching into a stretching routine. He kept one eye watching the top of the wall. He knew that the unu didn't patrol the side and rear walls. In their arrogance, they believed themselves invincible due to the combination of the torrential waters, the stone monoliths, and, as Rikard was now well aware, the biological protections. He watched the cloudy ball of the sun descend into the horizon and began to prepare for the final part of his climb. He lashed his daggers to his wrists with numb fingers and began to climb the wall. The apparently smooth walls were, in actuality, just the opposite, and the climb was much easier than his first one. The dark of night descended slowly upon him as he made his way up the wall. The massive blocks of stone that made up the wall had decayed from centuries of being eroded by the elements.

Slowly, Rikard glanced over the top of wall and saw the great city of Ornus sprawled out before him. To his left, he saw one of the castles nestled against the back left corner of city; the second castle was directly opposite of it in the front right corner of the city. The unu and their balance. The rest of the town was laid out around a central bazaar and the Anvil. The Anvil was the massive central arena where unu fought as gladiators in epic confrontations for glory, or for the right to be made clanmaster. Every building in the city was short and made from the same golden, sandy stone that the walls were hewn from. He looked to his left and right for any sign of the guards, but the way was clear. In a single motion, Rikard pulled himself up and vaulted over the wall.

He crept quickly across the ten feet and leapt across the chasm to the house that was directly in front of him and about six feet below him. He hit the roof with a wince and dropped into a roll to cushion the impact. There were rope lines with clothes hanging between houses throughout the city, and he made his way over to one of them. A roughly woven brown cloth shirt and trousers made for an unu child immediately caught his eye. He dropped down into the alleyway between two houses and pulled on the loose-fitting clothing. First order of business was done. He was not exactly looking forward to the second.

He began scouting through the back alleys of the city. Ornus had a strict curfew of sundown, and so he knew that he would be the only one on the streets besides the guards. Rikard stealthily made his way forward. He had been here many times before, and he knew his way around. More importantly, he knew where she lived. He navigated through the meticulously balanced streets until he finally came to a doorway that looked like so many others, instinctively knowing this was the correct one. He ran his fingers over the grain of the wood, and he took a deep breath. This would be…interesting. He quietly rapped twice in the top left corner of the door and twice more on the bottom right corner and once in the center. Then he waited and hoped that she hadn't been reassigned.

Rikard held his breath as he saw two hands slowly open the door. Before him stood a beautiful unu woman. Unu women were different than the men, though they retained the deep blue skin and slightly unnerving golden eyes and hair. They were thinner than the barbarian stature of their mates and had four arms instead of two. They also had longer bodies and faces and more pronounced curves in the hips and chests, like human women. The unu woman before him was of exceptional beauty, though at just over two meters tall she was considered exceptionally short for her kind. Two of her arms were opening the door, one was rested at her side and the fourth cupped her gaping mouth. Her blue skin shone in the candlelight, and her simple white dress perfectly accentuated her every feature. Her eyes were wide in a look of a surprise, and her unbraided hair cascaded down to the small of her back. He offered her his most Rowen-like smile.

"Hello, Breva." He said simply. She exhaled as if she had been holding her breath for all the years that it had been since he had seen her. Her voice was barely more than a whisper in the night wind.

"Dorian?"

45795808R00232

Made in the USA
Lexington, KY
10 October 2015